COLE

NYT AND USA TODAY BESTSELLING AUTHOR

TIJAN

Edited by Jessica Royer Ocken
Proofread by Chris O'Neil Parece, Paige Smith, Kara Hildebrand and Pam Huff
Formatting by Elaine York
Allusion Graphics, LLC/Publishing & Book Formatting
www.allusiongraphics.com

DEDICATION

To my readers!

CHAPTER ONE

I was surrounded—by champagne, crystal lights, and beautiful people. And I wanted to die.

Not really, but I *was* huddled in a corner with my back turned to the party. This was Sia's job. She was the event coordinator at this art gallery, the Gala. I wasn't even sure what event she was throwing, but I was here because she asked me to be. This was her thing, a typical Friday night for my best friend. The rich and gorgeous people came together to drink, socialize, throw money at some charity and mainly gossip. This was not my thing, and among all these paintings and socialites, I wanted to disappear.

I moved to Chicago two years ago, but that seemed like a lifetime now. We came for Liam's job. He was the newest counselor at the Haven Center, but a year ago he was killed, struck by a drunk driver on his way home.

A shudder went through me as I remembered.

Liam had left a message that he was stopping to get flowers—he was a block away. The local florist had a booth in our grocery store. I'd had the genius idea to walk Frankie and meet him at the store. Our ~~dog~~ furry child could wait in the car while we got food together. It was silly, but grocery shopping was a favorite "date" for me. Liam thought it was ridiculous. He always laughed, but he'd humor me. And Frankie loved it. He got out of the house and could wag his tail to his heart's content in the car. We lived in a nice neighborhood, and it wasn't too hot, so I trusted our child would still be there when we returned.

When Frankie and I walked around the corner, Liam's car was waiting to cross the intersection and turn in to the parking lot. He smiled when he saw Frankie and me, and he looked so happy. He'd lifted his hand to wave. So had I. When the light changed, Liam started across—I saw his smile fall away. I saw his hand grab for the steering wheel. I saw the blood drain from his face. He'd started to mouth, "*I lo—*"

My heart twisted. It was being yanked out, slowly, inch by inch.

As I'd watched, my husband's car was T-boned by a truck.

I bowed my head and gripped my champagne glass now. I could still hear the sound of metal being smashed, crunching and grinding. Then the car had started in a roll.

Once.

Twice.

It had rolled three times before stopping. *He* had rolled three times before dying.

The terror—I'll never get that image out of my mind. His crystal blue eyes, high cheekbones, a face I'd always teased would keep the ladies hitting on him long after he passed fifty, had never looked so scared. Everything happened in slow motion. His eyes went to the truck, and then they found me. Frankie was barking. I couldn't move. My heart slowed.

I was told later that I'd kept Frankie from running in to traffic, but I have no memory of that. All I can remember is Liam and the look in his eyes when he knew he was going to die.

My future died that day.

"Addison!"

I had one second to ready myself, and I wiped away the tear that had leaked from my eye. Sia rushed to my side, hissing my name in an excited whisper as she grasped my arm. She moved close, turning so she could speak quietly to me but still watch her friends behind us. Her dress grazed my bare arm.

"I just got the best news ever for you! Seriously, I'm gushing like a twelve year old because it's that damned good." She paused, her eyes searching my face, and her head moved back an inch. "Wait. What are you doing all the way over here?" She glanced over her shoulder. "The street's beautiful and all, but the party's behind you."

I had to stifle a smile. She wouldn't understand. I was indeed facing downtown Chicago. Traffic was minimal due to the impending blizzard. Already the snow was falling, piling atop cars, sidewalks, people, and signs.

It was breathtaking. That was the art I appreciated. Sia loved people, or more specifically, she loved connections. She didn't just see faces when she met them. She saw wealth, their friends, and potential connections. I was the opposite. I seemed to notice everything except those things—or I used to. I had during my Liam era, when my heart was full and open and welcoming. But that was then.

Now I was in the after-Liam era.

Everything was dull. Grey. Black. White.

I sighed. I even depressed myself.

I tuned back in to what Sia was saying. She hadn't stopped to wait for my response. "...number, and I have to tell you, you'll love it. It's one of the most exclusive places I've heard about. No one knows about the opening, but I got the number for you. Can you believe it? How amazing a friend am I?" Her eyes sparkled. "I'm fucking amazing, Addison. Ah—"

"Okay, I got it." I gently pulled her hand off my arm, keeping it in mine.

She squeezed back, her body dancing with excitement.

"Say it again," I told her. "What'd you get for me?"

She tucked a piece of paper into my palm. Her voice was so hush-hush. "I got the number for one of the most exclusive buildings there is. It's three blocks from here. There's never been a vacancy, but there's one now. The third floor is open."

"What do you mean, the third floor is open?" I unfolded the paper to find a phone number scrawled on it, nothing else.

"It's the silver building."

"The silver…" I looked up at her as it clicked which building she was talking about. It was a building a short walk away, covered entirely in something silver. Sia had first thought it was a business, but once she found out it housed residents, it took on a whole other appeal to her. Her interest was piqued, and when that happens, Sia's like a detective, going after every tip she gets. Only she couldn't find any information about it. There was an air of secrecy about who owned it and who lived there, which only added to its appeal.

I'd been hearing about this building for the entire two years I'd known Sia. We'd met early on when Liam and I moved to Chicago, and she'd been the one friend who stuck with me as my life fell apart.

I was speechless for a moment. She'd finally solved her mystery? "Who owns it?"

A grimace flashed over her face, momentarily marring the image of perfection I knew she wanted for tonight. She'd swept her light blond hair up into a bun and rimmed her dark eyes. They looked smoky, but alluring and sexy. Exactly how Sia was. She moved closer to me, pulling her wrap tighter around her shoulders as she checked behind her. No one was looking, so she reached down to tug the front of her ball gown up. It had ridden low, showing a healthy amount of cleavage, but that was Sia. I'd just figured that was the look she was going for.

"That's the thing," she said. "I still don't know, and it's driving me nuts. You can find out, though." She clamped on to my arm again. "This was passed to me through a friend of a friend of a friend, but if you call that number, you can request to view the third floor."

"It sounds expensive."

"It's perfect for you." Her hand moved to her chest. "I can't afford it, but you totally can. You have the money Liam left you, and you've been wanting to get out of that house. I mean, all those memories. I totally get it. I know you've been looking to move."

I was, though it was a shameful secret of mine. Liam had loved our house. We were going to have our family there. The thought of leaving made me feel like I was leaving him. I'd been putting it off for a year, but it was becoming too much. I could feel him in every room. I could hear him laughing. When I was upstairs, I swore he would call my name as if he were just coming home from work. Everything was him—the furniture, the stupid expensive espresso machine he'd vowed we needed to live and then couldn't figure out how to use. Even his juicer—I still couldn't believe he'd bought a juicer for us.

My throat closed. The tears were coming, and I had to shut them down. "Yeah, but downtown?" I murmured, my throat raw. "That's a big change."

"It'd be amazing. You'd live three blocks from here. I'm here all the time, and my place isn't far away either. You can cab that easily." Her eyes were wide and pleading. "Please tell me you'll call. Do it! Dooo it."

I glanced back to the number. "What if this is some elaborate scheme to trap people and kill them? You said it yourself: you don't know who owns the building. It could be the Russian mob," I teased.

"Even better!" She rolled her eyes and dismissed that with a wave. "Come on, if it was the Russian mob, I would've heard about that. Besides, I heard one of the residents is the CEO of Grove Banking."

"The CEO?"

"It's his place in the city."

"Oh." Coming downtown was such a hassle. I loved seeing Sia, but I hated coming here as much as I did. But actually living here…

I'd dodge all the parking and traffic. There was something peaceful about living among the finest restaurants, museums, shopping and so much more. And although things were busy during the workday, I knew there were also times when it was quiet. After hours, it was a sanctuary within one of the most active metropolitan areas in the country. "It'll be so expensive."

"Your inheritance from Liam is ridiculous. You'll be comfortable for the rest of your life."

Yes, my inheritance *was* ridiculous—but not because it was twenty million dollars, because I'd never known about it. Liam had never told me. In fact, he'd kept all sorts of secrets. I hadn't known about the wealth until his family told me at his funeral, begrudgingly. I knew his mother had hated doing it. His grandmother had been a household name, as she'd invented a popular kitchen utensil.

I still couldn't believe it, even though the money had been transferred to my bank account. Most days, Sia was the one who reminded me about it. I had done okay as a freelance writer before he died, enough to have a small nest egg, but I'd had to dip into his inheritance over the last year. Just a bit, but I'd have to dip into it more for that place.

"I'll call." Sia took the piece of paper from me. "I'll set it up. We'll go together to see it. You won't be alone, and that way I get to see inside that glorious piece of heaven. You can decide afterwards."

I gave her a rueful look. If I saw it, and it was gorgeous, I'd probably want it. I liked to live simply, but I did appreciate beauty. And evidently I could afford it.

I sighed. "Okay. Call and set it up."

She grabbed my arm with both hands. "Oh my God! I'm so excited!" She yanked me to her, but the movement caused her hair to scoot forward too, looking out of place on her head. She stopped and quickly patted everything back into place—hair, boobs, dress, everything. Her smile never faltered. "We have to celebrate! The best fucking champagne I can find." And she was off, in the same whirlwind as she'd come. She signaled for one of the waiters.

She moved gracefully through the crowd among all the sparkling dresses and black tuxedos. Sia's world was beautiful. It was much livelier than mine, and it was okay to come and visit. I didn't think I could handle living in it, though. Would that be what happened if I moved downtown?

Or even if this place were something I loved, if it was as exclusive as she'd said, would they take me? Surely they'd want someone else, someone who was *someone*. I was no one. Hell, half the time I wasn't even me. But I'd go. I'd see the place and let Sia down easy after that.

I could see her approaching now with not one but two bottles of champagne in her hands. I eyed the one she held out to me.

"Take it." She linked her elbow through mine as I did, and guided me back through the event she'd organized. "We're going upstairs to my office, and we're going to get smashed."

"What about your clients?"

"I've wined and dined with all of them already. They'll be fine. The staff will take care of them. It's best friend time." She pulled me up the stairs and winked over her shoulder, her voice dipping down. "And besides, I've already made my evening plans, if you know what I mean. When you go home and I'm feeling lonely—aka horny—I'm supposed to give Bernardo a call."

I didn't ask who Bernardo was; she had so many boyfriends. I just smiled and followed.

I would do what she wanted. And when my sides were splitting from laughing too much later on, I'd call a cab. I'd go home, and I'd curl up under my blanket knowing that for one night, the booze would help me sleep.

CHAPTER TWO

It took a month to schedule our showing.

Sia had to do it. She scheduled it; then I changed my mind. She scheduled a second one, and a repeat. What was I doing? How could I possibly leave Liam's home? It was ours. It was his. I couldn't leave. But after the third time Sia set up a meeting, she made a pitch that I just had to see it. *See*. Not commit. Not move in right away.

I was still scared shitless, but I agreed. Her slight guilt trip helped, too. She was my best friend, and I was the excuse for her to see the inside of the building. So here I was, finally.

We pulled up to the silver building, and I saw that it wasn't really silver. It was glass. The entire building was made of windows. As I got out of the cab and craned my head back, looking up, I couldn't deny that I was already impressed.

Sia grabbed my hand and pulled me toward the building. "Come on. The manager's expecting us."

There was no big double or circling door at the entrance like most places had. It had a single black door, instead, which opened for us once we stepped in front of it. I passed through and saw there was no doorknob. I couldn't imagine using that to get in and out, but once I stepped inside, I realized there was a doorman. His office was right next to the door, and he now stood beside Sia. I looked at him, and he bowed. *Bowed*. For real—just enough so I saw the top of his greying head.

He straightened back up. "Good afternoon, Ms. Bowman."

He used my maiden name. I hadn't been called Bowman for two years—even before Liam and I got married, our friends were calling me Mrs. Sailor. I caught Sia's reaction from the corner of my eye. She snapped to attention, her eyes jerking to me, but I didn't say anything. It sounded strange to hear my old name, but maybe it was time I started using it.

I nodded back. "You, too, Mr…"

"Kenneth. You can call me Kenneth."

"Okay. Thank you, and good afternoon to you, too, Mr. Kenneth."

He'd started to indicate behind us, but at his name, he paused. The corner of his lip tucked under, like he might have been holding back a grin. He was just slightly shorter than me, maybe around five foot six, and he wore a thick black sweater over black dress pants. I saw a coat hanging just inside the door and imagined him whisking it on as he stepped outside. He was a cute little man—reddened chubby cheeks, warm brown eyes, and a little pudge in the stomach area. He had a huggable, teddy bear appeal. If I somehow ended up living here, I'd be calling him Ken within the week, whether he wanted it or not.

I found myself grinning back, even though he was still trying to hold his in.

Sia looked between us. "Ookay…"

A door opened and closed, and I heard a low voice call, "Ms. Bowman, Ms. Clarke, welcome to The Mauricio."

A very quiet squeal came from Sia. I ignored her and nodded at the approaching man. He was tall, with a slender build. Unlike Kenneth, this guy gave off a no-nonsense vibe. He held out his hand and shook mine firmly. I wouldn't have called him handsome. His eyes were dark, and he had a big nose with a strong jawline. But although he wasn't pretty, he was authoritative. Sia's mouth opened an inch, and I knew she was instantly taken with him.

"You can call me Dorian."

I nodded. "Hello, Mr.—"

He interrupted, showcasing a blinding white smile. "Just Dorian. No Mr."

"Dorian it is, then." I spoke at the same moment Sia breathed out, a hand to her chest.

"Oh yes. Dorian," she murmured.

"Ms. Clarke, it's good to meet you in person, put a face to the voice." He turned to her.

"Uh-huh."

If I looked, I wouldn't have been surprised to see her knees shaking. She was enraptured, and I knew I'd be hearing about Dorian for the next two months, until she slept with him. Mr. Kenneth and I cast her a look, and when she didn't notice, still transfixed by Dorian, I cleared my throat.

"Thank you for letting us see the apartment," I said, hoping to break the spell. "And for talking with Sia to set this up."

Dorian's eyes had lingered on Sia, but as I spoke, he turned to me. A flicker of something passed over his face. I frowned, not identifying what it was. It didn't feel right, but then it was gone. He gazed back at me with only the utmost professionalism. Clearing his throat and with a quick nod, he extended a hand toward an elevator located across the lobby.

"Ah, yes. It's more than an apartment, though." He glanced at Sia, but went on without saying her name. "I'm sure you've been informed that we have a small number of residents. Most have an entire floor. The owner is private, so rent checks will be made out to The Mauricio, should you decide this is a place you'd like to live."

The elevator doors opened as we approached, though Dorian hadn't pushed a button. He paused before stepping inside and gestured behind us. "As you can see, Kenneth's office is right next to the front door. You'll never have to worry about waiting for entry. When you approach, if you live here, the door will automatically open, just like this elevator. If Kenneth or myself isn't here, the system recognizes our residents. You should never be left outside, and if you are, all you need to do is press a button. But we guarantee that will never happen."

Besides the elevator, the doorman's office, and the front door, there was only one other doorway in the lobby, situated to the left of the elevator. Dorian pointed to it. "The front lobby is not extravagant, but that doesn't mean all the amenities aren't here. Beyond that door you'll find the pool, the patio, and places where you can grill and socialize. We have a gym, along with a running track that winds around the building and basement. It's covered, so it looks like a tunnel when you're inside. Passersby won't see you. There's a garden and a fountain on the way to the pool. The owner spared no expense, and I think you'll appreciate his efforts, but first…" He held a hand toward the elevator, which had remained open for us the entire time. "I'll show you the third floor, which is the only floor open right now."

Inside the elevator, a B, L, and buttons numbered 2 through 7 were lit up in silver on the right side. Three black buttons sat above those. Dorian pushed number three and stood back as the doors closed. "There's a sitting room and a theater room on the first floor. Pool, mail, the gym, and the running track are also on the first floor. You'll meet the other residents in those areas, most likely." The elevator stopped at the third floor, but the doors didn't open. Instead, a panel appeared on the left side, and Dorian pushed four letters.

The doors opened then, straight into the empty living space. There was no hallway, but there was no need. I was spellbound by the beauty before me. As I stepped inside, I heard Dorian saying, as if from a distance, "We have cameras all over the building—the elevators, the lobby, the parking lots, and so forth—except not in your home. You will be given your own unique code for your floor. You can put it in once you get into the elevator, or when you arrive at your floor. It's up to you. And if others call to be let up to your floor, you can approve them by pushing a button. That will allow the doors to open for your floor because you're sending the signal from within your own apartment, if that makes sense?"

I crossed the hardwood floors and went straight to the street side. The views were stunning.

Dorian spoke from just inside the door. "You can look out, but no one can see in. It's very private. Your safety is important to us, and believe me, if you live here, you are absolutely secure. The entire building is alarmed. A basement parking lot is available to you if you drive, and you'll be given a code for the first floor exits and your own door, if you use the stairs. You'll also get your own code for everything on the main floor. We have onsite security, though you'll probably never see them. They remain invisible to the residents, but if something were to happen, you'd be protected within seconds."

"And how would I alert them?"

He moved to the island in the kitchen and put his hand beneath the counter. "There's a panic button here. There's one in each room."

I glanced at Sia, who was frowning, erasing her dreamy look. The heavy security seemed more than I needed, but these people were rich. And I supposed heavy security was always a good thing.

I drifted back to the view of the street. Everyone was so busy, rushing down the sidewalk or hailing a cab. Cars moved along, as it was close to the end of business hours. They wanted to go home, and I knew in a couple of hours, the street would be very still. A shiver went through me, up my spine, over my arms, down my legs. It was the excited kind, the good kind, and I wanted to make it last.

It hit me then: I wanted to live here—not just as a fantasy, but for real. I wanted to be tucked away and safe in this building, but still so much in the center of everything. Even with the little I'd seen of the space, I already knew everything was top of the line.

I scouted around a little more. Hardwood floors that went everywhere. Four bedrooms. A master bathroom with a deep hot tub. Two living rooms, one sunken like something out of a hotel lobby. A white brick fireplace nestled between two couches. Dorian said the fireplace was just for show, but it still looked beautiful. A state-of-the-art kitchen with granite countertops and professional-grade appliances. Three chandeliers accented the spaces. The place came unfurnished, but Dorian said the chandeliers could remain.

Dorian stepped into the elevator to give us some time to talk, and he told me the code I'd need to call the elevator when we were ready to go.

As the doors closed behind him, Sia turned to me. "Okay, before you say anything, he said it's only $25,000 a month. I know you can afford this place. I totally think you should apply."

I had been ready to say yes, but suddenly I couldn't. "Liam loved our home." I felt him now. He was with me, looking at the place, and I could feel his hurt. I was going to leave his dream home for this?

Sia rolled her eyes. "I'm not trying to be mean, but he'd want you to move on."

*It's only been a year...*echoed in my head.

"I don't know, Si."

"I do." She stepped close, her voice softening. She touched my arm. "This is a once-in-a-lifetime place. It's going to be snapped up, and whoever moves in here won't be moving out. I can tell you love it, and you won't get this chance again. I guarantee. I know. I've been watching this place for two years, and I've never heard of an opening here. Get in while you can. Plus, you'll be so much closer to me! I know you hate the long cab rides, and I know you don't like riding the train alone. Do it. Take this place."

I let out a ragged breath. "That's if they'll even accept me. I'm sure they have a ton of people wanting to get in here."

"They'd be lucky to have you as a resident." She squeezed my arm. "Take it. Please? Or, at least try. For me. I'm begging you."

"I..." I did want it. I really did, but Liam. I'd be leaving him. "I need to think about it."

I could see the disappointment in her eyes, but she didn't say anything. She gave me a smile and pulled me close, her cheek next to mine. "Okay. You take your time." She hugged me, and in that moment—with my heart wanting one thing, but loving another—I needed that comfort.

I went home feeling like I was crazy. How could I leave Liam's home, my home with him? I walked into the house, hung my coat on the rack beside the door, and went to the kitchen. It was dark and empty.

There'd been life here before. Liam's baseball caps. The pile where he'd dumped his gym clothes. It stunk up the entire first floor. He always promised to move them, and he never did. I did, and I was always irritated. He was always clueless how they got back into his drawers.

So many memories, but half of them were packed away.

I couldn't bring myself to get rid of everything. The pictures had stayed up, but not the ones from the wedding. Those I sent to my parents, along with Frankie. After the accident, I ceased eating, bathing, living for a while. I couldn't take care of myself, much less our dog, so I sent him to run happily around on the farm. Or that was what I told myself. I hoped he was happy. Liam hadn't been a hunter, but my dad was. Frankie was a bird dog, so maybe everything worked out for the best…for Frankie.

I gazed over the empty table, the empty counters. Then I opened the refrigerator and found it empty except for a head of lettuce, ranch dressing, and two slices of cheese. And wine. I pulled out an open bottle from the door. It was half gone, but I didn't remember opening it.

Sia had been here every day for the first full month after I lost Liam. Then it became every other day in the second month, every third in the next. It was the sixth month when she couldn't take it anymore. I think it depressed her too much. She never said so, and

I never knew if it was the house or just me, but I realized she didn't want to be here.

I took pity on her and never asked her to come to the house again. I always went to her now.

The neighbors had come over when they heard about the accident. They'd brought casseroles, flowers, and blankets. I don't know why I got the blankets, but it was fine. They went into a pile in the guest room, and those eventually went to my parents as well. I'm sure my mother washed them, and I'd have my pick to use the next time I visited.

I let out a sigh. It seemed to echo through the house.

Liam and I hadn't gotten to know the neighbors before. We were still in the honeymoon phase, and it was all about us... I wished now that I'd made friends with a few of them so I could run over for a glass of wine, or hell, if I ever bought enough to bake, I could pretend to ask for a cup of sugar. I hadn't been inclined to make friends after he died.

"Should I leave?" I asked no one, though I still half-expected a response.

Was Liam here? I closed my eyes. He was everywhere. He was coming home from work. Frankie was barking, running to the door. He was coming in to kiss my forehead, telling me about his day. Frankie's paws pitter-pattered on the floor. He barked, darting around Liam, hoping for food. Liam would've grabbed a snack and sat at the table across from me. He'd groan, complaining about what Marsha said, or what Amie did. His co-workers drove him nuts. Frankie would whine when it was time to eat. Then Liam would take him for a walk, and I'd have food ready for everyone when they got back.

A tear fell, sliding down my cheek. I left it there. I knew more would join it.

I asked again. "Should I leave?"

No one answered. I was alone...with memories of my dead husband.

I skipped the salad and finished the bottle. Wine was one thing Liam had loved. He drank it sparingly, but he'd loved collecting his favorite bottles and had accumulated enough to try his hand at a makeshift wine cellar in the basement. I went downstairs, pulled out a few more bottles, placed two of them into the refrigerator, and took one with me back upstairs.

That bottle kept me company for the rest of the night.

There was a buzzing in my ear. It was loud, drowning out everything else. The air was hot, and people were running around, but a fog descended over me. I could hear a dog barking in the distance. Someone was screaming. There were sirens. I couldn't make sense of what I was seeing, but I knew it wasn't right. None of this was right.

Liam's car was upside down, glass everywhere. The other car—a truck—I looked around for it. It was gone. That…that didn't make sense. The driver left? Drove away? I saw a hand outside Liam's car. An arm had stretched out and rested on the top of the doorframe. I started forward. I had to get to him.

Was that Liam?

My heart was in my throat.

I didn't want it to be him. It couldn't be, but still I came closer— running even though the dog's barking and the shouting intensified. I shook my head. I didn't want to hear them, but I couldn't silence them. The pounding in my heart grew louder, competing with the screams and sirens for my attention. I couldn't focus on any of that. I had to get closer.

Then I was there. I knelt down.

God—it was Liam. I saw his wedding band.

Tears flowed down my face. The wetness registered, but I also felt pain—and burning. So much burning. It was so incredibly hot, but I had to get to Liam.

My knees touched the ground, and I heard crunching sounds. None of that mattered. Liam—

I ducked down so I could see him. He looked right at me. His eyes so alert and clear, almost as if he felt no pain, hadn't been in a car accident. I knew he had been, and this didn't make sense, but then he choked out, "Addison."

"I'm here." I reached out my hand, fitting it into his. I wanted to pull him clear.

"No, Addison."

"Why not?"

There was glass under my hand. I heard the pieces crack under me, but I didn't think about it. I just needed to get to him. "Liam, please." I wasn't sure what I was begging him for. To come to me? To let me near?

"No, Addison. You have to stay."

"Why?"

He lifted his head. A pipe was lodged in the back of his skull, and I scrambled back, choking as I saw it. I tried to tell him to stop, not to move, but he pulled his head clear. The pipe had been thrust up from the back of his seat. It was sticking out of his headrest, and blood poured from back of his head.

"Liam, please." I sobbed. I felt the tears. I could hardly see him. My sobs sounded like they were choking me.

"Why are you here?"

"What do you mean?"

"I don't want you here." His eyes flashed, darkening in anger. "I don't want you here! Get out."

"Liam—"

"GET OUT!" he roared.

I fell back, startled by the sudden change, and I landed on the street. Pain sliced through me. Stabbing, searing pain. My hands were coated with blood. Pieces of glass stuck to them. Pain exploded all over my body. Every muscle ached. My insides were on fire, and I hurried backward, scooting over the street. More pain. More glass. More burning.

I was halfway to the curb when I heard his laughter. I stopped, my chest heaving.

Liam was laughing.

My heart squeezed in a tight grip as he began to move. He was crawling out of the car, coming to me. His eyes pinned me down, and then he was standing. I couldn't move. I was held immobile.

I knew I should run. I should yell for him to stop, but I couldn't do anything.

He came toward me, saying, "You failed. Why did you fail?"

I tried to shake my head. I didn't know what he was talking about. But he kept coming. His eyes were so accusing. Blood had soaked him entirely. It dripped from his face, his hands, his fingertips, even his feet. He left bloody footprints over the glass, and still he came.

"You failed me, Addison. You betrayed me. Why?"

"I didn't — " I was crying too much; no words could come out. My throat closed, and then he was over me. He seemed to grow in size, foreboding and intimidating.

He grasped my shoulders. His fingers dug in, piercing my skin. "Why, Addison?!" He shook me. "Why did you betray me? WHY — "

I woke up screaming and jerked upright in bed, my entire body soaked in sweat. My heart pounded, and all I could do was sit as my chest heaved up and down, taking in gaping breaths of air. I had to settle down. It was a nightmare…a nightmare. I closed my eyes, telling myself that over and over again.

My hands curled around the blanket, forming fists. That was when I heard his laughter.

I lifted my head. My eyes snapped open, and I heard it again.

It was the laugh from the nightmare. It had been eerie then, and it sent shivers down my spine now. I gulped. Liam's laugh was so clear, so vivid; it couldn't be my imagination, though this laugh lacked all of Liam's warmth.

I sat there, afraid to move, and he kept laughing. I lay back down, but my eyes never closed. My hands never uncurled. And Liam never stopped laughing.

My mind was made up.

It was time to move.

CHAPTER THREE

"I'm so damn happy you decided to go for this."

Sia was unpacking a box in my new kitchen, pulling out pans and plates. I sat in the living room, stacking the books I hadn't been able to leave behind.

"What changed your mind?" she asked.

I paused, holding on to the box between my legs. It'd been a few weeks since that nightmare. Since then, I'd been staying at Sia's. When I arrived, she hadn't questioned me, and I was thankful I didn't have to explain my temporary relocation. I had a few more nightmares, but I heard no more creepy laughing at Sia's. Thank God.

The movers brought in the last piece of furniture around nine at night, and it was nearly two hours later when my stomach started growling. I hadn't eaten all day.

Sia frowned at one of the pans. She held it up as I approached. "What do you use this for? I just realized I have some of these, but I've never used them."

I took it from her, placing it beside the empty box on the counter. "Step away from the pan and promise me you'll never use one unless I'm there with you."

"So they can be dangerous, huh?"

"Not normally, but you'd burn your apartment down."

Her eyes widened. "I'm not that bad."

"Yes, you are." I patted her hand as my stomach grumbled again. "And speaking of food, is there a restaurant around these parts?"

Sia checked her phone. "Gianni's is down the block. I go there for lunch when I'm working. I've never been there this time of night, but I know it's open."

"I'm easy. That works for me. You have to show me around the neighborhood anyway. I know where you work and where your apartment is. That's it. Ken mentioned a grocery store not far from here, too."

"Ken?" Sia grabbed her purse and coat.

I shrugged, hitting the elevator button. "My nickname for him."

"Does he know he has a nickname?"

"He will."

When we walked through the lobby, he came out of his office and held the door for us. "Ladies, you have a safe night now."

"Thanks, *Ken*."

He paused, and then a grin spread over his face as well. He nodded again. "Miss Addison. Ms. Clarke."

Sia stepped outside and shoved her hands in her coat. "Why does he use my last name, but your first name?"

I stepped out behind her, and the door closed. Shrugging, I nudged her shoulder with mine. "I get the special nickname. You know, because I'm special." I winked, and she rolled her eyes.

"Don't get a big head because the doorman likes you. You're the one who lives here."

"How can I not? He's adorable. And besides," I continued as we began walking side by side, "Ken and I have this connection. It was instant, and it was glorious. You've got competition."

Sia leveled me with a hard look. "I do, huh?"

I nodded. "He's going to be my best friend. At the rate our relationship is moving, I'm sure it'll take two days. I'll need that best friend bracelet back. I'll have to get it enlarged for Ken. I think he has bigger wrists than you."

"Stop." She tilted her head back and laughed. "You think you're so funny."

"On occasion."

She continued to laugh, but threw an arm around my shoulder and hugged me tight to her side. "I've missed this."

"Acting like you're my boyfriend?" I gave her arm a pointed look.

She squeezed me. "No, this. You. You're joking, and you're smiling, and you're...the old you." She grew somber. "Maybe moving out was just what you needed."

"Yeah. Maybe."

I could feel Sia watching me from the corner of her eye, making sure I was okay with what she said, and I was. Surprisingly. My chest felt lighter. My shoulders didn't feel an invisible weight on them. And she was right. I'd always been able to laugh or joke for a moment—many of our nights together had been spent that way—but this was different. I wasn't on a break, or hiding from Liam's ghost. I felt free.

My stomach rumbled again, this time louder.

Sia heard it. "We awakened the beast." An overhang stuck out from the restaurant's front door, and she slowed. "And we're here. I'm hungry now, too."

Dark red fabric covered the overhang, and as we swept inside, past the black windows that faced the streets, I could see that black and red was the theme inside as well. Large black leather booths lined the auburn walls, carefully spaced to allow privacy. It was cozy and warm, but I felt an underlying tension in the room. A hostess led us to a back booth, and I remembered coming to this place once before with Sia. It had been a weekday during the noon hour, and the feeling had been markedly different. The entire room had been lit up and every table busy. The tension wasn't there then, not like it was now.

Sia slid into our booth. "We're going to drink. Just warning you now."

The hostess waited, holding my menu as I slid in across from Sia. Then she placed the menu in front of me and asked, "Would you like to order a beverage right away?"

"Hell, yes, she will." Sia moaned, opening up the drink menu. "A glass of chardonnay for me, and a water too. Addison, please order some alcohol with me. I don't want to be the only one boozing it up, and we deserve it after today." She gave me the drink menu and turned to the hostess. "She just moved in down the street. I'm thinking we'll need to buy a bottle to take home, too."

"I'm sure that can be arranged."

By the time I'd picked my glass of Merlot, Sia was fast friends with the hostess, and two bottles were coming with us, on the house.

I waited till she left and raised an eyebrow. "I didn't take that long to order."

Sia shrugged. "She's a model. I've seen her at the Gala for a few events. Trust me." She leaned forward and dropped her voice. "The free wine is because of the connections I can give her, not how long it took you to order."

"You're a fast worker."

"No, no." Propping her elbow on the table, an action Sia would normally frown upon, she twirled her wrist in the air and pointed at the hostess returning from the bar. "She's the fast worker. She recognized me, too. That's how this world works. Connections. Networking. Get to know people, and they might do you a favor later on. This is her favor to me, and she's smart, because if a photographer or painter needs a model, I'll have her in mind. Everything that goes around, comes around."

When the hostess came back over with a server right behind her, I sat back and watched my friend work. Sia was sparkling, sophisticated, and mesmerizing. The hostess didn't blink an eye as she charmed Sia right back. By the time the two bottles had been set up on the table, chilling in ice buckets, and our glasses set before us, the ladies had exchanged cards. As the hostess and server left, Sia sat back and sipped her chardonnay.

She wiggled her eyebrows at me. "We should come here more often. Forget noon lunch. Late-night dinner is the way to go."

I shook my head. "You amaze me, and you always exhaust me. I couldn't do that, flip it on like you just did."

"You get used to it. It makes life fun and interesting." She set her glass down, resting her fingers on the base. She toyed with it, biting down on her lip before asking, "I know my job isn't your style, but what are you going to do now?"

I sat back and tensed.

"You moved to Chicago because of his job, and I know you had a column in an online magazine, but what now? You haven't written anything for a while."

I hadn't realized she was checking.

"I subscribed to your column. I haven't gotten any alerts." She leaned forward. "I'm not trying to be a pushy best friend, but I am trying to be encouraging at the pace you need. I feel like you need it now. Moving out was a good thing. Writing is a good thing, too. Are you going to start doing that again?"

Was I going to start writing? Even just thinking about it, some of the heaviness returned to my chest. I shook my head, letting out a breath of air. I read, and I went on walks, and I watched movies. I did anything to clear my mind, and that meant no writing. "I don't know. Maybe. One thing at a time right now. Moving is a big deal. I already feel like I've betrayed Liam once."

"Oh." She straightened back in her seat. "I'm sorry. Sometimes I don't think of it from your perspective. I know moving is a big deal. And you don't have to write. I mean, you're set with money, so that's good. You don't have to worry. But I think it'll help you, even if you just do it for yourself. You're right. One thing at a time." She paused and then looked deeply into my eyes. "For what it's worth, Liam was a really great guy. He loved you more than anything. I know he'd be proud that you're moving forward."

My throat closed up. I could feel the tears coming, so I looked down. I didn't want to cry, not again. Reaching for my wine, I murmured, hoarsely, "Thank you." The mere mention of him, the thought that I might be betraying him—my insides burned. The hole that had been in my chest since Liam died opened wide again. I groaned and took a few sips of my wine more quickly than normal. *Fuck it.* I threw the whole glass back, and when I set it down, Sia had a stupid grin on her face.

She beamed at me. "There she is. I love this Addison. Let's get drunk tonight!"

I managed a smile. "Sounds good to me."

She was waving the server down for a second glass before the words left me.

The next glass went down faster than the first, and so did the third. I paused on the fourth and let the food soak up the first three. The meal was delicious, but that could've been the wine talking. Everything about the restaurant was fun. Late night dinner might be my new favorite way of eating, too.

Today had been a hard day—hard but satisfying. It was time to relax and let some tension go, and so we did. A couple hours later we were in the process of having our food boxed up, as well as the two bottles of wine, when a group of men entered the restaurant.

They came in suddenly and walked straight through toward the back. The atmosphere around us shifted. Their presence brought the undercurrent of tension I'd been feeling to the forefront. Everyone could sense it now, even Sia. I was intrigued by the pack of visitors, and I heard her swift intake of breath.

The men were all tall, all over six feet, with broad shoulders. They looked muscular, like they could've been MMA fighters, and most had hard jawlines. It wasn't necessarily their appearances that drew them attention, it was how they walked, their strong and confident presence together. They seemed to have one mission, and they didn't waver from it. None of them smiled. None of them looked around the restaurant, but they were clearly familiar with it. The hostess and server quieted, but didn't approach them. They seemed used to their presence as well.

The men didn't walk past our booth—we were too far in the corner—but they came toward us, then turned left. As they did, I watched them. The guy in the middle was different. He was startlingly beautiful. His hair was dark, almost black, and cut short. He had chiseled cheekbones and dark eyes that weren't like the others'. The other men had dead eyes. They were there to take orders, and this was the guy who gave them. He was the leader.

Authority and confidence emanated from him, along with an aura of danger.

I could find no outward indication to prove my gut feeling, but I was sure of it. The others were well above six feet, whereas this guy was either six feet or an inch above. He moved with a grace the others didn't have. He was lean, with broad shoulders and a slender waist, but he wasn't skinny. The others walked, but he stalked in a sensual way. He moved like a predator.

I licked my lips, then realized what I had done and pulled my gaze away. When the group reached the rear of the restaurant, instead of pushing through the door into the kitchen, they turned. I hadn't noticed before, but I saw a set of stairs. I counted as eight of them went up, leaving two behind. They took position with their backs to the stairs and hands folded in front. They were the guard dogs.

I realized I wasn't the only one caught in some kind of spell. The hostess and server had gone quietly back to their work, but Sia's mouth was hanging open. She still stared at where they'd disappeared.

I waited for her to snap out of it, thankful for the time to compose myself. That man, whoever he was, he'd affected me in a way no other had—since Liam. And at the thought of him, a bucket of ice crashed over me.

"Addison." Sia finally managed, her eyes still locked on the two guys standing at the stairs. "Oh my—did you see that?"

I coughed, clearing my throat. "What do you mean?"

"That guy." She leaned forward. "He was *gorgeous!*"

The image of him flashed in my head. A different burning flared up. "He was. Yes." I could admit that much. "He was also scary looking."

"Negative," Sia declared with a quick head shake. "He was absolutely breathtaking. Forget your building manager. I want to know who *that* guy is and how can I be his wife."

A genuine laugh came from me. This was vintage Sia. She had a new project, and it wasn't me. Thankfully. I had no doubt she'd hunt the guy down, find out who he was, and do as she'd promised, or at the very least have a hot fling.

"Seriously." She fanned herself. "I've never seen that man before, and I know almost everyone around here. Who could he be?"

"I have no clue."

"I suppose not." She skimmed over my face. "Oh, babe. You look a little flushed. The wine must be hitting you, huh?"

I nodded, but it wasn't the wine. "Yes, let's go, please."

Sia laughed, sliding out of the booth. I followed suit, and we walked back to my new home, armed with our food and two bottles of wine. No one had better mess with us. Our wobbly knees would be the death of them. I was grateful when Sia threw her arm around my shoulders again. It made me feel steady. She transferred her food to me so she only had to hold the wine and rested her head against mine.

We went home that way, and when we entered my apartment I remembered: I had no clue where anything was.

CHAPTER FOUR

The next month was glorious.

I woke up every morning to bustling traffic and pedestrians darting back and forth on the streets below. The view took my breath away, and it never stopped. And it was quiet. That had been my only concern, having a resident below and above me, but I shouldn't have worried at all. I heard nothing to even indicate that I had neighbors.

However, I'd seen one a couple times when I went to the gym. She looked to be in her early thirties, and as soon as I entered to hit the treadmill, she grabbed her towel and bottle of water and left. I thought it was me, but the fourth time I arrived, she was just starting, and she stayed the whole hour. I saw her a few other times after that, but she kept her head down and focused on her workout until she left.

In a way, it was a nice break from all the attention I'd received after Liam's death. So many people had approached me to express their condolences. I knew very few of them. They were the stranger neighbors or Liam's coworkers. I hadn't realized how exhausting it had been—the smiles, the warm wishes back to each of them, all people I didn't know. This woman was frank. She didn't know me. She didn't care to know me. I rather liked it.

Once I realized that Monday, Wednesday, and Friday she went to the gym at eleven in the morning, and her Tuesday / Thursday / Saturday schedule was five in the afternoon, I adjusted my routine and went at a different time. Since then we'd passed once in the lobby. I was leaving the elevator, and she was getting on. She gave me her first smile, and I grinned back.

I felt like she was thanking me for leaving her alone.

I didn't meet another resident until my fifth week living here. I'd started a routine where I grabbed the mail as soon as it came, which was around eleven in the morning. I went to the pool area to open it with a cup of coffee. After that, I'd either go upstairs to read a book, or I'd work out. It depended on whether not-so-friendly neighbor was using the gym or not. In addition to the normal television and movies I watched, I became a CNN addict. There was a restlessness in me, like life was passing me by, and I didn't want to miss a thing.

Yet when I thought about finding a job or writing a piece, emotions surged up in me. I didn't want to feel those emotions; I didn't even want to name them. I just didn't want them, so I'd go back to doing something that numbed me. Anything.

But everything was different in the mornings. It was a fresh start. Those feelings were pushed all the way down, and this morning was the same. I felt somewhat cheerful as I opened a letter from my realtor. My house was still being shown. I figured. Anything pressing would warrant a phone call or an email.

Then a man entered the pool area behind me.

I glanced up, startled by his presence, and my elbow hit my coffee. "Oh, no." I bent quickly to snatch it up.

"Here." The guy came over, grabbing a handful of towels on the way. He knelt, blotting the coffee to absorb it. "Sorry about that," he said as he looked up.

Young. Tall. And when he looked up at me, close—personal bubble close. He was pretty, or that was how Sia would've described him. Tall, dark, and handsome. The cliché fit him perfectly. His body was lean, and judging from the swim trunks and white shirt, swimming was the way he kept himself in shape. He wasn't gorgeous like the guy from the restaurant. *Yes, I am still thinking about him.* He didn't have the same striking, intense eyes or physique. This guy had a rounder face. He was more filled out, but he was still good-looking, and he was waiting for my response.

I shook my head. "That was my fault." I frowned at the dirtied towels. "Is that okay? Do I need to let Dorian know it was my fault? They're stained."

He glanced down as if he didn't know what I was talking about. Seeing the towels, his shoulders shook with laughter. "No. The money this place gets, they can afford a few stained towels. These will get tossed anyway." He dropped them on a nearby table and held his hand out to me. "I'm Jake Parker. I'm on the seventh floor. You're the new resident, right?"

I shook his hand. "I am. Third floor. I'm Addison—" I was about to say my married name, but heard myself saying instead, "— Bowman." I'd told him my maiden name. Why did I do that—nope. I wasn't going to analyze it. It was done.

"Addison Bowman?" He pulled out the chair across from me. "Do you mind?"

"No. Please, sit."

He sat down, and I straightened up. It felt weird to be sitting with another man, even though he was a neighbor.

"You okay?" His voice was soft and concerned. He hunched forward, so he didn't appear so tall. His eyes looked into mine, and they were warm, like heated chocolate. "I can go, if I'm making you uncomfortable."

"No." I shook my head, holding a hand out. "Please stay. I mean it."

"You sure?"

"I am."

"Good." He relaxed in his seat, kicking out one of his legs. He didn't touch me, but six inches to the right and his leg would've been pressed right against mine.

"I'm a lawyer. My firm's a couple blocks down." A grin tugged at his lips. "Most of the partners have their own places outside the city, but I'm a workaholic. Figured it was better to be closer to work."

"You're a new partner?"

He nodded. "Two months. It paid to be there all the time." Pride filled his voice. "How about you? What do you do?"

"Uh…" I looked at the table, for just a moment. "I'm a freelance writer. I used to do a column."

"Used to?"

"I've taken some time off."

"Breaks are good." He lightened his tone, glancing around and frowning at the pool. "I've been in New York for work the last few weeks, and I've neglected working out." His gaze swung back to mine. His eyes narrowed. "I'm surprised I haven't run into you before now. When'd you move in?"

"Five weeks ago."

His head bobbed up and down. "Oh yeah, and I'm sure you were probably busying unpacking and everything."

I nodded, gesturing out the door to the gym on the other side of the hallway. "I saw another woman in there a few times."

His grin widened. "Let me guess, she took off as soon as you walked in? And kept doing it, making you think you have a disease or something?"

"She did that to you, too?"

"Oh, yeah." He rolled his eyes and began drumming his fingers on the table. "That's Dawn, but that's just how she is. She has to warm up to people. Gotta say, this place is perfect for her. Not many residents here. It's exclusive, safe, and she's protected. The first couple months I was here, that's how she was. Then it switched. She started smiling, talking, and now we've hung out a couple times. There are a few of us who do dinners together. Dawn's hosting the next one. I can ask her if you can come, but I'd be surprised if she okayed that. I'm doing the one after that. You should come to that one for sure. It's next month. I've got a mean slow cooker, just to let you know." He blew on his knuckles. "I'm known around these parts as Chef Slow Pot."

A laugh burst out of me. "Thank you for that, Chef Slow Pot."

"Mmm-hmmm. Ninja skills in the kitchen. I'm telling you." He winked. "But seriously, don't worry about Dawn. She'll warm up to you, and you'll find her buzzing your door with coffee every morning."

I lifted an eyebrow. "She does that for you, huh?"

"No. She'll do that for you." He gestured to my empty cup on the table between us. "She tends to show up with wine at my place, when I'm home. Because of her thing with people, she sticks like glue to the ones she knows. I'm the wine-and-movie friend. Half the time she zonks out and sleeps on the couch."

"You two are good friends?"

"I guess so. She's fun. Wicked obsessed with *The Walking Dead*." He leaned forward to rest his elbows on the table. "I know Dawn and I are single. How about you? There's a couple on the fifth floor, and the only other resident I've met is Derek. He's an IT guy, so if you've got computer problems, he's below me on the sixth floor."

"What floor is Dawn?"

"Second. I don't know who's on the fourth floor." He pointed to the ceiling. "And the big boss, too. I've not met him."

My mind was spinning, doing the math. "So there's you on seven, IT guy on six, a couple on five, four is a question mark, I'm three, and Dawn's on two. Who's the big boss? He's not on four?"

"No way. I'm sorry. I meant the owner. He's got the top three floors in here."

There were those three black buttons in the elevator. "Who's the owner?"

"Who knows." His shoulders lifted and dropped back down. He pushed his chair up to rest on the back two legs. He kept hold of the table. "That's the big mystery. No one knows who owns the place. We all go through Dorian for everything."

"Why the secrecy?"

He shook his head again. "You got me. I know Dawn's obsessed with figuring it out. She's a hermit in terms of the outside world, but she tries to stake out the elevator. Dorian or Kenneth always kicks her out. Technically, we can do whatever we want around here. That's their whole motto—that this building is our home—but you noticed there's nothing in the lobby, right?"

"I did. Yeah."

"That's because of Dawn. There used to be a couple couches down there, but she took them up as her favorite knitting spot. She'd sit there for an entire day and all night a couple times, knitting her blankets and listening to books on tape. I thought it was hilarious. She texted me to bring her food and relieve her so she could go to the bathroom."

"And during that, still no sign of him?"

"Nope. Not a glimpse. I don't think he's here that often, if it is a he. Who knows. Maybe it's a woman. I think he or *she*—" He winked at me. "—was here last month sometime. The shipping elevators were shut down."

"When you weren't here?"

"Dawn told me. She orders stuff a lot. She had a table coming that day and was super steamed because Dorian made her move the arrival date back. I was on the phone with her for three hours."

"Sounds entertaining."

He glanced back over his shoulder, eyeing the pool again. "I suppose." A deep sigh. "I have to meet clients tonight. I should get to my workout." He stood up, pushing his chair back in place. "It was nice to meet you, Addison."

"You, too." My stomach dipped as he said my name, his eyes lingering on my lips. "Jake."

"Yes. Jake. That's my name." He pointed to me, winking again. "Keep using it, and if you're not here when I finish, I mean it about the dinner next month. I'll drop an invite in your mailbox."

"Sounds perfect." *Sia.* "Wait."

He turned.

"Can I bring a friend?"

The corners of his mouth turned down, but smoothed out right away. He smiled. "Of course."

"You might regret saying that. I'll bring my best friend. She's...a handful, I'll just say."

His grin widened. "Perfect. Dawn will freak if there's a stranger, so we'll have a good show. She'll come back down once you're gone. She's already claimed a TWD marathon that night. Anyway, sounds good. I look forward to meeting this friend of yours."

He lingered, staring another moment before he pulled his gaze away and went to the pool. I still had more mail to open, but I checked my phone. The clock agreed with me. Grabbing my mail, I went to the front lobby. There was a back elevator, and I wasn't sure about the special codes. I'd stood at it one day and kept hitting the button. Nothing happened. So since then, I'd always gone to the front elevator.

Pushing through the door that connected the rest of the first floor with the front lobby, I stopped abruptly when I saw Dorian talking to Ken. Both wore similar grim expressions, but when they heard the door open, welcoming smiles instantly took their place.

"Ms. Bowman." Dorian approached, his hand stretched out toward the elevator. "May I ride up with you?"

I nodded as the doors slid open, and he stepped inside, holding them for me. I glanced to Ken and saw some of the seriousness had returned to his face. He didn't catch my look, but Dorian did. He cleared his throat, saying pointedly, "I'll be right back, Kenneth."

Ken looked up and saw my scrutiny. His warm and welcoming smile returned as he nodded. "Of course, Mr. Dorian. Ms. Bowm—"

"Addison."

"Hmm?" He was half-turned back toward his office.

"Use my first name, Ken." I added quietly, "Please."

"Oh. Yes." He chuckled softly. "I certainly will from now on."

Stepping inside the elevator, I swung a stern look toward Dorian. "That goes for you, too."

His head lowered slightly. "I will, Addison." He hit the third button.

After that, we rode in silence, and when I stepped out on my floor, I glanced over my shoulder.

Dorian hit one of the black buttons.

CHAPTER FIVE

Sia closed her eyes, humming "We Are The Champions" by Queen, as we waited for the elevator. Her head bobbed in rhythm when she got to the "on and on" part. The crescendo was building. Her hips swayed back and forth, and her shoulders had started to move by the time the elevator arrived.

"Oh." She quieted, straightening as the doors opened. Smoothing a hand down her hair, she flashed me a grin as we stepped into the empty elevator. "I'm getting all jacked up for the party. I'm going to conquer the shut-in. Mark my words." She paused. "She knits, right?"

I hit the seventh-floor button, holding a bottle of wine. "Yeah."

Jake had been true to his word. I'd found an invite in my mail, and we'd chatted more over the last month. Either his swimming time matched when I went through my mail, or he'd rearranged his schedule. Either way, it had become almost a regular thing to meet up in the pool area three times a week. Dawn had sat with us two of those times—in silence the first and grunting a few words the second. Jake assured me she was warming up and my presence at his dinner wouldn't be an issue, but we both knew Sia would be. The last we talked, the plan had been to wait and see, so that was what I was going to do.

"I need a problem about knitting."

"You knit?"

"No." She pulled out her phone. "But she won't know that."

"What?"

Sia was busy looking at her phone and waved a hand at me. "Don't worry. This is what I do. You said Dawn is the building shut-in, right?"

I nodded.

"I'm new. She just started saying hello to you, so she's going to bolt at the sight of a stranger. That puts pressure on you. I'm your friend, you're the new resident, and the other people are going to blame you. I don't want that to happen, so therefore, the shut-in needs to stay put. She knits. She must have a love for it, and little does she know—" Sia flicked her wrist, showcasing her face in a Vanna White wave. "She's about to meet her knitting soulmate. By the time that elevator door opens, I'll have enough in my head to bullshit my way through a problem only she can help me with." She leaned forward and dropped her voice. "Because, you know, us knitters need to stick together. No one else gets the frustration of a—" She checked her phone. "—dropped knot."

I could only stare at her. "Your powers cannot be challenged by mere mortals."

"Darn tootin'. I'm the Athena of networking. A shut-in is a snack before lunch for me. Give me a room of shut-ins, and I've got my dinner entree."

"I have no idea how you do it, but thank you." My voice softened. "I know you're doing this for me."

Her smile softened as well. "I know." She nudged me with her arm. "Love you, girl."

"Love you back."

"Now, shut up. I have to get more info in my head before those doors open."

But we were already there, and the door opened with Jake standing on the other side, two glasses in his hands. He raised them. "Champagne for my new guests."

"Well…" Sia stopped, still in the elevator, and looked him up and down. She wasn't subtle. Tucking her phone away, she exited, keeping her eyes on him the whole time. "You're a nice surprise. I'm Sia, Addison's best friend."

"Jake." He handed us each a glass and held out his hand.

"Hello." Sia shook it and moved closer, giving him a good view down her dress.

His eyes widened a bit, and the corner of his mouth lifted. He glanced to me, a question on his face. I lifted a shoulder. I should've thought about this. Sia had been searching for Mr. Gorgeous from the restaurant, but she'd come up with nothing. Her frustrations had been expressed over and over…and over again.

Whoever the guy was, he'd escaped certain heartbreak. Sia would've run through him like a snowplow and spit him out at the end. That was her way. Always looking for The One, she got a whole lot of hot sex instead, and the guys never lasted long. She had that look right now, still grasping Jake's hand. Her eyes narrowed like a predator who'd found the prey to beat all other prey. I was surprised she didn't lick her lips and stalk around him, giving him a good once-over.

"Hello back to you." Jake said to Sia, but he cast me a look, surprise in his depths.

I pretended to be ignorant. Sia was my best friend, after all. Their hands finally parted, and I handed over the bottle of wine. "I brought this with. I hope it works for dinner."

Sia continued looking him up and down.

I was a barrier between them, and Jake ducked his head, speaking so only I could hear. "Should I be scared?"

"Oh, yeah." I grinned. "Be very scared."

He laughed and squeezed my shoulder before gesturing toward the dining room. "Come on in. Make yourselves at home. I'm—" His eyes found Sia's again, and he faltered, running into his counter. "Uh, I have to check on some of the food real quick."

He moved away, and Sia closed in. "You didn't tell me he was gorgeous."

Jake? He opened the oven and bent over to pull out a pan. I looked at him thoughtfully. His ass was firm and tight. His pants showed it off perfectly, so why hadn't I... I shrugged. "Yeah. He's pretty, but I thought you were obsessed with the other guy. The restaurant guy."

Her eyes were still trained on Jake's ass. "I was, but whoever he is, he's not in my circle. That means he's either wealthy beyond wealthy, or he's a criminal." She sighed. "Goddamn. Why didn't you warn me about Jake? Wait." She stiffened. "Do you like him? I'll back off if you do. You haven't shown interest in a guy since..." She trailed off, her eyes darkening. "Sorry."

Liam.

I could sense an apology about to spill from her lips, but held up a hand. "Don't. I mean it, and yes, I thought Jake was attractive when I first met him. But it's dwindled since then. He's just another building resident to me now."

"Are you sure?"

"I'm sure." I glanced around. An older couple stood on the other side of Jake's place. Both held champagne glasses, and they were talking to another man. I assumed they were the couple from the fifth floor, and the other man was from sixth, the computer guy. I skirted around to take in the rest of the space. Dawn stood in the corner, hostile eyes latched onto Sia. She held an entire bottle of champagne in front of her like it was a shield to ward off evil spirits. Sia looked at her, too, and Dawn's eyes widened. She jerked. Her back hit the wall. "Um." My hand closed over Sia's arm. "You might get hit by a bottle if you go over to see Dawn."

"That's the shut-in?"

I nodded. "Let me do the introductions."

It was pointless. Sia headed right for her. Dawn looked around her—down to the floor, back to the elevator, and then to the windows. Then Sia was in front of her, her hand stretched out. I watched my friend in action. Dawn was a cornered wild animal, but as Sia kept talking, her shoulders relaxed. The weapon lowered. She sagged back into the wall instead of bouncing off it, and she began to nod. Suddenly, her eyes lit up, and a smile appeared. Sia had her. Just like that. Whatever lie she was weaving, it worked. Sia took the bottle and placed it on a nearby table. Her phone came out, and the two bent over it as they continued to talk.

"Holy shit." Jake breathed into my ear, stepping around to my side. "I wouldn't believe that if I hadn't seen it for myself."

"That's what she does."

"You're proud of her."

I paused, and decided he was right. "I wish I had skills like that. She has the ability to make everyone in this room feel like her best friend. I'm most definitely *not* that way."

"You and me both. I'm friendly, but I can't compare. Took months for Dawn to warm up to me. She's eating out of your friend's hand within ten minutes."

His voice dipped down, and I readied myself. I knew where this was going.

"I have to ask…" He leaned even closer. "Is your friend single?"

"And ready to mingle."

"Do you mind if I…?" He gestured with his head.

I could see it now. Sia would be at the pool. She'd be in the exercise room. She'd pop in every now and then. That'd be great, until the other shoe dropped. Then she'd pop in to vent, not to chat. She'd want to know if I'd seen Jake that day, if I'd heard laughter from his floor, if I thought another girl was with him. Sia's love affairs were hot until they got chilly. And if she was here, if she was my friend, and they broke up—that'd be awkward. She wouldn't want to come over. She'd be tense, wondering whether she was going to run into him or not.

A sense of impending doom slowly slithered all the way down to my feet, but I waved him toward her. "Have at it."

"Thanks, Addison."

Jake was smitten.

He couldn't stop staring at her, and then introductions happened. The couple was Doris and William, sixty-year-old socialites having the time of their life. They loved living so close to the museums, nicest restaurants, and concert halls. They recited all that with a slight nasally sound in their voice, and then Jake came around with more champagne. Their inner hippies came out shortly after that. Their son disapproved of their lifestyle, Doris informed me. They were supposed to volunteer for the nursing home he ran. Their daughter more than shared their love of the scene. She was a third resident on their floor, often staying longer than they wanted when she was in between boyfriends, and her little Shih Tzu too. I didn't know there was a dog policy, but based on how they suddenly grew hushed, I didn't ask.

Then Doris whispered loudly, "That's all on the downlow, though. Be a dear, sweetheart. Mum's the word. Hmmm?"

I felt like I'd just agreed to be their drug dealer. The next introduction was Derek, who wasn't just an IT guy, he was a computer genius. He created programs, and the "heads," he explained with finger quotations, liked to meet at their offices downtown. He was a geek in all the best ways: wrinkled T-shirt, baggy jeans cropped too short at the ankles, and champagne in his favorite coffee mug, which said, Don't Worry, I Won't Byte.

All the while, Sia kept Dawn occupied in the corner. Jake veered over at one point, and a dark look, filled with promise, passed between him and Sia. He ended up going back to open my wine. Somehow, a third bottle brought everything up another notch. Conversation flowed more easily. Laughter grew louder, and more frequent. Dawn was nearly bouncing up and down with excitement next to Derek, holding his arm, and Jake and Sia disappeared for a few moments. When they re-emerged, both flushed in the face, hair messed and lips swollen, Sia veered toward Doris and William. Jake joined Derek and Dawn, and I watched the three single residents in

TIJAN

action. Jake seemed almost like a mentoring big brother to Derek, or maybe the cool brother Derek wanted to be. Dawn nearly beamed. As Sia predicted, she'd found her knitting soulmate, at long last.

"The Age of Aquarius" blasted from the speakers, and instead of a full meal, Jake arranged the food as a snacking buffet.

"Doris took over the music." Sia collapsed on the couch next to me. "It's going to be a Beatles and John Lennon night tonight. Betting you twenty bucks the old couple brings out a joint within the hour. I got a good whiff from William. He just smoked up."

"Here?"

She waved down the hallway. "In the bathroom. He was coming out at the same time—" And she realized what she'd been about to say.

I gave her a knowing grin. "I saw your entrance. Don't even try to lie to me."

She groaned, but couldn't hide her smile. "I must look silly." She rolled her eyes. "Addison, I had no idea. I finally found my booty-call soulmate."

"Booty call?"

"Yeah." She stilled. One side of her mouth flattened. "What?"

She was in love. At long last, her future husband. She was going to move in with him. Those were her normal responses, what I was used to hearing from her as every steamy affair got started. I shook my head. Calling a new guy a booty call wasn't her usual approach.

"Nothing."

"No. What? You had a look," she pressed.

"It's just…" I glanced over at Jake. He was watching us—correction, he was watching Sia. I pointed at him. "I know that look. All your new boyfriends have it. It's going to be hot, intense, and I won't see you for a month or two until you break up." I gave her a hard look. "That's when it will get uncomfortable. I know how you are."

"What are you talking about?"

"When you two break up, you won't come here anymore. He's my neighbor."

She waved that off. "Oh, phooey. That's silly. I've been over to your place a ton and not run into him. It won't be a problem."

But it would be. I could read the writing on the wall from half a mile away.

"Addison." She touched my arm. "I won't let it affect you and me."

My hand went over hers. "Promise?"

She squeezed my arm. "Promise. I need you, too. It's not just you needing me. You're my sanity in this crazy life I lead."

I didn't believe her, but it meant a lot that she said so. "Thank you."

"Any time, best friend."

My arm rubbed against hers. Staring at the group, I couldn't believe these were my neighbors. This felt weird, but it felt good at the same time. A year ago, I couldn't remember to give Frankie water, and now I was sitting in someone else's home at a gathering. I let out a sigh.

"What's wrong?"

I shook my head, then gestured to the group. "I thought I was going to die a year ago."

"Ah." She got it. "You've come a long way."

For a moment, I couldn't talk. My throat closed up. Then, Simon and Garfunkel filled the room, and Doris started swaying her hips. Her arms raised, and her hands began circling in time with the music. William bopped next to her, and Jake pulled Sia to the dance floor. Derek grabbed my hand, doing an impersonation of a chicken around me, and even Dawn moved her shoulders in her corner.

For my first resident dinner, I'd say it was a success.

Doris and William danced happily off to their floor. Dawn and Derek were both giggling, clutching each other for balance as they caught the elevator right behind them. So it was Jake, Sia, and myself remaining.

I turned around. Nope. The two of them were already in the bedroom.

"So," I called. "I suppose I'll see you tomorrow?"

I waited.

Nothing.

"Sia?" I cleared my throat. "My best friend, who came with me as my date tonight?"

Soft laughter and a groan was my answer.

"Okay then." I hit the button for the elevator. I had a bit of a wait, as it had to drop both Derek and Dawn off before coming back up for me. "I'll just, uh, turn in."

A shoe hit the floor. A burst of giggling sounded, and then I heard footsteps rushing down the hall to me. The swishing of Sia's dress assured she was clothed—I didn't need to brace myself for a vision of her underwear or straight-up breasts. When she appeared, her hair was a mess and her lipstick faded.

"Addison." She hurried the rest of the way, her cheeks flushed and glowing. A good whiff of Merlot made my nose twitch when she flung her arms around me. "I love you, baby." She pulled back, then smacked my cheek with her lips. "I'm staying with Jake for the night."

"Lunch tomorrow?"

"Oh yeah. I'll pick you up. We can walk to Gianni's together."

"Okay." I hugged her as the elevator pinged its arrival. "Have a good night. Use protection."

"I will." She leaned in close, giving me another hug as the doors opened behind me. "Thank you so much for being the bestest friend ever. Love you, honey bunches." Her breath tickled my neck, and then she was off, headed back to the bedroom.

I stepped into the elevator, and after putting in my code, my finger paused over the button for three. I remembered I hadn't gotten my mail that day. I could ask Ken to bring it up, but I hit the lobby button.

I had my mail in hand, and I was about to return to the lobby when I heard the noises. A door burst open, not from the front lobby where I now stood, but behind me somewhere. My feet moved first. I didn't think as I headed back to the mail area. That back elevator was close by, and as I rounded the exercise room, I saw the men.

Five of them. All tall. They weren't talking. They reminded me of the men from the restaurant, their hard jawlines set in stone. They were clearly no-nonsense, and as one moved aside, his jacket opened, and I saw a gun in a holster under his arm.

The back elevator opened, and two of the men rushed toward it. I held my breath.

My feet quickened. I clutched my mail in a tight grip, almost squishing it into a ball.

"Clear," one of the men announced.

Someone else spoke on the other side of the man I could see. They filed one by one into the elevator, leaving only the one with his back to me. He glanced behind him before he joined them, saying the word, "Clea—" But as he saw me, the word died in his throat.

I wanted to see.

The elevator was closing.

I hurried up. Who were they?

The man stepped inside. He moved, trying to block me, but I saw their faces.

It *was* the men from the restaurant. My feet planted, and my body teetered forward before finding balance again. I could only stare.

There was the leader. He stood against the back wall, holding up another man by the arm.

I was locked in, staring back at Sia's mystery man. I couldn't help but note the irony. She'd given up on him—and was now probably writhing underneath my neighbor—just as he appeared.

Once again, he was dressed as the others—black jackets, black shirts, and slacks—but he was different. I'd never heard him speak, but I knew he was the alpha. He was strong, authoritarian, and somehow I knew he was intelligent. A darkness began swirling in me, filling me up. I didn't know where it came from, and I couldn't make sense of it, but it was addicting. My blood began to buzz, and my heart picked up its pace. I couldn't look away. His eyes narrowed, and he stared right back at me as the doors started to close.

I moved forward again. I wanted to see more. Just before the doors closed, I glanced down and saw the pool of blood at his feet.

The doors closed. I stepped back to watch.

The elevator stopped on the floor above Jake's.

CHAPTER SIX

Mrs. Sailer,

I enjoyed your email, and yes, we'd love to have you back on the team. Your column position was filled last year, so unfortunately, we'll have to bring you in on an assignment-based capacity until more openings occur. Please send me any ideas you have, and we can proceed from there. I'm excited to get in touch and talk further.

Sincerely,
Tina Gais
Editor-in-Chief
Onlooker Online Magazine

    I read that email once, then again, and a third time. I'd received it this morning, and I was trying to create a list of ideas, but found myself going back to read it all over again. There was no mention of Liam's death, what I'd been through, or why they'd had to fill my position. Yep. No word on how they'd promised I could take all the time I needed to mourn. No one could replace me, and they were thinking of me always. No mention of any of the supportive messages they'd sent me when I let them know I needed more time. Being a relationship advice columnist when the love of my life had just died hadn't been one of those things I could bounce back into.

My gaze shifted from the email to my list of ideas. So far I had a number one…and nothing else. That blank number one had taken a whole hour to figure out. I felt it was promising. I rolled my eyes. Who was I kidding? I still wasn't there. My column was taken. I had to send back new ideas, not my old ones. No more stories on why Mr. Settle-For-You would never compare to Mr. Perfect-For-You. I was such a sap.

I hunched back over the computer and typed:

Ten things to do if your husband dies.

#1. Move out of your shared house. It saves time on being haunted.

#2. Hide the booze from others. You'll want it on those nights when everyone leaves you alone, and that happens faster than you think.

#3. Smile. They may be perfect strangers, but they don't like to be reminded they are.

#4. Get plastered every night so you don't play your husband's death over and over again in your head. This ties back to #1.

#5. ---------------

I shoved back from the computer. I couldn't send that. Going into the bathroom, I looked in the mirror. That person staring back, she was most definitely a downer. Sad eyes. Bags under those same dark eyes. Hair that used to shine in the sunlight—that was what Liam had said. It was a sandy-color blond that fell past my shoulders. It looked like a limp mop now. I shook my head, cleared my thoughts. Yes, whoever was staring back at me wasn't me. She was grieving, but me, I was trying to live again.

Sia had said to try to get back to work. That would help. This morning was my first real try at it.

It was a big-time fail.

I was supposed to meet Sia for lunch at Gianni's, and instead of us walking together, I'd gotten a message from her earlier just to meet her there. That meant I had three hours to kill before walking down the block, and writing had been supposed to fill that time.

I eyed my sneakers and headphones. I'd been avoiding Dawn in the gym, but she was friendlier lately. Chewing the inside of my cheek, I considered… I could do a hard workout and still be done with stretching and even cool down before she entered the elevator. It wasn't that I wanted to avoid Dawn. I just didn't want to push my luck with her. Sia was her new bestie, or so she thought, and I didn't want to be pulled into the middle of that either—just like Sia and Jake and whatever was going to happen with them.

I grunted. Even Sia was better at living my new life than me, and thinking about that, my decision was made.

Changing clothes, I grabbed my sneakers and laced them up. My headphones in one hand and my phone in the other, I headed downstairs. The doors slid open at the lobby, and I stepped out, turning toward the door to the back area.

"You're going for a workout, Miss Addison?"

"Addison, Ken." He still refused. "Just Addison."

Ken stepped out of his office and chuckled, his wrinkled face immediately rounding. His cheeks colored, and he pulled his hat off, tucking it against his chest. "Might you feel up for a run today, Addison?"

My name came out so reluctantly. I could imagine his teeth grinding together. Wait. What did he say? A run? "Is the gym closed?" I usually used the elliptical, then the treadmill for my cool down.

"No, ma'am."

"Ken," I warned.

"No, Addison." His gaze shifted to my left, over my shoulder. "Our running track's nicely heated, though, if you were to feel up for a real run today."

"I…"

He turned back into his office, and I trailed off. That was different. I turned, and with a last glance over my shoulder at him, I pushed open the door. I paused on the other side. My hands found my hips and rested there, but then I shrugged. He wanted me to run on the track. Well, I liked Ken. I figured he said it for a reason.

Jake said he'd used the running track a few times, and it was long and winding. It dipped down next to the basement parking lot and back up to go along the side of the building before it circled back inside.

I opened the door to the track and had to pause again. Jake never mentioned that the track was literally a clear tube. It had two lanes, and beyond the tube I could see the gardens that decorated the pool area. Ken was right. I was beginning to feel more and more like a run.

I was popping my headphones in after a quick stretch when I heard soft footsteps on the track—the sound of someone running. They were coming in quick and strong, and then they rounded the last turn, coming right for me. The runner's head was bent, his hood pulled low. I was off to the side, so when he zoomed past me, I couldn't quite see who it was. It wasn't Jake, or I didn't think it was. He was probably at work, and the guy was taller than Derek. I doubted it was William. Maybe the mysterious fourth-floor resident?

Then the image from last night flashed in my head: Mr. Gorgeous holding his comrade up, pool of blood on the floor. Could it be? The runner had the same physique, but two times in two days when no one else had seen him? Ever? I shook my head. It was probably the fourth floor guy, and with that decided, I started off at a light jog.

Okay. Well. The first lap took longer than I thought. And I was wheezing. I wasn't as fit as I'd thought. Still, I could do another lap. My lungs weren't bursting, so I circled around for the second lap. At the end of it, I vowed to bring my pedometer next time. I wanted to know how far each lap took me. This was longer than a normal track, much longer. I was panting like a beached whale when I circled back around toward the door again, and that was when I saw him.

He'd stayed.

His arms folded over his chest, and he was watching me.

A thrill coursed through me. He wasn't even stretching. He was just waiting for me. I slowed, forcing my breathing to calm as I walked in. I needed time to adjust because it was *him*—Mr. Mystery Gorgeous Man from the back elevator. Like last night, as our eyes met and held, my blood started buzzing. A whole host of emotions circled like a tornado in me. I didn't like it, but as adrenaline and excitement zipped through me, I had to admit that I didn't *not* like it either.

He wore a warm smile, and his sweatshirt clung to him, showing his broad and muscled shoulders. God. His body—it was toned. Even under black sweatpants and a sweatshirt, I could tell how ripped he was. His hood was pushed back now, and as I got closer, I noticed his hair had been cut since yesterday. It was buzzed short. It fit him. His hair didn't seem as dark as before, yet somehow, it made him seem even more primal and dangerous. He could do damage. I didn't want to know what kind of damage, but I knew without a doubt he was not someone I wanted as an enemy. I didn't fear him; I actually felt drawn to him, my body sizzling. Yet I was wary of him, and of myself at the same time.

His dark eyes never left mine. He studied me, and I got the feeling he knew exactly what kind of sensations and thoughts were going through my head.

A glimmer of a grin showed on his face before he held out his hand. "I'm Cole."

I eyed his hand. I've never been a hands lady, but his showed strength. Fitting my palm to his, I learned his hands weren't rough. He gave me a firm handshake, and a rush of blood went through me. My knees nearly buckled. I closed my eyes. What was happening? I'd never reacted like this—ever. Not to Liam. Not to any guy.

Get yourself together, Addison.

"Addison," I managed to respond.

He nodded as if he already knew. His eyes sparked, and I got the distinct impression he was laughing at me. He glanced down the running track. "You did good. Almost a mile."

"Is that how far two laps go?" I asked, my voice too loud. "I was trying to figure it out. I've never run here before."

I wasn't a schoolgirl, but he made me feel like one. I was too old to be reacting like this. Shifting on my feet, I reached over and kept one arm across my chest like a barrier. I grabbed my other arm, which was pressed into my side. There. I felt some semblance of control now, which was ridiculous. My arm over my chest wasn't a barrier at all.

"Do you live here?" I asked.

One side of his mouth lifted, and if I'd thought he was gorgeous before, the half-smile made him breathtaking. I wasn't prepared for the sight, and I rocked back on my heels.

Good God. That was enough. I could hear Sia's voice in my head saying, *You need to get laid.* She was right. That was why I was reacting like this, so even a damned half-smile made me wet. It was time to do the deed and suffer through a one-night stand. Apparently my hormones were making this announcement in the most embarrassing way possible.

"I'm a friend of Dorian's."

Lucky Dorian. He hadn't answered my question, but I didn't push it. "Okay."

"You must be the new resident? He said someone new moved into the third floor."

"Yeah. That's me." I had to avert my eyes. It was like he could stare into my soul. I didn't like that.

His head moved with mine so he could still see my eyes. "Am I making you nervous?" His voice softened.

"A bit." I'd admit that. A wry laugh followed. "I'm, uh, to be fair, you're…" I waved my hand at him. "…a lot. And I haven't been around guys like you in a while. My, uh, husband—"

Stop, stop, stop! I yelled silently at myself. *"Guys like him?"* What the hell was I saying? And I was about to tell him about Liam? Not first-time meeting material. I shook my head, grimacing, and managed to stop.

"I'm sorry. I'm, I saw you last night in the elevator." I looked up. He had inched back a step, putting a bit more distance between us, and my chest loosened. "Is your friend okay? He was bleeding."

He continued studying me, and he seemed more closed off. A wall that hadn't been there a moment ago was erected between us. "He's fine. Dorian patched him up." His half-smile faded, but it soon sparked back up, just another glimmer. "He had a bit too much to drink last night, took a bad spill on the street."

"That's good that he got fixed up."

I was confused. Did Dorian live on the top floors? Jake said the owner did, though Cole made it sound like that wasn't the case. Cole was obviously connected to the building somehow, but I wasn't going to figure it out here.

I pointed to the door. "I'm meeting a friend for lunch, and I still have to change. I should get going."

He nodded. "Do you run every day?"

I started to step around him, but paused. "What?"

He watched me with those intense eyes. The feeling of being exposed to him returned. He was looking into me, through me.

"Uh. No. Ken suggested it today, but I liked it. I'll do this again."

"I'll be here every day at this time, if you want to run together."

My eyes widened. At the suggestion, my heart pounded against my chest. "Um." My face was heating up. I averted my eyes, trained them on the door behind him, and lifted a shoulder. "Maybe. I'll see if I can. I'm not sure, you know, about my calendar. I might have something going on." My eyes darted back to his, and they widened once again.

He hadn't moved, but he felt closer to me. His presence was overwhelming. "Okay," he murmured. "Well, you'll know where I am, if you want a running buddy."

Then, just like that, I felt him pull away. He didn't move, but I could breathe easier again. Now that he'd said what he wanted to, he released me. My legs were unsteady as I forced myself to walk forward.

I spoke over my shoulder, my heart racing, "Maybe I'll see you tomorrow."

My heart thundered as I approached the exit. As I touched the metal door handle, I heard him speak. "Yeah. Maybe."

I sucked in my breath. That voice, those words spoken so softly— they reached inside me and wrapped around my heart. I felt him. He had power over me, and none of this made sense. He'd branded me, claiming me. I looked back over my shoulder, air suspended in my throat, but he wasn't watching now. His hood was back up, and he kicked off, starting another lap.

My shoulders sagged. I twisted around so my back was against the door and watched him go. This man, whoever he was, whatever kind of man he was, could affect me like no other had in my life.

Something had happened here, and I had a feeling everything was going to change. I just didn't know if it would be for the better or for the worse.

Straightening from the door, I shook my head. I was being ridiculous.

CHAPTER SEVEN

Gianni's was already busy when I got there. Nearly every table was filled, and unlike the last time we were here, the restaurant was brightly lit. The shades over the front windows had been raised, and men in business suits, women in suits and dresses had taken over the space.

I gave the hostess my name and went to the booth reserved for us, not knowing what I'd say to Sia. I was kind of a mess. All the while I'd been showering, changing, and getting ready to meet her, my mind had still been back on the running track with Cole. I was pretty sure I'd washed my hair with my face cleanser. It didn't have its regular volume after I dried it, but then it was too late. I'd wasted too much time in Cole La La Land, so I put it in a braid and clipped it up. It looked messily rumpled, just the way Sia loved it. She went nuts when my hair was like this, calling it "a sexy mess."

I expected the same reaction this time, but instead, Sia rushed over, a scarf wrapped around her neck, and slid in across from me. Her sunglasses stayed on as she reached for her water.

"Oh my God." She leaned back and let out a loud sigh. "You have no idea how thirsty I am today."

"Hung over?"

She nodded, gulping half the water and scanning the table. "Why's there no coffee yet?"

I raised an eyebrow. "That's *my* job?"

She groaned. Her head fell to the table, cushioned by her arm. "I'm sorry. I'm the worst best friend. You're right." She sat up and took her sunglasses off, squinting from the brightness. "I'm hung over like no other."

"You didn't seem that bad when I left."

"Oh no. Because I wasn't." She shook her head. "But we kept drinking. After the first really hot round in bed, we decided it was a great idea to have shots. So the shots started, and kept going. Then we broke the table. That meant more shots. We did it on his couch."

My nose wrinkled. "I liked that couch."

"On his kitchen island."

"Too much information."

"On his kitchen counter. Against the elevator doors. And then, with all the sex and all the booze, you'd think we'd be tired this morning. Nope. We did it in his shower, too."

"Is that possible? I thought guys took forever to get it up again."

"Not him. He's got the penis of a racehorse. And I am so fucking exhausted." Her eyes shifted over my shoulder, and she straightened up. A transformation came over her. It was like the bags under her eyes diminished. She pulled out a lip gloss and fluffed her hair back.

I narrowed my eyes. "Your scarf is sideways."

With one quick tug, it jerked back in place, and Sia smiled as she watched someone coming to our table. I had a sinking feeling I knew who it was. This was confirmed when she gushed, "Jake! How are you feeling?"

He sat beside her and dipped his head rather than answering. They kissed. No, they weren't kissing. They were devouring each other. They were trying to say hello with their tongues in the literal sense. Jake tried to pull away, but then their mouths opened wider over each other.

I averted my eyes. A moan started. I cringed. He groaned. I bit the inside of my lip. This was a tad bit awkward, just a bit. I shifted on my seat, feeling a tightness in my chest. It was growing. *Nope. Don't say anything. Let them be. It'll be over real soon…maybe now…no, not yet. Okay, now. Nope.*

"Okay." I planted both my hands on the table, fingers spread out. I leaned forward with a forced smile on my face. "That's lovely, you know." They broke apart, shooting me guilty grins. I rested against the back of the booth and waved a finger at them. "The two of you. My neighbor." My finger moved to Sia. "My best friend. All kissing and giving me way too many details about your sex-fest night."

Jake frowned and glanced sideways to Sia.

She pressed her lips together, shooting me a look.

I ignored both reactions. "Enough with the kissing in front of my face." I held up my hand. I'd put my wedding ring back on after I showered. It was a last-minute decision, and it felt right. I felt comforted. "Remember." I wiggled my finger. "I lost the love of my life a year ago. I'm happy for you both, but please, stop. Just…stop."

Time seemed to stand still for a moment as they stared at me, and I realized what I'd done: officially thrown a tantrum, right here in Gianni's Restaurant.

My hand covered my face. *Where had that come from?* "I'm so sorry, Sia." I shot Jake a pleading look. "I'm sorry, Jake. I'm not normally like this."

He perked up. "You mean Sia makes out in front of you all the time?"

She whacked his arm. "I do not." She gave me a meaningful look. "I do not. Tell him that."

"No." I shook my head. "She doesn't, not normally, but I have no excuse for having a fit."

Jake frowned before a slight smile showed. "Pretty sure we were making the scene, not you, Addison. You have no reason to apologize."

"Maybe not, but I'm still embarrassed."

"No, really. *I'm* sorry." Sia laid a hand on my arm. "And I know we were going to have our own lunch. I meant to explain earlier that Jake was coming too, but I was beyond busy this morning, and well, you know how rude I was when I first got here."

Jake gave her a look.

She waved him off with her free hand. "I was annoyed we didn't have coffee, like it was Addison's job to read my mind and have it ready. I was a bitch. I'm apologizing right now." She squeezed my arm once before pulling away, and tucked her hand in her lap. "Being beyond exhausted, hung over, and sore in places I never knew I even had isn't putting me at my most gracious."

I snorted.

Her eyes went to mine. "Having said that, I want to apologize again and also say you have no need to apologize. I should've been more sensitive. Way, way, way more sensitive. I'm a huge asshole. The hugest! And selfish. I am beyond selfish right now."

Okay. She was going to start flogging herself. She apologized. Jake apologized. I apologized. I considered the whole sorry-fest over. Picking up my water, I brandished a smile. "Can we toast to that?"

Sia reached for her water, but Jake beat her there. They gave each other another adoring smiles and raised the glass together. It was almost sickening; that was how cute it was.

I was having a hard time not smiling. I liked this stage in Sia's relationships. Despite the initial irritation today, she was kinder and softer. I already knew what I'd be hearing once Jake left: she was in love. She had the best night, ever. He was The One.

She'd downplayed him the night before, calling him her perfect booty-call soulmate, but things were clearly already past that, and as I watched them gaze into each other's eyes, I had to admit that this seemed like more. When Sia proclaimed her love, I might believe it this time. And good for her. I meant that. Truly.

Sia and Jake laughed and talked with each other, and I had a feeling there would be no space for me to interject about meeting Cole. And that felt fine. I wasn't ready to say anything about it, not yet.

A waiter brought water for Jake and refills for the rest of us. Sia got her coffee, hallelujah! The food came soon after we ordered. It was a light lunch, but the salad filled me up. Sia and Jake ordered sandwiches and devoured them, probably starving from their cardiovascular activities the previous night. Not long after we finished, Jake slid out of the booth to head back to work. Sia went with him to say goodbye. They walked out holding hands.

Young love. I remembered those days... Then Cole flashed in my head—the image of him standing there, watching me, waiting as I walked toward him. My mouth watered, and my stomach flipped over on itself.

Cole, whatever his last name was, affected me and in a big and intense way. And thinking of his invitation, I knew I couldn't do that. My body was tired after just one brief meeting with him. If I ran with him, next to him the entire time—my hand pressed into my stomach, trying to forcibly calm the nerves.

A server distracted me, reaching for my glass to refill it.

"Could I get the bill?"

"It's on the house." He set my water back down.

"What?"

But he turned and moved on to the next table.

Sia slid back into her seat at that moment. Folding her hands over each other, she leaned in close. "I'm so sorry, again. I know I apologized before, but this really was supposed to be our lunch, and you had no idea he was coming. And then you had to sit and endure our whole gushy-gushy stuff just now." Her hands pressed against her chest. "I'm not that selfish friend. I don't want to be. I owe you HUGE. What can I do to make it up to you?" She sat up suddenly. "Friday night! I have Friday night off for once. No event. No fundraiser. No showcase. Nothing. We should do a slumber party. You. Me. Lots of wine." She winced, then waved that away. "I'll be back on the wine bandwagon by then. Ooh. Can we do that? Are you up for it?"

"No Jake showing up in the middle of our slumber party?"

"Only if we start drinking tequila. You know how I get frisky when I drink that stuff."

"No tequila."

"Just wine." Sia beamed at me.

I nodded. "Just wine."

"And pajamas. Nice, big, comfortable pajamas. Nothing tight or constricting."

I shook my head. "Definitely not."

"Then it's a best friend, Friday night, slumber party date." She reached for her purse and raised her hand in the air. "And lunch is on me."

"I tried."

"What?"

I motioned. "Lower your hand. It won't matter."

"You asked for the bill?" She scanned the table. "Where is it? You didn't pay it already, did you?"

"I asked for it, but the server said it's on the house."

"Are you serious?" She sat back, hitting the back of her seat with a soft bounce. "This place isn't cheap, and I've never had my bill..." A light bulb went on. Her eyes lit up, and she sat upright. "That hostess from the other night! She must've recognized our reservation and said something ahead of time. I bet it was her. Man, if it was, I really need to pay her back. I'll reach out to a designer who's looking for models, give her name. That was really nice of her." She was in awe. "I've never had a hostess be that nice before. Usually they try to network by offering to work for free at an event or something. Yeah, I'll make sure to get her a job because of this."

I reached for my own purse. "Mystery solved."

Once we stepped out onto the street, Sia linked her elbow with mine and pulled me close to her side. We walked that way, like we had the other night, back to my building. She only had another block to go for her job, and we paused outside the front entrance. "Next lunch is just the two of us. I promise. Wait. Was there something you wanted to talk about today?"

An image of Cole appeared in my mind—my seared memory of him in the elevator, watching me as the doors closed. The blood on the floor from his comrade. Him running. Him waiting for me as I finished my last lap. *"I'm Cole."*

My fingers closed over her hand, and I cleared my throat. "Nope. Nothing."

"You sure?"

"I wanted to hear about you and Jake, but I got one better. I saw it first hand, like a private Broadway show."

She groaned. "Again. I am so sorry."

"I know. I'm just torturing you now."

"Okay." She twisted around, peering up at my floor. "So, if I don't talk to you all week, plan for Friday. It's a definite for me."

I narrowed my eyes. "Today's Friday."

"Wha—" Her mouth opened and stayed there. The wheels were turning in her head. Then she smacked herself in the forehead. "I meant next Friday, and holy shit! I'm insinuating I won't be around all weekend too. I am so—"

Our arms were still linked. I unlinked them, but pressed both my hands over her arms. "Stop. I know how you are with your guys."

Her eyes closed tight, but she opened one. "Really?"

I nodded. "I'm an adult. I'm thirty years old. I can manage just fine. Heck—" I tried for a joke. "Maybe Dawn and I will meet up for drinks tonight."

Sia laughed, relaxing. "You can take up knitting."

"I'll be her real knitting soulmate, not a pretend one like you."

"Don't tell her my lie," Sia whispered.

"I won't." I shoved her forward, gently. "Now go. Have fun. Have lots of sex, and if we don't talk before next Friday, I'll meet you at my door. I'll be the one wearing pajamas already."

"Okay." She moved forward, reluctantly, then turned around. She pointed at me. "Slumber party."

I yelled as she was swallowed up by the crowd, "Friday night!"

Her eyes widened—

"Next Friday night," I clarified.

She was still pointing at me, but switched to give me a thumbs-up instead.

My weekend came and went. It was fine. I found a bookstore and spent Sunday there, curled up with a book in one of the chairs. The next week passed just as uneventfully. Every morning, I looked at the clock. Cole was on my mind. I could've gone to run with him, but I never went. I was a chicken shit, but then one day I wasn't. I actually stood. My mind was made up. My chest tightened, and butterflies whipped around in me as I grabbed my sneakers and dressed. I had my headphones in hand and got to the elevator, only to *not* push the button.

I couldn't do it.

I was too nervous.

I hadn't heard from Sia since yesterday, and today was slumber party day, but I hadn't expected to. She had an event at the Gala last night. I loaded up on wine, and got tequila for her. Promising a slumber party was one thing, but actually following through was another. If the situation were reversed, I'd have a hard time staying four floors under the new man in my life. I figured she'd spend the evening with me, maybe even stay late, but once the tequila was in full effect, she'd sneak up to his floor. I planned to let her know she didn't need to sneak.

Seven o'clock rolled around, and she sent no word. I texted, asking if she was running late.

Eight o'clock.

Nine o'clock.

She should've called me by now.

I waited till nine thirty, then checked my phone. No text. No call. No email. I got on Instagram and went to her page. There it was: a selfie of her and Jake wearing Hawks jerseys. They were at the hockey game.

I'd been stood up.

CHAPTER EIGHT

Maybe my subconscious took me there.

Maybe I needed to run off some steam. Maybe I needed to get out of my apartment… I couldn't think of any other reasons, so maybe, just maybe I went to the running track looking for Cole. There. I admitted it. My friend stood me up for a boyfriend, and I went in search of the man I'd been too much of a coward to seek out all week.

I pushed through the door and jogged a few feet before stopping. Then I just stood there. I wasn't dressed for running. I was barely dressed for anything. Pajamas. A white tank top over short sleeping shorts. Thank God, I'd grabbed a robe. I was dressed and ready for what was supposed to have been my night.

I knew he wasn't here. It was foolish to think he would be. He ran in the mornings. He told me himself. And it was Friday, almost ten at night.

A bitter laugh escaped me, sending a puff of white breath into the air. It was chillier than usual in here. I closed my eyes, feeling the cold now, and I turned around to head back.

"It's Friday night." His voice stopped me. He stood right inside the door, and his eyes raked over me. "And you're wearing panda pajamas." He shook his head, his dark eyes twinkling. "You know, sometimes I wonder how smart I am, but I'm deducing you didn't come in here to work out."

I didn't answer. I couldn't. I just stared at him, taking him all in. He wore nice, custom-tailored-looking jeans and a black shirt under a black leather jacket. He was beautiful in his rich, bad-boy way.

"You're going out." My hand lifted toward him, then fell back at my side.

I cursed myself. Even now, even knowing what I was getting myself into when I came down here, I was still reduced to a teenager. I felt a blush in my cheeks, like I always had when I talked to a crush. I swallowed and forced out a quiet sigh. I really did need to get a handle on my hormones. They were too old for this ridiculousness.

He chuckled and shoved his hands into the leather jacket's pockets, pulling it tighter against his shoulders. My mouth watered.

"Unlike you, who must have fun plans this evening, I promised a friend I'd check in on his restaurant. He's out of town and just recently bought it." His eyes narrowed, and his head cocked to the side. "Are you going to bed like that, or are you going to a pajama party somewhere?"

My blush was at full force. I felt it creeping down my neck. "Neither. I don't know what I'm doing."

"You don't?"

"I thought a friend was down here."

"Friend?" He pointed to himself, stepping forward. "Me?"

"No. I—" This was stupid. "Yes. You."

A smirk showed on his face, and he took another step closer. "Well, isn't this a coincidence then?"

"You're gloating."

He laughed. "Of course I am. You avoided me for an entire week."

"I did not."

"Really?" He stopped, standing so close now, and I looked up at him. His eyes stared right down into mine, and I could've touched him. All I had to do was reach out. Hell, I could've pretended to trip, and he would've caught me. I didn't know this man, but I knew he would do that. I could fall, and he would keep me steady.

I wanted his touch, yearned for it.

"So, what'll it be?" he asked, his gaze falling to my lips.

I coughed, unable to talk at first. "What do you mean?" I bit my bottom lip. My knees were growing weak.

"I'd like someone to go to this restaurant with me. You must've sensed my dire need. I mean…" He gestured down the running lanes. "You came here looking for me. I think it's destiny. You're supposed to keep me company so I don't die of boredom tonight."

"Ha!" I was grinning now. My cheeks hurt from how much I was grinning. "You think I sensed that you needed a sidekick tonight, and the gods sent me for you?"

"No." He reached out and touched one of the pandas on my pajamas, right where my tank top rested over my shorts. The material lifted, and I felt the heat of his hand there, right on my stomach. "Just the panda gods. They must've heard my prayer."

My head tipped back. "You're funny." God, his hand felt good there.

His eyes darkened, and the smirk lingered. "I have lots of talents, but I mean it. I'd love a *date* for this restaurant tonight."

I stopped laughing. I got his message. He wasn't interested in a friend, a sidekick, or a companion. He wanted a date. My body reacted to his straightforwardness, and for a moment, I didn't trust myself to speak.

Clearing my throat, I pulled my eyes away. "Uh."

"It's Friday night." He was still touching one of the pandas on my pajamas. His hand was against my stomach, and he pulled me closer to him. The cloth felt like nothing now. There was no barrier between us, and I looked down, unable to tear my eyes away from his hand. "I'd like you to have dinner with me." He tucked a strand of my hair behind my ear with his other hand.

When I looked up, his hand fell away, but he still held on to me. He was bold, and I didn't want his hand to move. I heard myself saying, "I need to change."

He nodded. "Meet me in the lobby. One hour?"

My head moved up and down, and then I pulled away and went around him. Every part of my body was aware of him. Like it wasn't just mine anymore, it was a part of him. With each step I took, I sensed who I was leaving behind.

This wasn't normal. This didn't happen in real life. It took months before I'd felt this burn for Liam. With Cole it was the second time we talked, and the fourth time I'd seen him.

Everything melted inside me, and I had no idea what I'd picked to wear until I was stepping back into the elevator and hitting the lobby button. I glanced down, and my hand went to my hair. I'd put on an outfit Sia once chose for me. She'd laid it out on my dresser, saying I needed to dress sexier, and it had stayed there for two weeks. I looked in the mirrored wall to see my hair. It was pulled up in a messy braid, similar to last Friday's lunch. Sia would've approved.

The elevator came to a stop, lurching in sync with my stomach.

A date—I wasn't ready.

I reached inside my purse and found my wedding ring. I didn't put it on, but I held it. Some of the nerves calmed inside. Then the doors slid open, and I looked up.

It wasn't how good Cole looked that gave me pause. It was the look in his eyes when he saw me. It'd been so long since a man looked at me like that, like I was breathtaking to him, like he wanted to protect me, take me to bed, and laugh all night, all at the same time. I felt beautiful as Cole took in the sight of me. The feeling washed over me. I blinked back a tear, held my breath.

Liam... I missed him with an impossible heaviness.

Then I could hear him whispering, *"Whatever this guy's going to say, I agree. You look stunning, Addison."* He would've leaned in to kiss me. *"I love you. Live your happy, Addy."*

It felt so real—feeling him, hearing him. *Live your happy.*

The heaviness lifted, and I stepped from the elevator, my head high as I walked toward Cole.

He drank me in. "You look beautiful."

It was a simple dress, a simple sweater, but with the black boots Sia had picked, and I knew my getup made me look sexy, too. *Thank you, Sia,* I thought as Cole held out his hand for me and I took it, feeling his fingers close around mine.

Ken was waiting by the door. He held it open for us, pushing out toward the street. He nodded as we passed. "Have a fun evening, Mr.—"

Cole shot him a look.

"Cole and Miss Addison," he finished.

I turned to give him a reproach for the 'Miss' part, but Cole led me quickly around a black SUV and opened the passenger door. I got inside and waited until he'd rounded the back to get in the driver's seat.

"You drive yourself?"

He started the engine. "Hell yeah, I do. You didn't think I would?" He turned into traffic, and his wolfish grin showed me another side of this mystery man. He loved driving. No, it was more than that, but I couldn't pinpoint exactly what.

"For some reason I thought you'd have a driver."

"Ah." His hand moved over the steering wheel. He leaned back, keeping one hand there and resting the other on the stick shift. "You're right. I normally would have a driver, but this week has been my vacation from regular life. That means no driver. I get to do it myself. And driving a stick shift—" He changed gears. "—is a rush all its own."

He was dangerous. He was strong. And now, he loved adrenaline. Cole was everything Liam hadn't been. "You like the rush," I mused.

He moved between cars and glanced over at me.

"Is that in all aspects of life?" I asked.

His eyes narrowed, but he didn't reply. I saw the corner of his mouth lift up. Then we switched lanes again and came to an intersection. The faint grin was gone by then, and he turned onto another road before sliding to a halt in front of a brick building. He unclipped his seat belt. He didn't get out, not even when the valet opened his door. He watched me. "Does that unnerve you? The rush?"

My mouth dried. "Maybe in some aspects of life."

His eyebrow lifted. "Like the bedroom?"

My eyes widened. "You were bold when you said this was a date, and now you're bringing up the bedroom? Maybe you get a rush from making women uncomfortable?"

He was too close, too soon. I'd lashed out, and I regretted it, but I wasn't used to this. Cole was honest, but maybe too honest? That didn't sit right with me.

He didn't reply, not at first. He continued to watch me, studying me, then he said, softly, "I don't enjoy making women uncomfortable, but I also know you're not uncomfortable. I enjoy being honest, so here's my honesty right now." He paused, making sure I looked right back at him. "I'm not interested in being your friend."

O—Oh!

My pulse sped up, faster than it already was, and his gaze lingered a moment longer before he got out of the car. A second valet driver opened my door. I couldn't move, not at first. I didn't think my legs could hold me. When I did, Cole was waiting for me, and I rested my hand on his arm. He steadied me, and my God, I hated that while I liked it so much.

I was a mess inside, but it was a good mess.

The restaurant's inside was dark with minimal lighting. Candles rested on the window frames and the front desk. A hostess stood behind it, and as we came inside, she came out from behind. She was tiny and beautiful: Dark eyes. Dark hair. A rack most guys would love, and she folded her hands in front of her tight-buttoned shirt and skirt. "Mr.—"

"Cole."

She blinked once. "Cole. It's wonderful to have you tonight. The usual seating?"

He nodded. "That'd be great."

The back corner booth was big enough to seat six comfortably. Cole waited until I slid in and then sat beside me. The hostess handed us two menus before heading back to the front. A server came over right away, pitcher of water in hand, to fill our glasses. He disappeared, only to return with a bottle of wine. Two more glasses were soon filled with wine, and the bottle sat beside the table in an ice bucket.

Cole handed me one of the menus. "Did you want wine? Or would you like something else?"

I cracked a grin. "Uh, wine will go right to my head. Maybe coffee? Is that an option?"

The corner of his lip twitched. He stopped a server walking by. "Could we get a pitcher of coffee as well?" He asked me, "Cream and sugar?"

I hadn't thought my cheeks could get any redder. I was wrong. "I'm sorry. I was joking." I glanced from the server to Cole. "Sorry. Bad joke."

The server left, and Cole shifted to face me. "Are you nervous?"

I laughed. "Have you ever been around yourself? You're a bit much."

"I am?" His eyebrow lifted.

"Your whole presence. You're just…I'm not used to people like you."

"Dorian mentioned you have a friend? Sia?"

Of course he'd know about Sia. "Sia Clarke."

"That name sounds familiar."

"She's the event coordinator at the Gala down the street. Do you know her?"

"No. Dorian mentioned she had a 'forceful presence.'" Cole's eyes twinkled in amusement. "I imagine she propositioned him or something like that?"

"I wouldn't be surprised. She can certainly be direct."

"See?" His hand touched mine. It was a soft and gentle tap. "I can't be the only one."

"But you're the only one I want to—" I caught myself and closed my eyes, horrified. I was going to say I wanted to sleep with him.

My hormones had been asleep for a year, but Cole woke them up. They screamed for attention. "Nothing. Never mind."

"Nothing?" The half-grin he'd been giving me stretched to the other side. He knew damn well what I'd been about to say.

I groaned. "I'm already embarrassed." I waved between us. We weren't touching, but we were side by side. "This is a lot for me." Water. I needed to quench my throat. I scooted around the corner of the table so we weren't right next to each other anymore.

Cole moved into the space I left and sat back.

God, those eyes. They never left my face, and the longer they watched me, the more I felt I was losing some sort of battle. Over my will power. Or his intentions for after dinner. Whatever battle it was, I knew there was little chance I could withstand it.

We didn't talk. Minutes passed, and still we gazed at each other. The pull between us was crazy, and the longer I held his gaze, the faster my heart beat. I reached for my napkin blindly and pulled it into my lap. My hand fisted it into a ball, and I held onto it so I wouldn't do anything else. I had no idea what, but it was useless.

I was going to sleep with him.

The understanding spread through me.

"Would you like to leave?" His eyes darkened in stark hunger, and he leaned forward. He saw my reaction.

Okay. There it was. We were going to talk about it. "And do it in the car?"

"I was hoping for your place."

A dry laugh ripped from me. "I don't do this."

His eyebrow moved up again. "Seems like you're going to."

"No, you don't understand." I gestured between us. "You and me. I am not used to this sort of thing."

"One-night stands or casual sex?"

A second laugh bubbled up. "You're already labeling it that way?"

"Well…" He looked around, but no one was near. His hand lifted.

I didn't look. I didn't know what he was gesturing for, and I didn't care. He was right. We were two minutes from walking right back outside, and I wasn't going to regret it. I couldn't. This power, whatever he had over me, it was making me do things I never thought I would. But after this past year—I didn't care anymore. The pain. The sadness. The loneliness. I wanted it wiped out, even for just one night. One goddamn night.

"We've just met," he continued, his voice dropping low. "There's a lot we don't know about each other."

"You know where I live. Do you live there, too?"

His eyes grew hooded. "There are things about my life I can't share. I'd like to, but I'm in a position where I can't. Not until I trust you."

"You can't tell me where you live?"

"No."

"You're unbelievable. You want to have sex with me, but you won't tell me where you live?"

"I'm close to Dorian." His hand rested on the table between us. It curled into a fist, and his jaw clenched. "That's all I can tell you right now. But I want to tell you more." He leaned forward. His hand stayed there, still balled up. "I really do want to."

"You have a job you can't tell me about. You live somewhere you can't tell me about, but you *can* tell me you're friends with my building manager? What am I supposed to do with that?"

"I was hoping you'd give me time. I can tell you; I just can't do it now."

A month ago I would've laughed in his face. Hell, two weeks ago I would've laughed in his face, but this wasn't two weeks ago. I had endured an entire week of wanting to see him, be around him, but I had been too scared. Tonight was different. Sia had stood me up. I couldn't blame her. She had a life. She was out there. She was living, and I hadn't been. I'd been holed up in my house, and now I was holed up on my floor. I'd been healing—or was it hiding? Thirteen months, and one meeting with this man set my world ablaze.

I was smart. I was educated. One-night stands weren't me, but looking back at him, I was quickly losing my capacity for rational thinking. My body had made up its own mind.

Thump.

I couldn't believe this.

Thump.

My pulse pounded in my eardrum.

Thump.

He was waiting for my response.

I sighed, then nodded. "Okay."

CHAPTER NINE

Cole got up to check on the restaurant for his friend, and when he came back, we left. We didn't touch on the way out. We didn't need to.

I was already imagining him over me, sliding inside, thrusting and pulling back, only to go deep once more, stretching me. The ache between my legs wasn't going to go away.

The drive was the same. I didn't see the scenery. I could only concentrate on his hand. He positioned it on his leg, half turned up. Maybe it was there for me to hold if I chose. A part of me was glad he didn't put his hand on my leg. The other part of me wanted nothing more. And when my mind continued its play-by-play of what would happen once we got to my place, it got to be too much. So I tried to change my thoughts.

Sia.

That picture of her and Jake at the hockey game flashed in my head. My body cooled, just a tiny bit. But then Cole reached for the stick shift to change gears, and I went right back to fixating on that hand—what it would feel like, where it would touch me, how his fingers would be inside of me.

I was wet, beyond the point of embarrassment.

"You okay?" Cole's voice was soft.

I looked up and nodded, seeing his desire. "I am."

He held my gaze for another second before turning back to the road. I was reassured. Any tiny doubt that might've tried to tunnel its way into me was stopped in its tracks. I was ready.

Instead of parking in front of my building, Cole turned to the side street and pulled into the parking lot. Really? I smiled. Yes, he could say again that he knew the code and the parking lot because of Dorian, but I suspected it was more. Too knowledgeable. Then he wheeled into the building manager's slot. It was labeled on the pavement. I didn't know what Cole did, but he was someone.

He got out of the car, and I didn't wait for him to open my door. I climbed out, and we walked beside each other to the elevator. The closer we got to my place, the more my blood pumped through me.

Once inside the elevator, I stood to one side, watching him. He returned my gaze.

We still did not touch.

My chest tightened, hoping no one would call the elevator at that moment. We sailed past the lobby, the second floor, and stopped at mine. I put in the code, and the doors opened to my home.

I drew in a breath, filling my lungs again. God, it was time.

Stepping out with shaky knees, I bypassed the light switch. The full moon lit up my entire floor. I went to the kitchen and paused at the island. "Did you want something to drink?" I caught sight of the tequila and wine on the counter. There was more than enough.

Cole stepped up behind me and followed my gaze. "Were you going to have a party?" he asked, his breath coating the back of my neck.

I shivered, closing my eyes for one delicious moment. "I stocked up. I thought a friend was coming over tonight."

His hand rested on my back, nudging my sweater aside to touch my skin. "He?"

"She. Sia." I looked over my shoulder. He was so close. "She stood me up for a date."

A faint smile showed. "I need to send her a thank-you card."

"Please don't sign it."

"Why not?"

I turned around, easing my back against the island. Cole placed his hands on either side of me, trapping me in place.

"Because she's slightly obsessed with you, though she's in love with someone else now. She could circle back," I joked.

"Me?"

"We saw you one night."

"When?" He leaned away, but his hands remained on the counter. It was like he was giving me breathing space on purpose.

"At Gianni's. We went there the night I moved in."

He didn't move, but I could feel him pulling away. A protest started in my head, but I bit back the words. He didn't reply. He was waiting for me instead.

I continued, "You came in with a bunch of men and went upstairs. That was it."

His eyes narrowed. "Did you talk to anyone?"

"What do you mean?"

"The staff?"

"About you?"

"About anything."

My forehead wrinkled. "Sia networked with the hostess. They exchanged cards. Sia said the girl was a model. She recognized her from the Gala. That was it. Oh, well, another server sat with us for a drink later on. But they mostly talked with Sia about the Gala and about photographers—stuff like that."

He relaxed, his hands loosening their hold on the counter. I was scared to ask what he was so worried they'd told us.

"I don't know who you are." I lifted a hand, placing it on his chest. His heart was racing, just like mine. My mouth parted in surprise. "If that's what you're worried about."

He glanced down at my hand and held still. He was thinking something over. I held my tongue, worried it was me, that he was second-guessing this night for us. I wanted to tell him there was nothing to worry about, but it sounded ridiculous. I really had no idea. So I waited it out, my heart pressing against my rib cage.

When he looked back up, the hunger was in his eyes again—dark, primal, and more evident than ever. He took my hand and leaned in, closing the distance between us. With his other hand, he cupped the side of my face. "I wasn't second-guessing this. I want you to know that." His touch was tender.

"What were you thinking about?"

"Something else, but it wasn't you."

"This is one of those moments where you wish you could tell me, but you can't? Not yet?"

The corner of his mouth lifted. His eyes moved from mine to my lips. "Something like that, yes."

"Mmmm-hmmm," I started to tease, but then his head dipped down, and his lips were on mine.

I gasped. The pleasure was immediate. His mouth was gentle, but as he felt my body's reaction, he applied pressure. His touch grew more demanding, then I was kissing him back. I wanted more. Someone groaned. That was me.

His hand slid around to the back of my neck. He held me in his grip as his mouth explored mine, opening over me and slipping inside. My hands grasped his shoulders, just holding on. All I could focus on was his tongue. I met his with mine and reveled in the sensation. But it wasn't enough. Need shot through my whole body.

My hands slid under his shirt and moved over his back and shoulders. His body was just as powerful as his presence. I felt the shift of his muscles. They trembled under my hands. The feeling was intoxicating. I had power over him, and I wanted more. I wanted to see how much power I actually had.

Pulling back, I studied him.

He was panting lightly. So was I.

I could see him wondering what I was going to do, so I reached back to the counter and started to lift myself. His hands caught the backs of my thighs, and he lifted me the rest of the way. Now sitting on the edge of the island, my legs parted, and he was back between them. His mouth went right to mine.

I couldn't get over what I was doing. I didn't care.

I didn't think I would care the next day, the day after, or however long this lasted. I had no clue. I only knew I had one night. One long night.

Another groan left me. Cole began trailing kisses down my throat and between my breasts. He pushed my sweater off. It fell to the counter, and his hands went to my legs, resting above my knees. Still his lips lingered between my breasts. The dress was a barrier.

I wanted it gone.

I wanted his mouth on me. I wanted to kiss him back, and I began tugging on his shirt, pulling it from his jeans. He lifted his head, helping me for a moment and then bent back to my chest. My hands returned to his back. Instead of feeling, I gazed down. I couldn't help it. I was captivated. I had felt those muscles rippling under my touch, but seeing them now, my breath was gone.

He was perfect. There were no other words. He could've been a weapon himself, just his body.

"Cole," I murmured.

He looked up and nodded, sliding his hands further up my legs. He waited, resting them on my waist beneath my dress. As he continued to hold my gaze, one of his hands moved lower and his finger slid inside my thong.

My body jerked, exploding at his touch. I didn't climax, but dear God, I almost did. I clamped around him as he buried his finger inside me.

He pulled out, then leaned down. His lips found mine, and my legs wound around his waist. My arms clenched his back. His finger moved out, then back in. And again. Again. He kept going.

I was helpless against his onslaught, and I didn't want to stop him. I started trembling, but I didn't want to come, not yet. I wanted to wait, to hold off—but he never stopped. In and out. Slide in, pull out, and back in again.

"Cole." My lips brushed over his.

He kept going.

"Cole, please."

"Please what?" His voice was just as hoarse as mine.

I grabbed for his wrist, trying to pause his caresses. In response, he went even deeper. A second finger slipped in, and I could only gasp, my mouth hanging open as the pleasure went through me. Wave after wave coursed through me, coating me completely.

I couldn't—I didn't know what I couldn't. He kept going, and going.

"Cole—my God."

He lifted his lips to my ear and murmured, gently as if it were a caress in itself, "Let go. Please, Addison." He kissed me there. "Let go."

"But you—"

"You're not done. Let me do this for you." A third finger went in, stretching me farther than I had been in so long. His fingers moved together, going deep, sliding back, going in again. He started to speed up.

I was breathing heavily, panting loudly into the room. All I could do was cling to him, my legs and arms straining around him. And then, one last thrust and I soared over the edge. Tremors wracked my body, and Cole held me as I rode each wave. They kept going until finally the last one ebbed, and I was complete. My body was satiated.

But even as I thought that, I knew it wasn't true. An ache formed, just a tiny one, between my legs. Cole's fingers were still inside me. I turned so our eyes were inches apart.

I didn't say anything.

His need sparked in his eyes, and it was deep, more ravenous than mine. His jaw clenched as he swallowed. His free hand flexed and then tightened on my thigh. For the first time, I saw into him like he had been seeing into me.

He waited, letting me regain control of myself. When I had, I gave him a small nod, and he picked me up, whisking me off the counter. He didn't react to holding me. It was as if I were a doll.

He carried me down the hallway to my bedroom, then placed me on the bed. I sat up and pulled off my dress, then reached behind me to unclasp my bra. Finally I wore only my thong. My eyes traced over his shoulders, down his chest to his abdominals. He was lean, but he was muscled everywhere.

I had thought of him as a weapon before, and I know how true it was. I remembered the first time I saw him. I thought he stalked in a sensual way, like a predator, and my mouth watered once more thinking of how he'd feel inside of me. How he'd feel over me.

I sat up. His gaze went to my breasts, lingering there.

They reacted under his attention. His eyes smoldered, and he moved toward me. He leaned down, and I closed my eyes, knowing he was going to touch me again. The bed dipped under his weight, and then his lips were on my breast.

I gasped again, arching my back.

His mouth opened, taking my nipple inside. As he kissed and caressed me, he helped me move farther up the bed as he joined me.

I opened my eyes and watched as he continued his kisses, switching to my other breast. I writhed beneath him, wanting the feel of his body on mine. I wanted that heaviness, then to feel him entering me—not his fingers. Him. But for now he kept tasting me, touching me, and I continued watching.

What the morning would bring, I didn't know, but I didn't want to sleep to meet it. I wanted to be awake. I wanted the feel of Cole over and over again. Unable to hold back anymore, I slid my hands up his body, enjoying the dip and valley between each of his muscles until I wound my hands around his neck and grabbed his jaw. He answered my touch, lifting his head to look at me with wild eyes. He loved this as much as I did. He blinked and focused on me. When he saw what I wanted, the side of his mouth lifted.

He moved over me, bending now so he wasn't crushing me, and his forehead rested on mine. He pulled out his wallet. Grabbing a condom, he tore the wrapper and then made quick work of his pants and his briefs. He kicked them off, putting the protection on, and reached between my legs. I gasped at his hands on my inner thighs and he paused, looking into my eyes.

I felt his unspoken question, and I nodded. I was ready.

He grabbed my underwear and ripped them. One second later, he slid inside, and my entire body lifted in response. He paused, letting me adjust to him, before he began to move. And then everything changed. Sometime during the night, I claimed him as well.

CHAPTER TEN

My alarm was going off.

No.

My phone? Wait. No.

Slowly I came out of sleep. It was the elevator. Why was it ringing at—I twisted under Cole's arms to see the clock—six in the morning?

Sia.

I bolted upright, but before I could say anything, Cole was out of bed. He pulled on his pants and reached for his shirt. I scrambled to join him.

"Are you expecting anyone?"

I shook my head. Last night—oh, man. I surveyed the bed. We'd pulled the bottom sheet off. I had no thoughts about that, not right now. Reaching for the robe slung over my dresser, I pulled it on as the buzzer kept going.

"Addison." Cole went to the doorway and paused. He'd left his jeans undone. He asked again, "Are you expecting someone?"

"It could be Sia."

The frown he'd worn last night when I told him about Gianni's returned.

"I have a box of—" I stopped talking when I remembered. I'd put some of Liam's things together and stored them in my closet. It was sentimental stuff. Things I could pull out if I was missing him too much. I stepped into the closet and grabbed Liam's favorite robe, offering it to Cole. He was dressed, so I don't know why I was offering a robe.

I didn't know what I was doing.

His frown deepened. "Whose is that?"

I didn't think. I answered, "My dead husband's." The buzzer sounded again, and I hurried out, pressing the camera. Cole moved behind me and peered over my shoulder. It was Dorian. I hit the accept button and started to ask, "Why is my building manager—"

Cole's hand touched the small of my back. I stopped talking once again.

"He's here for me."

"Oh." Well, of course. That made sense. I registered that Cole hadn't put on the robe. He was in his shirt and jeans, barefoot.

The elevator doors started to slide open. Cole glanced down. "Can you give us a minute?"

"Oh."

I sounded ridiculous. I went to my bedroom, cursing myself. I already knew what I was going to do. I tiptoed to the edge of the hallway, keeping to the side so neither of them could see me.

Their heads were bent together, and I could hear murmuring. I pulled back, just in case they looked over.

"...sure?" Cole's voice rose a tiny bit.

"I'm sorry."

Dorian didn't sound it, though.

Cole grunted. "I'm sure you are."

"I didn't tell you to sleep here."

"Lower your voice."

Back to murmurings. I waited, but after another thirty seconds of whispered conversation, I knew I wasn't going to hear anything else. I began edging backward, tiptoeing soundlessly all the way to my bed. I sat. I folded my hands in my lap, and it was then that the events of the previous night began hitting me.

Sex.

Hot sex.

All night long.

We'd only stopped forty—I glanced at the clock again—or so minutes ago. I winced. It was more like thirty minutes.

Raking a hand through my hair, I caught a whiff of my breath and recoiled. No wonder Cole wanted space. Going to the bathroom, I closed the door and started the routine I did every morning. Showered. Brushed my teeth. I was getting ready for the day. It'd be a sluggish one, but I wouldn't be able to sleep anymore.

I was wrapped in a towel and grabbing my clothes when I heard the elevator doors close.

I waited for the soft sounds of bare feet, but none came.

Suddenly, Cole was in the closet doorway.

I shrieked. "Holy fuck, fuck! Seriously?" My heart lodged itself in the back of my throat. "I just had a heart attack. Make some sound next time, please."

Cole propped a shoulder against the doorframe and folded his arms over his chest. He smirked, his eyes showing his amusement. "You're cute when you're worked up."

I groaned, ignoring the little flip my stomach did when he teased me. "Whatever. I'll return the favor and see how you like it."

The amusement vanished. "You can't."

"What?"

"You can't scare me like that. Ever."

"Why not?" I clutched my shirt and jeans.

"Because…" He ran a hand over his head. "I'm a trained fighter. I could hurt you. I don't want to ever hurt you."

Oh…Oh! "Is that what you do for a living?"

"What?" He looked confused for a moment. "No." He folded his arms over his chest. "Just don't scare me like that. I can't promise I won't react. I mean it, Addison. I never want to hurt you."

I could feel a *but* coming. Not about me, but about him standing there, looking appetizing, and not staying. I sighed. "And you have to go?"

He nodded. "I do. I'd like to see you again. Tonight? We'll stay for dinner this time."

I almost smiled. Almost. "No running today?"

"Not today. Seems my little vacation is over. I'll be gone all day."

"Okay." I rubbed at my forehead. "It's Saturday. I won't have anything going on tonight."

The chuckle grew to a soft laugh. He crossed to me and leaned close. I closed my eyes just as his lips touched my lips. That felt nice, nicer than it should've. He rested his lips there, then pulled away. I could feel his reluctance.

"Tonight." He didn't move all the way back. He gazed down at me.

"Do you know what time?"

"Not yet, but when I do, I'll call." He frowned again. "And if you want to make plans, go for it. I can wait to see you another night. I understand."

"Yeah. Sure." That wasn't going to happen. "Me, social creature here."

The corner of his mouth lifted again. "I'll see you."

"Tonight."

He began walking backward. "Tonight."

Then he turned the corner. I heard the elevator take him away, and I was back to being alone.

CHAPTER ELEVEN

Well.

To say I had things on my mind would be an understatement. There was a complete hurricane in my mind—but no. I'd promised myself last night that I wouldn't regret anything, and I was sticking to it. I'd just also chosen this time to finally finish the last of my unpacking. Anything that wasn't put away already got a spot, and was categorized. Then color-coded.

I didn't regret my night with Cole. It was the opposite.

I kept glancing at my phone. I told myself it wasn't because of him. This wasn't high school. This wasn't a crush, but the fluttering in my stomach didn't reassure me. The other person I kept expecting to hear from, which was more logical since I'd texted her the night before, was Sia.

She'd stood me up, and it had been crickets since. That wasn't normal, even when she was enthralled with a new boyfriend. She'd only forgotten me one other time, and the apologies had started immediately, with flowers. I was going to ask for chocolates this time, but evidently I wasn't going to have the chance.

My phone was silent.

It was a little after noon when I ventured downstairs. My body was exhilarated, but exhausted at the same time, so no exercise for me. I planned to head out for a little exploring. I hadn't felt like meandering the streets since I'd moved in, and it was past time for that to happen. I was coming back from the mailroom when I saw Dawn peeking through the door. She was watching someone in the lobby, so I cleared my throat.

She didn't startle, but turned her head. Her eyes went flat. "Oh. It's you."

I gave her a look. "I thought we were friendly...ish?"

She looked back, raising up on her tiptoes. "I'm mad at you."

Huh? "At me?"

"Yeah." She gave me another dark look. "You."

"Why?"

"You introduced them."

"Who—" *Sia and Jake.* The light bulb clicked on as I heard laughter coming from the lobby. Male laughter. Female laughter. Laughter I recognized. "Sia and Jake are out there?"

"Things were going according to plan until you brought *her* to the dinner." Her nose wrinkled. "Thanks a lot for that."

I blinked. "I had no idea, Dawn. I thought you liked Sia."

She lifted a stiff shoulder, peering through the door again. "I was seduced by her. Not many understand the frustration when you don't use a stitch square. The results can be catastrophic. Sia understood." Her eyes narrowed as she turned back to me. "But I'm on to her. Did you bring her intentionally to take him away?"

I had no words for a moment. "Uh." I shook my head. "Dawn, you're a little scary right now."

"I'm the building's shut-in. I have a lot of time on my hands." She looked back for a moment and then announced, "We have to hide."

"Wha—"

She grabbed my shoulders and pushed me backward, steering me along the way. We were moving fast, then we stopped.

"Wher—"

"Sssh!"

"...I don't know where it is. I didn't check it after the game, but I brought it down when we were swimming. I know I did, but I don't remember having it after that." Sia's voice grew clear as she walked past us. "I should stop and see Addison. I have this feeling we were supposed to do something together this weekend."

"Really?" Jake's voice wasn't as clear. They were moving beyond the door. "We could ask her…" They were out of earshot.

I waited, but Dawn never opened the door. I reached for the knob. She grabbed my hand and hissed, "They're coming back. He's getting his mail, just like you."

"Were they out all night?"

She inched forward. I couldn't see her face. "They were at brunch just now, but I think they stayed at her place."

"How would you know that?"

"Instagram. Hello? You never post on yours, by the way. You should post more."

"Duly noted."

Sia's voice approached. "…it's bugging me. I remember having it before we went swimming."

"I don't know," Jake said. "Maybe. We were both buzzed, but it would still be down here. Or Kenneth would've given it to us if someone else found it first. It was late when we were down here."

"I know." I could hear the confusion in her voice as they walked past again. "Let's buzz Addison's place. Maybe she found it and is holding it for me?"

"Maybe."

So Sia still didn't remember our plans last night. And they were buzzing my place while I was trapped in a dark closet with Dawn. I started to move forward again, reaching for the door, but she blocked me.

"No. They could come back."

"Dawn." I grabbed her arm. Two could play at this. "Either move, or I will move you."

"Just wait. Okay? They're going to come back and look for you."

"Really?"

"Yes," she snapped at me.

"And why do you think that?"

"Because you don't go anywhere, like me. If you're not in your place, they'll know you're down here."

"Oh, good grief." I needed to get a life. Now. "Move away from the door. I want to talk to them."

"Just wai—" A ping sounded in the closet, followed by a myriad of bells ringing.

I knew that sound. "You have Sia's phone!"

"No, I don't."

But she did. The sounds kept coming, which Sia had set on purpose. She never wanted to miss something. Dawn pulled it out from wherever she'd had it hidden. It lit up the closet, and I saw enough to grab it and push past her at the same time.

"No!" She came after me.

I hit the accept button for the text message and read the message from Jake: **Where are you, phone? If someone finds this, please call my number.**

I'd had enough. I hit the call button and lifted it to my ear.

"No!" Dawn tried to grab the phone from me.

I held her off, leveling her with a warning. "You are unbelievable. At first I thought *you* thought you were too good for me. Then I felt bad for you. You were shy. That's what Jake said, and now I find out you stole my best friend's phone? Were you down here while they were swimming?"

If looks could kill, I'd have been ashes.

Then Jake answered his phone. "Hello? You have Sia's phone?"

"Hi, Jake. Yeah. It's Addison."

"Addison?" I could hear him pull away from the phone. "Addison has your phone," he told Sia.

I could hear her in the background. "Oh, thank goodness. Hi, Addy!"

He came back. "Are you home? We just tried buzzing your place."

"I'm in the lobby."

"Oh good." He pulled away again. "She found your phone downstairs."

"She did?" Sia questioned, her voice distant. "That's so weird. I wonder where I left it. Where was she? We were just down there."

I returned Dawn's glare. As she heard the conversation, horror bloomed in her eyes, and she began shaking her head. "Don't tell him. Please. Don't tell either of them."

"Okay," Jake said. "You want to come up here or should we come down there?"

I didn't answer right away, mulling over my best course of action.

Dawn mouthed, "Please. Please!"

I groaned. "I'll come up there." Then I forced a lightness in my voice. "Are you guys dressed? Do I need to cover my eyes when I come in?"

He laughed. "We're dressed. We were already out and about today, too."

"Addison, we need to have drinks tonight!"

"Yeah. Drinks sound great. Be up in a bit." I hung up and placed my hands on my hips. "What the hell were you thinking? Did you break her code?"

"No." Some of the fight seemed to have left Dawn. She moved back a step and her head hung slightly. "I could just read the texts the way you did now. You know her code?"

"I'm her best friend. Of course I do."

"That's nice." Her shoulders drooped. "That's really private. She must trust you."

"Yeah, and you know what? I'm going to tell her you stole the phone."

Her head shot up. "You can't. Please. Please don't."

"Why not?" I felt like I was bartering with a child. "Give me a good reason why I should break her trust in me?"

"Because..." Dawn's hands came up in a helpless gesture. "I don't know. I've loved Jake for a year, and it's hard. You have no idea how hard it is. He finally looked at me. You have no clue what it's like to always be around, but never have someone look at you, really look at you. He did. A month ago. There was a moment, and then you moved in, and you brought *her* along. Now it's back to how it was before. He doesn't even see me. He walks right past me."

Okay. My heartstrings tugged a little, but only a little. I held up the phone. "So you stole Sia's phone?"

"Yeah. Because…I don't know. I was hoping for information."

"What kind of information?"

"Like…" She shrugged, looking away. "What does he like? Does he flirt on the phone? How did she get him? She's not prettier than me. I might be weird, sometimes, but I can look good. I know I can. Derek thinks so."

"So date Derek."

"No way. He's weird."

"So are you." I cringed as soon as the words were out. "I'm sorry. I didn't mean it like that, but the two of you are similar. Jake and Sia, they're similar."

"No." She shook her head. "Don't say that. Opposites attract."

I…had no words. This wasn't the hostile and guarded Dawn; this was the real her. She was in love, or thought she was, and she wanted that guy to love her back. A part of me felt for her. We all wanted to be loved, or to have that back again.

I tucked Sia's phone into my pocket and started for the door.

"What are you going to do?"

I turned around, hitting the door with my back and pushing it open. "I don't know."

I saw the pain and hurt in Dawn's eyes, but my heart hardened. I felt for Dawn. I did. But she'd gone about things in a bad way, and Sia was my family. Even after forgetting about me the night before.

CHAPTER TWELVE

"You stood me up!"

I went up there to tell Sia about Dawn, but then I saw how happy she was. They were eating cheese from a platter. Jake had his arm around her waist, and she was snuggled into his side. If they hadn't been so adorable, they would've been nauseating.

Dawn could wait.

She was putting a piece of cheese in her mouth and froze. "What?"

"We had plans last night."

"Oh…" I saw the wheels turning and then she groaned, her head falling to the counter. She rested her forehead there, gently hitting it one more time. "I am such a shitty friend. Holy shit. I suck. There's no other way around it." She moved around the counter, lifting her arms up. "First the whole make-out in front of you and now this." She pulled me in, hugging me tight. Her voice dropped to a murmur, "I'm so beyond sorry. I'll make it up to you. Slumber party tonight. I don't care what I have going on. It's canceled, and prepare for an entire month of me groveling. You'll be getting chocolates, wine, whatever you want. Every single day."

I laughed, hugging her back. "I'm okay, and I don't want any of that. Just don't stand me up again. Okay?"

Sia continued to apologize, but I was more interested in hearing how fun the hockey game was. Then I heard about their spontaneous decision to go swimming in the middle of the night, and a small guilt began gnawing at me. I didn't want to get Sia mad about Dawn. She was ridiculously happy with Jake. If anything, I'd tell Jake later, but for now I wanted to do damage control, so I excused myself to the bathroom. I knew her passcode, and I deleted my calls from her phone, then the two texts, too. None of them had been seen yet, and once I was done, she'd never have any idea they'd been there in the first place.

I checked for any creepy messages from Dawn as well. There weren't any, and after I finished, I left her phone on a table by the elevator door. Sia hadn't asked for it yet, though normal Sia would've wanted it as soon as I stepped off the elevator. Happy and in love Sia seemed to have forgotten the whole thing already. Probably how she lost it in the first place.

When I returned, they invited me to dinner with them at Gianni's at seven. I gave them a maybe, saying I wasn't sure how I'd be feeling. I was going to wait to see if Cole really did call me before deciding on my plans, but of course I didn't tell them that.

Once I got back to my place, the waiting began.

As time passed, I began to wonder if he'd follow through. Maybe he just wanted to get away without any awkwardness. But I couldn't deny that I wanted him to call. I wanted to see him again, and I hoped I wasn't being stupid at the same time.

Halfway through the afternoon, I realized he might not have my number. I tried to shove that aside, but figured he knew where I lived, but probably not my number. I should go with Sia and Jake. I wasn't going to wait here in case he rang my floor. Literally.

That worked. My decision was made…for thirty minutes.

Then my mind started whirring again.

Did he have my number? Something told me he could find it.

Cole knew Dorian.

Ken had called him Cole the night before.

I had to know.

I was moving to the elevator before I realized what I was doing. Hitting the lobby button, my heart raced.

When the doors opened, I didn't step outside. I looked up, and Ken was there. He looked too.

"Does he have my phone number?" I asked, straight to the point.

He nodded once. "He does."

No other questions asked; no other answers needed.

I nodded in thanks and hit my floor again. I leaned back and closed my eyes. I felt like a nervouås school girl. Was this how dating was? How hooking up felt? I had a new sympathy for Sia.

The elevator stopped, and I started to get off, not looking at the floor number.

Dawn stood in front of me, her arms crossed over her chest.

I stepped back, my eyes flicking to the lights. She'd called the elevator.

"Did you tell?" she asked.

Annoyance flared in me. I jerked forward, hitting the button to make the doors close as I said, "No. Consider yourself lucky, okay? You owe me."

She let out a breath of relief, and jerked her head in a shaky nod.

"But if you don't leave 'em alone, I will."

Four o'clock came and went with no word from Cole.

Five o'clock.

Five thirty, and I needed something to do, so I checked my email. Not much there. I scrolled over most until I saw one from my realtor.

Addison, I've been in touch with a lawyer representing Liam's family. Can you give my office a call? We should plan a meeting.
--Heather, Coldwater Realty Services

I frowned. That didn't sound good, but maybe his family wanted to buy the house? Maybe they were upset I was selling it in the first place. We weren't close. His mother had never wanted us together. For the first year we dated, she brought another woman along every time she met Liam for a meal. They were always the same: older twenties or early thirties, single, beautiful. A few were co-workers. A few were daughters of her friends. One woman was in her walking club.

Liam's dad hadn't been much better.

The first year he'd hit on me himself. The last couple years, he'd ignored me and only talked to Liam at get-togethers. Liam's older sister was married, lived in the suburbs, and kept asking when we were going to have kids, but her interest never felt like it was genuine. There was a younger brother, too, but I never met him. He lived in San Francisco and never came home to visit, not the entire time I was with Liam.

I put my realtor's email on the I Really Don't Want To Deal list. It'd be nice to see Heather, but anything about Liam's family brought my walls up and claws out.

And I'd officially been distracted for ten minutes.

I watched the clock. Six o'clock came and went, and I'd officially had enough. I went out for dinner and drinks with Sia and Jake. Despite the urge to check my phone and constant effort to keep my thoughts on the conversation, not on a certain person who hadn't called yet, the evening was similar as our last time there. Well, except there was much less kissing. I figured Jake and Sia were holding hands under the table. They'd stop talking suddenly and share a look, one of those dreamy kinds, but other than that, it was an enjoyable dinner.

At the end when we asked for our bill, none came. Each of us took turns asking, but we all got the same response. It was on the house.

Sia was fine with it. Jake wasn't.

His eyebrows furrowed together, and I could see his wheels spinning. He wanted to know what was going on. A nagging voice kept saying Cole's name in the back of my mind, but that didn't make sense either. Cole said he knew the owner of that other restaurant, but I remembered how he'd walked into Gianni's with his friends. They knew the place like they ran it, like it was a second home to them. That didn't make sense either. I'd just brought up the restaurant with him last night, and my lunch date with Sia had been taken care of the week before.

"Maybe we should hold off going there?" We were nearing home, but I paused. Sia and Jake both stopped and looked at me. Sia gave me a blank expression. I added, "I mean, until we know why. Unless it doesn't bother you."

It bothered me. I wanted to know why we weren't getting a bill there. It felt like we owed someone something. I wanted to know what, and I wanted to be the one to sign up for it, not have it put upon me.

Jake didn't say anything at first, his eyes skirting to Sia. "I'm with you. It's weird."

"It's free food. Who turns that down?" Sia gave us both confused looks. "I say we go there every day."

"And if it's a creepy guy who wants to get in your pants?" Jake asked.

She shrugged. "Let him try. We never asked for free food. That's on him."

I didn't like it, but I didn't have a good argument against free food. If Sia found out if there were invisible strings, she'd be the first to give the middle finger to whoever was holding them. Then she'd snip those strings off. That was how she was, but I was more cautious.

Not with Cole, a voice said to me. I took a breath. That voice was right. I was reserved, though not last night. I glanced up at the building, wondering if he was up there somewhere. If he wasn't, where was he? I couldn't help it. I pulled my phone out, and it was still blank.

My hope sank in me. Maybe I shouldn't have been all spontaneous last night. Maybe I should return to being cautious and boring Addison? Nothing like going home to an empty apartment to make the transition back, and I turned as the doors opened.

Walking inside, I expected to find Ken waiting for us in the doorway. He wasn't.

Dorian was there instead, and he gave us all a polite nod.

I paused mid-step. The same disapproval was there from this morning—I saw it in his eyes. His face was blank, almost unemotional.

I frowned, feeling a nagging worry in my chest. Why did that bother me?

"Addison?"

Jake and Sia had gone ahead. They waited for me in the elevator.

Something didn't feel right. Ken was always here. Where was Ken? I stepped into the elevator, my mind whirling.

"You want me to come in for a while?"

I'd been chewing the inside of my cheek when Sia asked. I looked up, realizing they were waiting for me to get out at my floor.

"Nah. I'm going to bed soon. I'll see you later."

Sia suggested lunch on Monday, and I might've accepted. I wasn't sure. I was distracted, as a certain someone kept popping up in the back of my mind.

And I tried further distracting myself from that someone with a book and a glass of wine, but after reading the same page for an hour, I quit.

I was getting up, ready to go to bed, when my elevator buzzed. Cole?

I rolled my eyes at myself. The hope that burst forth was annoying. It wasn't like we were in the early stages of a relationship, where it was fun and exciting and everything left me breathless. That was not this, no way.

But I couldn't ignore the fluttering inside as I crossed the room and hit the voice button. "Who is it?"

I didn't check the camera because I knew. I'd tried telling myself it was probably Sia. She forgot something. She wanted to check on me. She wanted to apologize again for standing me up, but my body knew. There was nothing holding back the butterflies in my stomach. They were flitting around, worked up about an impending storm.

"It's me."

It was Cole, and everything clicked in place inside of me. It was like my intuition was laughing at me, *Told you*. My body knew it was him before I'd even stood from the couch, and now that I heard confirmation, my nerves had settled.

There was a weariness in his voice when he asked, "Can I come up?"

I hit the button allowing him access, already frowning, already wanting to know what was wrong. Then I jerked to the hallway mirror. I looked ridiculous. I was trying to smooth my hair back when the sounds of the elevator sunk in. It was coming from above, not rising from below.

Then the doors slid open, and any questions evaporated at the sight of him.

Bags were under his eyes. Dark smudges covered his face like he'd run his hand over it and left trails of dirt. His black sweatshirt reminded me of the first time I'd seen him on the running track, and he wore black athletic pants. Both molded to his frame in the right places, outlining his leanness, but I couldn't look away from the pained expression in his eyes.

"What happened?"

He shook his head, stepping inside. He didn't answer, just pulled me to him and rested his forehead in the crook of my neck and shoulder. I stood for a second, just holding him. He remained long after the elevator doors had closed again. I waited, unsure what to say, but I knew this embrace was for comfort, nothing more. He needed me in the truest way; he needed a friend.

He smelled of smoke and a faint tease of sweat, like he'd been running before he got here. They weren't overwhelming scents, just clinging to him in a nice way.

After another few seconds, I pulled back. His gaze was hooded. I rested a hand to the side of his face. "What happened to you?"

He shook his head, pulling completely away. "I can't tell you."

There it was. Again.

"Of course."

He shot me a look, but didn't say anything.

I turned to the kitchen. "Do you want a drink?"

"God, yes."

I could hear how tired he was, and a part of me ached for him. "Tequila? Rum? Something harder?"

He'd gone to the couch, laying his head on the back. He rolled it to look at me. "Whiskey?"

My heart leapt for a brief moment, and I had to pause. It felt right to have him there, sitting on my couch, waiting for me. I reached for the closest bottle, and my hands gripped it tightly, like I needed something to hold on to. That shouldn't be happening, the sensation of him being at home, like a piece of the puzzle had been put in place to complete the picture.

I felt a lump form at the bottom of my throat, but I asked around it, my voice hoarse, "You want to burn tonight?"

"It's better than what I'm feeling right now."

Instead of one glass, I pulled out two, and I pushed my wine aside. Whatever had happened, it was heavy. I went over and settled on the couch beside him, the bottle and two glasses in hand.

"Thank you." His voice was soft.

He sat up and took the bottle and glasses from me, placing them on the coffee table. He poured for both of us. The liquid covered the bottom third of the glass, and after a good whiff, it cleared my nose right up.

"You're right. This is going to be painful."

He gave me a sideways grin. "I know why I'm drinking. Why are you?"

"You're not the only one with ghosts."

I didn't wait for his reaction. I closed my eyes and threw it back, hissing as I felt the burn in my throat. Damn. I wanted another. I held the glass out. Cole took it, his soft chuckle blanketing me as he poured another shot.

He downed his, then leaned back to sip the next glass. He had no reaction when he drank. Nothing. I watched him, but the dullness in his eyes never lifted. He didn't wince. It could've been water.

"I'm sorry I didn't call earlier, but things got away from me, and…" He hesitated before saying, "I lost a friend today. That's where I've been, taking care of…" Another hesitation. "Things for him."

He wanted to say more. I could feel it, but he couldn't. I sat back beside him, my knees pulled up, and I clutched my glass in front of me.

"A close friend?" Was that why Ken was gone from the office below? Did he know this person, too? Was that why Dorian hadn't been happy both times I saw him?

He nodded.

"I'm sorry."

"No, I'm sorry." He finished the rest of his second drink, wincing slightly. "It's hard to not say anything to you. What I do…"

I waited. I'd been waiting since I first saw him.

"What I do is dangerous. That's why I can't tell you, at least not yet. I know it's not fair." He waved around my living room. "I show up here, and you're supposed to comfort me without knowing anything? It's unfair of me, but I didn't want to go anywhere else. This felt right." He looked up, his eyes boring into me. "Coming to you felt right."

I couldn't look away from him, nor did I want to. I held tight to the glass in my hand, and I said the only thing I was thinking at that moment. "I'm glad you came."

"Thank you." His hand rested on my leg.

His hand seared through my thin silk pants. I had changed into something soft and comfortable when I got back. I was now aware of just how thin the cloth was, and that I was only wearing a tank top, one that was loose but showing too much. I wasn't self-conscious, but my body was already yearning for him. It wasn't a live flame, like it had been last night, but a slow broil. It was there. It was heating up, but it was containable.

I glanced down at my glass. "You're here. You're hurting, and normally, I would ask what happened, and you'd tell me. We could go from there, but that's not the case. And I'm...I'm at a loss for what to say."

He cleared his throat. "You mentioned a husband?"

I looked back up. His eyes were sparkling from the moonlight behind me. The rest of his face was shadowed.

"Liam. Yeah. He died."

"I'm sorry."

"I'm sorry about your friend."

Another moment of silence. Cole began running one finger up and down my leg, moving over my thigh. "He was loyal. I've had people, people who *should* be loyal to me, plot against me. He was one of the good ones."

"Did you know him long?"

His gaze was on me, weighing before he answered. "I guess so. I knew him when I was younger. Then I went away and didn't know anyone from my old life. That changed a year ago. He's been by my side since."

"Was Dorian close to him?"

Cole nodded. "Ken knew him, too."

I grinned. "I thought I was the only one to call him Ken."

"No." Cole smiled. "Some people call him Kenny even."

"He wasn't downstairs tonight."

"He was with me. I was telling him about—" Cole hesitated. "—about our friend."

So he knew Dorian *and* Ken, though that wasn't news to me. It was just confirmation. Whether Cole lived upstairs or Dorian did, he was connected to the owner of this building. There were so many secrets around him. I didn't want to become one of them myself, but as he looked away and I studied his side profile, I had a feeling I already was.

I reached forward and took his hand, linking our fingers together. "I used to sit and hold Liam's hand like this."

Cole gazed down at our hands, but he didn't say anything.

The air was so damn thick. I was about to make it even heavier.

"I know you can't say anything, but maybe I can? I can tell you about me, and someday you'll tell me about you?"

I felt his gaze on me, but I didn't look. I didn't dare, or I'd lose my courage. Speaking about Liam was hard enough, but saying it to Cole, I felt ice moving through my veins. I forced myself to speak, knowing it was good to air some of this out, even just for myself.

"My family lives far away, so when Liam and I moved here, he became my family. He didn't get along with the rest of his family. His mom didn't like me, and his dad was just…absent. I guess that's the best way to describe him. His sister hated him, and he had another brother I never met. He never came home, not even for Liam's funeral. I don't know what I'm really saying here, but when Liam died, I died, too. Or it felt like it. Sia's been wonderful to me, but right now, she's four floors up with her new boyfriend, and I actually feel like he might be the one for her." What was I saying? I was rambling.

Cole squeezed my fingers lightly.

I felt encouraged by that small pressure. "I guess I'm just saying you can trust me, even though this—" I gestured between us. "—is something I have no way to understand right now. And I'm not trying to pressure you. I just want to say…" I stopped talking, feeling my eyes well up as I stared at our linked hands. "I'm a mess. I didn't mean to make things awkward between us. This is stupid. I was just trying to say I liked that we could hold hands. That was it—"

"Addison," he murmured.

"What?" I looked up.

"Shut up." Then his mouth was on mine, and he lifted me onto his lap.

I wanted to die again, but for a whole other reason.

I woke to the feeling of kisses on my neck. There was no thought. I opened my eyes, saw Cole, and rolled to my back. We didn't speak as he moved so he was above me. I rested my arms over his shoulders, looping my hands, and closed my eyes, just enjoying the feel of him. It wasn't long before he reached for a condom and slid inside me.

This was the way every morning should be: waking up to Cole inside of me. As he thrust in and slid out, over and over, I arched my back. Waves of pleasure rolled through me. His hand skimmed down my rib cage to cup my hip, and he used it as an anchor to go deeper.

This man, who I knew little to nothing about, knew my body in a way only Liam had. This should've alarmed me—waking up to him in my bed should've alarmed me—but it did the opposite. I felt safe and protected. And when I felt him coming, I didn't want it to end.

Afterward, as both of us trembled, he breathed into my ear. "You're bad for my work ethic." A low chuckle sounded.

"What do you mean?"

He pulled out to lie on his side, facing me. He traced a finger down my side, leaving tingles in its wake. "I have to leave town because of Robbie's death. The funeral will be somewhere else, and I have…" Again with the hesitation. "…There's business to deal with. I might be gone a while." His eyes raked over me, and he groaned and buried his face in my neck. "I don't want to go."

I skimmed a hand down his bare back, enjoying the feel of his muscles. "But you have to."

He nodded. "I have to."

He spoke those words against my skin. I felt another rush go through me.

"I'm sorry for you," I told him.

He pulled back, gazing down at me. His eyes clouded.

I pulled my hand against my chest. "I mean the funeral. You'll have to go through all of that." I remembered Liam's. "Trust me, it's going to suck."

The cloud disappeared. A new emotion lurked there—one I couldn't name.

"Funerals always suck," he said, almost roughly. He rolled in one smooth movement to sit on the edge of the bed. I sat up with him, pulling the sheet to cover my breasts. He glanced over his shoulder. "I've been to too damn many of them. You?"

"Liam's."

The corners of his mouth turned down. "Hey, I didn't say it last night, but thank you for telling me a little about him. Your husband."

My throat swelled up. "Yeah."

"I lost my family when I was little."

I lifted my head.

"I know what it's like to lose your family." His hand covered mine on the bed between us. "I'm an ass—coming in, sleeping with you, and not telling you much about me."

I laughed. "Trust me, I've asked myself more than a few times what the hell we're doing. But you came back." I clutched the sheet tighter and shrugged. "And here we are. Again."

"You're okay with this?"

"I…It is what it is."

"What does that mean?"

"Go to your funeral." I scooted forward and pressed a soft kiss to the back of his shoulder. "Bury your friend, and then come back to me. Maybe we can figure it out more then."

"I like that idea." His eyes darkened as I pulled away. Another time, another day, and we would've lain back down in that bed—when he didn't have to bury a loved one.

Cole dressed, and I stayed in bed, content to just listen to him moving around. I closed my eyes at one point. It was nice to hear another person in my home, one I knew was alive. I hadn't realized how the emptiness had bothered me, but that wasn't why I'd allowed Cole into my bed. Why I was doing that, I wasn't thinking about. He came over, and I wanted this. Every time. I knew I'd be waiting for the next time he rang my elevator. I'd let him up, and it wouldn't matter whether he gave me answers or not. Maybe I was a fool, or maybe I was at a place in my life where I didn't need to care. I was ready to just be.

I'd think later. I'd worry later. Right now, I'd just feel.

He came back to leave a lingering kiss on my lips and another on my forehead before he left. "I have your number," he said as he turned away. "I'll text you from the plane."

A moment later, I heard the elevator going up.

CHAPTER THIRTEEN

Two weeks went by.

It was fun at first. We texted each other. He sent a picture from an airplane seat—another tidbit he let slip. I wasn't a world traveler, but I'd been inside enough regular airplanes to recognize a private airplane when I saw one.

The texts started off flirty: What was I wearing? How tight was his suit? How lonely were my nights? I reciprocated, asking if he'd found a new "friend" to replace me. I'd thought the text was teasing, but as soon as I hit send, I realized I meant it.

Cole was gorgeous. He could have his pick of women. Why had he picked me?

The question plagued me, and I immediately heard Sia's screech in my mind. If she'd heard my question, she would've corrected me. He didn't pick me. He got *lucky* with me. Men weren't the hunters in her life. They were her prey. I also felt a stab of guilt that I was still keeping my involvement with Cole a secret from her. I wasn't ready to say anything, though. Plus, it'd been two nights. That didn't constitute something to talk about, yet. She would've had questions. Who was he? What did he do? How serious were we? What was I feeling about the relationship? All solid questions, but no solid answers. I couldn't reply to any of them, especially the one about how I was feeling about whatever it was between Cole and me.

I had no idea.

I liked him. I got excited about him. He made me feel alive. He put my blood on a constant simmer, where it could flame up and boil at any moment. That was how our two nights had been. I'd felt alive, but I was starting to go through withdrawals. He was like a drug. One hit and I was addicted, or close to it. Maybe a few hits? Who was I trying to kid? I was completely addicted and going through detox, but it was a detox I hadn't signed up for.

When was he coming back?

That thought ran through my head a few times a day, and every time it did, I felt foolish. I was a mature woman. I wasn't a young twenty-something. Or a teenager. Two nights together shouldn't be making me feel this yearning for him, or have me replaying how it felt when he stepped off my elevator and held onto me, or what it was like holding hands with him on the couch.

But it did. And every time I thought those things, my level of missing him went up a notch.

Sia was happy with Jake, and I was thankful. That kept her distracted enough not to worry too much about me or even focus on me when we got together for lunch or drinks a few times each week.

Cole seemed to sense that I hadn't been entirely kidding with that text, and his messages grew more serious after that: **Never. I want to come back as soon as I can. Business is getting in the way.** The rest of his texts were similar. He really did seem to want to know how I was, if I slept okay at night. He texted once, **Dorian said you were walking the track late last night. You okay?**

He'd been asking about me. A warmth spread through me, tingling all the way to my toes. I immediately wanted to shake that off and roll my eyes, but I couldn't. Instead, I thumbed back, **My bed seems empty now. Your fault.**

A few more days. I'll make it up to you. ;)

The few days turned into two more weeks.

The texts grew random and slowed. It was what it was. The detox was in full effect. After no communication in the fifth week he'd been gone, it was time I dealt with some of my feelings. I wasn't going to date anyone else. I wasn't even going to date Cole, but I wasn't going to wait for his texts anymore.

I went to see my realtor one day. We were in her office, and I wasn't thinking about Cole. Nope.

"Addison."

I'd been thinking about Cole. Cursing myself, I turned back to Heather's voice.

She hadn't come alone into the conference room. Three men followed her.

I stood and managed a half-smile. "Hello."

The first man looked me over, a smile plastered on his tanned and weathered face. His hair was dark, unnaturally dark. He looked to be in his later fifties, and he was tall, probably close to six feet. A gut stuck out beneath his suit jacket. The other two, both scowling, walked in behind him. They ignored my outstretched hand and claimed their seats, leaving the seat across from me open. They placed their briefcases on the table.

"Ms. Sailer." The first one finally shook my hand, giving it a firm pump. "I'm Alfred Mahler. I'm from Mahler and Associates. I'm representing your in-laws, Mr. and *Mrs.* Sailer. It's a pleasure to have met you." He glanced around the room. "Heather, I thought Ms. Sailer would have legal representation with her?"

Heather was a petite woman, but she'd been a force when she sold the house to Liam and me. She took the seat at the head of the table. "We weren't aware that lawyers were going to be needed." She adopted the same scowl as the other two. "You said Carol and Hank wanted this meeting."

"Yes." His smile was still there, but his eyes were dismissive. "They wanted this meeting, and we are representing them."

"I don't understand why we're here. You were vague on the phone." Heather folded her hands together, resting on the table. "What is it that you're here to say?"

Mr. Alfred Mahler didn't answer, not right away. He took his time before signaling his colleagues. The farthest one unclipped his briefcase and pulled out some papers. He handed them to the second lawyer, who handed them to Mr. Alfred Mahler. But no, that wasn't right. Mr. Mahler cleared his throat and tapped the table. The papers were placed there and then slid over until they were right in front of him.

I glanced away to roll my eyes.

Heather said under her breath, "This is ridiculous."

"What was that?" Mahler asked.

"Nothing." Her voice grew clearer. "I'm assuming these papers are for Addison?"

"Yes." He leaned forward, his finger still resting on the papers. "They're for *Ms.* Sailer."

Heather looked at me. "Do you mind?" She indicated the papers.

I shrugged.

She pulled them out from under the lawyer's finger and began reading. The more she read, the deeper her frown became. By the third page, I was worried.

She looked over.

"What is it?"

"They're suing you for the house." She regarded him, her neck already red and the color spreading to her face. "You have no basis. She was his wife."

"What?" I…what?!

"Yes, we assumed you would say that, but her name's not on the title, and my clients feel their money was used to purchase the house." Mr. Mahler stood up. The other two scrambled to stand with him. "This meeting was more a formality. We wanted to make sure you were served these papers, and next time we meet, bring legal representation." He turned toward the door. They walked out, one after another.

"Why do I have the urge to throw an eraser at him?" I asked, glowering at Mahler's retreating form.

"Because he's a pompous ass." Heather sighed. "Addison, oh my God. Whose money did you use to buy your home?"

Liam's, but... I took the papers from her and began reading. The more I read, the more my stomach sank. The money had come from Liam, but it was my house. It had been our house together. Our home. It was my choice what happened to it now.

They couldn't take the house away.

"I'm his wife, though. I thought that mattered."

"It does. This is complete bullshit." Heather lifted her hands in the air. "With lawyers and the courts..." Her hands dropped to the table. "Who knows what they can do. Liam didn't put you on the title. He said he was going to add you later, but he never did. Do you know why he did that?"

"Fuck." I had no idea. A headache was forming. I pressed on my temples, but knew it wasn't going to go away. "He had a new job. He was busy. And I didn't think about it. I mean, who would ever think about this? Liam had the money. He said he had enough saved up. We bought it outright. There's no mortgage or anything. I didn't even know about his money until the funeral, but I mean—" *What should I do?* "What can I do?"

Heather leaned close, a hard look in her eye. "You get a lawyer. You know any?"

"I..." I did. "My neighbor's a lawyer." I'd forgotten for a moment.

"Does he specialize in property law?"

That nice relieved feeling I'd just gotten vanished. I slumped back in my chair. "I have no idea."

CHAPTER FOURTEEN

Jake welcomed me from the elevator that evening with a look of surprise. "Hey, Addison." He still wore a business suit from work. A pot of coffee had started to sputter alive behind him. "Sia's not here, if that's who you're looking for?"

"No." I shook my head. "I'm looking for you. I might need legal help."

His eyes lit up. "Well, in that case, you came to the right place. Come in." He gestured to the living room. "Do you drink coffee— no. You don't, but Sia does. That's right. She told me you're not a big coffee drinker."

The elevator doors closed, and I waited on the couch as he got organized. He hung his suit coat on a nearby chair and sat down across from me.

"Okay. What do you have for me?"

I took out the papers. "I was given these a few hours ago."

"Yeah?" He took them and leafed through.

I hated this. I hated that Liam's family had put me in this position. I glanced around. This was my neighbor. I wasn't supposed to be a client, not this way. I clasped my hands together.

This was the worst part. The waiting.

"Okay." He finished reading and placed them on the table. "Um, well, first, how are you?"

"What?"

"How are you?"

"I'm…" I cocked my head to the side. "What do you mean?"

His eyes went to the floor, then came up as he cleared his throat. "Sia told me about you and Liam, how much you really loved him, and these are your in-laws doing this. So, I guess, how are you? I'm not asking as your lawyer, but as your neighbor and the guy in love with your best friend."

"Love, huh?" I sat back.

"Yeah. I love her. I haven't told her, but this isn't about that." He tapped the papers. "How are you feeling about Liam's parents doing this?"

"I'm furious." My voice was monotone.

"Okay. Yeah." He coughed into his hand. "I can see that. My firm does work in property law. You paid for your home in full?"

I nodded. "With cash."

"And who primarily paid for it? Was it you and Liam? Was it mainly just Liam?"

"It was Liam." I slid my hands under my legs. They were beginning to tremble. "I paid for the insurance, and I helped with the furniture, but it was mostly his money." I had to swallow a lump in my throat. "It was all his money."

"Okay." His eyes drifted from me to the papers, then to the floor. "Your name isn't on the title, but you're his wife. They don't have a case. However, if you wanted to make this go away more quickly, you could show them a copy of your accounts—where it shows that it was Liam's money, and not money put into his account by your in-laws. That would be enough to make this completely go away, but you don't have to do that. As your lawyer, I wouldn't advise you to show your bank statements for any reason."

"And as a friend?"

"If you want to make this go away so your in-laws aren't fucking with you, I'd just show them the proof. They have to go away then."

I wanted them to go away. *I* wanted to go away. I nodded. "I can do that. Liam got his inheritance when he turned thirty. So that money would've been in there before."

"And that's how he paid for the house?"

I nodded. "I didn't know it at the time, but yes. He got twenty million from his grandmother's estate. I found out about it at the funeral. Carol, his mother, told me. The lawyers came over later with all the paperwork."

"Okay. Those were her lawyers or Liam's lawyers?"

I tried to remember. "They were lawyers. I don't know if they were Liam's or his parents'."

"They should've been Liam's, but sometimes family members use the same firm. Did Liam get along with his family?"

"No." This conversation was ripping me open. "He and his younger brother didn't get along with their parents. There's a sister, and she did, but Liam didn't get along with her either. I mean, Liam had lunch with her sometimes until she began trying to introduce him to other women. She didn't like me." My voice sounded so strange right now, like it was another person talking.

"Do you remember who came over with the inheritance papers?"

"No." I shook my head.

"So, okay. I think if you can remember the name of the firm Liam worked with, I'll have my firm reach out to them. That would help because we don't want them coming back and suing you for validity of inheritance. We'll make sure everything is in order. This shouldn't be a problem. I don't know how it even could, to be honest. People can sue for anything these days. Most claims are bullshit, but if you don't want to prolong this—"

"No. I know. I'll do that. It's fine." I nodded, and that was it. We made plans for our next meeting, which would be held at his actual place of business. I was about to head for the elevator when he asked, "What about Sia?"

"What do you mean?"

"Technically this is confidential information with attorney-client privilege, so you tell me. I don't have to say a word to her, if you don't want me to."

"Oh." I blinked. Sia hated Carol. "Maybe not, for now. I don't want to be sued for my ex-mother-in-law's death. Sia tends to look for pitchforks whenever she talks about Carol."

Jake laughed. "That sounds like Sia. Okay. I think we're set then. I'll see you in a few days. My office will call you tomorrow."

"Thank you, Jake."

"Not a problem. We'll take care of you."

Those words—*take care of you.*

I hit the button for my floor and leaned back. It'd been a long time since I'd heard words like that. When the elevator stopped, I was expecting it to open on my floor, but I looked up and realized I was at the lobby instead, and Ken stood right before me. His hands were folded in front of him, and his head was slightly bowed.

He cleared his throat. "There's been a request from our mutual *acquaintance*. He'd like for you to pack an overnight bag and your identification. There's a car waiting for you outside."

"What?"

"You'll be driven to the airport. Mr. Cole is unable to come here, so he'd like to bring you to him instead."

CHAPTER FIFTEEN

The car drove me to the airport and dropped me off in the private planes section, pulling up outside a hangar. A Ken look-alike waited for me—similar greying hair, his hands folded in front of his dark blue suit, kind eyes warming as he nodded a small smile to me.

He held his hand out, gesturing toward a set of stairs that led to a private plane. "Ms. Bowman, I imagine?"

I nodded, still dazed from what Ken had said. "Uh, yeah."

"The plane is prepped and ready. You'll be landing at JFK shortly, and another car will be waiting for you there." He bowed, just briefly. "Have a wonderful trip."

"Uh." I was still dazed. "Thank you."

He didn't tell me his name, but he took my small bag and carried it to a flight attendant waiting at the bottom of the stairs. I trailed after him, and as the attendant took the bag, he gave me another professional nod.

"Safe flying, Ms. Bowman."

Then he was gone, disappearing back inside the hangar.

The attendant waited, a similar smile on her face. She indicated for me to go ahead, and as I did, she put my bag in a compartment.

"Would you like anything in particular to drink or eat before we take off?" she asked.

I shook my head. This was all… I looked around. Private plane. I mean, I knew Cole had been on a private plane, but I didn't know it was his, and this one must've been. Maybe he just chartered it? For some reason, that helped settle my nerves. That made sense.

Still, when we arrived at JFK and I got inside the waiting car, I didn't ask the attendant or the driver. A part of me didn't want to know. What would those details indicate about Cole? He looked too young to have all this, but then again, maybe that was what he thought about me? I wasn't working, and I could afford to live in The Mauricio. It was obvious I had money, but he never questioned me. And why was I even wondering about this?

I was nervous.

My thoughts bounced around, and when the car headed into the city, I crossed my arms over my chest. Deep breath. Maybe a second one. I wanted to calm the knots inside, loosen them up.

When the car pulled over and the driver opened my door, I got out and craned my neck. We were outside a building similar to The Mauricio—all silver colored and made of pure glass. This one stretched much higher than the one I lived in, and it seemed friendlier. Unlike The Mauricio's door, which was small and almost drab-looking on purpose to help with the exclusivity, this one was a circling glass door.

A doorman approached with the same polite nod and smile as the others. "Ms. Bowman." He took the bag the driver offered him and gestured toward the doors. "I'll show you to your room."

I didn't know what to expect, but when we went inside, I was still surprised.

It was a hotel. One desk, one worker behind it, and a small fountain in the middle. That was it. The walls were dark with red trim, and the floors were dark marble tile. It gave off a swanky feeling that mingled with anonymity. The doorman passed the desk and led me around the corner to the elevator. He rode with me, pushing the top button on the panel, and I had déjà vu. Cole often came from a higher floor in The Mauricio; it seemed fitting that he had the top floor here.

"Miss."

The doors opened, and the doorman held an arm out, waiting for me to go first. I stepped out, and he swept behind me, disappearing into a room. A second later, he returned and pressed the button for the elevator again. It opened, he nodded to me a last time, and was whisked away.

Turning around, I found the suite immense and impressive. The living room was a step down in the middle of the room. The kitchen was something I'd seen in a magazine, and there was a veranda. It stretched from the kitchen past the living room and wrapped all the way around. I hadn't even looked for the bedrooms. I'd just started, heading down the small hallway, when the phone rang.

I picked it up. "Hello?"

"Ms. Bowman?"

"This is."

"This is Thomas from the front desk. I'm calling to inquire if the room is okay?"

"Oh, yes."

"Is there anything you'd like brought up for you?"

"No. Thank you, though."

I was about to hang up when I heard, "One more thing, Ms. Bowman."

I frowned. "Yeah?"

"I have a message to pass along from Mr. Cole."

I straightened.

"He sends his apologies that he's not in the room right now. He's currently in a meeting and unable to get away. If you'd like, there's a dress laid out in the master bedroom. Mr. Cole will be arriving shortly and wonders if you'd meet him in a private box at The Octavia? We have staff that will accompany you until he arrives, if you'd like any added direction and guidance."

"Oh." This was a little *Pretty Woman*-esque, but I shrugged. "Sure. When do I have to be ready?"

"Thirty minutes." That came out in a flat voice, and he hung up right after. So, not *Pretty Woman*-esque. The guy sound annoyed with me.

I rolled my eyes, but moved to the master bedroom. The dress stopped me in my tracks. It was white, with a translucent covering. I lifted it up, and it looked like something a Greek goddess would wear. I could only imagine having my hair up in braids and a light coating of glitter makeup.

I suppressed a shiver—not a bad one, just one that didn't feel right to me. This stuff happened to Sia. This was a story she would've told me after meeting a brand new boyfriend. This stuff didn't happen to me.

I laid the dress down and sat. I...I didn't even know what to think about all of this. *Who is Cole?*

I sighed and sat back when I heard another phone ringing. This time it was mine, and I searched for it in my bag, which had been placed on the bed next to the dress.

Cole's name was sprawled across the screen when I found it. "Hey."

"Hey, are you at the hotel?" He paused one second. "Ken did tell you about coming to New York, right? Are you still in Chicago?"

"No. I'm here. I'm in New York." I laughed. It felt good to hear the small fear in his voice. I reached over, fingering the dress. The fabric was so soft. I knew I'd never worn something so extravagant. "Cole."

"Hmm?"

"What is this? This whole thing?" I glanced around the hotel room. "Are you trying to wow me or something?" He didn't have to. I'd seen him naked. That was wow enough. "This is too much."

"Wait. What are you talking about?"

"The private plane. The dress. What club is The Octavia?"

He groaned. "Okay, I'm sorry. The private plane was because if you agreed, I just wanted you to come as soon as possible. That was me being selfish. I've been in business meetings all day long, and I only have tonight free. I just wanted to see you.

"You didn't pick out the dress?"

"No. I asked one of my staff to handle the details. I had no idea he'd pick out a dress for you."

"A guy picked this out then?" I didn't know what was worse, thinking Cole had picked it out or knowing another man did. Another man, definitely the other man. If Cole had picked it out… again, that good kind of shiver happened. "You haven't seen the dress?"

His voice dropped low. "Do I want to? And the note said to meet me at The Octavia?"

"It wasn't a note. The front desk guy, Thomas, called me."

He barked out a laugh. "That wasn't the front desk. Thomas is one of my guards. We have about twelve Thomases working for us. I've no doubt that was an inside joke. I'm sorry. Listen, I was going to go to The Octavia for a bit, but you don't have to come. It's a nightclub my buddy owns here."

"A nightclub?" Another place and adventure that Sia would've had, and would've told me about. I sat up, forgetting the dress. "I'll come."

"Wait—"

"No. I want to come."

"Are you sure?"

"Yes." I couldn't remember the last time I went to an actual nightclub. A restaurant, one of Sia's events at the Gala—those I'd go to, but not an actual dancing club. Something stirred in me. I was waking up, and I said again, "I want to come."

"Uh." He hesitated. "Okay. The club's next to the hotel you're in. That's why I wanted a room there for you. Give me a bit, and I'll come over."

We hung up, and I didn't have time for the nerves to explode. I knew they would, but that was ridiculous. I knew Cole, kind of. I'd slept with him, no kind of there. Definitely. So nerves didn't make sense, but as I picked up the dress and went to the bathroom, the back of my mind called bullshit on me.

This was new. This was out of my comfort zone. This was… my hands were shaking, and thirty minutes later, I stood back and smoothed down the front of my dress. This was surreal.

The dress wasn't long so it looked appropriate for a club, ending between my thigh and knee. A good amount of thigh was showing, and the loose, see-through fabric that covered the rest of the dress shimmered in the light. It really was beautiful, something I never would've picked to wear, and it meant more now.

I wanted to surprise Cole, just like he'd surprised me with this trip.

I gazed in the mirror. My old sandy-blond hair was back. It had been a drab mop for so long, but it had changed. It was shining now. I touched some of the looser strands that had fallen down to frame my face. The rest was pulled back into one large, messy braid. My makeup was minimal, though I had pulled out a shimmering lip balm.

Yes. I studied myself. I was satisfied. I saw a spark in my eyes that I hadn't seen for so long.

I heard the door open, then Cole called out, "Addison?"

I moved through the bedroom, stopping in the doorway.

He was yawning, a hand scratching behind his ear when he turned, asking, "You here…" His voice trailed off when he saw me. "Whoa." His hand fell to his side. "Wow." A wolfish grin curved over his face, and he came toward me, his hand coming to rest on my side. "I might need to have Thomas pick out more of your clothes. Wow."

Warmth spread through me. Whether it was his reaction, or seeing him, being near him again, I wasn't sure.

"Is Thomas looking for a job?" I murmured. "Personal shopper?"

Cole laughed softly, the sound ending as he looked into my eyes. He touched the side of my face. "Do you know how beautiful you are?"

My heart skipped a beat. I couldn't talk.

His eyes darkened. He cupped the side of my face, and his gaze fell to my lips. "I am so very, very happy I asked you to come here. Even if it's just for one night." He leaned in.

I held my breath.

His eyes flicked back up to mine. "Are you okay with this?"

"With what?" I rested my hand against his chest. I could feel his heart, a strong thumping against me.

"Coming here, being whisked away. I have to go back to my meetings tomorrow, but all those weeks were becoming too long." He looked torn, a hesitancy filling his gaze. He leaned back an inch. "We don't have to go to The Octavia. We can have a nice meal somewhere, then come back."

"What? No. I want to go to The Octavia. It sounds fun."

"Are you sure? It's loud, and dark, and…"

"What?"

"It's sex."

I raised an eyebrow. "How's that a problem?"

"You're more than sex."

Oh. I fell quiet, so conscious of his hand holding the side of my face.

"I know that's how we started, but it's more already," he added, his voice growing softer. "You're not someone I'd fly in, just for sex. You're worth an expensive dinner, quiet time together, any view you want. It's your company I wanted tonight, because I was missing you. I just want you to know all of that. I don't…"

I covered his hand and swallowed over a lump. "I know. It's the same for me."

He stared into me, searching, and for a moment, I felt like I got a glimpse of the real Cole. He was dangerous, mysterious, and mesmerizing, but he was more. Kind. Considerate. I saw a glimmer of someone who cared.

A jittery sensation grew in my stomach, and I licked my lips. Confusion, euphoria, exhaustion. All of those emotions slammed into me, and I didn't want to think about them. I pressed my hand harder against him and leaned forward. The feel of him—his other hand had moved to my waist—anchored me. I was getting swept up, but I needed my feet on the ground.

I heard myself saying, my voice a hoarse rasp, "Let's go to The Octavia." The sudden need to experience this club was powerful.

He nodded, his hand dropping into my mine.

He'd told me I was beautiful. He'd told me I was more than sex to him now.

But he hadn't kissed me, and I was suddenly drowning for the touch of his lips on mine.

He led me out the door, and two men fell in step with us. One walked before us, standing a few yards away, and the other walked behind. They were far enough away to give us the sense of walking without them, but they were there, and I clutched Cole's hand.

Who is Cole?

That question grew more and more urgent, nagging me, but when he glanced over and I saw the lust in his eyes, the question dissipated. I was beginning not to care who he was, as long as he was with me.

We went through a back door into The Octavia, and even though it was dark, I knew the instant we changed buildings. We'd gone through a back hallway that connected the two. As soon as the door opened, techno music hit our ears. A makeshift wall rose in front of us, and neon light flashed behind it. The smell of dry ice filled the air, along with sweat and, as Cole had said, the smell of sex, too.

We went down a hallway, seeming to circle around the main dance floor, and sex was all I felt. I heard moaning behind closed doors, then heard moaning in the music itself. We passed a clearing, and I looked over. It was like we were rounding a stadium, except there were no seats. The stadium floor was for dancing, and there were sections cut off that circled the building and led up to where we were, at the top of the entire thing. All those separate sections had their own bars, with the floors lit up in the same neon color that flashed in rhythm with the music. Some sections had couches. Others were filled with people dancing, and a lot of people were on the stairs talking. The stairs connected everything, except the top floor where we were. Two thin poles ran the length from each makeshift wall so we were kept from going below, or they were kept from coming to us above. I had a feeling it was the latter. A few people nursing drinks glanced up when they saw us, and they looked surprised. It was like they hadn't realized people could walk above them.

I squeezed Cole's hand harder. I knew I'd said I wanted to come here, but I hadn't known. This place was huge—not as huge as a real stadium, but bigger than any other nightclub I knew about. Who was his friend? And if his friend owned this, what did Cole own? Or maybe he helped manage these places? Maybe he was just connected to someone wealthy. But as the guy who'd been leading us turned back and spoke to Cole, I didn't feel like that was the case.

I could see his mouth moving, but I couldn't hear the words. The music was too loud, and a second later, Cole nodded. He changed our positions, so I was holding his left hand instead. I felt like he wanted his right hand free. He was walking closest to the makeshift wall now, and as we kept going, another man materialized out of nowhere. This guy wasn't walking right next to me, but close enough. I was smack in the middle. The two others had closed their distance, so now I was surrounded by four men, in a diamond shape.

I couldn't even process this switch, so I held on to Cole's hand. That was it. I focused on him, and a moment later, he ducked inside another room. It was a private box, directly above the DJ's booth, which was three floors below us.

Cole spoke to the three men before he shut the door behind us. I was relieved.

He noticed me watching the door as he came over, his hand touching the small of my back. "What?"

I didn't ask who they were. Gut instinct told me he wouldn't answer. "I thought they were coming in with us."

"No." His hand tightened its hold on my back, his fingers pressing in. "But two of them will stay out there. It's just typical security measures."

I held his gaze. "Really?"

He stared back, not blinking, no reaction, until his hand fell away. "They're a part of the stuff I can't tell you about."

That was what I thought. "Don't bullshit me, okay?"

One corner of his mouth curved up, and his hand came back to my waist. "I won't." His finger tucked into a part of my dress where there was an opening, and he tugged me back until I came into full contact with him. He pressed right up against me, and his arms came around, holding on to the box's wall as he dipped his head down to rest on my shoulder. He spoke right next to my ear. "I'm sorry."

I closed my eyes, not caring about the hundreds of people beneath us. The entire club was dark. The lights had been flashing over the dance floor, but I knew no one could see us from below. I leaned back, winding my arms up around his neck. My back arched, pushing my breasts forward. My dress had a low V-neck, so I knew he could see. I wanted him to see. I wanted him to touch, to caress. I wanted all of it.

"Addison," he murmured into my ear.

I could hear his desire, and an almost drugged smile crossed my face. The security guards were gone from my mind. The feeling of sex that penetrated the club's atmosphere had slipped past my walls, and I wanted what I'd wanted back in the room. I wanted Cole to kiss me.

I wanted more, as well, but until then… I turned around, my arms looping around his neck. I leaned back so I could see him. The club was now our backdrop.

The same primal want stared back at me. I touched the side of his face. "I'm going to go back to my life tomorrow."

His eyes grew hooded.

"But this night, being here, this isn't normal for me. I don't do this kind of stuff. Thank you."

He frowned. "For what?"

"For pulling me out of that life, at least for a bit." *For waking me up.*

His hand gripped my hip, and he moved in, pressing against me. I felt him grind into me, and a drunk feeling coursed through me, though I'd had nothing to drink. He dropped his head down, brushing a kiss to my naked shoulder.

He murmured against my ear again, "It should be me thanking you. You have no idea."

I stilled. His tone wasn't normal. He wasn't guarded, and he wasn't teasing.

Then he said, with an eerie seriousness, "My life I can't talk about, but this—you coming to me—is like a breath of oxygen. I can breathe again." He dropped his mouth, lingering on my shoulder. "Something pure among so much tainted."

I closed my eyes. I wasn't going to ask what he meant. He wouldn't tell me, but I reached back, took hold of the wall, and used it to push myself forward, even closer to him. I caused a small opening behind us, and Cole wound his arm around me, lifting me in the air.

I gazed down at him, half-laughing, my arms around his neck. "What are you doing?"

He grinned back, his eyes so dark and wanting as he turned me to sit on top of the bar in our box. I thanked goodness we had no bartender, and then Cole stepped between my legs. He touched my face again, tilting it as he came in. His lips pressed to mine, and right there, another tingle went down my spine. He was where he was supposed to be—with me, touching me, being with me.

I pulled him in, and I didn't care who could see us. As he deepened our kiss, I let go of everything. There was only this moment. I was only with him. Tomorrow I would think about the future. Tomorrow I would think about Sia, about my life back in Chicago, but right now, for this moment, it was only Cole.

It was only Cole and the sensations he had unearthed inside of me.

CHAPTER SIXTEEN

We stayed in that box for half the night, just making out. And when we couldn't hold back any longer, we went back to my hotel room.

Cole woke me early in the morning with more kisses and touches, but he had to leave around six. He had more business to attend to, and the plane was waiting for me when I woke again later.

On the flight home, I thought about the night. The entire thing had been like a daydream. I'd been transported into a different world—Cole's world. I'd visited his life. Even for just a moment, and even if I didn't know what life that was, it had been worth it. So worth it.

I refused to think of any price I might pay, and once I got home, I went back to life as normal. Or I tried. Cole remained in the back of my mind, but the first thing: my meeting with Jake's law firm.

It went well. I gave them the paperwork they needed, and that was enough. They said they'd be surprised if Liam's parents proceeded any further, especially since it was a "bullshit suit." Those were Jake's and his colleague's words.

I never told Sia that I'd left town for a night, but she must've noticed I was acting differently. She asked if everything was fine, and instead of believing me when I said it was, she invited me to attend an event with her.

"The Gala is sponsoring the event, so I'm supposed to go, but I didn't organize it so I don't have a lot of work to do," she explained. "I just need to talk to a few people—you know, network. But the event is going to be huge. It's at the Haldorf, not the Gala. We're just one of the sponsors. I'm sure a few celebrities will be there, and anyone influential in the city will be there. Do you want to come? You don't have to. But I'm making Jake come, too."

Maybe it was because I didn't want to be alone. Maybe it was because Cole had woken me up, and now I was restless. Things had been gray before, but the world was in color now. I wanted things to be in bright lights, neon like the club. I didn't want everything to be dimmed anymore. And maybe it was for that reason that I found myself agreeing to go.

Twenty-four hours later, I was back among beautiful people, crystal lights, and champagne. Lots and lots of champagne. Sia had said it would be bigger. She hadn't lied. It was like one of her events, but on steroids, and multiplied by ten.

I wanted to die. Well, almost. Not quite. See? Progress. I was only experiencing a mild form of irritation and regret. I clutched my champagne glass tightly in front of me like it was a shield against anyone who tried to talk to me.

The Haldorf was one of the most prestigious hotels in Chicago, and the clientele for the evening was more diverse—star athletes and celebrities, as well as most of the usual socialites the Gala always invited. My corner view through the window gave me a look at the front entrance and the impressive lineup of people entering. It was my own private red carpet.

"Hey." Jake sidled up next to me, drink in hand. He turned his back to the window and surveyed the crowd behind me. "This is impressive. Did Sia have a lot to do with it?"

"I'm not sure."

"She's off flitting around." He glanced down at me. "Is this what it's like coming to a party as her date?"

Patting his arm, I turned to watch the crowd inside with him. "Yes, yes, it is, my dear friend. You have joined the dark side. I call it Sia's Neglected Entourage. For a while there, it was a sad club with only one member, but I welcome you, a new member now."

"Can I get a pin?"

"I'll buy you one of those things pageant winners wear." I sobered. "Just so you know, she's never brought a boyfriend to one of these events."

"Yeah?" He studied me.

I nodded. "You're the first. She never cared enough about the others." I nudged him gently with my arm. "I think that says something."

His chest puffed up. "Damn straight. I'm awesome in bed."

I burst out laughing.

"No way!"

I looked up, distracted by Jake's sudden proclamation. He stared at a crowd to our left, his mouth open. "It's Mahler."

"Who?"

I looked but saw only a bunch of black tuxedos and shiny dresses. No one stood out to me until a couple moved aside and I saw him. The lead attorney for my in-laws. I looked over to the couple beside him, and my blood ran cold. "Oh, no."

"That's the piece of shit trying to sue you for your in-laws, or who tried. Biggest piece of crap lawsuit I've heard about in a long time."

Jake had no clue who was next to the piece of shit. "He's not alone."

"Huh?" He followed my gaze. "No way. Are those—?"

"Liam's parents. In the flesh."

"They must've come on his ticket. What do you want to do?" Some of Jake's heat faded. "I was ready to go over and pick a fight, but I'll follow your lead. Avoid? Ignore? Laugh like we're better than them? Walk by and accidentally knock my elbow into his dad? He doesn't have a firm grip on his drink. We could go for the winner, see if he'd spill his drink on himself? I'm game. You choose."

"Pick a fight?"

Jake shrugged. "Okay, but my style. The lawyer way. We fight differently than everyone else."

I was about to change my answer to *avoid*, but Mahler looked in our direction, and then it was too late. He saw us. His eyes got big, and a smarmy, smug look came over him. His face was red and sweaty, and when he waved us over, I noticed his eyes were glazed.

"Look who we have here!" he said. "Jake Parker. Your office sent over papers today. How thoughtful and cooperative you all are being."

Jake groaned under his breath. "Come on. We have to go over now."

I didn't move, but Carol and Hank both saw me, and Carol had visibly stiffened. I was distantly aware of Jake's hand nudging me forward.

"Mahler." Jake sounded as stiff as Carol looked. "I could've saved money and delivered those papers tonight."

Mahler let out a deep laugh, clamping a hand on Jake's shoulder. "None of that. Tonight's for pleasure. We're raising money for some cause—horse tails, maybe?" He tossed back a good portion of his champagne. "Where's your drink? You, too, Ms. Sailer. Where's your drink? You need to be enjoying yourselves with us—" Then he cut himself off and seemed to remember who he was standing with.

The only satisfaction I got was that my in-laws looked as uncomfortable as I was.

Carol looked down, lifting a tiny hand to pat her greying hair, which was pulled up in a diamond-encrusted barrette. She'd always been beautiful, and her aging had only made her more stunning. Liam got his looks from her. They had the same blue eyes, soft cheekbones, and heart-shaped face. Liam used to make fun of himself, saying he would've been a pretty girl, but I loved how he looked. And a lot of other ladies agreed with me. I was staring at the reason so many had tried their hands at catching him.

"You look lovely, Carol."

I sensed Jake's surprise, but she'd brought Liam into this world. I owed her that much.

She seemed just as surprised as Jake. "Thank you, Addison." She looked me up and down. "You as well. The black is beautiful on you."

I repressed a retort, pressing my lips together.

"*Really, Addison,*" she'd said after the funeral. "*You must stop wearing black. It's depressing. I know most girls wear it because it's slimming, but you're all bones. You should be wearing white. That'll make you look healthier. Trust me, most of the girls will be envious. I know Liam loved white. Wear it for him, or wear something else. Some color. Blue even. God forbid you wear something more lively than black.*"

The guilt in her gaze told me she remembered this as well. I forced my smile to hold, though my cheeks protested. I could've taken a cheap shot. Her silver sequins matched her greying hair, but that was another comment I suppressed.

"Hank." I nodded. That was all I said to him.

Liam's father was the same age as Mahler, but he did not have the same beauty regimen. While Mahler's hair was dyed jet black, Hank's was mostly grey, just like his wife's. That was something I remembered about them. They believed in keeping chemicals and toxins out of their bodies as much as possible.

Hank nodded back to me. "Addison." His hand curved behind his wife's arm, the same way Jake held on to me. "You're dating a lawyer now?"

"What?"

"Oh." Jake withdrew his hand, laughing. "No. We're—"

"—friends," I finished, adding, "Jake's a good friend. He *helped* me with the case." I stressed the word *helped* because as far as I was concerned the case was over. I raised my chin, daring any of them to disagree.

Hank put his hands in his pockets. Carol sighed and turned, raising her head to scan the rest of the room. She kept her fingers clasped together around her glass, like it was too heavy for her and she needed both hands to hold it up. I eyed her, noting a droop to her shoulders I hadn't noticed before. Her makeup couldn't hide the bags under her eyes either. They seemed larger than I'd ever noticed before.

Jake was silent.

Mahler let out another hearty laugh. "I'm still thinking we need drinks for you two. Where's a damn waitress when you need one?" He scanned the room for a moment. "Holy shit!" Everyone turned to him with the change in his tone. "Talk about a ghost from the past."

He stepped backward and reached out as two men slipped by in the crowd. He tried to grab the first man's arm, but he twisted at the last second and caught Mahler's wrist. Mahler blinked a couple times before he burst out with another booming laugh.

"Carter Reed. I couldn't believe it, and I can barely believe it now." He eased his arm out of the man's grasp. "As quick as you ever were." He lifted his hand as if to clasp him on the shoulder, but the man narrowed his eyes in warning. Mahler's hand fell back to his side. He cleared his throat. "How are you, Reed? I didn't know you came around these parts anymore."

"Fuck."

I was the only one who seemed to have heard Jake's quiet curse, and I glanced at him. His eyes were wide and trained on this Carter Reed person.

Reed had wolf-like blue eyes, dark blond hair, and a dangerous air. If Sia had been here, and not been with Jake, she would've been gushing over him like when she first saw Cole at Gianni's. This man was powerful. That was obvious. Carol and Hank seemed frozen as well, their reactions close to Jake's.

Who is this guy?

"I have to say, it's not a good surprise to see you, Reed." Mahler spoke again since the other man refused to respond. "Where you go, bodies tend to pile up." When everyone else remained silent, he laughed at his own joke. He was the only one.

Reed only watched him, an icy glint in his eyes. He didn't seem annoyed or scared, just like he was waiting for the idiot to shut up.

Carol jerked into motion. She reached for Mahler's glass. "I think you've had one too many, Alfred."

"Oh, come on." He was still laughing. "It's funny. Besides, what are you nervous about? Reed's out of the game. Right?" He reached for the man's shoulder again, and he was evaded again.

"If you try to touch me one more time, I will break your hand."

The soft threat shut him up. It was as if Mahler suddenly realized who he'd been poking, like a child pointing a stick at a cobra. His face became even more flushed.

"Uh." He took a step back, cramming his hands into his pockets as he tried to recover. "Who are you here with?" He craned his neck to see who had been standing behind the taller man. As he did, Reed's companion moved forward, and Hank and Carol moved aside. They kept their eyes focused elsewhere.

I should have, too.

Reed's associate came into view, and I felt punched in the diaphragm.

It was Cole.

I could only stand there and stare. I hadn't thought he'd be here. I hadn't thought he was even in the state. I'd just been with him a few nights before, and he'd said nothing. He'd texted a couple times since then, asking how I was, but he'd given no indication he was coming back to town. These thoughts were racing in my mind, but all I could do was swallow, feeling a knot moving up my throat.

I tried to keep my mouth from falling open and gaping at him, but that was where my jaw should've been, on the damn floor. I couldn't help noting how he looked and how my body was already leaning toward him, like it wanted to go into his arms, like that was the most natural thing in the world.

Like that was where I was supposed to be, and why the hell was I still only standing here, not going to him?

I knew that wasn't rational, and I tried to shut off that side of my brain. Anger, annoyance, and some other sensations I didn't want to identify churned in me. If I let myself feel them, it'd be a recipe for disaster. I would not make a scene here. I would not demand answers. That would be later, but not in front of my in-laws, or in front of anyone, for that matter.

Instead, I took in how striking Cole looked. His friend was striking as well, but I preferred Cole. He was dark to his friend's light. Each balanced the other, drawing attention from everyone around us and other groups beyond them. They had an animal magnetism. They were affecting the crowd. People grew restless, feeling a shift in the air.

Both were deadly. Both knew it, and both gazed at Mahler like he was their next meal.

Mahler was finally struck speechless. He could only stare at Cole, as could I. Cole narrowed his eyes at Mahler, then Jake, then swung his gaze to me. He lingered a moment before returning to Mahler.

Complete silence settled over the group. What was going on? They couldn't have known about us. Reed was staring at me now, and I froze for a beat. Curiosity mingled faintly with an amused look in his eyes before he shifted backward to stand shoulder to shoulder with Cole.

"You were full of drunken stupidity when you saw me, Mahler," Reed spoke. "Now you can't say a word?" He glanced to Cole. "Or maybe you weren't aware that Cole was in town?"

Mahler sputtered out some words, but none made sense.

My ex in-laws didn't seem surprised to see him, or maybe they'd gotten over it faster. Both had their eyes trained on the floor, their shoulders slightly hunched forward. They were the vision of demure and timid.

I tilted my head to the side. This didn't make sense. Nothing was making sense. I turned to Jake, but he couldn't look away from Cole. His jaw clenched, and his Adam's apple swiftly jerked up and down.

What…?

"Well, I mean—" Mahler had found his ability to speak. Unfortunately. He coughed once, a deep burst of air that cleaned out his pipes. "I don't think anyone was aware that Cole Mauricio was back in town."

Mauricio—I felt another kick to my stomach. The Mauricio. Cole Mauricio. He was the building's owner. He had to be, and he'd been quiet about it the whole time. I stared at him, accusing. His eyes flicked to mine, and I caught a brief flash of amusement mixed with an apology before it disappeared and his face shifted back to an unreadable mask.

I narrowed my eyes. I didn't share the sentiment. I felt the opposite, and I still had to clamp down on the emotions twisting around me, like an angry tornado.

Reed studied Hank and Carol. "I think your companions did."

Mahler glanced to them, then at Jake and me. "Oh. Well…" He shrugged. "Maybe they saw Cole earlier."

"We just arrived."

All eyes turned to Cole. His eyes darted to mine once before returning to Mahler. They narrowed, then swept over Carol and Hank, too. "Maybe they were aware for another reason."

I frowned. What was he talking about?

Both Carol and Hank turned bright red, and my ex mother-in-law reached for her husband's arm. "It's been a wonderful event, but I've grown tired all the sudden."

Mahler snorted.

She paused, shooting him a dark look. "It's been lovely, Alfred. And it was a pleasure to have met you, Mr. Reed. Mr. Mauricio." She stopped, realizing who else she needed to address. She looked up, barely meeting my eyes. "And nice seeing you as well, Addison."

Liam's mother was just as fake as she'd always been. I couldn't muster up anything polite to say in return. So I said nothing. I just wanted them to go away.

They turned to go just as Cole said, "Bea Bertal."

They stopped. But they didn't look back, not at first. Two seconds passed before Carol turned back to Cole. She swallowed visibly. Her hand clutched Hank's arm. "You knew my mother?"

"Cole." Mahler started forward, but Reed blocked him.

I glanced to Jake, and found him captivated. Unaware of my gaze, he inched forward, as if to hear better.

"I've been hearing rumors about your father," Cole said evenly. "Tell me, Carol." He leaned closer to her. "Are they only rumors?"

Her bottom lip started to tremble. "I don't know. Bea is dead, you know. My husband and I, along with our children, don't speak to my father anymore."

"Was that a recent change?"

"No." She seemed to wilt under his gaze. "We haven't spoken to my father for years, since my eldest was born, in fact." As she mentioned Liam, she looked at me before turning back to Cole. "As I mentioned before, I've grown quite tired. We'll wish you all a good evening."

Hank hurried off, with Carol right behind him. Their exit seemed eerily similar to an escape.

I looked at Cole. Who was he to Liam's parents? Who was he at all? The need to find out now burned in me. If I didn't find out…I couldn't finish. I didn't know what I'd do. I didn't want to think about it because then all rational thought might actually shut down. I couldn't go there.

Jake's hand came back to my elbow. "I think the Sailers had the right idea. I think we'll be going as well—"

Jake was going to say more, but Mahler burst out, "You can't come around here and threaten my clients. I won't have it!"

Reed and Cole moved as one to close ranks around Mahler. It was startling to watch; they were so fast. Reed reached for Mahler, but Cole beat him to it. He turned his back to us, and Reed adjusted his back toward the rest of the room. They'd closed everyone out.

I surged forward, shoving into Jake. I wanted to see what was going on. I got a glimpse of Cole reaching forward. I couldn't see the rest, but Mahler suddenly stopped talking. His eyes bulged, and his cheeks rounded. Either he couldn't get oxygen, or he was keeping himself from crying out. And Cole spoke softly to him.

Mahler scrunched up his face and jerked his head up and down repeatedly. "Okay. Okay!"

Reed touched Cole's arm. "That's enough."

Cole stepped back. Nothing else was said. Mahler clutched his arm, swung around, and barreled through a group of people. Cole peered at me a moment before he and Carter Reed continued ahead. The crowd parted for them, and a moment later, they were beyond sight.

A shiver went down my spine. They were known, and while I saw lust in the women's gazes, I couldn't look away from what I saw in the men's eyes. Fear.

"Jake?"

"Hmm?"

"Who was that?"

"I'm pretty sure he's our landlord. That's Cole Mauricio."

"I know, but *who* is Cole Mauricio?"

"He's the head of the Mauricio family."

My mouth dried up. "What does that mean?"

Then I heard Jake's response, and my world was pulled out from under my feet.

"Mafia. He's not in the mafia, Addison. He *is* the mafia."

CHAPTER SEVENTEEN

Jake went off to find Sia.

His plan was to let her know he was riding home with me, then coming right back for her. It was ridiculous that he was insisting on taking me home, but he was.

Once Jake pushed through the crowd, I went to flag a cab. Then I texted him. **I'm already in a taxi. Stay with Sia. Have fun. We can talk later.** I lifted my arm for a cab, and one pulled forward. A valet from the hotel opened the back door, but someone called my name from behind me.

"Mrs. Sailer?"

A black SUV was parked in front of the building with a man standing beside its open door.

"I'm supposed to give you a ride home, ma'am," he added.

"A ride home?" Why was he using my married name? How did he even know that name? Who was this guy? This was a private service. The man was big and muscular—and I recognized him. "I saw you at Gianni's one night."

"I don't remember, but you saw me at The Mauricio, too."

Cole. The back elevator. He'd been holding up his friend. "You were hurt." This was the guy who'd been bleeding.

He nodded. "Yes, ma'am. Mr. Dorian patched me up."

"You're one of Cole's men." Because he had men. They weren't his friends. They weren't his co-workers, although maybe they were. My stomach began twisting and churning. "Cole told you to wait for me?"

"Yes, ma'am. I'm to give you a ride wherever you want—" He stopped himself. His hands came around and joined in front of him. "Can I give you a ride home?"

I took a step closer, folding my arms over my chest. The night wind had picked up. I hadn't chosen the right coat. I went with stylish and lightweight—the one that looked nice over a formal dress. I shivered now, wishing I'd gone for something heavier.

"What else?" I demanded. "Why did you just use my married name?"

"Ma'am?" His eyes widened, and his mouth formed a small o, like he'd been caught at something. It was there, then gone in the next instant. "What do you mean, ma'am?"

"I'm Addison Bowman. Not Sailer. Who told you my last name was Sailer?"

"It was a mistake. My apologies, Ms. Bowman." Then his mouth closed, and I knew he wasn't going to say anything more.

"I won't get in there until you tell me."

He frowned. "I'm supposed to keep you safe. That's all I was going to say."

This was Cole's man, here on Cole's order, and where was Cole? Back in that party, standing next to another man just as deadly. Jake's voice sounded in my head again, *"Addison, he is the mafia."*

The mob. Cole. I couldn't digest that, not yet anyway, but it made so much sense. I thought? *Does it make sense?* I shook my head. One thing at a time, and right now, I let loose the fury that'd been waiting on the bottom of my stomach. This guy wasn't being honest, and I was officially fed up with it.

I glared at him, letting all the anger I'd reserved for Cole blast him. I shook my head. "No way."

He looked unsure. "Ma'am? Addison?"

I gave him a fake smile, sweetening my tone. "I'm sorry. I misspoke. I meant no *fucking* way. I'll find my own ride home. Thank you."

I hurried into the open cab and gave my address to the driver.

We pulled out, but a second later the driver told me, "We're being followed, Miss. That car is right behind us."

My head fell back against the seat. Of course he was.

"Should I call the police?"

What would happen if he did? If the police came and questioned Cole's man, what then? He was following because his boss told him to give me a ride. They'd laugh at me. There was no danger—or maybe they'd recognize him? Maybe they'd search his name and find he had a record. The cops would find out he was mob, and what then? He'd get arrested, just for doing his job? Would Cole come bail him out? Or would he send someone else?

I wasn't aware I was laughing until the driver asked, "Miss? Are you okay?"

I cringed. There was a faint note of hysteria there. I let it go and gave him a reassuring smile. "I'm fine. Sorry. Just tired is all."

He didn't look away from the rearview mirror right away. But he had to watch where he was driving. I quieted and tried to relax the rest of the way. The Haldorf wasn't too far from The Mauricio, but tonight, it felt like an hour's drive. When he pulled up in front, the SUV stopped behind us.

I stayed on the sidewalk as the cab drove away.

Cole's man got out, but he didn't walk around to me. He held up a hand. "Sorry, ma'am. I have orders. I couldn't stay behind. I'll be out here if you need a ride somewhere else."

"For the rest of the night?"

"No." He lowered his hand to rest on the SUV's doorframe. "I'll be out here indefinitely. Myself or another driver."

Indefinitely? "What?" I must've heard that wrong.

The door to The Mauricio opened behind me, and I heard Ken's voice. "He'll be in the basement parking lot, Miss Addison."

Ken was in full doorman uniform tonight, his coat buttoned all the way to his neck with a dark scarf tucked inside. He even had on

142

his hat, pulled low to protect his forehead. His hands were folded in front of him inside white gloves.

"I gotta go down there?"

Ken nodded at the driver. "No parking on the streets tonight, Carl."

I laughed bitterly. *Carl.* Ken knew him by name. And Carl obviously knew Ken well enough. His voice changed once Ken came out, relaxing, moving to a familiar tone. He wasn't strained or guarded like he'd been with me. Even his shoulders seemed relaxed as he swung back into the SUV.

"He's just going around the block. He'll pull into the basement." Ken hesitated. "If you need him for a ride somewhere else tonight."

This was another world. "He'll always be down there?"

"Him or another fella, Jim. The two will switch off, but yes. They're your personal drivers."

"Because Cole gave that order?" I watched him intently. I wanted to see his reaction.

There was none. He didn't even blink, just offered a nice, friendly smile. "Yes, Miss Addison, he did. He does that for people he cares about."

I couldn't believe any of this. "Cole owns this building?" It wasn't really a question. I wanted confirmation. No, I needed confirmation. I needed to be told something concrete. There'd been too many questions raised this evening. Were Dorian and Cole only friends? Who was Carter Reed? And how on Earth did Liam's family factor in here?

Who was Cole, whose job was a secret, whose job was dangerous, whose life took him away for an entire month at a time, and who took a private jet to bury a friend? I'd been okay with the mystery before, but not now. Not anymore.

Ken gave me a curt, silent nod.

I ground my teeth together. "Is *he* coming tonight?"

He nodded.

I brushed past. "Good." I'd get all the damn answers I wanted tonight. If I didn't, I'd find them myself, regardless of the consequences.

Once I got up to my apartment, Sia called to make sure I was okay. Judging by her slurred speech, Jake hadn't filled her in on our evening's excitement, so I didn't either. I wanted to hear from Cole first. I reassured Sia and then tried to wait for Cole. Reading. TV. Even drinking wine—it was all pointless. Nothing could distract my anger.

Okay. A bottle of wine could maybe help.

But what had Jake said? Cole wasn't just *in* the mafia. He *was* the mafia. I supposed people like that were important. They had to have meetings, do whatever it was Cole and that other guy had been doing tonight. Maybe chat so they could decide who to kill and who to beat up? I snorted, reaching for the glass in front of me.

I mean, *fuck*. Who was even in the mob? A whole host of old movies came to mind. And that other guy, Carter Reed—who was he to Cole? Who was he at all? And he and Cole knew Liam's parents. *Bea Bertal*, Cole has said. That was Liam's grandmother. She and Liam met for lunches every now and then. I remembered when she died. I'd thought Liam would be upset, but he wasn't, at least not the way I'd expected.

Liam came in from the study, pausing before entering the kitchen. I waited. Listening. He said nothing. I was stirring soup and still heard nothing, so I glanced over my shoulder. Something was wrong.

His phone was in his hand, and he just stared at it.

"Liam? What is it?"

He lifted his eyes. Bleak, so bleak.

"Liam?"

"My grandmother is dead."

I waited, remaining by the kitchen, but again, there was only silence. He frowned, and his eyes—they looked so lost.

My heart ached. "I'm sorry."

He shook his head and scanned the room. His hand lifted to rake through his hair. The phone dropped to the floor with a dull thud.

"I…" He blinked. Once. Twice. "I…"

"Liam?"

"I have no idea what to say."

"Are you—" I frowned. "—upset? You guys were close."

"She never met you." He said that quietly, like he regretted it. "She wanted to meet you, but I was scared. Then you'd know. " He shook his head. "I don't know what this means for the family."

He'd been sad, but more scared. That never made sense to me. It did now. I would've known…about what? The Bertal name? I still didn't know anything about it, except that Liam's parents were scared of Cole. I knew that much.

And fuck this.

If Cole wasn't coming to give me answers, I'd get my own.

I booted up my computer.

An hour later…

I wasn't prepared. There was no way I could've been.

CHAPTER EIGHTEEN

The elevator buzzed.

I didn't move.

It buzzed a second time.

I couldn't even look away from the computer screen. Carter Reed's picture was smack in the middle of it, and Cole's name was everywhere. As I continued reading, the elevator starting moving, but I couldn't focus on it. The need to know had faded in me, but now I was trapped, unable to stop gathering details. I almost wished I didn't know.

The doors opened, and there was Cole, dressed as if he'd been on the running track: black hooded sweatshirt and black athletic pants. And like that first time I saw him, he looked damn good in them. He was one of the best-looking men I had ever seen, but tonight, his appearance stuck a dagger into me. I felt like a toy being played with.

"Of course you have the codes for my floor," I said calmly. "You're the owner. Right?"

He stopped just inside my place, the doors closing behind him. I couldn't read his face, what he was thinking and feeling, but I was beginning to recognize this look. He'd worn this look so many times, and it was the same unreadable mask he'd worn at the event earlier.

His shoulders lifted in a silent breath. "You're mad."

"Wouldn't you be?" My blood was boiling. This guy—damn this guy. "I only had sex with you, and now I found out that you're in the mob?! I mean, I have no reason to be upset. You're right, *totally* right." A bitter laugh escaped me. "You said you couldn't tell me, but I never thought mafia. All the mystery about you? I had no clue, and I should've. I mean, yeah, you were honest. You said you couldn't tell me, but give a girl a clue next time? The mob. The mob, Cole! That's dangerous." *And scary.* I held that thought back. I had other questions on the tip of my tongue, but I held those back, too.

Did he kill people?

I snorted. Of course he did.

Did he order people to be killed? A second snort as I raked a hand through my hair. What else? Prostitution? Gambling? What crimes did he commit? Did he beat people up, demand payment from them? Did he demand a cut from store owners? My mind raced through all the mafia movies and stories I'd heard growing up. All those characters had been cloaked in an alluring draw, romanticized, but none of them were saints. None of them.

I stared at someone I didn't know. I went to bed with him. I spent time with him. I ran with him. I laughed with him. I felt with him. I became alive with him. And God, staring at him now, all I wanted to do was throw myself in his arms again. Fuck everything else.

The truth hit me then. "I didn't want to know the truth."

A hollow sound slipped out of me. I didn't know if it was a laugh or a grunt, but whatever it was, it wasn't right. I was gutted. I needed to calm down. Two nights. That was it. That was all we'd had. I had to keep reminding myself of that. I needed another goddamn drink. The bottle was empty. I rose to get another, but the room swayed.

Cole started for me.

I waved him away, grabbing the couch to steady myself and easing myself back down. "No. I'm drunk. I didn't eat today."

He came closer, closing the distance until he stood on the other side of the coffee table from me. "You have every right to be upset with me. What I do, where I come from, that's not something you should have to learn about at some high-society party. I'm sorry that happened to you."

God. I gulped, meeting his eyes. I didn't want to see the sympathy there, but I did, and somehow, it broke down a wall in me. A tear slipped from my eye. Much of my pain over this had nothing to do with Cole. "I feel like I've lost him all over again."

Cole didn't say anything.

I lowered my head. "I had no idea." I pointed to my computer. "None of this. Liam kept it all secret from me, too. And now it makes sense—why his family never accepted me, why he had meals with them alone, why his younger brother never came home."

"I'm sorry, Addison—"

"Did you know?" I demanded. "Did you know who I was? Who Liam was?"

He shook his head. "You applied for this place while I was gone. I'm not here that often, so I'm not kept abreast of everything that happens. Dorian runs the building. I trust him. He told me there was a new resident, but I never questioned him about you. It wasn't until..."

"Until?"

"Until I saw you tonight. I recognized your in-laws, and everything came together." He hesitated. There was something more he was going to say, but he held it back. He only said, "I didn't know either. I never even thought..." He let out a deep sigh, taking the seat next to mine on the couch. "Addison, you did nothing wrong. *Nothing.*"

I pointed to the article on the screen. "It says the Mauricio family and Bertal family are enemies."

"*Were* enemies."

I snorted. "You didn't look too friendly tonight."

The corner of his mouth lifted. "Yeah. Well, there's a long history of bloodshed, but as of now, the peace still holds between us."

"That's good?"

"It is."

But his eyes were wary, his jaw clenched. His mouth pressed in a solemn line, and I felt a heaviness from him. "You're lying." I saw behind his mask.

His eyes widened, sharpening on me.

I sat up, leaning closer to him. "You don't let me in, but I'm starting to be able to read you. Just a little bit. Something is going on, isn't it? Between the Bertal family and yours?"

"Addison."

"Tell me the truth." Then a whole other idea hit me. "Unless you think I'm part of them. Is that what you think?"

He shook his head. Pain flared in his eyes before he masked it, like he always did. He pushed himself back—an inch, maybe two, but it felt like a rejection. "That's...that's the other problem we have."

"What?"

"I want to tell you. I want to tell you about me, about my family, about my friends. But I can't."

"Because of Liam?"

"Because of his family."

A lump formed in my throat. "They said they're not a part of that."

He shook his head. "They're lying. Liam's grandmother was a direct descendant of the founding Bertal family."

"What does that mean?"

"Liam's great-grandfather started their family business. There were other siblings, but Bea Bertal was active. She ran the books. Even if Liam's parents claim they aren't a part of the business, the money trickled down to them, down to Liam, too."

The inheritance. "What does that matter? You said there's a truce. What does that have to do with you and me?"

"There might not always be peace."

His words took mine away. I could be an enemy? Was that what he meant?

"It just means things are complicated," he added after a moment. "You and me. We're complicated now."

My mouth went dry. "You and me?" *There was a we to even be complicated?* "You've been gone for a month."

"I couldn't get back until today. Things…got complicated for me."

"And you can't tell me about that. You stopped calling and texting. You can't tell me why? Just like you can't tell me anything about yourself or about your family, or even about your friends. None of that, right? Because I'm connected to the Bertal family even though I'm not a part of them." I could feel a flush rising up, covering my neck. It wasn't the happy kind of flush either. "You're keeping me out because of people who could be my allies? Am I getting this right? Allies that never showed me any support, that are suing me."

I shoved off the couch and started to pace. Back and forth. I hugged myself, wrapping my arms tight. "This is ridiculous. All of this. I loved him. I loved Liam *so much*, and they want to—I don't even know what they want. They want the house? Is that why they're suing me? They didn't give a shit about the house. They didn't give a shit about me, not until lately."

"What are you talking about?"

"And you." I flung a hand out, pointing at him. "You—all hot and hella good in bed. I mean, fuck. Like, *fuck*. Pun intended. I haven't felt anything for anyone until you. You swooped into Gianni's, and my best friend went gaga for you, but I did too. I mean, you're gorgeous, and you're ripped. And I always knew you were dangerous. I could just tell. *Listen to your gut*, that was what Liam always told me. He said if I don't know what I'm doing, I'm supposed to listen to my gut. Well, my gut took me to your penis, and now look where we are. Your family wants to kill my family, and my family—I don't even like my family. I'm a Bowman, dammit. I was a Sailer, and your driver called me Sailer. Why did he call me Sailer?"

"My what?"

"The driver downstairs. He called me Sailer."

Cole frowned. "I don't know. That order came through Dorian."

"I thought he said you told him to drive me home."

"The order came from me, but it would've been Dorian who called him."

"Oh." I cleared my head. I could still feel that flush; it was covering my ears. "I was a Sailer, but I'm not anymore. I'm a Bowman. No matter who I've been with, I've always been a Bowman. I'm *not* a Bertal. I am *not* with them. I was haunted every day and every night after Liam died, and it only stopped when I came here." I stared at Cole, but it was more than staring. I had so many damn walls.

I was tired of the walls, of the secrets, of the not knowing. My voice grew hoarse. "I stopped hearing his voice after I came here. I can still feel him, but in a good way—like we're laughing together again, or he wants me to be happy. And the nights with you... I haven't felt like myself in so long. You gave that to me. I wasn't Liam's wife or his widow those nights. I was me. I was Addison. That's all I was, and I loved it."

Tears fell down my cheeks

I whispered, "I came to you, and the ghosts left me."

His eyes darkened, and he stood. He moved close, stopping just out of reach. I could feel his heat. My walls were down now, so were his. The mask was gone, and I saw the lust inside of him. I saw more, a whole lot more, but I clung to the lust because my body was starting to react. My mouth watered, and that ache—the ache that hadn't been filled in a month—began to throb once more.

I wanted him.

He grinned, faintly, before taking the last step. His body touched mine, and I closed my eyes, savoring the feeling. Hard. Strong. And more, so much more.

"I'm going to pick you up," he murmured. He spoke to me like I was a wounded animal. Like he wanted to comfort me, but he didn't want to scare me away. He was soothing and seducing me all at the same time.

And that was exactly what I wanted.

Bending down, his hands touched my waist, and he stood again. I wrapped myself around him and held tight. I couldn't have made myself let go, even if I wanted to. I was his. He was mine. I didn't care what would happen. I couldn't deny this feeling. I needed him.

He looked up into my eyes. "Now I'm going to walk you back to the bedroom."

"I have an idea where this is going."

He drew a deep breath, his eyes growing soft. "I'm going to do everything you want me to do. I won't do anything you don't want me to. If you want me to hold you, I'll never let you go. If you want me to kiss you all night long, you'll have to buy me chapstick in the morning. Anything you want, I'll do." He carried me to the bed and laid me down. His arms never let me go. He bent over me, my arms and legs still wrapped around him. His forehead rested against mine, so softly, matching his voice, "Except leave. That's the only thing I won't do." His eyes searched my face, studying every detail.

"I'm going to help you become Addison once more. Just you. Just me. No one else." And then, as his mouth touched mine, gently, tenderly, he did as he'd promised.

CHAPTER NINETEEN

Cole was in the mafia. The motherfucking mafia.

The sun had begun to creep in. It was probably around seven in the morning, and I lay there, wide awake, as he slept next to me. The sheet trailed down, resting a little higher than his waist, giving me a good eyeful.

I knew his chest and back were contoured with muscles, but I didn't know about the scars. I saw them clearly now, scattered all over him. There were two holes in his chest: one by his shoulder and another lower on his side. I leaned over and touched the latter. It was bigger than the other and had been stitched up, leaving a little ridge where the stitches healed.

This man—I studied his face again. His eyes were closed, his body relaxed, and he looked peaceful. I realized how little I knew about this man. He was the head of his family, but what did that mean? The articles I'd found on the web said Carter Reed had run the family until last year. One blog went into more detail than the others and said he'd been the one to name Cole as the new leader.

My mind raced.

If there was peace between the Mauricio family and the Bertals, why did Liam's parents seem guilty of something? They were scared and tense, and all that jazz, but there was more under the surface. Carol had gotten the same look on her face the one time I confronted her about the women she kept pushing on Liam. I went to her house, told her to stop bringing them around. She'd looked ashamed that day, but only that day.

I saw that same look last night.

Maybe it wasn't just that peace doesn't always last, as Cole said, but that it was already ending?

I skimmed a hand down Cole's side. He rolled over on his stomach and buried his head under my pillow. One of his arms came to rest on my waist, scooping me closer to him. I waited, but a second later his breathing evened out, like he'd fallen back asleep.

"Your thinking is waking me up." One of his eyes opened. "Stop thinking. It's annoyingly loud. I haven't slept in three days, and all I want to do is stay in bed with you. Go to sleep, Addison."

"What does it mean?"

"What does what mean?" His arm tightened its hold around me. It felt nice.

"Can we be like this? I mean, with my connection to the Bertals and yours to, well, you know."

Could Cole get in trouble? Could I? And what did trouble even mean in his world? Death? I shuddered at that thought.

"It means…" He caught my hand at his hip, lacing our fingers together. "…that I can't share anything with you."

"And if you do?"

He rolled to his back again and observed me. His eyes darkened. "And if I do, then you're in. You're all the way in."

My stomach flipped over. "What does that mean?"

"You're officially a traitor to your in-laws and everyone else connected to Liam's life."

His hand traveled up, covering my side, over my arm, leaving shivers in its wake. Or maybe those were from his words. I was starting to not discern the difference.

"Does something happen to me? If they cast me a traitor to them?"

He shook his head. "You mean, do they kill you or something?"

God. I couldn't answer. I could only move my head up and down.

"No."

The ball of tension that had formed in my stomach loosened a notch. "Are you sure?"

"I'm sure. They'll only put a hit on you if you have something to give me, something they don't want me to have." His eyes narrowed. He seemed to be waiting for something.

"What?"

"Nothing." He caught my other hand and pulled me over on top of him. My breasts rubbed his chest and he wrapped his arms around my waist, anchoring me in place. "We can't go public, not unless you're ready. It has to be your decision."

"What do you mean?"

"They'll cut you off. There won't be an order on you, but I meant what I said. Any ties you had to Liam's family will be severed. Is there anyone you care for?"

I laughed. "No. I don't even have to think about that question. I've always talked as little with his family as possible. His dad never cared about our marriage, and his mother hated it. Liam didn't get along with his sister, and I never met his younger brother. We felt like it was us against the world sometimes."

Cole's gaze drifted to my lips and lingered there. He traced my bottom lip with his thumb. "They didn't like you because you weren't Bertal-approved. I can tell you that."

I lifted my head, and he let go of my lip. "I don't even know what that is."

"They like to marry within their structure of associates. I'm sure Carol had other women she wanted Liam to wed. You're an outsider. Outsiders are…" He hesitated, eyeing me. "They can be a risk."

"I read some articles that talked about an Emma person? She's with your friend Carter, the one from last night. Is it the same for her as it is for me?"

He shook his head. "No. Emma was an outsider from the beginning. She wasn't connected to another family, and Carter has known her a long time. They kinda grew up together. It's more difficult with you because you're connected to the enemy. If we went public and this, whatever it is, didn't work out, you'd still be looked at as a traitor. You chose the enemy."

It seemed logical in some stupid, schoolyard way. "I'm not connected to them anyway, so I can't imagine feeling any worse. I guess it doesn't matter to me because Liam's—"

I moved off of him to sit on the bed. Cole turned to watch as I rested the side of my face to the tops of my knees. I couldn't hide my sadness. "Grief is a bitter fuck-you pill, isn't it?"

He grunted. His hand went to my leg and began caressing it— for comfort, nothing more. "I wasn't lying when I told you about my family. I lost every family member, one after another, until it was just me. Grief and I go way back." He smirked. "We're old pals."

"I'm sorry." I couldn't imagine that. I didn't want to. "I wanted to go with him."

"Addison," Cole murmured, sitting up beside me.

I tucked my forehead into my knees. The little girl in me wanted to close my eyes and disappear.

"It hurts to start living without them. I get it."

I was tired of the invisible weight on my shoulders. Cole lifted it, always, but this time I decided I was ready to choose to let it go. I tried for a smile. "So I guess there is a *we* if we're talking about how *we* can't go public?"

"We can be a we," he teased, "if you don't care what your in-laws do."

"Even on good days, I don't give a damn about them."

"You said they're suing you?"

I nodded. "They're fighting my right to sell our house. They're saying Liam bought it with their money, but he didn't. He got some inheritance from his grandmother, and he used that money to pay for the house."

"Was there a buyer ready?"

I shrugged. "Not that I know of."

His glanced away, and I felt him pulling away, too.

"Hey." I touched his hand. "What are you thinking?"

"Nothing. That's just odd is all." He sat up and pressed a kiss to my forehead. "I'm sure it's nothing."

I caught his arm. "Why do I get the sense you're about to get out of this bed?"

His face cleared. Whatever had been troubling him disappeared, and the softness from last night came back. He smiled, and his eyes darkened as he leaned down. His lips touched mine, holding there softly, like the promise of a caress, and he murmured, "We don't have to stay in bed all day. There are other places we can go."

"Like whe—" I let out a surprised shriek as he swung me in the air and carried me to the bathroom, where he turned on the shower.

I was ready for him, even as he waited for the water to heat up, even as he lowered me to the floor, even as he pressed me back against the wall. His head dipped, his lips found mine again, and I kissed him. But this was more. It wasn't sex anymore. It wasn't whatever he'd had before. There was laughter, teasing, but there were feelings.

There was more. We were more.

I think we already had been, even before he left the last time.

CHAPTER TWENTY

Cole left two hours later, and so did I.

Sia texted, asking me to come up to Jake's floor, but it was Jake who met me at the elevator with his hands in the air. He wore pajama pants, socks, and a wrinkled T-shirt. Half of his hair stuck straight up, and he held a finger in front of his mouth.

"Sia doesn't know," he whispered.

"Know what?"

He waved his hand in the air, as if pushing it down. "Lower your voice. I really don't want to get into it with her."

"What do you mean?" I was almost whispering, but I glanced toward his bedroom. The shower was on. "I don't think she can hear us anyway."

"I know, but just in case." He motioned to the farthest corner of the floor, and I followed him through the living room. Jake turned with his back to the window so he could look over my shoulder. Then he crossed his hands over his chest. "Okay. Here's the deal: she's upset."

"What'd you do?"

His eyebrows shot up. "Me? Nothing. This is on you."

"Me?" My eyebrows went up, too. "What'd I do?"

"It's what you didn't do." He bent his head closer to mine. "She found out from someone last night about your in-laws. One of her socialite buddies eavesdropped on the conversation at the party."

"But we didn't talk about the case."

"No, but evidently this person told her you and I 'looked friendly.'" He used his fingers for air quotations. "And she got

Mahler's name, and Liam's parents. I guess they weren't on the guest list, so she's been on the phone for an hour this morning already trying to figure out how they got in."

"Mahler probably brought them."

"That's what she found out, but she's pissed. Majorly pissed. She wanted to know what they said to you." He shrugged. "I didn't know what to say, so…"

My mouth dropped. "You said nothing? Please tell me you said something."

"I didn't know what to do." His shoulders raised nearly to his ears. "I said there was attorney-client privilege, and she needed to talk to you."

I groaned. The urge to smack my forehead had my hand twitching—no, it was the urge to smack Jake in the forehead. "Why'd you say that? She probably thinks it's worse than it is."

"Why haven't you told her about the lawsuit?"

"Because…" I searched for a reason. "I don't know. I haven't really seen much of her lately. She's been happy, and if I told her what Carol and Hank are trying, she'd be pissed. There's nothing she can do, so I didn't want to burden her with it."

"Oh." He straightened. "That's really thoughtful of you."

I shrugged. I was already lying about Cole. Lying by omission to Sia was nothing compared to that. "Don't give me too much credit—"

"I can hear you." Sia's voice interrupted us.

She stood in the bedroom doorway, dressed in jeans and a sweater, her hair in a ponytail—looking ready to go for a casual lunch. She seemed refreshed, except for the look on her face and her arms crossed over her chest. She was pissed.

"I want to know what the hell happened last night." She turned to focus specifically on me. "My girlfriend calls me up and tells me something was happening last night between you, my boyfriend, and an attorney. Then I find out Liam's parents were there, too." She softened her voice. "Are you okay? Did they say something to you?

They weren't supposed to be there. Alfred Mahler brought them as his guests, and he's a high-powered attorney. Beth told me she was scared to tell him his guests couldn't attend."

"It was fine."

Her nose wrinkled in disbelief.

"I mean it, Sia. They didn't even say much. I didn't keep this a secret on purpose. You've just been…" I swung my gaze to Jake. "Preoccupied."

"Addison." Her voice softened. "You can tell me anything at any time."

"I know—"

"Just tell her!" Jake threw his hands in the air. "Sorry. I want her to know so we can talk." He gave me a look. "So we can talk about the other thing."

"The other thing?" Sia echoed him, confused.

The other thing was Cole. My insides twisted in a knot. I figured Jake had guessed that Cole was our landlord, but I didn't relish the idea of having conversations about him.

"Yeah." I took a breath. "The other thing."

Sia looked back and forth between us before shaking her head again. "Okay, someone start. I'm dying to know what I'm missing. Missy mentioned there were two delicious-looking guys at the party, but she didn't catch their names." Her forehead wrinkled. "Wait. She told me one, but she didn't know the other…" Her wheels were spinning, and then it hit her. Her eyes got big and wide. "Oh, holy shit. No way. You guys talked to Carter Reed?" She turned to Jake. "*The* Carter Reed, the mob guy?"

He nodded.

"So?! You guys have to tell me everything now."

"Okay. Okay." I held up a hand. "You need to sit down because I know you're going to get worked up about the first part."

"She might get worked up about the other part, too," Jake mumbled, scanning his place. "You can't throw anything, Si. Promise me that."

"Huh?"

I ignored that and waited for Sia to sit. Once she did, I took another breath. "First, you have to promise me you won't do anything."

"Why would I do that?" She shot Jake a look too. "Why would I throw anything?"

"Sia, promise."

"Okay. I promise." She drew an invisible X over her heart. "You get my drift."

One breath. Then I started. "My in-laws were there with Mahler because he's representing them against me."

She turned to look at Jake, but kept quiet.

"And Jake is representing me against them."

"What's the case?"

I kept going, not skipping a beat. "They're suing me about the house, but it's a bullshit case. They have nothing legal to stand on."

"What?" Her mouth dropped.

I nodded. "They're saying I don't have the right to sell the house, that Liam bought it with their money."

"Assholes!" Sia said. "What complete, utter assholes. Who do they think they are?" She jumped up and started pacing. Her hands were flying in the air. "And let me guess, next they'll say you don't get Liam's inheritance? I bet they'll try. I bet that's why they started with this lawsuit. Don't tell me—they had to see your bank statements?" She didn't wait for an answer. Her head bobbed up and down. "I'm *livid* at them. I want to cast them out of every social event in the city. Wait." She stopped in her tracks. "Can I do that? How connected are they?"

"And that brings us to the other thing," Jake announced.

"What thing?" Sia turned to her boyfriend.

Jake glanced to me, and his shoulders rose slowly before he said, "Our landlord."

"What?"

I fought against squirming in my seat. Sia read body posture like no other. If I started fidgeting, she'd know immediately something more was going on. I tried to keep a stone face.

"Cole Mauricio," Jake said.

"Who?" The ends of her mouth dipped down. "That's the name of this building."

"We met him last night, too," he added.

"I'm confused." Sia's gaze skirted between the two of us.

Jake was waiting for me, but I shook my head. I was smack in the middle of this "other thing," but I wanted no part of talking about it. I looked at the elevator with longing. I could escape. I just needed a valid reason to go. Jake could explain all of this without me here, including Liam's connections to Cole's rival family. But when he started talking, I didn't have a good enough excuse. I had to sit and listen, and Jake loved telling her everything.

By the end, her mouth was on the floor. "No fucking way."

Jake's eyes gleamed with excitement. "He's our landlord, Sia. The head of the Mauricio family owns this building."

"But you aren't sure?"

"I'm mostly sure, but we can dig it up. There are public records."

"Whoa." She leaned back in her seat, fanning herself. "Addision, you had no idea?"

"About Cole?" My words were out before I could stop them. *Shit.* I hadn't meant to say his first name, like I knew him. "I mean—what?"

"About Liam and his grandmother."

"Oh." The knot that had twisted in my chest as Jake talked loosened slightly. "No. I had no idea, but it makes sense."

"Yeah. He didn't like his family, and you're right. He kept you away from them for so long. That does make sense. A lot makes sense now."

I nodded, silently hoping she wouldn't start in about Cole, but I knew that was senseless. He was powerful, elusive, mysterious, dangerous, and wealthy. He'd be Sia's new project for months, and Jake looked just as excited. He should've been scared. Cole was in the mafia. What if someone did something to our building to get back at him?

"You're okay living here?"

Sia voiced my question, but she directed it at Jake.

Surprise flashed over his face. "What do you mean?"

"The mafia is a big deal. Like, a really big deal. Aren't you scared something could happen?"

He shrugged. "I was pissed at first, but I'm not in the mob. The guy's never here, or I don't think he's here. This building's been fine since it opened. What are they going to do? Hurt the building's shut-in? I think we're the furthest thing from being in danger. All the security makes sense now, too."

Jake's response was weird. Sia narrowed her eyes, so I wondered if she thought the same.

"Besides." Jake gestured to me. "She's a Bertal, and she's living here."

"I'm not a Bertal."

"Basically."

My mouth opened. "I am not. Liam's parents aren't either."

Jake snorted. "I hate to break it to you, but they are. Mauricio himself alluded to that last night. They're still in, Addison. They just haven't brought you in."

"Jake," Sia said softly.

"What?" he asked.

He didn't get it. This wasn't real to him. But Sia was concerned. So was I, more than they knew. Whichever way I turned, I was headed toward someone in the mafia. My own money had come from the mafia—something I hadn't let myself think about. I didn't know how I felt about that, or how right it was to keep the money. I'd have so many problems if I gave it back. I'd have to move out, and I really would need the money from selling the house.

I felt a headache coming on. No. I would stop worrying until I knew more. Until things went past the point of no return.

They already are, a voice said in my head.

"I have to go." I stood abruptly.

Concern clouded Sia's face. "You okay?"

"Yeah. Uh, I just have to go." My hand flicked between them. "You guys seem like you need to talk anyway. This is couple stuff."

Sia stood up with me. "You live here, too. Do you feel safe?"

In Cole's arms, yes. Outside of them? Still yes. But as we went to the elevator, I lifted a shoulder. "I don't know. This place seems separate from that life. We would've noticed something by now if it wasn't, and there's also Dawn. If something iffy was going on, she'd know."

Yeah, Dawn. The realization had merit. The Dawn who hid in closets, who staged a sit-in to find out who owned the building and had her bench removed because of it. The Dawn who snuck around, stole phones, who probably knew everything or most of everything that went on in this building. I didn't think she knew about Cole.

I hoped not, anyway.

"Yeah, I guess."

Sia's tone didn't agree with her words.

I hit the button to call the elevator. "Are *you* okay?"

"Huh?" She'd been chewing on her lip.

I pointed at it. "You do that when something's on your mind."

"Well, I mean—" She peeked over her shoulder at Jake, who was sitting at his desk now, and quieted her tone. "Cole Mauricio. Even that name is scary. I saw the news coverage about Carter Reed. There was a mob war, and some of it happened here. That guy was their hit man, and now what? Is he out? We don't really know anything. Yeah, I'm worried. I'm really worried. I don't want to lose my boyfriend and my best friend."

He was their hit man. I'd read that online the night before, but hearing those words out loud sent chills down my back.

"Jake's a mob nut. The geek inside of him is doing somersaults. He can't see this as reality. Someone really dangerous lives here."

Carter Reed was dangerous. Cole was dangerous. My throat closed. Cole could kill someone, probably already had…and he'd been inside me just hours ago. And I knew he'd be there again tonight. And the night after, and any other night as long as I let him. I didn't think I could stop. I didn't think I wanted to stop.

"Why aren't you scared?" She grabbed my arm, holding it lightly as she moved closer. "Why am I the only one who's nervous?"

Because… I had a vision of Cole holding me in the shower as he thrust inside of me. His hips moving, holding mine as I moved right along with him. My body heated, and that ache came back. It was always there. It just took a thought, that was it.

He was my drug.

"Addison?"

I shook my head. "I don't know."

"You're insane. Both of you," she said. "You guys have lost your heads."

I couldn't speak for Jake, but maybe I had.

I said my goodbyes, promising to meet Sia for lunch on Monday, and as the elevator closed, my eyes did the same. I leaned back against the wall and felt the car carry me down.

Maybe I was crazy.

Maybe I had lost my mind.

Maybe I had fallen more than I realized.

Just maybe.

CHAPTER TWENTY-ONE

As Jake predicted, Liam's parents dropped the lawsuit two weeks after I saw them. Mahler said it was because they realized they'd caused me enough grief. Jake and his partner laughed at that once the doors closed behind Mahler and his team. A judge would never have allowed the suit to proceed, and everyone knew it. I continued to hope Sia's prediction wasn't true, that they hadn't used it to look at my bank statements as preparation to come back with a lawsuit for Liam's inheritance. Jake and his partner promised that wouldn't happen. The inheritance would be protected.

I was pissed at Carol and Hank, but that had faded to annoyance, and the more time that passed without hearing anything from them, even that was starting to dissipate. I preferred not to think of them at all.

For the first two weeks after Sia learned about Cole, she and Jake slept at her apartment. Then, even though the facts hadn't changed—Cole Mauricio was still in the mafia, and he was still Jake's landlord—somehow Sia's concern faded. They were back to sleeping at Jake's. Sia and I met for lunch every other day, and I had dinner with them at Jake's a couple times, too.

But I never invited them to my floor—because of Cole.

He came over every night, or almost every night. Each time was different. Some nights we ate dinner, watched movies. Other nights we went straight to bed. And still other times, it was even later. Cole would slide into bed next to me. There were times I couldn't let him go, and nights when he acted like he'd been starving for me.

We did what normal couples did, but we weren't a normal couple. I tried not to think about how much I missed him when he wasn't there or how my body ached to touch him, to feel the answering pressure of his body against mine.

Today was one of those days. I was trying not to count the hours away until he came back. I needed a distraction, and checking my email, I got the perfect one.

Addison,

We have an opening for our column this week. Could you put something together? Let me know asap if you can. If not, we'll run someone else, but if you can, we'll save that space for you.

Sincerely,
Tina Gais
Editor-in-Chief
Onlooker Online Magazine

And crap.

I needed to do something. I couldn't sit around anymore. I'd been more and more restless, and maybe it was time I tried writing again, so I found myself typing on the computer:

Five Ways to Keep Him Out of Your Heart (until you're ready to let him in)

Okay, ladies. You all know *that* guy. He's the guy after the guy. Whether you've lost a husband, a boyfriend, a lover, or had a crush that completely crushed you, life goes on. You have to move on too, and whether it has taken you days, weeks, months, or even years, eventually you get there. That's when *that* guy shows up.

You start slow. Maybe you just see each other in the hallway. Then you find yourself seeing more and more of each other. You exchange smiles. You stop and talk to each other. After that it may be something more. You make plans. You follow through. You start seeing each other, and bam! After a few times, you've officially done what you didn't think was possible.

You've. Moved. On.

But here's the tricky part. How do you continue moving on without relapsing? How do you protect your heart, keep yourself from being crushed again and experiencing the same agony you just got over, all over again? Use these tips to ensure you don't get crushed by *that* guy.

◆ **Know your limits.** Don't kiss on the lips or look into his eyes when you have sex. This causes feelings. You'll feel intimate with him, and that wall around your heart will begin to melt. Back up. Retreat. Don't go there!

◆ **Don't tell him your deepest, darkest fears.** When you share something close and personal, you're opening up. This makes you vulnerable. Keep the lips shut. Change the topic to the weather, to sports, to a sale your favorite store is having this weekend. Think about superficial things, like clothes, trips, hockey. Don't go personal at any cost, not until you're ready. When you do, he'll worm his way in even farther, and that wall will soon be half melted.

◆ **Do not introduce him to your friends.** This is key! Even if you're trying not to get too personal with that guy, they will. They'll want to know details about him. What does he do? What's his family like? Are you going to get married? If you do, will you live at his house or your place? Does he have kids? Does he want more kids? They'll claim to mean well, but it's a rare friend who can read the signs and keep things on the surface for you. And really, whatever happens is your fault because you introduced them. So like 1 and 2—don't do it! Be selfish. Keep him all to yourself.

◆ **No family gatherings.** If you can't introduce him to friends, why would you introduce him to family? They're the definition of up close and personal. Family is friends on steroids, and they'll ask even more probing questions: about religion, how you'll raise your children together, if you'll invite Aunt Timbuktu to the wedding and whether your cousin from Aunt Timbuktu's family is going to do the solo at the ceremony. I'm yelling at you and waving my hands in the air: *don't do it!*

◆ **Do not leave your belongings at each other's places.** Your belongings are representations of your feelings. If you leave them, you're leaving part of yourself behind. Keep all of yourself together. When you walk out the next day for work, take your overnight bag with you. And don't let him leave his stuff behind either. The only approved item for the drawer on his side of the bed is a condom. That piece of rubber could be used for anyone, so there's no sentimental attachment.

So there you have it. Follow these five steps, and your emotions should be guarded until the moment you're ready to let that guy in. And if even this sounds too risky, there is one surefire, 100%-guaranteed way to keep your heart intact: dating abstinence. Just don't date! Buy a dildo for the lonely nights, and fill up your evenings with friends. Use alcohol as needed.

I was the biggest hypocrite in the world, but staring at the screen, I was proud of what I'd written. I read back through, made a few tweaks, and sent it to Tina. This was the first real thing I'd written since Liam's accident.

A sudden need to celebrate had me reaching for my phone. I didn't think. I texted Cole: **I want to do something fun tonight.**

Good. I'll plan it. Get in the car at nine. Carl will drive you.
My phone buzzed a moment later. **Dress in jeans, a sweater, and cowboy boots.**

Cowboy boots?

Do you have a pair? I can have some sent over.

I have some. But cowboy boots?

Trust me. I think you'll love it. I'll meet you at the place. It takes an hour to get there.

And at nine that night, Carl was waiting for me in the basement parking lot.

I'd tried several times to get Cole to let him do something else; I didn't need a driver, but he insisted. He said it was a small worry he didn't have to be concerned about anymore. When I met Sia for lunch, I walked with her, but if we went somewhere other than Gianni's, I lied and made sure to let her know I would "order" a car for us. In a way I did: I let Carl know when we'd need him.

A little voice nagged at me whenever Carl drove us. Sia was scared of Cole, and one of his drivers was driving us around. I wasn't ready to tell her about him, and I knew Carl had orders. If I went anywhere without him, he would follow me anyway. So my way of appeasing everyone was to lie. I hoped when Sia did find out, she wouldn't hate me, and as Carl drove into the night, taking me outside the city limits, I hoped once again that Sia would forgive me.

She'd called earlier, wanting me to go to dinner with her and Jake. If I said I was sick, she'd want to check on me, and if I made any other excuse, they'd have called relentlessly for me to join them at Jake's after dinner.

I'd needed a reason that took me out of their reach, so I'd lied once more.

I'd told her I was checking one last time on my house. I knew she would give me space to deal with that. She always did. Once I told her that, I'd realized I really did need to check on the house. I planned on asking Carl to take me there tomorrow.

Right now, I sat back and watched the city lights fade as Carl drove. I grew sleepy until the car turned on to a gravel road. We were in the country. On both sides of the car were green meadows, fenced in by wooden posts. The fences were painted white and the grass trimmed low. We were at a ranch. The car stopped, and Carl came around to open my door.

We'd parked right in front of a large wooden barn—bright red and two-storied. Its big door was opened, and I could see stalls lining both sides of the barn with a large cement pathway in the middle. Another barn sat to the right and a large track to the left.

"What is this place?"

Carl didn't answer. He went back to the car and began to reverse.

"Addison."

I twisted to find Cole coming toward me in jeans and a black zip-up sweatshirt that molded to him perfectly. He didn't look like a mobster now; he was more akin to a ranch owner. I glanced down and scowled.

I pointed. "You don't have cowboy boots on." I tapped my boot-clad feet. "You told me to wear cowboy boots."

He laughed. "I know." He caught my hand, lacing our fingers.

There. I felt the tingle, like always.

"I wanted to see you in them. I thought they'd be cute."

I tightened our hold, not having a retort ready to go. Everything was melting inside of me.

The barn was heated as Cole led me inside, and the first few stalls held horses. Some looked back at me with heads over the stall doors. Others turned away, their heads hanging down. A few munched hay that hung in the stalls' corners.

"What is this place?" I asked, drawing closer to Cole.

He gestured to a horse wearing a long, draped coat. "I own a race track, but I also board horses. This is one of our boarding stables."

"You own these horses?"

"A few, but most belong to other people." We progressed through the barn, coming to a side door. It was open, and Cole pointed to the racing track. "Some are trained here. Some are just ridden here by their owners." He gestured to the woods. "There are riding trails out there."

"Who are the other owners?"

He shrugged. "It depends. Most of them are people in the city. The other barn holds the racing horses, but some owners have their own stables."

The stables felt intimate and warm. A set of stairs wound down from the second floor into the middle of the stalls. Cole kept moving toward the opposite end of the barn. A horse—all white with black spots—hung its head over its stall and watched us come. It was larger than the others, and as we got closer, I could tell it was a special horse. It held its head high with a thick and muscular neck. Power rippled from the horse's body.

He reminded me of Cole.

Cole moved closer, extending his hand to touch the horse's neck. "This is one of our stallions. We keep the mares in the other building and the geldings in the front, where we came in. Those are the guys who got the bits snipped, if you didn't know. This guy here we keep separate from the rest so no fights break out."

"Is he dangerous?" I didn't know anything about horses, but I could see that Cole loved him. And the stallion allowed Cole to touch him.

"He can be; that's for sure. But if he's handled right, he's a happy guy." Cole gestured around the stable. "He's only in here at night. We let him run with the breeding mares during the day. We've got a few other stallions, but we keep them elsewhere."

"He's beautiful, Cole."

He grinned at me, resting against the stall door. "You wanted to do something fun, but since we're confined to privacy, I thought I'd bring you here. I can't tell you anything about my life as a Mauricio, but for a time, I wasn't a Mauricio. This place—well, not this specific place, but another stable—I spent a lot of time there. I lived with a family for a few years and helped take care of their horses. I bought this place when I came back. It reminds me of my home, or one of my homes anyway."

My mouth dried. There was so much I wanted to know, and I couldn't ask. I hadn't said yes yet, to letting my in-laws know I'd officially chosen sides. I hadn't thought about it, to be honest; but I'd been holding back. I wasn't sure why, maybe I was just trying to be cautious? Maybe I just wanted to know before I was all in, but I wanted to say it now. I opened my mouth, and I almost said it, but I didn't.

Cole tightened his hand on mine. His thumb brushed over my hand, back and forth. Tingles shot up my arm. "I've got dinner planned up there. It's the sleeping quarters."

I wanted to know why Cole had brought me here. I knew there was a reason, and it wasn't just privacy. I'd heard him on the phone enough, interacted with him enough to know he was decisive. He never wasted words, and everything he did had a purpose.

He took me upstairs, and I got another surprise.

The second floor included a living area, a kitchen, and a table set up on one side with a hallway leading past the stairs. Cole pointed in that direction and said, "There are three rooms for sleeping back there. If a mare is foaling, the owners will sleep here or have a worker sleep here. I have a general manager who runs this whole place, and he sleeps there, too, when his wife kicks him out of the house."

"And tonight?"

Cole paused, his eyes darting to my lips before darkening. "Tonight is my turn. I told him I'd watch the horses."

There was no doubt that he intended both of us to stay, and that thought had my usual ache coming back. I could already anticipate the feel of him over me when he stepped close. My eyes flicked up.

He focused on my lips, and I held my breath, knowing what was next. I closed my eyes as his head lowered, and a second later, his lips touched mine. My pulse skipped before speeding up as his mouth opened over mine, taking charge. I gasped, surging up on my toes to press more fully against him.

"Addison," he murmured, his lips moving over mine.

That sent a whole other rush through me. "Yes?" I didn't open my eyes. I wanted to stay there, right where we were.

"Do you want to go to bed or do you want to eat?"

That was a no-brainer. I wrapped my arms around him. "Bed, please. Now."

CHAPTER TWENTY-TWO

Coming back down, I could only lie there as Cole trailed kisses down my throat all the way to my stomach before pulling out and resting beside me. Even my eyelids were exhausted. I watched him with heavy eyes as he grinned at me.

I chuckled softly, but had no words. I didn't feel the need to say anything. Cole wrapped an arm around my waist and tucked his head into my shoulder. His eyelashes grazed my skin as his eyes closed. It felt right to be here in silence—just us and someplace beautiful and private.

It was later, much later, when I realized I must've fallen asleep. Cole had left the light in the bathroom on, but that was off now.

"Cole," I whispered.

His arm had moved farther down to my hip. He was stretched out beside me on his back. "Yeah?"

I heard the sleep in his voice, but asked anyway, "Did you turn the light off in the bathroom?"

I didn't need to say anything else. He was off the bed in one smooth, quick movement. I couldn't hear him, but I could see his shadow in the dark. He went around the bed to the window, first pressing against the wall next to it. He stayed there, peering outside, and my chest grew tighter with each passing second.

Something was happening. Something that wasn't good.

"Cole?" I kept my voice low.

"Shhh." His was even lower. Then his hand moved, and the moonlight bounced off something hard. He pulled it closer, and I saw the end of a gun.

He had a gun. Cole was the mafia.

It hit me in the chest like a battering ram. I'd forgotten, or I'd forgotten about the dangers that came with it, until now. The blow was fierce, and it bowled me over. I could only stare at his gun.

"Get dressed, Addison."

He didn't move from the window.

I rolled off the bed and dressed on the floor, making as little sound as possible. When I reached for my boots, he said, "There are shoes in the closet. Crawl there and grab a pair."

I heard him moving as I did, and figured he was doing the same. Once inside the closet, I felt around on the floor and found some sneakers. Pulling them on, I crawled back out. My heart was trying to pound its way out of my chest as I did.

My hand brushed his once I got to his side, and his own came to my shoulder. He urged me behind him, just a little bit.

"Sir." A voice spoke from the stairs, through the closed door.

Cole turned swiftly, blocking me, with his gun held out straight. "Don't move."

"It's me. Carl."

Cole lowered the gun, but kept his arms straight. He rested the gun at his side, pointing to the ground, and took a few steps toward the bedroom's door. "You okay?"

"I am." Carl didn't come into the room or even open the door. "There's no movement out there. Both barns lost electricity, and the house down the way is out, too."

"Still." Cole's hand came to my shoulder and squeezed lightly. "We should head back to the city. I'll let Ruby know I didn't stay the night."

"Okay. I'll be in the car, sir."

Carl left, and this time I could hear him moving down the stairs. After a moment the front door to the barn opened as he left, crossing the yard to the car. Cole waited, watching him go. Once Carl was inside the vehicle and safe, Cole's hand dropped from my shoulder. "Okay, let's g—"

Later, I would remember that we were given warning: the lights went out.

Later, I would think how there should've been more warning. Like a feeling, or a premonition.

Later, I would realize that there'd been none of those, just the lights. That'd been it.

It was jarring when it happened. And I knew the sound would never leave my mind. I'd hear it over and over again for the rest of my life.

Before Cole finished speaking, I heard the sound of glass shattering mixed with quick pops. The more those pops sounded, the more glass shattered. I froze. Everything in me paused. I couldn't think. I couldn't breathe. I couldn't move.

Cole pushed me to the ground, turning himself back to the window. As soon as my face hit the floor, I knew what those pops were. Gunfire. My brain took another beat to catch up. Someone was shooting at us, but no, that wasn't quite right.

A buzzing sounded in my ear, starting to drown out the repeating shots and glass, but eventually the glass stopped breaking. They had broken everything.

Cole left.

I couldn't cry out. My throat wasn't working, but I didn't want him to go.

In a moment he was back and pressing something into my hand. "Can you shoot?" he asked, hurriedly.

"No." My hand closed over metal.

He cursed, but lifted my hand. "Sit here. Keep your back to the wall. If someone comes up those stairs, you pull the trigger." He spoke quietly, but fiercely. "Do not point this gun anywhere except at the stairs. If you do, get your finger off the trigger. Okay?"

I nodded. I had no idea what he was saying.

"Stay alive." He pressed a hard kiss against my forehead. "And don't shoot yourself."

Stop! My brain kicked back into drive, and I grabbed his arm as he started to leave. "Where are you going?"

"Those men aren't done. Carl came out from this barn. They're going to look for us. They're coming."

They're coming. His words echoed in my mind. I was still processing that when he was gone. He'd slipped down the stairs before I could say anything. Now that it was just me, I looked at what was in my hand: a gun.

My eyes widened, but that was it. That was my only reaction until everything snapped back into place. When my brain caught up, I knew what was happening. There were men here. Men who'd shot something, and were coming to shoot me.

I scooted back against the wall and bent my knees. Resting my arms on my legs, I held the gun with both hands, and I did what Cole said. I kept it pointed right at the stairs. I couldn't save Cole. He knew how to save himself, but I'd be damned if I was going to go down quietly. I'd piss my pants later. For now, I was going to stay alive.

COLE

I could see six of them, but that didn't mean that was it. I watched as six men surrounded Carl's car and shot out every window. They'd done this before, but with only four shooters. I'd survived that attack, but I knew Carl hadn't survived this one. And as the six men turned toward the barn, I knew they'd be thorough.

They were coming for me, but I knew they'd find Addison, too. That couldn't happen.

Addison had given me shoes, but I kept them off on purpose. I padded barefoot down the stairs and through the stalls. I needed to hit them with the element of surprise. I hoped they'd split up to search for us, and after I slipped into one of the geldings' stalls, keeping a calming hand on the horse, I heard them call softly to each other and knew they'd done just that.

The door opened slowly with a squeak, and I saw the silhouettes of two men coming inside. I lowered myself and pressed against the stall's door. The horses started neighing as the men approached, and a few began kicking at their stall doors. They could feel the tension in the air. My horse stepped from side to side, but he never pawed at the door. He wouldn't hurt me, but his eyes were growing wild in the moonlight, and he began to shake his head.

"Every fucking stall has a horse. What are we supposed to do with that? Search each one?" grumbled the guy closest to me.

"I don't know," his companion replied. "I guess so. Markay and Gus are going to sweep upstairs. They're waiting for our signal that this level is clear."

They would come from the side door, then head upstairs.

I couldn't wait.

The men turned on flashlights and shined them in the stalls. They were making quick work, not bothering to go inside. I watched as they kept coming, clearing the stalls next to me, and then pointing their lights at my horse. They lit him up, and he reared back from being blinded. I held my breath. Right that second, the horse was more dangerous to me than the men. They passed their flashlights over the back corners of the stall. The gelding moved toward them, and toward me, but they turned their flashlights to the stall behind them.

It was time.

I slipped over the stall's door and dropped to the floor. I came up behind them and pulled a knife out of my pocket, keeping it tucked against the palm of my hand.

The two men were almost to the middle of the row of stalls.

I slipped up behind one, then reached around and slashed his throat. His blood sprayed over me, and before his companion could react, I grabbed his shoulder and did the same to him. Both men fell to the ground. They couldn't speak, and they'd be dead within minutes.

"Hey! Bannon? Carl? You guys okay?" a voice called from the far end of the barn.

One of these assholes was named Carl. Ironic. I grabbed their flashlights and held them apart. "We're good," I yelled back, making my voice deeper to match what I'd heard earlier. "One of the horses spooked us."

There was silence for a second. Then the guy hollered again, "Yeah, okay. Check every stall. Keep going."

The other two flashlights were coming toward me. I had to get behind them, take them down the same way. I knew the final two would be coming through the side doors at any moment, but so far the doors were still closed. They weren't locked. I'd closed them before taking Addison upstairs, but meant to come back down and lock everything up for the night.

Turning the flashlights off, I locked both doors, darting from side to side.

"Hey!" The other two guys came running.

I flattened against one of the stalls and waited. They rushed past and separated, going to the doors. The closest one pushed at the door. "Fuck! Did he go this way?"

I moved quickly, slicing his throat in the dark, too.

The other guy swung around, and his flashlight blinded me. "Stay there, you fucker!"

I moved so the stairs were between us.

"I said STOP!" he bellowed.

I waited now. He'd need backup, whether that meant calling for his friends or unlocking the doors. I stared at his feet, memorizing where he was until I heard him fumbling around. Then I launched myself at him. He had a gun trained on me, but his mind wasn't focused on pulling the trigger. I used that against him, soaring around the stairs. He saw me go left and his gun moved that way, but I ducked to the floor. The flashlight couldn't keep up with me, and I kicked at him. He pulled the trigger and the bullet hit the floor next to me, but he was down. I grappled with him for the gun, kicking at his face.

The doors were rattling now. The other men shoved against them, trying to get in.

"*Thirty seconds…*" I could hear Carter's voice in my head. I had thirty seconds before they remembered the other two entrances were unlocked and open. Then they'd act, and be on me.

The guy fighting me was stronger than I'd thought, so I flipped over, putting my knees on either side of his head. His gun was up, but I had the advantage now. I slammed his hand on the ground, and it opened with the impact. Grabbing the gun, I shot him in the face.

He was dead instantly. I rolled off of him and scooted back against the stalls so I was partially blocked. The doors were quiet now. They'd quieted as soon as they heard their friend die. My heart pounded, but I stilled my breathing.

They'd have to come all the way to the middle stairs to see me, but that was my only opening. They had the advantage. I had to think of something. As I waited, I pulled my second gun out. I had one gun in each hand now. They'd have to find me.

One fallen flashlight pointed down the hallway. They'd be coming that way, but they'd keep to the dark. I positioned myself with my gun and my eyes focused on that spot because there was no other way they could come. Not unless they'd doubled back and were coming from behind.

I'd have to risk it.

I heard them before I saw them. Shoes scraped against the cement floor, and I shot into the darkness ahead of me. A hoarse scream came from that direction, and I thumbed off two more bullets, pointing the gun slightly higher than my shoulder.

A third gun went off, and then there was silence.

A body fell to the floor with a thud. All six were dead, but there could be more. I waited.

"Are they dead?"

I whirled to face the top of the stairs and scrambled to find a flashlight. I shined it up into the darkness to find Addison perched on the top stair, her gun in hand. She still had it pointed at the man lying dead just beyond my shoulders.

I cursed, taking note of her pallor. Her face looked drained of blood, and tears streaked down her cheeks. She asked again, not even flinching against the flashlight, "Are they dead?"

The adrenaline of the fight still pumped through me, but it ebbed at the tiny sound of her voice. I didn't want to answer—not because of what I'd just done, but because I hadn't acted alone.

She'd helped me. She killed the last one.

"Yes. They're dead," I told her. I couldn't spare her any comfort. "More could be out there," I said harshly. "Stay here."

She nodded, and she kept nodding. Over and over again.

"You can stop, Addison."

"Okay." And she did, her eyes still on the guy behind me.

"I'll be right back."

I stood, my legs a little shaky. This wasn't my first or even my second attack. I'd been in so many, and I'd survived. I'd lived. That was what I did. But this was the first time, or the first that I remembered, when I was scared.

Addison could've died.

I turned, going for the door. I had to see if anyone else was out there, and because of her, I knew I'd be more brutal.

The need to kill was stronger than it had ever been.

CHAPTER TWENTY-THREE

ADDISON

I stayed.

I didn't move.

I didn't dare move.

My arms were straight, and I held the gun steady. I tried to keep my breathing even, but what if there were more out there? Cole was on his own—No. I pressed my eyes closed. I couldn't focus on that. Cole knew what he was doing. *Trust Cole. Do what he says.* And that was what I did.

After a few minutes he came back. I saw a spark of pride in his eyes as he looked at me, and a jolt of satisfaction coursed through me.

"Okay." Cole stopped inside the door of the barn. His hand went to his shoulder. "I need you to do some things for me."

I stood and hurried down the stairs, still holding the gun. He was breathing a little heavy, but that seemed normal. We'd just been attacked. Right?

"Were you shot?" I heard myself ask. His hand never moved from his shoulder. It wasn't an ache he was rubbing.

"I was."

"What?"

"But it went right through me. I'll be fine. I promise."

My alarm lessened, but just a bit.

"I need you to do some things."

I nodded and handed the gun to him, carefully. "I'm ready."

"Okay. First." He motioned to all the doors. "I need you to lock all of the doors."

"Okay." I reached for the one next to him.

He blocked me. "Not this one. We have to leave through this one."

"Yeah. Got it." And I was off. I fumbled with the first one, not sure where the lock was, but once I found it, I made fast work after that. I hurried back and waited for the next order.

He gestured upstairs. "Take a flashlight and go grab my keys, wallet, and phone."

I frowned. "Why weren't those in your pants?" He always kept them in his pockets, even when he slept.

A rakish grin was my answer. "Because I was more focused on getting in your pants."

I laughed, and that felt better. I wasn't as tense as I grabbed one of the flashlights. Cole also had one in his hand now. He must've grabbed it while I was doing the doors. "So where is your stuff up there?" I asked.

"On a counter in the kitchen."

"On it." I didn't want to waste time, but I circled the upstairs, making sure we weren't leaving anything behind. I had no idea what Cole was planning. With his items in hand, I went back to find him waiting for me, standing in the open doorway.

He motioned to my hand. "I need my phone." Then waved for me to keep the keys. "My car is behind the other barn."

"Oh." He wanted me to drive. Check. I could do that. I started to step outside, but he blocked me once more. His hand touched the door in front of me. "What?"

He didn't answer, and I couldn't see his eyes. The moon behind him cast his face in shadow. His voice was soft when he finally spoke. "I need you to keep your head down when you go out there."

"Why?"

"Do you remember when they first started shooting?"

I nodded, but my mind was blank. I'd switched from panic to fear to 'let's get this shit done, whatever that shit is,' and I was still in that mode. I could follow orders, but… I remembered now—they hadn't shot into the barn. The horses would've bolted. What had they fired at…?

Carl.

My knees buckled.

Cole grabbed my hand. He pulled me toward him, adjusting so my back faced Carl's car. "Don't look. Please. I don't want you to think of him that way."

I lowered my head, but I wasn't seeing Carl in my mind. I was back watching Liam. He was in the intersection, waiting. He saw the truck coming, saw me, and he mouthed, *"I lo—"*

"Addison."

"What?" I looked up.

"You're okay?"

"This isn't the first time I've seen bloodshed."

Cole winced. I caught the faintest glimmer of it before he turned and led me across the clearing to the second barn. I wanted to look, but didn't. When Cole pulled me the rest of the way around the corner, I sagged in relief.

Cole had begun to limp. He directed me to the driver's side of his car. "Can you drive?"

I nodded. "Yes." My voice was so damned even. I wanted to fold, but I didn't. I couldn't.

Cole studied me, but my answer must've appeased him. He gave me a clipped nod and went to the passenger side. We both got in, and I started the engine as Cole gave me directions. When we were on a highway, heading back to the city, he got on the phone.

"I need you to check on the horses. We had to leave," he said. There was a pause. "There was an incident. You might want to wait a couple hours for it to be cleaned up… Okay. Thank you."

His second call: "We were attacked. I need you to take a team; clean up the stables… Yes, it's the one outside the city."

The third one: "We're coming back. Have the med kit upstairs ready… Yes. I was shot. It went through my shoulder, but there might be fragments. My breathing is more labored than it should be."

He was so calm. When I thought about why he shouldn't be, some of my control slipped. My hands started to shake, and I glanced over.

He noticed my look. "You okay?"

I drew in a breath. His tone was so soft, so caring. It broke more of my wall down. I jerked my head in a nod, refocusing on the road again. "I'm good."

"You're trembling."

I was? Oh, yeah. My hands. I clamped them tight to the steering wheel and forced a smile. "See? All better. I'm good to go."

"No." He pointed to the side of the road. "Pull over. I can drive."

"You're shot!"

"I can get us a little farther along. One of my men can meet us halfway." He pointed again. "Pull over, Addison. Come on."

"No." I meant it. "I'm good." I rolled my shoulders back, sat up, and shoved all that shit out of my head. "I got this."

"Addiso—"

I shot him a fierce look. "I said I got this."

Our eyes caught and held, and I swear I saw a new emotion unveil itself in his eyes. I blinked, feeling that emotion answer in me, but I couldn't focus on that either.

I cleared my throat. "Just…help me out."

"What do you need?"

"I—" What did I need? My body was going into shock. I had to think about something else. "Let me talk about something else. I can't think about what just happened or my body will start reacting. I—"

"That's fine." Again came that soft tone from him.

My throat swelled, and I blinked, pushing the threatening tears away. That really wouldn't help.

"Go ahead," he added. "Whatever you want to talk about."

I didn't want to talk about anything real, so I began spilling every little detail about Sia. Her men. Her job. How I hated going to her events. Jake. That he was a good lawyer. That he was in love with my best friend.

Nothing was off limits.

Even Dawn. How she'd accused me of bringing Sia in on purpose, how they'd bonded over something called a cross-stitch, how I didn't really remember what they'd bonded over. How she'd stolen Sia's phone. How she was the building's shut-in, and did he even know that?

But I didn't wait for a response. I kept going. Doris and William's daughter. Her dog.

Did he have a dog policy for the building? If not, he should. Dogs were good. People loved their dogs. I could bring Frankie back.

Then it became all about Frankie.

The city lights moved past overhead, lighting our way as the car sailed down the highway. "He would just lie next to me," I explained, continuing on about Frankie. "I was either in bed, or if I couldn't stand the smell of Liam's pillows, I'd sit in one of the other rooms. I just sat on the floor, and Frankie would curl up next to me. He barked sometimes. He wanted food, but I couldn't get up to feed him. I knew that was what he wanted, but I just couldn't make myself to get it for him. Everything was work. Moving. Sitting. Going to the bathroom. It was all just work."

"Here's our exit," Cole murmured.

I turned on the signal and followed the lane, transitioning to the next road. His direction brought me back to reality. He must've sensed that.

"Are you okay?" he asked.

I moved my head up and down. The shock had worn off, because now I felt exhausted and numb all at the same time. We rode the rest of the way in silence. When we neared The Mauricio, I turned the corner. Cole hit the button, and the bottom parking lot door opened. Pulling the car inside, I parked in Cole's spot and turned the engine off.

We went inside, and I expected we'd go to my place. We didn't. When I started for the elevator, Cole caught my hand and pulled me another way. His hand fell to my hip, and he opened an exit door in the corner, revealing another elevator. I knew no other code would work for this one.

Cole said, "Open."

The doors obeyed, and we stepped inside. There were only three buttons to choose between. He touched the middle one, and we were moving. When the doors opened again, Dorian stood waiting for Cole. His head jerked back when he saw me, but he pressed his lips together in a tight line.

Cole sat down in a chair, and Dorian went right to work.

I didn't look around. I knew this was Cole's place, but *he* was my focus in that moment. My determination lasted thirty minutes. The exhaustion was hitting me hard, and at one point I almost fell to the floor before catching myself.

Cole grinned at me. "Go to sleep, Addison."

"I don't know how to get there."

He pointed behind him. "Follow the hallway. Take the stairs to the top floor, and you'll see the bed."

He wanted me to sleep in his bed. I could only blink at him. That meant something.

"I'll be up in a little bit."

I could tell Dorian didn't approve. His face had told me when I came in, and now he stiffened and sucked in his breath when Cole sent me to his bedroom. I looked over at him, then back at Cole. Cole shook his head.

Okay. That was my cue to do as he said. I walked around him, my hand touching his good shoulder briefly as I passed. I looked down. It felt wrong to explore Cole's home without him. When I came to the stairs, I followed them all the way up. There was a door right ahead of me. It was the only place to go, and when I opened it, I saw the biggest bed I'd ever seen in my life.

I almost cried out with joy. Almost. I refrained, figuring Dorian would try to kick me out if he heard. Instead I staggered into the bathroom and tried not to drool over everything inside. There was a Jacuzzi bathtub in one corner and a glass shower along the entire opposite wall. A basket of towels sat between two sinks. They looked large and warm enough to heat me like a blanket.

I stripped, showered, and grabbed one of those towels. I was right. They were heated, too. I didn't waste time looking for a shirt to wear. I crawled under Cole's sheets still wrapped in the towel.

I tried to stay awake. I wanted to wait for him to join me. There were things I wanted to say and lying here, I thought about what all was happening. Right now, men were heading out to the stables. They would clean up the bodies, the glass. They'd take care of everything, and my job—I looked to the doorway. Cole was there, his hands rested on the doorframe as he stared back at me.

Cole was my job now.

We'd changed. We *had been* changing, but we had graduated to a new level tonight. Cole took care of me. I took care of him. We were a team.

We were *together* now.

I felt sleep coming on, and knew I wouldn't be able to fight it, but as my eyelids started to drop, I whispered to him, "I choose. I choose you."

CHAPTER TWENTY-FOUR

I woke and could only lie there.

I'd shot a gun last night. I might've killed a man. Cole did kill five of them, and maybe that last one, too. They came, they shot Carl, and they tried to hunt us down.

At the end of it all, I chose Cole.

Everything was different now.

The first time Cole and I were together, I felt possessed by him. And I claimed him back. That night had been intense, but it was just the beginning. We'd grown closer and more connected each time we were together. After last night, there was no going back.

I was his. He was mine.

There should've been a red alarm going off in my head. Cole was dangerous, so dangerous, and I should've been hysterical or curled up in a fetal position sobbing. Last night had not been a normal night, for anyone, but here I was—disturbed mostly by how undisturbed I was. The only thing alarming to me was how nonchalant Cole had been last night.

I looked over and found him right next to me. His eyes were closed, those long eyelashes resting against his cheek and his head turned slightly toward me. He was beautiful, like a fallen angel, but so lethal at the same time. The bandage over his shoulder was a stark reminder of that fact.

A shiver went down my spine. He'd never hesitated last night. He was calm the entire time, only showing some impact after he was shot.

"What are you thinking?" He spoke as he opened his eyes, looking right at me.

He was looking *into* me.

I didn't hesitate. "You scare me."

There'd been a twinkle of amusement in his dark eyes. It fled now, and he lifted his head slightly. "I do?"

I nodded, moving my head against my pillow. "We were attacked by six men last night, and I feel like it was just another day for you. Yeah. That scares me."

He grew pensive, lowering his head back to his pillow. His voice dipped low. "Because it was."

I bit the inside of my cheek. He had more to say. I wanted to hear it all.

"I told you about my family, but I didn't go into detail." He closed his eyes, just for a second. When he opened them, I saw his ghosts. They were right there, and he remembered each and every one of them. His voice grew hoarse. "They killed my dad first. He was going to my sister's piano recital. They gunned him down in the streets. That was a message from them. They were coming for us."

"Cole." I laid a hand against his cheek.

"My mom was the next week. That was the joke on us. We thought it was done. The Bertals declared war when they killed my dad, but we never realized what was coming next. How could we?"

A tear slipped from my eye. It slid all the way to my jawline and lingered there. I didn't dare talk. Not yet.

He kept going, his words biting now. "She was in the fucking grocery store. My brother Ben was with her, but he'd gone to the magazine section. He liked to check out the babes." He lifted his mouth into a half-grin, one that didn't reach his eyes. He wasn't seeing me. He was looking through me, remembering. "They didn't know Ben was there, or they would've gone for him. Maybe. She was asking a grocery clerk about bread when they shot her. Twelve times, point-blank range. Ben ran out the back, and they never heard him. They couldn't hear anything except their own gunshots. Twelve fucking bullet holes in her."

"Cole," I whispered. My throat felt closed. "You don't have to tell me."

His hand covered mine on his cheek. He saw me again. "I do. I need you to know who I am."

So he told me.

His brothers were gunned down, one after another, one a week. Then his older sister, the one who'd had the piano recital where their father was killed. They went into hiding after the first brother was killed, but it never mattered.

I heard the pain in Cole's voice, and I couldn't do a thing to appease it. He'd been stripped of his family.

I had to listen, and I couldn't do a thing. Not a damn thing to take that pain away.

Then he got to the last. Two little sisters, twins.

They were in a safe house, but no matter where they hid, the Bertals found them. One sister hid in a closet, clinging to a stuffed manatee. She loved that manatee.

Cole laughed, but even that sound broke my heart. It was more a brief reprieve, like laughter from a dying man when he reads a fortune saying he'll live a long and prosperous life. It was a hollow sound, but he kept on. The other sister had gone to the roof. They found her clinging to the side of the house. Who would look over the roof's edge? They had, and she wasn't shot. They'd stepped on her fingers until she let go.

"I was next until Carter went off the books."

"What do you mean?" It hurt to breathe.

"He was supposed to guard me, but he saw what was happening. There was a rat in the family, so he took me away. He didn't tell anyone. I lived because he defied orders."

"That was when you worked with horses."

He nodded, breathing in deep. "Carter saved my life. I stayed away for five years until they found me. They fucked up. They sent four men and circled the car, like they did with Carl. I was with friends that day, normal friends who had no idea who I was. They died. I lived. I got out, and I killed the fuckers. Then I came back and killed more of them." A hard glint appeared in his eyes. "I took back my place in this family. My dad was the head. Now I am."

He stared hard at me.

"It's not going to work," I murmured, my hand still resting against his cheek. I rubbed my thumb back and forth, tenderly. "I should be scared off. I know. I should've been scared when I first saw you walk into Gianni's. You and those men—I knew right away you were dangerous. And I should've been scared when I saw you in the elevator, when you were holding Carl up. He was bleeding. The blood itself is scary enough, but it never happened. The fear never came. The only thing that scared me was when I talked to you, when I felt how much you could affect me." I smiled, faintly. "Still does, to be honest, but no. I'm not scared of who you are. I'm not scared of what you can do. I'm not scared what it means to be at your side. I'm only scared of how much I can't be without you. That terrifies me, all the way to the bone. But I'm still here. I can't walk away from you."

A light entered his eyes. It burned brighter with each word I spoke. "People die around me."

"So be it."

"You could die."

"Not long ago, I was halfway there."

He closed his eyes and exhaled a long, shaky breath. He looked back at me, and that light hadn't dimmed. "I kill people."

"I might've killed one last night."

"No." He shook his head against the pillow. "Your shot didn't kill him. It was mine. I shot him twice in the head. That's not you. Don't take that on you. It's not yours to carry."

My hand shifted, and my thumb went to his lips. "Thank you for saving my life last night."

His eyes darkened. "You were in that situation because of me. Don't thank me for that."

"I don't care."

"You should."

But I didn't. No thoughts held weight inside me when I was around Cole. My body was drawn to his, had been from the beginning, and as he moved over me, his lips finding mine, I knew what I'd said was true: I couldn't walk away from him.

His lips moved down my throat.

Nothing could drag me away.

CHAPTER TWENTY-FIVE

A few hours later, we woke again. Cole's elevator was buzzing on repeat, like someone was leaning on the button. Cole slipped from bed, cursing under his breath. He pulled on some pants and padded barefoot out of the room.

Checking the clock, I saw it was past noon. Good gracious. It was time to get up. I'd showered the night before, but I showered again. I found a pair of shorts in Cole's closet and grabbed a shirt. I didn't think he'd care. Then I tried remembering where all of my stuff was from last night.

I'd grabbed everything when I got his keys, wallet, and phone. I'd taken my purse to the stables, and I'd had it slung over me—his car. I'd put it in his backseat. Everything would be in there, including my phone. I was hesitant to leave the bedroom. Somehow it had become our private sanctuary, but I had to face the real world.

I was coming around the corner when Cole almost ran into me, coming my way.

His hands caught me, holding me at the waist, and he stopped me from careening into his chest. He winced, but that was it. He'd been able to be with me earlier as if his wound didn't bother him at all. I saw now that it did.

"Sorry." My hand rested on his chest. "I should get going. I think my purse is in your car."

"I was coming to get you."

"You were?"

He gestured over his shoulder. "Dorian's here for you."

"For me? Dorian?"

He nodded.

Time slowed. There was nothing dramatic about this, but I knew it wasn't good. Dorian wouldn't have come for a "Hey, how are you?" There was a storm coming. I felt it in my gut.

As I turned the corner and approached him, my gut was right. He was closed-off. I'd thought Dorian liked me initially, but since that morning he'd woken Cole up at my place, things had gone downhill.

"Your friend has been trying to get ahold of you."

"My friend?"

"Ms. Clarke."

My alarm spiked. "Sia? What's wrong?"

"Do you know where your phone is, Mrs. Sailer?" He glanced at Cole as he said my married name.

Cole grunted, leaning back against a kitchen counter. "Stop being catty, Dorian."

He didn't reply. His shoulders lifted in one slow motion before relaxing back down. He didn't even blink as he said to me, "She called me ten minutes ago with the request that I open your doors. She's concerned something is wrong. You've not been answering your phone since last evening."

"Oh, no." I stepped back. That wasn't good. "Sia's been calling me since last night?" I cursed and turned to Cole. "I need my phone. I have to call her."

He nodded, straightening from the counter. "I'll get it for you." He took his keys and squeezed my shoulder as he passed between Dorian and me.

As soon as the doors closed behind Cole, Dorian spoke again. "She said the police called her. There was a break-in at your home— your other home."

I grew wary. "Why are you telling me this?"

"I don't think a small excuse that you felt unwell last night, or forgot your phone at the running track will satisfy your friend. She's been very insistent that I find you if you're in the building."

"Is she at Jake's?"

"No. She's at the police station."

"Shit." It was worse than I'd imagined. "A break-in? Really?"

His head barely moved in a nod, and after a minute of silence, the elevator broke the tension. Cole had returned. He had my phone in hand, along with my purse.

"Here you go." As I took it and thumbed in my passcode to call Sia, he said to Dorian, "Was that it?"

"*Mrs.* Sailer can fill you in with the rest." Dorian left in all his uptight, stiff-neck-and-back gloriousness. He gave me one more searing look of disapproval before the elevator took him away.

"What'd he say?" Cole asked.

But just then Sia answered, and I turned around.

"Hello?! Addison!" She sounded hysterical.

"Yeah." I hit speaker, holding the phone out so Cole could hear. "I'm here. I'm so sorry. I lost my phone last night. What happened?"

"Your house was broken into!"

That still made no sense. "What?"

"One of your neighbors called it in, and when the police couldn't reach you, they called me. They had my information from Liam's accident. Addison, where have you been? I've been calling nonstop since last night."

"Dorian said you're at the police station?" I ignored so much there.

"No. I was."

Oh, no. "Where are you now?"

"I'm at Jake's. We tried getting into your floor, but it's impossible. The elevator wouldn't budge. I finally called and harassed your building manager. Addison…" Her voice calmed, but grew cautious. "The cops were asking me all sorts of questions."

I frowned. "Like what?"

"When I told them where you were living now, they got weird."

A different form of alarm rose up. I shared a look with Cole and gripped my phone tighter. "What do you mean?"

"I mean, like, at first they were acting like it was some regular kind of break-in, almost like it was no big deal. Then the second I mentioned you were living at The Mauricio, their heads literally jerked up. One of the cops left the room and came back with a detective. Is that normal?" She whispered into the phone, "They asked if you knew Cole Mauricio."

My throat grew dry. "What did you say?"

"I said yes. I mean, you *did* meet him at that event."

"But that was it? That's all you said?"

"What else would I say? It's not like you're bosom buddies with the guy."

I was a shitty friend.

"Oh, yeah. And Jake." Her voice rose again in volume. "They talked to him, too. They pulled him into an interrogation room. Of course, they said it wasn't an interrogation, but it sure felt like it. I could see the whole thing from where I was sitting. Jake told me they were asking how long ago he moved into the building, had he met Cole Mauricio before that, all sorts of questions."

"Did you tell them about Liam's parents?"

"No. Why would I? Wait. Should I have?"

"No, no." My hand loosened its grip on the phone. "Okay. Um, did they give you a number I should call?"

"Yeah. Hold on. I'll get it." There was silence, then she spoke again. "Wait. I'll just come down. They want you to call, and they want to meet you at the house. You need to go through it and let them know if anything's missing. You still had some things there."

"Um…" A headache began to form. I was going down a wayward path, and it led to a nasty intersection with Cole's world.

Cole mouthed to me, *"Tell her to wait. You'll call her back."* He made a motion of holding a phone to his ear and hanging it up, then pointed to my phone.

I nodded. "Give me—I just woke up. Let me dress and shower. I'm kinda in shock. I'll call you in a bit. Okay?"

"Are you sure you don't want me to just come down?"

"I'm sure. I'll call you."

"Okay."

Cole took the phone and hit the end call button. "They're going to ask about me."

"I'm aware."

My stomach was in knots. It had been twisting, tightening the more Sia told me, but this was inevitable.

"I chose you last night," I reminded him.

"Things were heated. I saved your life. You helped me. You might've said something you regret now. Your friend called you, and you could be remembering how life was without me." His voice softened. "I wouldn't blame you if you wanted to walk away. You can. There's still time."

"And what? Lie about knowing you?"

He shook his head, his eyes holding mine. "Tell the truth. You knew me. We had a fling, and that was it. It ends now. Everything ends now. You can still get out."

But I didn't want out. "I know that's the right thing to do. And I know what it meant last night when I chose you. I still do. And I know I should leave, but I can't." The knot loosened with each word I said. "And even if I do, and we end this—it will take one night of loneliness, and I know you'll be in my bed. One night. One call. That's all I have to do. We'll start this up all over again."

His eyes grew hard. "Not if I walk away from you."

Those words stung. They shouldn't have, but they did. I drew in a sharp breath. "I don't know if I could handle that."

His eyes softened again. "I don't know if I could walk away either."

"Well." My head hung. "There you have it." I started toward the elevator.

"Wait." Cole grabbed my arm. "I have cops on my payroll. Your friend is going to find out, but I can delay it."

"What are you talking about?"

"They're going to ask you questions, but I can get my guys in there. They can separate you from your friend when you're being interviewed."

"I—are you sure?"

He nodded. "Let me do that for you, at least. You can tell your friend on your own terms then. You can control that, at least."

"Thank you." His hand slipped down my arm to my hand. I squeezed.

I was very aware that if this happened a few months from now, Cole would be at my side. He would walk through my home with me. I wouldn't have to do it alone, but now it was too soon. Too early. I had to do this without him.

A little while later, I met Sia in the lobby, and we rode together in a car Ken "called" for us.

I didn't look at the driver. I knew it wasn't Carl.

CHAPTER TWENTY-SIX

Nothing was missing.

I walked through the house with two detectives. One was tall and the other was medium height, maybe an inch taller than me. Each was in his mid-forties, or so I guessed based on how haggard they looked. They had beady eyes and hawk-like focus centered right on me. It was uncomfortable, but I was relieved to find nothing gone.

I had taken everything that had sentimental value with me when I moved, I explained. Nothing left was particularly important to me, but it was still a relief to know I hadn't been robbed.

And true to Cole's word, when the detectives began to question me, a police officer came and directed Sia away. I couldn't hear the reason he gave her, but she threw me a confused look and followed him from the room.

I was ready. The hard questions were coming now.

"You're sure, Mrs. Sailer, that nothing is missing?"

"You can call me Addison."

"You don't go by your married name anymore?" The taller one cocked his head to the side. He had introduced himself as Reyes. I tried to remember the other one…maybe Smythe?

"I go by Addison."

Smythe, or whatever his name was, asked, "Is there a reason for that? Usually when people change their names, there's a reason. They're seeing someone new, or they don't want to be associated with the old name. Anything like that?"

I knew what he was asking, but I didn't react, despite the irritation starting to boil inside me. "My husband died over a year ago. I guess I'm slowly getting used to being just Addison right now. What does that have to do with someone breaking into my house?"

"We're just trying to understand your circumstances, find a connection or motive that might explain this," Reyes said smoothly.

"So, you think this is *my* fault?" I countered. Unbelievable.

They ignored me.

Reyes gestured over his shoulder, where Sia had gone. "Your friend said you moved into The Mauricio downtown. That's a pretty expensive place."

His partner grunted. "And exclusive. I'd have no idea how to get in there even if I wanted to."

They grinned at each other, perhaps thinking I didn't know where they were going with these questions.

I raised my chin and rolled my shoulders back. "Just ask what you want to ask."

The feigned amusement was gone. Their hawk eyes returned. The taller one narrowed his. "Do you know Cole Mauricio, ma'am?"

Ma'am. They even dropped the first name. A cold feeling crept in. "Yes, I do."

"Your friend said you met at some hoity-toity event. One of those fundraisers. Is that true?"

"He was there, yes."

They studied me, and I felt them reassessing.

Smythe asked quietly, "Is that where you met Cole Mauricio?"

"He wasn't introduced to the group. Alfred Mahler conversed with him and his companion. Then Cole said a few words to the other people standing with us."

"Other people? Who were they?"

Deep breath, and here we go. "My dead husband's parents."

"In-laws?" Both looked at me, long and hard. They hadn't expected that.

I nodded. "I prefer ex-in-laws. There's no relationship."

Reyes wrote something down on a pad of paper. "Is that how you know Cole Mauricio?"

"I know him because I live in his building."

"Your friend is dating one of the other residents, and she didn't know him."

I lifted a shoulder. "There's a running track inside. We were both running one day. That's where I met him." I was willing to tell the truth, but I'd be damned if I just handed it over.

The medium-height one shifted on his feet, peering at me. "Your friend said you and your husband were estranged from his family."

"That's true. Yes."

"Did you ever meet your husband's grandmother?"

They were going the Bertal route. They weren't going to ask whether I knew Cole on a personal level. The relief almost overwhelmed me. My knees grew weak, and I moved my head from side to side. "No. I never did. Liam was—he didn't want me to meet her. That was obvious."

"And you never questioned him?"

"I loved him. If he didn't want me to meet her, there was a reason for it. I trusted him."

Reyes put his pad of paper in his jacket's inside pocket. "Were you aware Liam's grandmother was a Bertal?"

"Yes, but not until the night of the event." I could say this. I knew it had no bearing on me. "Cole Mauricio said that name, and I didn't understand the implication. I looked up Bea Bertal on the internet that night."

"The internet?" Reyes' mouth twitched. "You found out about your deceased husband's family from the world wide web?"

"Yes." I frowned. "Why are you surprised by that?"

"You'd never thought to look up his family before?"

"Why would I? We were happy. Liam was a counselor. I wrote freelance. There was no reason to be suspicious."

He shrugged. "I guess so."

They shared another look before swinging their gazes back to me. "Is there anything else we should know, Addison?" Reyes asked.

"About the break-in?" I shook my head. "No. Can I ask you a question?"

"Go for it."

"Why are there two detectives on this case? Wouldn't normal protocol be that one police officer take my statement?"

Both reacted, unreadable masks slamming down on their faces. Reyes coughed. "We're just being thorough. If you find that anything was taken, let us know. Otherwise it looks like no harm done. We don't have much to go on."

"Yeah. Could've just been teenagers looking for an empty house to party in." Smythe pointed to a corner devoid of furniture. "Sometimes they'll look on real estate websites and watch to see how long a house is listed. They'll scope it out, and if it's empty, they'll throw a big rager. Although," he mused, "doesn't seem like that either."

They left soon after that, and Sia joined me in the kitchen, watching them go through the window. "That was weird."

I grunted my agreement.

"So, nothing's missing?"

The detectives got in their car and pulled away. The squad car that had come with them followed behind. I turned toward Sia. "I really don't think so. Nothing stood out to me."

"Oh." She chewed her bottom lip, glancing around the empty house. "This place gives me the chills sometimes." Her eyes got big. "Oh, I'm sorry, Addison. I didn't mean it like that."

I shook my head, sighing. "It gives me the chills, too. Come on." I linked our arms together as we walked to the door. "It's been a weird day. Let's go do something fun."

She grabbed my hand, intertwining our fingers. "I thought you'd never ask. Gianni's?"

"Let's try somewhere new."

"I have the perfect place." A smile stretched over her face as she went down to the car.

I stayed behind to lock the door. I knew eventually she'd question me about where I was last night, but so far she just seemed relieved that nothing was missing and I was okay. Maybe she'd forgotten where I'd told her I was going. I slid in next to her and glanced back at the house as the driver pulled away. I wanted to come back later, but with Cole instead.

I looked over at Sia, smiling until I remembered my alibi for the night before.

I told her I was going to be at my house last night.

Once we were back in the city, Sia should've gone to work, but she didn't. She took the day off, declaring it Best Friend Day. For me. For the ass best friend. For the friend who had been lying to her.

We went to a new restaurant. We laughed. We drank. Fuck—we got drunk. The day, for all the craziness that had happened, was fun. Sia got my mind off of everything: Cole, the attack, my house. The only thing that wasn't fun about the day was me. Sia was intent on celebrating me, while I was lying to her face.

How could I make that right in my head? How would I even try? I couldn't. There were no words, no ways. At the end of the day, as we were giggling and tripping over ourselves going into the elevator, I knew who the bad guy was: me. Sia was being my friend, like she always had. I wasn't doing the same. Nope. Douchebag. That was me.

She helped me into my place, and I fell on the floor.

"Oomph!" I felt nothing. I was just startled, and laughter pealed out of me.

Sia fell down beside me, laughing too. "We're horrible."

"No." I pointed at her, my finger pressing into her skin. "We did what every burglarized person should do."

She snorted, fighting back a grin. "Get wasted?"

"Yes." I offered an emphatic nod. I meant business. "And when you get burglarized, I'll do the same."

"Spend a paycheck on cheap whiskey?"

I sat up and drew in a breath. "You spent a paycheck? A whole one?"

She rolled around, arching her back as more laughter came from her. "God, no. I love you, Addison. I probably spent two hundred dollars tonight."

I touched her hand. "I'll pay you back. I promise."

"No." She shook her head, almost knocking herself over as she struggled to sit up. "I owe you, and I'm doing what a friend should do. I'm taking your mind off things."

I let out a sigh. "You really are." I pulled her hand to my chest. "Thank you, friend."

"No problem." Her laughter dried up. Her voice grew somber. "You'd do the same for me."

"Would I?"

"Addison." She tilted her head. "You know you would."

"I don't know anymore," I said, talking mostly to myself.

"Oh, Addy," she murmured, scooting forward. She wrapped her arms around my waist and laid her head on my shoulder. "You lost your real best friend." She moved her hand to rest over my heart. "He's in here now. I can only hope to do him proud, but you're selling yourself short. Addison, you are an amazing friend. You're allowed to grieve the loss of your soulmate, no matter how long that takes. And trust me, I'm trying to play catch-up here. I've been slacking, you know, since a certain neighbor of yours came into my life."

I laughed softly, leaning into her. "Thank you, Sia."

She rested her chin on my shoulder, holding me once again.

"Thank you for making me feel better."

"No problem." She pressed her cheek to mine. "That's what real friends do for each other, no matter what shit has hit the fan."

CHAPTER TWENTY-SEVEN

"I'm a bad friend."

Cole was in my kitchen, making scrambled eggs on my stove. He paused to frown at me. "What do you mean?"

"Sia's been there for me so many times, and I'm lying to her about—" I waved at him. "You know."

"Cut yourself a break." Turning the stove off, he put the scrambled eggs on a plate and came toward the table. He grabbed two forks on the way and sat down. He gestured to the plate and passed me a fork. "Dig in. This is our breakfast."

"Chef Cole extraordinaire, huh?"

"You know it." He grinned, fork in hand and ready to dive in. He paused to stare at me a moment and seemed to grow thoughtful, lowering his hand to the table. "This is what I lived on when I was on my own for a while."

"The family you stayed with didn't cook for you?"

"They did, but I stayed in the stables. If they came for me, I didn't want the family to die, too." He shook his head. "That's ridiculous thinking now. The Bertals would've cleaned house. They would've killed the family first and then come looking for me when they couldn't find me in the house."

"I'm sorry."

"They weren't your family." He shrugged, raising his fork again. "But going back to the eggs, this is what I ate a lot of the time. I had dinner once or twice a week with the family. The other times, there was a small kitchen area in the barn, and I ate lots and lots of eggs. Somehow I got it in my head that that's what you eat to get big."

He laughed before spearing some eggs and popping them in his mouth. He ate half the plate in a few minutes before leaning back in his chair, rubbing his stomach. "I hated eggs when I first came back. I wouldn't eat them. Carter never said anything, but I knew he wondered. We'd have dinner every now and then when I came back, and if there were eggs in the meal, I always picked them out."

"Jake and Sia said Carter was your family's hit man?"

He nodded. "Yeah, for a while. He rose up in the ranks, killed everything in sight. He was a fucking badass. I worshiped him; then I worshiped him even more after he saved my life. I learned later that he kind of ran the family until I came back. He's a good guy. I owe him everything."

I put my fork aside and leaned back in my chair, mirroring Cole. His legs stretched out under my seat, and I lifted mine, tucking them alongside his. It calmed me.

"There's a lot on the internet about your friend."

"The media loves him." He winked at me. "He's gorgeous, you know."

I laughed softly. "So are you."

Cole's eyes darkened, and he leaned forward. He picked up my hand and laced our fingers together before looking back at me. "He wants to meet you."

"Huh?" I tried to pull my hand away, but Cole only tightened his hold.

He flashed that killer smile again, rubbing his thumb over mine. He'd grabbed my hand on purpose. "Yep. He wants to meet you all official like."

"Just him?" A dark room flashed in my head. Men in dark business suits lined up against the far wall as I was led to my death. "Or will others be there?"

Cole's eyes narrowed, and he cocked his head before shaking it. "Nope. I love the guy. He's family, but I know he's scary. I thought maybe if it was over dinner, that'd be less intense. And Emma will come, too."

"Who's Emma?" As I asked, I remembered. "Emma Nathans."

Cole nodded. "She's nice. I think you'll like her. She's the one who tamed the Carter beast." He smiled, and I heard the fondness in his voice.

He liked Emma. He cared for her—or maybe it was something else. He respected her, just like he respected Carter Reed. I knew it, but I still asked. "You really care about them, don't you?"

He nodded. "I do. I owe my life to both of them, actually. Last year—" His voice dropped. "I know there's a lot of scary shit on the internet about Carter, and I don't know what they say about Emma, but it's not all true. Carter's dangerous, and he's killed, but he's not a bad guy. He's like me."

Cole let go of my hand and leaned back in his chair again. His arms spread wide, and the carefree Cole returned. "Only I'm younger, funnier, and way better looking."

I remembered how they'd looked, Cole and Carter, at the banquet. How they'd moved as one. Cole might be younger, but he was just as deadly. He'd showed me how dangerous he could be, and thinking about that night again, a shiver went through me, cooling my blood.

"You in?"

"Huh?"

Cole watched me.

"Oh yeah. Dinner with Carter and Emma." I nodded. "I'm in."

"Nothing big. Just a get-together among friends."

That didn't appease my nerves.

Cole held my hand the next night, leading me into the restaurant he and I had gone to once before. I knew this wasn't going to be anything like "nothing big." The hostess led us past crowded tables, and conversations stopped. I remembered the feeling of being watched from the last time, but I'd been overwhelmed just being at dinner with a guy who wasn't Liam. I couldn't imagine how it was worse this time than then, but it was. My nerves were shot.

I kept my eyes forward, and halfway through the restaurant, Cole squeezed my hand. That helped. He was calm, and I tried to take on some of that. By the time we got to the back and started up to the second floor, I could breathe a little bit easier, though I still had a death grip on Cole's hand. When we got to the second floor, he maneuvered us so I was first. He now walked behind me, and a second later, I realized why. His hand came to the small of my back, and he began rubbing small circles, comforting me.

The floor was empty except for a table set up beside a stone fireplace. Two people sat there. I recognized the man as Carter. He rose to shake Cole's hand, his ice blue eyes resting on me the whole time.

Cole spoke to him, joking about something, and then he stepped away from my side to converse with the woman, who'd stood as well. She didn't come around the table. She waited by her seat, smiling and laughing at whatever Cole said to her.

Meanwhile, there was me, feeling like an idiot.

"I'm Carter. It's nice to meet you." He held his hand out.

The rebellious kid I used to be wanted to cut tail and run. I didn't know where she'd come from, but I shoved her down and shook his hand. It was strong and authoritative. Okay. I got it. He was protective of his family. I was having a hard time making eye contact. Cole's eyes were dark. Pain mixed with playfulness in them, but they were always warm when they looked back at me.

 Carter was different.

I saw death when I looked at him. He was guarded, cautious, serious, and when I turned to Emma, I wondered briefly if this was a joke. Were these two actually together? She had none of those qualities. She was beautiful, with dark hair that fell to her shoulders, and her smile lit up her face. She was more slender than me, but when she shook my hand, she wasn't weak. Not at all. She was strong as hell.

She waved a hand to the chair beside Cole. "Please, have a seat, Addison. It's so nice to meet you." She sat back down, her eyes flicking to my right for a moment. "Cole's spoken highly of you."

He snorted, sitting beside me. His hand rested on my leg under the table. "Like I'd have anything negative to say. I'm dating her, Ems. What do you expect?"

"I know." She pulled her cloth napkin out and folded it on her lap, jerking her head to the guy on her right. "You've never introduced us to a woman before. I'm pretty sure Carter scared the shit out of her. I'm trying to make her feel more welcome."

Carter stiffened. "I didn't do anything."

"You don't have to." Emma laid her hand on top of his. She spoke with such love that I was taken aback for a second. "You have resting bitch face, honey."

Cole laughed "RBF? Nah. It's more like the cold killer face. Stone cold, Carter. Stone cold."

The ends of Carter's mouth turned down. "You guys are making fun of me."

"Yeah." Cole nodded. "That's what family does. We tease each other." He laid his arm on the back of my chair, his hand falling to rest on my shoulder. "Addison's the only one who gets a break tonight. She's just met you guys, and we're too new. Well…" He watched me from the corner of his eye, holding back a grin. "No. I get to tease her, but not you guys. You have to be nice."

A server came over and poured Cole a glass of wine before moving around to serve the rest of the table.

"Don't fight it, Carter," Cole said, raising his glass. "Teasing you is a privilege, one that I hold dear. It's an honor to be able to make fun of the Cold Killer to his face."

"Cole." Carter's eyes flashed a warning, darting to the server, then landing on me.

Cole took a sip before setting his glass down. He waited till the server left, then leaned over the table. "Really? You don't think your own employees know what they used to call you?"

Emma had been quiet, but she started laughing now. "The look on your face. You look like you want to shoot Cole and hug him at the same time."

Carter's shoulders lifted in a slow breath, and then a small smile showed. "You've always had that effect on me."

"Because I'm like your little brother." Cole winked at Carter, his hand drawing circles behind my shoulder. "And half the time you want to kick my ass; the other half you're damned grateful you can call me family. That's my effect on you. Consider it my thank you gift for all those times you saved my ass."

I knew what Cole was doing. He knew Carter made me nervous, and he was trying to lighten the mood, drawing the attention from me to Carter himself. It was working. Carter turned his hand upside down and linked his fingers with Emma's. They shared a warm look. They clearly adored each other. Once he was holding her hand, Carter relaxed. He rested more fully against the back of his chair. His shoulders loosened, and his grin seemed more natural.

Cole was also protecting me. He'd inserted himself into the conversation so any questions for me had to go through him in a way. I didn't know how he'd done that, but he had. And the others took note.

Carter's eyes flicked to me and lingered.

Cole noticed. "Don't worry about Addison. She was at the stables with me."

At the mention, I knew the slight break in tension was over. Carter's eyes snapped back to attention and his grin disappeared. A faint scowl took its place. "Are you kidding me?"

"No."

Cole's light-hearted tone was gone as well. He leaned forward slightly. I started to lean in as well, but Cole's hand splayed out on my shoulder. He held me back.

"She was there, and she saw the whole thing," Cole said.

Emma closed her eyes before her gaze fell to her lap.

Maybe I wasn't supposed to know something? Maybe I wasn't supposed to be at those stables? I didn't know, but I knew I couldn't say anything. Whatever was going on, it was between Carter and Cole.

"It's done, Carter."

"You could've kept her in the dark."

Cole snorted. "Right. The next time I have to…" He hesitated. "…do what we do sometimes, I'll lock her in a bathroom or something."

Carter didn't reply. He looked to me before returning to Cole.

"They came in. We were there. It's done," Cole said.

They were talking half in code. I could follow because of what I'd seen at the stables. I wondered if the servers could guess. I glanced over my shoulder, saw the server coming back with a pitcher of water, and coughed, clearing my throat. "Water, anyone?"

The conversation was dropped, but I had a feeling it was over anyway. Once the water was poured, Carter ordered for himself and Emma. Cole made sure I was okay with what he ordered for us, and once the server was gone again, Emma took charge.

She leaned forward, reaching for her wine glass. "So, Addison, Cole said you two met because you live in his building?"

That was her signal. Whatever Carter and Cole were arguing about, it wasn't to be brought back up. She gave both of them pointed looks, and they nodded in response. After that, the conversation was smoother. I told them all about the other residents. Emma's eyes got bigger and bigger, especially when I mentioned Dawn and her affection for Jake.

"And that's the guy your best friend is dating now?"

I nodded, finishing my second glass of wine. I was done eating as well. My plate was still a third full. The chicken, scallops, and asparagus would've made my taste buds dance on a normal night, but this wasn't normal. The nerves had lessened when Emma took charge, but they were still there, and that kept my appetite at bay. Carter didn't approve of me, or he didn't approve of something about me, and Cole didn't care. The undercurrents had been tucked down, way down, but I knew I was reading them right.

Once Cole finished eating, his arm rested behind me again, and his hand never left my shoulder. I was thankful. That tiny touch helped assuage some of the tension.

I leaned back into his hand now. His fingers splayed out, and his palm rested on my skin. A small tingle coursed through me, helping to ease a bit more of the knot in my stomach.

"Yes," I said to Emma. "Jake's the one. I haven't told Sia about Dawn yet. I should."

"Don't." Emma sounded sure.

"Don't?"

"Tell him what happened."

"What do you mean?"

"Tell *him* Dawn took the phone. The friendship is between him and Dawn. It will be easier on Sia if he puts a stop to it; then she won't be in the middle. He should protect both of them. It's his friend and his girlfriend, so it's his job. Not yours, not your friend's."

I'd never thought of telling Jake. I was floored. "Thank you. I think I will."

"Shit, Emma. When'd you get all wise on me?" Cole teased.

She laughed, sinking into Carter's side, slipping her hand through his. "It's all because of this guy. Once you go Carter, you always become smarter." She held her laugh, raising her eyes to wait for Carter's reaction.

When he heard the rhyme, he groaned, shaking his head. "You didn't just say that."

"I did, and it's true, but—" She held up her glass of wine. "It's probably more because of this. I think this is my third glass. I'm officially a lush." She rested her head on his shoulder. "We might need to fly Theresa and Amanda out here. I'm feeling in the Octave mood. Surely there's something like that around here?"

"Octave?"

"The club Carter owns back home. Speaking of," he said to Carter, "when are you going to open one here? I took Emma to Octavia in New York, but I think doing another one here would be smart. That's one of your best business ventures."

Carter lifted his arm so there was no barrier between him and Emma. She sank farther into his side, and he held her close, his hand resting on her other arm. "When you'll open it with me."

"I'll put in money."

"I don't need money."

This was another conversation for just the two of them. Emma seemed content to listen, so I did the same. I wasn't nestled into Cole's side, but his hand was still on the back of my shoulder, like he was silently holding me up. As he talked with Carter, his hand went back to drawing circles.

In the end, Cole remarked, "I don't know. Maybe. We'll see."

"Good enough for me." Carter's smile was much less strained than in the beginning. He glanced down, and his smile grew even softer. "Emma's about to fall asleep if we don't head out."

"I'm up." She yawned. "I'm totally awake." Her eyes closed… and didn't open. "See. I'm ready to dance. Nightclub, anyone?"

"Right." Carter shifted and swept Emma into his arms.

She squealed. "What are you doing?"

"You were falling asleep."

"Put me down. I can walk. I promise."

"You sure?"

The two were talking, but they were laughing at the same time. Carter carried her toward the stairs.

As he did, Cole turned to me. He pulled me into his side now that they had gone downstairs. "You okay?"

I nodded. "Your friend is intense. I feel like I just ran a marathon, backward." My legs felt like lead. Even my arms were heavy.

"Don't worry. Carter's just protective. I'm a little less cautious than he is, but he'll relax. He knows a good thing when he sees it."

"Really?" I scoffed.

Cole nodded, his eyes warming as he held my gaze. "Really." He pressed a light kiss to my lips. "You ready to head back?"

"God, yes." I groaned. "But don't pick me up." I stood, seeing a mischievous glint in his eyes.

This was a new side to Cole—a Cole that poked at his friend, trying to get a reaction. I knew the dark and silent Cole. I knew the dangerous side of him, and when we were at my home together, I'd started to see his joking side, but this one was altogether new and unpredictable. I was cautious, learning new terrain, until he leaned in close and dropped his voice low.

"When I pick you up, it's not going to be because you're sleepy from too much wine." Cole stood behind me, his body brushing against mine. "It's going to be because your legs don't work for a whole other reason." As he spoke, he trailed a finger down my spine.

I caught my breath. One touch was all it took to awaken my body.

I murmured, huskily, "Yes. Let's go home."

His eyes darkened at my response, and his hand fell to the small of my back. He urged me forward. "Yes, let's."

CHAPTER TWENTY-EIGHT

I was surprised to learn Carter and Emma were staying at The Mauricio, so we all rode back together. Emma and I got out first, while Carter waited for Cole. Ken held the door open for Emma and me as we stepped inside the lobby.

"We stay here sometimes," she told me. "The first was a year ago. We used the fourth floor, and Carter said Cole had residents here as well. I was told not to talk to them, because he keeps his presence here a mystery, so it's nice knowing you're here."

"Yeah. Same here. You know, if you're here long, we could have lunch together or something?"

Interest sparked in her gaze. "Your days are free?"

I nodded. We were alone in the lobby. I turned to glance behind us, but Ken had closed the door.

"Carter's nervous about you," Emma said. "You're close to Cole. It's obvious how much he cares about you." She glanced sideways at me, a lingering look. "Cole's not as guarded as he is. I think he wanted to hash some stuff out before we go up for a nightcap."

I nodded. That made sense.

My gaze lingered on the closed door, though.

Emma touched my hand lightly, drawing my attention. "We're here for another few days. After what happened at the stables, Carter wants to make sure everything is fine. So if your offer is genuine, I'd love to meet for lunch one day."

"It is, and my days are wide open. I'm not working."

"Yeah?"

I was sure she and Carter knew about Liam, and about his death, but I was about to explain my lack of day job anyway when I heard the elevator ping its arrival. I'd just started to explain to Emma when I heard my name—and I turned to see Sia standing there.

The world tilted sideways for a moment.

Jake came up behind Sia, and they looked between Emma and me.

Sia said again, "Addison?"

I was frozen. My two worlds were colliding, and I couldn't say a damned thing.

"I—" I choked out. That was it.

Emma looked between us and understanding dawned over her face. She swung around, holding her hand out to Sia. "Hello. I'm Emma. You'll have to excuse me. I was coming in and saw—" She pretended to ask me, "Addison?"

I nodded, grateful.

"I saw Addison's shoes and stopped to ask her where she got them. I'm so sorry if I held your friend up. We started talking about restaurants around here. I asked her for a recommendation."

"Oh." Sia drew closer, some of her curiosity satisfied. "Did she mention Gianni's?"

"Gianni's." Emma's eyes lit up again. We could hear Carter and Cole coming in from outside, and she said hurriedly, "Yes. Actually I knew about Gianni's already. My friend owns the restaurant."

"Your friend?" The door opened and her gaze passed over us to the two coming in. Sia's eyes widened dramatically. So did Jake's.

Emma jumped in, raising her voice. "Yes, my friend Cole." She turned to them. "You guys are here. I've been entertaining myself. I ran into Addison, and she recommended your restaurant, Cole, for us to eat at tomorrow." She paused. "Have you met Addison or her friends?"

Cole didn't skip a beat. He held out his hand. "Hello, Addison." After we shook, my grip a little shaky, he held his hand out to Sia and Jake. "The both of you look familiar." He pretended to mull it over before he gestured to Jake. "You were at the fundraiser a while ago. That was almost a month and a half ago, I think? Carter, you were with me."

Carter sidled up next to him, shaking Sia and Jake's hands as well as they stood there, slack-jawed.

"I don't think we were introduced, but I remember," Carter said. "You were with Mahler."

"Yeah." Jake blinked a few times, closing his mouth. "I, uh, it's nice to meet you."

"Carter." He pointed to Cole. "And this is Cole." Emma moved next to him. "And you already met Emma."

"Yes." She clasped his arm, pulling him toward the elevator. "It was nice to meet you all."

Cole lingered as the other two stepped inside the elevator. He was waiting for my signal. With Jake and Sia's attention still focused on them and not me, I nodded briefly. Cole nodded back and followed his friends.

In silence, we all watched as the elevator went up. It stopped on the fourth floor.

"Whoa. Carter Reed stays there," Jake exclaimed. "That was, wow. I mean, maybe Carter Reed owns this building? You think? He was in the Mauricio family, too."

Sia didn't respond. She'd turned back to me. "You look pale. Are you okay?"

"Huh?" Jake frowned.

She ignored him. "Addison?"

"Oh." Jake shook his head, raking a hand through his hair. He stepped back to give us space.

Sia asked again. "I called you earlier. We're going to a get-together. One of Jake's colleagues is celebrating his birthday. Do you want to come with?"

She asked me to come along.

Because I was alone.

Because they ran into me in the lobby.

All the guilt from yesterday rushed back to me, doubling because, yet again, I'd lied to her face. I couldn't do it, not anymore. Sia deserved better, and I let out a deep sigh.

"Sia," I started.

"Yeah?"

Please, don't hate me. "I've been an asshole friend."

A half laugh came from her. She shook her head. "What are you talking about?"

"I've been lying to you." The words were hard to say. I felt like I'd swallowed bark, and it was coming back up, scraping the insides of my throat.

"Okay." She cocked her head to the side. "What are you talking about, though?"

I looked to Jake. "Can I talk to her? It might take some time. I have a lot of groveling to do."

He glanced between us and asked, "Do you want me to wait?"

"No." She waved toward the door, adjusting her hold on her purse. "You go ahead. This could take a while. Is that okay?"

"You'll call me?"

"I will. Go and have fun. I'll let you know if I get a car to come on my own."

He bent down, giving her a quick kiss. "Okay." He gave me a confused look. "This will take a while, huh?"

"I'm afraid so."

And it did.

When we got to my floor, we sat down, and I told her almost everything: The first time I met Cole. The night she stood me up, how I went to the running track to find him again. How I'd been scared, but how I'd wanted to see him for an entire week, and that night, I finally had the courage to try. I told her about seeing him in the back elevator, and that I'd slept with him the first time we had dinner.

"I didn't care, Sia." My hands twisted together, pushing down on my lap. The harder I pushed down, the more the words poured out of me. "I was so beyond caring. I wanted to feel something other than grief. He made me feel better. For that night, I was alive. That was the first night I didn't have a nightmare."

I kept going. I told her how he'd come late the next night, how his friend had died and he'd flown out the next morning for the funeral preparations and business. That I didn't see him for another month, and I'd thought it was over until I saw him again at the event with Jake.

Once I was done, she sat, quiet. I waited. A heavy cloud hung between us. I couldn't say a thing. I could only hope she understood in some small way. I prayed for it.

"I see."

I winced. Her voice was quiet.

"The night your house was broken into?"

"I was with him."

"Okay. That's the only part I wasn't sure about."

I heard her wrong. I must've. "Huh?"

And she floored me when she shrugged. "Hate to break your illusion that I'm completely oblivious and an idiot, but I knew something was going on long ago. A best friend would have to be daft not to know something's up. I knew you lied to me. Hello. You told me you were going to be at your house, then I'm the one telling you it got broken into? I was more relieved to know you weren't hurt than pissed you lied to me at that moment."

I could only blink at her.

"And all the other stuff?" She snorted. "Like I'm not going to notice that every time we go to Gianni's, we don't get a bill if you're with us. Even Jake stopped talking about it. He knew it was you, but we just hadn't asked about the connection. Or that suddenly you always order the car when we go out, and it's always the same car, always the same driver. I have to be observant for my job," she said with a shrug. "I thought you were seeing the driver, not Cole Mauricio himself. That's the only part I didn't pick up right away."

I sat up in my seat. "You thought I was seeing Carl?"

"There were two guys, right? I knew it was one of them. I didn't catch their names."

"Jim's the other one."

"Carl's cuter." She grinned. "My personal choice for you."

Carl...

My throat started to swell up. I swallowed, clearing it, and changed the topic. "When did you know it was Cole?"

"I didn't until the other morning." Her voice quieted again. She bit her lip. "I was worried about you. I saw a car go around the corner and turn into the lot. I was watching from Jake's floor, and I thought maybe it was you. Turns out I was right. That's when I saw the two of you together. You guys looked so beaten down, but there was something to how you moved with each other. You moved as a unit, and then he touched your hip, and I knew he was the guy you were seeing. You guys looked like death warmed over."

She'd known. She'd known something almost the whole time, and she'd known who Cole was... "That was why you didn't bat an eye when the house was broken into. I'd told you I was going to check on it the night before."

She nodded. "It didn't seem right. But I figured you'd tell me when it was." She leaned forward, taking my hand. "I get it, Addison. I really do. He's the first guy since Liam, and considering who he is—I really *do* get it. I wouldn't have said anything either."

I started crying. I didn't know why. Maybe it was relief from unburdening myself, or maybe because I wasn't going to lose my best friend after all.

"I'm sorry." I waved my hands in front of me, fanning myself. "I hate crying."

"I know." She held my hand again. "I'm scared for you. I'm worried. I'm concerned, but he's *the* guy, isn't he?"

She wasn't asking if he was the guy I was dating. "Yeah."

"Then I'm happy for you." She squeezed my hand, shaking my arm in the air as she pretended to squeal. "The head of the Mauricio family. Holy fuck of all fucks, Addison!"

I gave her a choked laugh. "I met the hit man for their family tonight—if he's still their hit man, I don't know."

"Yeah." She grinned, her eyes wide. "Holy fuck, indeed."

I laughed again, and once I started, I couldn't stop. I didn't know what I was laughing about, I was just laughing. And Sia joined in. A slight chuckle, then more, and finally she was laughing almost as hard as I was. We sat at my kitchen table, holding hands and crying together. We must've looked crazy.

But I didn't care. Not one bit.

I had my friend back, and only now did I realize how much I'd missed her.

Cole slid into my bed.

I woke as soon as I felt the covers lift. The cold hit my naked back, but his warmth soon replaced it. The feel of his body against mine, and I rolled over, a *hmmm* on my lips. I didn't open my eyes.

"Hey," he murmured, dropping a kiss to the side of my mouth. He wrapped an arm around my waist, his hand sliding over my hip. "Hmmm back. I like this." I was naked for him. His hand moved down my leg and back up to my breast. "A lot."

I shifted, sliding one leg over his and the other between his legs. I pulled him close so he was pressed against me. I laid back, my head resting against the pillow, and looked up at him. "I figured. It's my present for you."

He pinched my nipple, then rubbed his thumb over the tip. "Happy early birthday to me. I should always leave you alone with your friend." He leaned close, sniffing. "You guys had a few drinks, huh?"

I rested my arms on his shoulders, keeping him over me. "We did, and it was glorious." A yawn slipped out. "I told her everything, Cole."

He stiffened before dipping his mouth to my shoulder. I felt his lips move over my skin as he asked, "Everything?" His hand dropped to my hip and tightened there a moment.

"Not the stables. Not what happened."

His hand relaxed, sweeping over the outside of my leg before coming back up on the inside. My pulse picked up. My blood warmed, and soon lust pulsated through my body. Would I always want him this way? I lifted myself, locking my legs around his waist and pulling him down at the same time.

Cole's eyes widened, but he pushed back, a satisfied smirk on his face. He rubbed against me, letting me feel how much he wanted me, too.

Yes. I silently answered my question. As his lips came down to mine, and I switched our positions to straddle him, I knew that my need for him wasn't going away, at least not any time soon. And with that in mind, I rested one hand against his chest and took control. This time, it was about what I wanted.

Cole could dominate me next time. I shivered in anticipation.

CHAPTER TWENTY-NINE

Addison,

The editors loved your article. We're running it in next month's issue. I'll send the link when it goes live. You'll have to fill out the forms attached for payment. We have another opening two months from now—would you be interested in doing another article? You pick the topic, but keep it similar to what you turned in. If this sounds like something you'd like to do, let me know. And again, great job!

Tina Gais
Editor-in-Chief
Onlooker Online Magazine

I stared at the screen, reading that email. It felt good. It felt *damn* good. Life was becoming normal—or as normal as it could be—and tonight would be another big moment.

I'd met Cole's friends, so it was his turn to meet mine.

Emma and Carter had stayed for three weeks, but I didn't see Carter again. Thankfully. Cole was content to come to my floor, and I assumed he met up with Carter during the day. I tried not to think about the attack, or what it meant for Cole. Would he retaliate? Was that why Carter was here? They didn't tell me. Emma and I met for lunch a few times during those weeks, and if she knew, she never said a word either. It was the topic that wasn't discussed, and right now, where we were, I was all right with that. I preferred it even.

For the last couple lunch dates, Sia had joined us, and while she'd been hesitant, Emma was warm and welcoming. It was a sight to see. The roles reversed. Sia, who was usually the social butterfly, was withdrawn and shy at first. Emma, who I realized was more reserved than I'd thought, was the one to make sure Sia relaxed.

I'd expressed the same thought to Cole one night, and he'd explained, "She didn't do it for your friend. Emma did that for you."

"What do you mean?" I'd rolled to my back, looking up at him.

"I care about you, so therefore, Emma does, too. It's what we do. You care about Sia, so Emma made sure she was happy. For you."

"You just said she did it for you."

He'd shrugged, smirking. "She was nice to you in the beginning because of me, but she likes you. She wouldn't continue to hang out with you if she didn't. Emma's not the fake type."

I was quiet for a moment. Then I'd flattened my hand against his chest and murmured, "It goes both ways."

His eyes had warmed. "Good."

It hadn't been long after that when conversation ceased, and soon we'd both been groaning.

"There you are!" Sia exclaimed, opening the bathroom door. We were at another one of her events, and it was *the* night. Cole would meet Sia and Jake in a more real way. He would come, pick me up and the four of us would go to Gianni's for a late-night dinner. Cole had the second floor reserved just for us.

The sounds of music, laughter, and conversation swirled into the small room along with her before the door closed again, dulling the noise. Her heels clacked on the floor as she made quick work looking into the three stalls. They were all empty. I watched her in the mirror, noting how her sequined black dress accentuated her body. I had on a soft blue dress. It was light and comfortable—all I cared about. I looked good, but I wasn't sexy, not like Sia. There was a slit up the side, so as she walked, she showed a good dose of leg.

When Jake had seen her earlier, he'd groaned. "How am I supposed to handle seeing that all night?"

Sia had laughed, trailing her finger over his chest, a twinkle in her eyes. "You'll have to restrain yourself until we get back home."

Home.

Jake's eyes had shifted to mine, and I knew what he'd been thinking about. She'd said the H word. He'd confided in me two days prior that he was considering asking Sia the big question: if she would move in with him. He came to me for advice—did I think it was a good idea, how had Sia been with guys who'd asked the moving question before, had she lived with other boyfriends, how did she feel about the landlord. At that point, the conversation had taken a slight hit. Jake never talked to me about my relationship with Cole. Sia assured me he was fine with it, not weirded out, but it hung in the room between us.

"Jake, uh—" I'd started, but he cut me off.

"You think she'd be open to it? To moving in with me?"

A small boulder landed at the bottom of my stomach. There was weirdness. I'd seen it then. Sia lied to me. But it was obvious Jake didn't want to talk about it. So I found myself nodding and feeling a little sad at the same time.

That was a conversation I wanted to try again with Jake. I never did tell him about Dawn's sneakiness with Sia's phone, but this conversation—I was determined to have with him.

Sia stepped up next to me, looking in the other mirror. "I'm ready to puke, piss, and have an orgasm all at the same time," she announced. "Shit. How do you do it?"

"Do what?" The Jake conversation faded to the background of my mind.

"Be around him."

"Who?"

"Cole Mauricio. How do you do it? He just came in, and I swear, the entire room either got wet or wanted to piss their pants. I'm all of the above. That man is like walking sex. Good Lord, do you think Jake can join the mafia with him for a while?"

"Jake?"

Sia half-rolled her eyes, tucking some of her hair into a barrette. "I love Jake, but he's no Cole Mauricio." Her eyes narrowed, growing thoughtful, and she tilted her head to the side. "Come to think of it, though, no. I like Jake just how he is. If there was no you or Jake in the picture, I'd fuck Cole Mauricio. I'm sorry. I'm being a bad friend, but I have to be honest. However, in saying that, I can also say that'd be it. He scares me too damn much for anything else. I'm pretty sure those two massive guys that came with him are carrying guns."

My head spun. I grabbed Sia's arm and focused on the most important piece of information: "You said the L word."

She went still. Her eyes locked on mine. "You caught that, huh?"

"Sia!" I pretended to shake her arm, grinning like an idiot. "You love Jake!" This was huge, huger than huge. "I'm so happy for you."

Her hands rested on the counter. "I know. I do. I'm really happy. I mean—" She waved to me. "I'm worried about you because hello, the mafia—but yeah, I'm happy. I really do love Jake."

"You've never said that about a boyfriend." I frowned. She had. "Not in the real sense, I mean, where you actually do love him."

She laughed, digging in her purse. "I know what you mean, and you're right. I've not said it for real. It's real." She pulled out her lipstick. "It's so real and so amazing, and I know I'm going to fuck it up somehow."

"No." I shook my head. "No way. I know you won't."

"I hope not, but let's be honest. I'm the love 'em and ditch 'em girl. I'd usually be on boyfriend number two after Jake by now." She closed her eyes, taking a deep breath. "I can't mess this up. That's all I know."

I touched her hand and squeezed. "You won't. I know you won't."

"Let's hope not." She grinned wryly at me. "But enough about me; are you ready for tonight?"

I laughed, letting go of her hand. "I think I should be asking you that question. Are you ready to officially meet Cole?"

She groaned, shaking her head. "No. Not a chance. Yes. Oh, God. That's really happening tonight. I saw him and had to come get you. I—I'm nervous, Addy." Her voice dropped to a whisper.

"Don't be." I raised my chin and squared my shoulders. "You can do this, and you want to know why?"

Her eyes met mine in the mirror. "Why?"

I knew Jake was nervous; well, I didn't know what Jake was feeling. But while he'd been geeking out before, the plan to meet Cole in a real-life way had him suddenly quiet. I was optimistic, hoping his closed lips had more to do with him calculating when he'd ask Sia to move in with him, but I knew some of it was about Cole. Sia switched roles again, back to being the one more open to meeting Cole as my—I went blank. Boyfriend?

Lover?

Significant other?

None of those seemed to fit. Cole was mine. I nodded to myself. That felt right. He was mine.

"Addison?"

Sia had been waiting for me. I pulled out of my thoughts. "Oh yeah, because I love you."

"I'm going to handle meeting your super hot and scary boyfriend because you love me?" She scoffed.

I nodded. "Yes. Well, no. It's because you love me. Cole will see that, and he'll like you."

"Because I love you?"

I rolled my eyes, matching her half-grin. "I know. I know. My thoughts are a bit jumbled, but that's the gist of it. Besides, if he didn't like you already, I doubt I ever would've gotten the floor."

"What do you mean?"

She'd been about to apply her lipstick when she paused.

"You know." I shrugged. "You were the one who got the number for the apartment, remember?"

She turned back to looking at herself in the mirror. It was like she hadn't thought about it that way, or something...

I paused now too, my frown matching hers. "Sia?"

"Huh?" She was deep in thought.

"What'd I say?" I'd said something wrong.

"No. Nothing." She shook her head, putting her lipstick away. "Never mind." A bright smile formed on her face, and she rolled her shoulders back, fixing one of her straps. "You ready? I've got thirty minutes left to dazzle the best of them, and then we're off to Gianni's."

"Yeah..." What had just happened?

"Great." Her smile spread another inch. "We should go. I locked the door so we could have our girl time in here, but I've got a feeling some of the socialite housewives aren't going to be happy with me."

"Just tell them you had to fix something."

Sia crossed to the door, unlocking it and pushing it open. She groaned. "God. That's even worse. They'll complain that the Gala isn't 'up to code' or 'appropriate' enough for them. I'll have to hand out champagne for the gift baskets at the end."

She was right. Two ladies, both decked out from head to toe in diamonds, waited outside, and both looked annoyed. One had her arms crossed over her chest and was actually tapping her fingers along her arm. The other harrumphed, "About time," as she swept past us.

Sia met my gaze, a hidden smile lurking there. "Your sexy and very powerful—" She raised her voice on that last word. "—man is in the back section. I sent him there while I came to get you."

I got the message and nodded, trying not to laugh. As soon as the grumpy woman heard *powerful*, her irritation seemed to vanish, replaced by curiosity. She eyed me now, and I could see the wheels spinning. Who was I? How much money did I have? Where was I on the totem pole compared to her?

But then Sia swept in, putting a hand on the lady's arm. As I left, I heard my best friend doing what she did best: charming the pants off that lady, or at the very least charming away any potential complaint she might've had.

I glanced around the crowded room. I'd come early to support Sia, and people had been trickling in ever since. It was nearing the end of the event, and usually people started to leave around this time, so I was surprised at how packed the main floor remained. I didn't see Jake anywhere. Snagging a champagne from a server, I started for the back room. It was darker, with lots of hidden corners, and I knew that was why Sia had sent Cole there. He and I could stand back there and be part of the event, but also be on our own.

I was passing a side entrance when I heard my name.

"Addison."

I turned, a polite greeting on the tip of my tongue, but I swallowed it when I saw Liam's mother. I grew cold. "What are you doing here?" She knew this was Sia's event. This was my territory.

Carol stopped. Her mouth opened as if to speak, but instead she closed it and started toward me.

I looked her up and down. She wore shimmery black pants and a black sweater that crossed over her waist. She looked nice, but she wasn't dressed for an event like this. I couldn't hold back my sneer. It wasn't often that I got to sneer at her. I wanted to take advantage of it when I could.

"You look...nice." I stepped back and made sure she saw my appraisal. Then I wrinkled my nose.

I thought she'd react. I was waiting for it, and I even had another veiled insult ready to go.

She glanced over her shoulder, reaching inside her sweater and she moved closer to me. "I'm so sorry, Addison," she said. "I actually am."

"Wha—"

Her hand flashed out, and I felt the prick of a needle in my neck.

I shoved her away, but I was too late. She blurred in front of me. Two large shapes moved around her as I started to fall. The world was falling with me. Something caught me just as everything went black.

CHAPTER THIRTY

I heard voices first. A woman and a man—and she was pissed. I couldn't make out their words, or even tell where they were, but they were somewhere nearby.

"I said no!" the woman yelled, then she stormed away.

I felt her footsteps underneath me, and a door slammed, making my headache the second thing I noticed. It pounded behind my forehead, like I'd been hit.

I tried opening my eyes, but closed them right away. The light made it worse.

What had happened to me? I tried moving my hands, but I couldn't. They were tied behind me, and I was sitting in a chair. A cool draft chilled my face and feet. I moved my feet around and felt a blanket. The backs of my arms were warmer. I felt heat back there.

I'd been at Sia's event at the Gala.

Cole had been there.

...and Carol. I'd been going to see Cole when I saw Liam's mother—and then felt the cold prick of a needle.

That bitch drugged me.

"Is she waking up?" a male voice spoke, sounding far away. It had echoed a bit.

I heard a shuffle of feet and a second voice. "Nah. Sometimes they fidget in their sleep."

"You sure?"

"Oh, yeah. She'll be out for a while."

"Boss said she's high priority. We can't fuck this up."

"We won't. Stop worrying. It's your turn." Knuckles rapped on a table. Poker chips rattled. "What'll you call?"

The first voice grumbled, his chair creaking. "Fuck if I know." His chair screeched, shoved against the floor. "I swear she's awake."

"She hasn't moved."

That was a third voice. How many were there? The woman, who'd left, and the guy she'd been arguing with and then these three. Their voices sounded from the other side of the room.

And *fuck*. My head was really pounding. I winced, then went back to slack jaw. I couldn't do anything different. No sounds. No movement. Nothing but breathing. I had to breathe normally, as if I were asleep—

Suddenly, my chair was tipped over, spilling me onto the floor.

"Ow!" I couldn't hold back. My eyes whipped open, and I lay sideways, staring at a table of four guys playing poker. A pair of combat boots stepped in front of me, and the arguing male voice said, "She's awake."

I tried to look up, but his face was in the dark. The light above him blinded me, and I heard him say, "Back to sleep, princess."

I saw it coming. His boot lifted and *oh shi*—the world went black again.

"Okay." Something was ripped from my face, and the light was blinding. "Wakey, wakey."

I screamed. Pressure throbbed through my head as I closed my eyes as tightly as I could. I whimpered now, but holy shit. Pain sliced through me, like tiny knives being shoved into my head. A low throb had started at the base of my skull, too.

"None of that."

Someone jerked my chair around. I was upright again and wheeled around to face the other way. The poker table was behind me, but it was empty, or so I thought. My glimpse of it had been so brief but now I stared at three people.

One guy leaned against the wall, tall and lean, with his arms crossed over his chest. This was a fucking Sunday tea party to him. He readjusted, cocking his head to the side. I couldn't make out his face in the shadows. Another guy stood in front of him—the one who'd whipped my chair around. He was dressed in black, from head to toe. A ski mask covered his face, and his voice was disguised by some automated thing.

Like what kidnappers use. My blood turned to ice at that thought.

"What do you want?" There was another person, a woman— maybe the woman from before? I couldn't see her. The room cut back into a small alcove, where she was sitting. She wore clothes similar to the others—black pants and sweater—but she didn't wear a ski mask. I didn't think. I got a flash of white from her neck and her hands folded together in front of her. No gloves. I lingered on the blue ring she wore—it was Carol.

I sneered. "Bitch, you drugged me."

Both men snickered.

Her hands jerked apart. She stuffed them behind her, but she didn't say anything.

"Enough with the pleasantries." Kidnapper guy leaned over me, staring right into my eyes. I tried to recognize his eyes, the only part of him I could see. Maybe I knew him? Maybe I would know him? A flicker of hope sprang to life in me. Maybe that meant they were going to keep me alive? He reached behind me and rested his hand next to my shoulder—the one I was trying to ignore because it hurt. It was the one I'd fallen on. His thumb moved over and lightly brushed it.

The stabbing pain in my head was nothing compared to what I felt in my arm. And with his touch it tripled. It felt like my arm was on fire. A whimper slipped out before I clamped everything down.

A slow, satisfied smile looked back at me. "Good." His eyes darkened. "Now that I know that you hurt, let's get started. Shall we?"

"Fuck you," I spat.

"Ah. Maybe one day, huh?" He kicked my chair again, moving me until I was directly in front of the light. He motioned behind him. "Turn the other lights off."

The room plunged into darkness, except for the light on me. He moved behind the light and pulled his ski mask off, holding it in his hands. "I'm going to make this real simple for you. Answer my questions, and stay alive. Don't answer my questions, and don't stay alive. It's as easy as that. Okay?" But he wasn't waiting for my response. The cool sensation of a blade touched my neck. "You feel that?" He applied pressure, enough to cut my skin.

I cried out, then stifled the sound right away. *Jackass. Asshole. Monster.* I was pissing my pants, but they weren't going to see fear on my face. No fucking way.

"Oh." He laughed softly. "You're a badass, huh?"

"Fuck you." My throat moved against the blade, bringing it tighter. I felt my skin tear, just slightly, and a wave of splitting pain coursed through me. Another wave of curses went through my mind. I gritted my teeth. This asshole—he was going to die. Somehow.

That damn chuckle. It grated on my nerves. Someone removed the blade, and a tether replaced it. My head was pulled back as the tether went tight behind me. My head was locked in place, and the man squatted next to me. I still couldn't see his face. I couldn't look over, just catch a blurred glimpse through the corners of my eyes. His hand came back to my shoulder and lay next to my burning arm. God. So much ached, but I held my breath. I knew what he was going to do.

"So." His thumb rested lightly over where my arm hurt the most.

Just the gentle graze was like a hot poker. I stifled another scream, biting down on my lip.

"Let's get started." He came even closer. I could feel his hot breath on my skin. Even that fucking hurt. "In case you're going to play dumb, I'll spell everything out for you. Over a year ago, your husband had a certain patient from our family, and we're pretty sure that patient shared some information, information he shouldn't have shared."

"What?"

"Your husband."

"Liam?"

"Yeppers, indeedy. That man of yours. He had a patient who told him some things. We're aware it's all supposed to be confidential, right? Patients and counselors, right? But we don't believe this was kept secret, and it don't matter that your husband was one of our own either."

His thumb still hovered over my arm. The burning was building, throbbing now. I blinked, trying to clear my head. I needed to follow what he was saying, but my God, I was hurting. And Liam—why was he talking about Liam? Was this why Carol did this to me?

"Carol?" I called. My voice was hoarse. "Carol, what is going on? Liam? This has to do with your son?"

"Don't." She was a sobbing mess.

The guy next to me barked, "Get her out of here!"

"No! No. I won't say anything." She struggled with someone. "No!"

Then a door opened and slammed shut. Her sobbing was now muffled. "I won't say anything. I promise."

"Shut her up! *Now!*"

The door opened and slammed shut again, this time with extra force. I felt the bang through the floor. Carol screamed, and then it was quiet. It was eerily quiet after that.

"Don't worry. Your mama-in-law isn't dead, just silenced. Now, you're going to tell me what your hubby told you so long ago."

"What?"

"You heard me. What did he say to you?"

I felt his thumb lowering to my arm, his touch growing firmer. I wracked my mind, trying to remember anything Liam had said—I had nothing. "He didn't—he didn't talk about his patients."

"I find that hard to believe." Another centimeter. His thumb began brushing back and forth.

I let out a deep, guttural scream. I had no choice. My hands spasmed, opening and closing, and my whole body jerked on the chair. The pain was crushing me.

"All you gotta do…" His voice was calm, sickeningly calm. "…is tell me what Liam told you. It would've been right before he died."

Died—I bit my tongue. Something didn't make sense. This whole thing didn't make sense. My head felt full and heavy. My neck was weakening to the point that I couldn't hold it up. I strained to see who this guy was, but I couldn't. He stayed just inside the shadow.

"Addison," he murmured. "Tell me what Liam said to you."

"I don't—" My voice was garbled. I could taste my own blood. "I don't know. I swear. He never talked about his patients."

"Come on, Addison."

The man's hand left my shoulder, but he only scooted closer. I could feel his body pressed against my arm. Tears slipped down my cheeks. He lowered his voice; it was almost soothing.

"I know he told you. You can just tell us, and we'll let you go. That's all we want. We actually *want* to let you go." His hand trailed up my arm, sending fresh waves of pain slicing through me. "But in order to do that, we need to know what your husband told you because, you see, we've been watching you. For an entire year, and now three months, we've been keeping track of who you talk to, who you email, who you call, who you see—all of it. When you thought you were alone?" His hand ran down my arm. My body shuddered. "We've been there the entire time. All those nightmares? We have to wonder what caused them. And they've stopped, haven't they?

When you moved, whatever was haunting you stopped haunting you—am I right?"

"Who the fuck are you? You're spying on me?"

He laughed. His breath coated me, choking me. "You were so sad when he died. I got chills watching you at the crime scene. You couldn't move. You were standing on that street corner, your dog going crazy, and you couldn't stop looking at him." His voice was almost seductive. "You must've really loved him. He shattered you, didn't he? You sent everything about him away, even his dog. You sent everything away that reminded you of him, didn't you?"

I drew in ragged breath, feeling tears hot on my face. They slid over cuts, and I winced. I was helpless to stop them.

Liam...

"Yeah." His hand went away, and he drew a knife over my arm. Up and down, like he was trying to comfort me. "But you have to put yourself in our shoes, Addison. You see, we were okay with letting you live. You didn't do anything. I mean, why make two deaths happen, you know? And Carol, she fought hard for you. She really did. We were going to pull you in, make you a Bertal, but she was adamant. She said Liam didn't want that. You were to remain out, but imagine our surprise when you moved into The Mauricio. You went into the heart of our enemy's territory, and suddenly you could sleep again. Makes me think maybe you unburdened yourself. Maybe there was something on your chest, and you had to get it off? Is that what happened? Did you tell Cole Mauricio something you shouldn't have?"

"Did I what?"

The knife stopped. He brought it to my throat and pushed hard—not the sharp edge, but the dull edge. I couldn't breathe; he was crushing my windpipe.

Cole...

"Stop playing around," he hissed. "Answer me! Did you tell Cole Mauricio what your husband told you?!"

"No—"

The knife cut me off. He yelled in my face, his spit landing on my cheek. *"Did you?!"*

I coughed, and kept coughing, He was pushing down so hard, and suddenly I could make no sound. I was choking. I couldn't get air inside.

When you're about to die, all the movies make it seem like time slows down, you get flashes of your life. Maybe those memories are supposed to comfort you. Maybe it's the brain shooting on its last synapses. I didn't know. I knew there were scientific theories, but that was not what happened to me.

I couldn't breathe—that was it. I. Just. Couldn't. Breathe. My eyes bulged, and I flailed in the chair. My arms were everywhere. Despite the pain, I broke through their ropes. My back arched off the chair, but my head was still tied in place...then I was falling...

I hit the floor with a smack.

After I hit the ground, I couldn't do anything. My body shook, all on its own. My mind was slipping away. There still wasn't enough air. My vision blurred, and there were voices. I heard them through a fog again.

A light—one single light burned right through me. Faces blocked it. Shoes hurried closer. I felt them pounding on the floor. A woman screamed. There was shouting. People were shoving, and someone fell.

Then Carol was on the floor, her head turned toward me. Terror lit up her eyes, and she was pale. I would've laughed, if I could. *She* was scared, and *I* was going to die. I saw movement at the door. Hands were touching me, putting me back in the chair. The light was blocked. The hallway door opened, and light spilled into the room. For one brief second, I saw him. I saw the man who had interrogated me. I saw his back, then his profile as he turned down the hallway.

I saw him.

Someone moved in front of me, and the rope around my neck fell away. Then I could breathe in ragged gulps. Someone lifted me, and my eyes rolled.

Blackness closed in again, but I'd seen him now.

I saw Dorian.

CHAPTER THIRTY-ONE

Cold water woke me up.

I turned my head and saw Carol beside my bed. She sat in a chair, a bucket next to her, and she was washing my face with a rag. She wasn't looking in my eyes. She was only focused on my skin. She brought the rag to my shoulder and began moving it lightly down my arm. As she got to my hand, she paused. A line marred her forehead, and she let out a deep sigh. With gentle hands, she picked up mine and examined it, turning it over so she could see better in the light.

There was a draft in the room. She brought the washcloth to my knuckles as I looked around. I was on a cot, tucked into the corner of a small bedroom. A single light bulb hung from the ceiling. I could see into the open closet door. Only a pile of blankets was inside.

Heavy footsteps sounded in the hallway. They grew louder, and I tensed—until they moved past the door.

"You're awake?" Carol now looked at me.

I must've moved my hand. I tried to nod, but it hurt too much. I felt half paralyzed when I croaked, "What did you do?"

Shame darkened her eyes, and she hung her head. The washcloth fell from her fingers, hitting the floor. She cursed and bent to grab it. When she sat back up, she placed it on the table next to the bed. Grabbing the bucket, she rose. "Hold on. I'll be right back."

I wanted to plead with her not to tell the others. *Don't let them know I'm awake! Don't let them hurt me again!* But no words came out. I couldn't get them out, so I lay there and waited, feeling like an opened wound.

She came back moments later, kicking the door shut with her heel. She placed the bucket beside me, pulled out a new washcloth, and brought it to my cheek. I held my breath, waiting for the cold and knowing it would add to my agony, but it didn't. Warm water greeted me instead, and I was relieved for the first time since being captured.

"Thank you," I finally got out, wondering if I should thank her for anything. My voice was a mangled mess.

She didn't respond. She washed the rest of my cheek, then moved to the other one. She bathed my jaw, and up to my forehead. After cleaning my nose, she sat back and dropped the rag into the bucket. Her shoulders slumped and she looked down. "This is all my fault," she said softly. "Every part of it."

My throat swelled. I didn't think it was from physical pain. I couldn't talk anymore.

"I was their eyes and ears on you," she continued. "No one else."

She met my gaze, maybe for the first time ever. The sadness in her eyes—it should have moved me. It didn't. I had no compassion for her.

"Liam gave me a key to the house, and after he died, they asked me to check on you every now and then. I didn't know why. I thought they were worried about you, and that seemed so kind of them."

Who is them? The Bertals?

She moved the washcloth up my arm. I closed my eyes, clinging to her words to block out the burning sensations.

"We weren't a part of them," she said. "Bea always wanted her kids out of the family business. She said it was foolishness. The only way out was a hot bullet, she used to say. I didn't know she did their bookkeeping, not until she died and everyone got their inheritances. Liam got the biggest one. She loved him the most, and there's another part coming to you." She looked up, a half-smile on her face. It was so haunted, it didn't look like a smile at all. "If you get out of this alive, I mean."

She rested her hand on my forehead and moved my hair to the side. "I'll get you out of here alive. I promise, Addison. I'll do it for Liam." Her voice grew watery. "I have to make my son proud, because I know he's ashamed of me. He has to be. I would be. I *am*." Her eyes grew fierce. "I swear I had no idea why they wanted me to watch you. They never said a word. I was just supposed to report if something weird happened, and you moving to The Mauricio was weird. That's when I found out."

Found out what? My mouth opened. I tried speaking. Still nothing.

"They think Liam—no, they *know* Liam had a Bertal as a patient. It was before they realized Liam was estranged from us. Everything went to the shitter after that." She met my eyes again. "There was a war going on back then, and they couldn't determine whose side Liam was on." She swallowed before adding, "The trouble started when Cole Mauricio came back. There'd been peace for a while, but he killed four of our men. That was it then."

I remembered what Cole had said. *"They sent four men... They died. I lived... I came back, and I killed more."*

"We got pulled into a war we didn't want, not at first. We were pissed. Oh yeah. They were pissed. And more of our men died. That Carter Reed, he killed almost all of us. The families all thought he was coming after us, like—"

–like *they* had for Cole's family. *They killed my dad first... My mom was the next week.* Then his three brothers. His older sister. His two younger sisters, the twins. One after another, week after week.

I wasn't crying, not for her. Her hand went to my neck, and she began to wash there. The tears that slid down and fell on the top of her hand were for Cole, for the man whose family she'd helped murder.

A seed started to grow in me. It was small, but it was powerful. It was my hate for this family, the one Liam came from.

"Anyway." She huffed, clearing her throat. Her hand lingered on my collarbone, but I didn't think she really saw me. "They're worried now that you told. That's why we sued you. I didn't want to. We knew Liam bought that home with his inheritance. We had no say in that money. Bea made sure of it. But they needed access to your bank accounts. That was the whole reason, and they have computer guys. I don't get it. They tried to explain it, but none of it made sense to me. They just wanted your bank statements, see if you got paid off by Mauricio, if that was why you were living in his building."

Who was they?! I wanted to know their names, their positions. I wanted to know everything.

"They couldn't find anything, said there were no suspicious transactions."

What? No. I couldn't speak. I couldn't defend myself. Instead my hands curled into fists, and my nails cut into my skin. The pain lessened some of the other pain. I kept digging them in.

"I kept telling them no," Carol said, pleading now. "I know you have every right to hate me, too, but I still love my boy. I wouldn't have done that to you, but they made us. They threatened us, threatened the rest of our kids. We had to. I'm so sorry, Addison. We had to."

She sat back, her hand falling to her lap. She held the washcloth, and it formed a wet spot on her pants. She didn't seem aware of it. "When they couldn't find any incriminating transactions, they went through the house. I tried to tell them there'd be nothing. I knew you took everything personal with you, or it went to your parents."

New horror filled me. I opened my mouth, trying to ask if she'd told them that, but only a whispered scream burst out.

She looked up. Her eyes rounded, and she shook her head. "Oh, no. I didn't tell them that. Just that the dog went to them. They wanted to know, but no way. I wouldn't put your mother in harm's way like that. I told them you put your stuff in storage, but I didn't know where. That's what they were looking for. They wanted to find a key or where you stored it all. They didn't find anything, like I knew they wouldn't."

A lost look entered her eyes. "And when they couldn't find anything, they said there was no other option." She looked at me again. "That's why you're here. They made me get close to you. No one else could, and I knew I only had a little window. You were going back there to stand next to Mauricio himself. He put guards on you. They've been watching you for a while, but always at a distance. Did you know that?" She nodded to herself. "They blended in, but we figured out who they were. For once, none of them were by you. I had to move, or it wouldn't have worked. I think maybe it shouldn't have worked. I should've taken the needle myself, made something up, said you overpowered me, but I knew it wouldn't work. They would've just killed you if I hadn't helped them take you this way."

She put the washcloth in the bucket, and her hand covered mine. She leaned close. "I'll get you out of this. I'll fix it. I promise. But, Addison, you have to tell me—what did Liam say to you?"

I shook my head.

"He must've said something. Why did you move into The Mauricio? Of all buildings, why that one? There was a reason. You went there on purpose. You have to tell us why. What did Liam tell you about the Bertals? What don't I know?"

I had no response. Even if my vocal chords had worked, I still wouldn't have told her a thing. There was nothing to tell. I lifted my shoulders and tried to shake my head again, side to side.

Carol sat back. "You have to know something."

I didn't.

"Addison—" She shot forward again. "You have to tell me. You tell me; I tell them. We're both safe. They said that. He said that. If you tell, they'll consider you family again. Everything will be fine. They'll protect us. Mauricio will never find us. Even Carter Reed, if he joined that family again, he won't find us either. We'll be safe. We could even go together—you, me, Hank. They wouldn't hurt my other children. They'd be safe, and we could be safe too. Just tell me."

I didn't know! If I could speak, I would've been shouting it. *I. Don't. Know!*

She held still, reading my eyes, before slumping back in her chair. "You really don't know, do you?"

She was defeated. She finally understood that I knew nothing. Liam never said a thing.

Her hand rested at the base of my throat, but she was talking to herself now. "This isn't good. They're going to kill you. They won't believe you. If you didn't tell them anything, then why did you move in? It wasn't a coincidence. Nothing's a coincidence." She focused on me again. "Why did you move in there?"

I lifted my hand, pretending to write something in the air.

"Oh!" She shot up out of her chair. "Hold on." And she was gone. She returned with a computer, which she placed on my lap, helping me sit up. The wifi was disabled. I couldn't send an email.

"Here you go." She brought up a blank screen and moved her chair around so she could see what I typed. "Tell me how you ended up living there."

My friend was approached, I typed.

"How?"

She was given a phone number. We called to look at it, and I loved the building. I paused, frowning, then added, **I thought the house was haunted with Liam's ghost. I couldn't stay there any longer.**

"Who was approached? Was it Sia? Was she the one?"

I pulled my hands from the keyboard. I wouldn't answer.

"Addison, come on."

I shook my head.

"They'll want to know. We have to tell them."

I typed out, **No fucking way! Piss off, bitch.**

Carol pulled away. "You don't have to be rude."

My hands were sore, but I extended my middle fingers. Both of them. When she saw, I moved them around in the air. She wasn't going to get Sia's name from me. My hands went back to the keyboard. I was going to type that they could kill me before I'd say, but she murmured, "Maybe *he'll* know. I bet he'll know."

Dorian.

Fear rushed through my body. I was paralyzed for a moment, then I lunged, as best as I could, and tried to type again, but Carol pulled the laptop away.

She tucked it under her arm and leaned close, pressing her lips to my forehead. "I'm so sorry, Addison. I know you love this friend, but he'll know. If it was Sia, he'll know, and if it wasn't, don't worry. She won't be harmed. I have to tell them."

I tried to hit her with my head, but she moved away. I couldn't do a thing to stop her. I was still tied down, just to a bed instead of a chair.

She went to the door and looked back. "I'll make them free you. Get ready. You're going to go home with Hank and me. We'll disappear together. Everything will be fine."

But we wouldn't be. We were so far beyond fine that there was no going back. She was deluding herself, and after she went to him, he would kill Sia. He would kill me, and he might even kill Carol herself.

No, we weren't going to be fine.

CHAPTER THIRTY-TWO

COLE

The tip came in through Ken.

He wasn't told who took Addison. We already knew that. He was told where she was, and we didn't hesitate. We were moving within the hour. I was in the weapons room when one of my men gave me the news I'd been expecting since Addison was taken. He coughed. "Sir, Carter Reed is at the door."

I stopped, knife in hand, and looked at my soldier. He fidgeted in the doorway, and I knew he wanted to run. Right now I wasn't the nice boss, the boss who joked around sometimes, the young boss everyone underestimated. I was the assassin the Bertals had created, the weapon Carter himself helped hone.

I was the fucking head of the Mauricio family staring back at him.

"You're new," I said.

His eyes narrowed before he nodded. "Yes, sir."

"You've killed before?"

Another jerk of his head. "I have, sir."

I pointed my knife at him. "And if they attack right now—if Carter's actually a traitor and he's going to try to kill me, what do you do?"

To give him credit, he didn't hesitate. He rolled back his shoulders and tucked his hands behind his back, spreading his feet evenly. "I'd kill him instead."

The door to the room opened and Carter walked past the soldier, but he paused and glanced at him. "You would, huh?"

The soldier's eyes went wide. His Adam's apple bobbed up and down. "I would. Sorry, sir." His eyes flicked to mine. "Other sir, I mean," he corrected. "But I would. I'm loyal to the head of the Mauricio family and…" He hesitated, glancing to me again before returning to Carter. Their eyes met and held.

My respect for him went up a notch.

"You are not in the Mauricio family in the official capacity anymore, Mr. Reed, sir."

Carter was holding back a grin, but he wasn't here to goad my soldiers. He was here for a whole other reason, and as I remembered that, the moment passed. I tossed my knife in the air, caught it by the handle and sent it soaring past my soldier. It stuck in the wall behind him.

He'd gone still, his eyes not even moving to the knife.

I gestured to it. "Take it. You're going to need more than a few guns tonight."

He stepped to the side, grabbed the knife, and yanked it out of the wall. He nodded to each of us before stepping out into the hallway.

Carter waited until the door closed, then turned to me. "You got his ear. Did you know that?"

I threw him a look. Of course I knew. I wasn't feeling particularly talkative. "What are you doing here?"

His eyes narrowed, looking over the assembly of weapons I spread on the table. "Are you ready to do this?"

"To do what?"

I knew. He knew. I wanted him to say it.

"Start a war."

There it was. "Like you did?"

"That was different."

"How?"

He crossed the room and stood on the opposite side of the table now. He lowered his eyes, studying me. "Do you love her?"

Emotion flickered in my gut, hardening everything again. I scowled, picking up another knife and shoving it into my shoulder holster. It hung beneath a 9mm. "You started a war for the woman you loved."

"I did."

"You finished a second one, too. For her." My eyes cooled. My jaw hardened.

"I did." Carter was waiting.

"So, you flew all this way to ask me if I love Addison?"

"Don't go to war if you don't," he said quietly. He leaned forward on the table. "She's *theirs*. They took one of their *own*. You broke in to take one of theirs—that's how they'll spin this. Are you ready for the fallout afterward? Businesses will be affected. Lives are going to end. Families will be torn apart. You could die. She could die. Are you ready for that?"

"She could be dead already." I waited, keeping myself controlled. There was another question still coming.

He asked it. "Is she worth this?"

A second passed between us. Another. And a third. I waited, and so did Carter. He'd said his piece. This was why he'd come, to test me. I leaned forward, my weapons ready to go, and said what needed to be said, "Yes. She's mine."

Nothing else mattered. Addison was *mine*.

Carter stood back as I took one more weapon and left. He wasn't in the family, not as one who would kill beside us, so he remained behind.

I swept out of the room, down the hallway, and out to the warehouse where my men waited. My arrival was the signal. Everything had been planned. Everyone knew their places, and as I went past them, they followed.

We were going to get what was mine.

We knocked once on the back door of a whorehouse. The door opened, and the bass from the main floor vibrated in the night. Some of the smoke and dry ice floated out, and the person who'd given us the tip stepped out into the alley.

I stared down at her. Hard. "Are you doing this to save your life?"

Addison's former mother-in-law, Carol, flinched, folding her hands together in front of her. She'd pulled on a light jacket but still wore the same clothes I'd seen in the Gala's security footage. I noticed dried blood on her sweater, and before she'd said a word, I noted, "That better not be Addison's blood."

Her head lowered, and I looked down at the top of her hair. But now she glanced back up. Fear lined her eyes. "She's been hurt. I can't lie about that."

"She's in the basement?"

She nodded, unable to hold my gaze. "Yes. I locked the door going to the main floor. None of the girls will bother you. There's a room right when you go down. Four guards are in there. They're supposed to be up here, but they're watching a game right now. Keep going. I counted maybe eight others down there. Addison is in the back room, all the way down on the left side. There's another room back there where the guards take their girls. I couldn't open it to see who was in there, so there might be more men."

"They're going to hunt you down."

Her skinny shoulders shrugged. She looked pathetic. "I'd like to take Addison away with me. She's family." She sounded pathetic, too.

"Not going to happen." I leaned forward. I wanted her to see the disgust in my eyes. "She's not your family. You never accepted her before, and you're using her to get rid of your own guilt. If you were my family?" I held a finger out and touched it to the top of her head, pretending to shoot her. "I'd put two right here." I stepped back. "But that's how I deal with traitors. Addison might be more forgiving."

She drew in a shuddering breath. "Yes. Well. Please, just get her out." Carol took off after that, running down the alley between my guys. I waited for the perimeters to check in, and once they signaled everything was clear, we moved in.

Killing isn't a big deal to me.

It happens. People are here, then they're gone. Carter told me one day my viewpoint was skewed because of my family's past. Fuck if I care. Usually for a job like this, the head of the family wouldn't be in the lead. But I wasn't like the previous head, or even Carter. I wanted to go first. I started to thirst for it. Maybe it was the element of surprise. Maybe it made me feel like a badass. Or maybe—two guys stepped around the corner, and I fired off two bullets, one for each of their foreheads—maybe it was this moment. As their bodies hit the ground, maybe I savored the feeling of stepping over them and continuing on, like they were nothing, like they'd always been there and I was going on with my day.

Whatever it was, I felt alive.

Kicking down the first room's door, I stepped in and put two more bullets in the first guy I saw. One of my men stepped up next to me and took out the second guy. Then we were both yanked backward. We heard the cock of guns readying behind the door, right on the other side of where we'd been standing. As we fell back into our men, someone blasted two holes through the door. I recognized the clip of an assault rifle and lunged forward. I slid past the door on the ground, and shot as I cleared it.

I got one. The other fell as one of my men shot through the holes in the door.

"Let's go." Another of my men slapped a hand on the wall. He was revved up. They were all revved up, and I nodded, jumping to my feet. They didn't wait. They were already kicking down the next door.

I turned and waved for some of the others to move forward. "Keep clearing out rooms." I pointed to five of them. "You guys, come with me."

There was gunfire from the next room. We waited until it cleared, then sprinted all the way to the end of the hallway. I came to the last two rooms. Carol said the one on the left was Addison, but the right one was an unknown.

I hated fucking unknowns.

"Cole." One of my men, Ford, grabbed my arm and held me back. "Let us clear it." He gestured to Addison's room with his gun. "Get your girl."

I nodded, but I had to wait as they kicked down the right door. I heard gunfire as I did the same to Addison's door. And as I stepped inside, my heart stopped. All the adrenaline and buzzing simply left me.

She was strapped to a bed, covered in bruises.

I almost fell to my knees.

I loved her.

I couldn't move, not at first. They had beaten her. Half her face was swollen. One of her eyes wouldn't open. Her throat was black, blue, and a grotesque yellow color. Her hands—I took the three steps toward her, I was falling with each one—her hands had shoe marks on them.

They'd stepped on her.

My mouth dried.

I gripped my gun more tightly, needing the feel of my knife in the other. I wanted to turn around, find one of their men, and gut him. I wanted him to bleed slowly, and I wanted his blood all over the floor when the Bertals came back for their men.

But then Addison's good eye opened, and a shaky calm came over me.

Tenderness like I'd never experienced covered the rage inside. It was like a thin sheet, veiling the blood lust, and I swallowed hard, forcing my mouth into a smile. She had to see me smile. She had to know everything was going to be okay. I would say anything, promise anything, do anything to make this woman feel safe once again.

"Hey," I said softly, kneeling at her side.

Tears welled up and fell down her face, sliding over the bruises.

"Hey." I lifted my hand. I was going to wipe some of the tears away, but I hesitated, holding my hand in the air. I didn't want to hurt her anymore. I loved her. It rushed through me, coating my lungs, my voice, my thoughts. "I have you. I love you."

She just kept crying.

"Addison?" I wiped my thumb over her face, hoping to God that I hadn't hurt her with that slight touch. "Addison, can you talk?"

Her head shook an inch, barely. She couldn't talk, and she just kept crying.

"I love you."

Keep going. Get her safe. Come back and murder who you have to. Those were my objectives. I made quick work untying the ropes. Once the last pulled free, I slid my arms under her and lifted. She was so light, so goddamn light—like she'd lost weight in the day she was gone. I almost stumbled heading back for the door, but took a deep breath and held her tight, securing her so she'd never feel unsafe again. Two of my men were waiting for me. They saw Addison, what they'd done to her, and everyone fell silent. The men stood next to the rooms they'd cleared and watched silently, letting me pass by.

The door that led to the main floor was open now, and a group of girls stood there. They were barely dressed. Some only wore thongs with their breasts hanging out. A few wore lingerie corsets, and all had heavy makeup and their hair done up. When they saw Addison in my arms, I heard quiet gasps. Two of them started crying. Another covered her mouth as they stepped back to let me pass.

One woman stepped outside. One of my men held her back, and her eyes widened. She pointed to Addison as I walked past, heading for the car that had turned down the alley. "They did that to her?"

"Yes," I ground out.

The car stopped beside me, and the back door flew open. Carter was there. "Give her to me so you can get in."

I held her tighter, unable to bear letting her go, even for one second. I climbed in and sat, cradling her in my lap. The driver shut the door, and we were off. My men would follow behind. Once we were clear of the whorehouse, I turned to Carter. "Why'd you come?"

His eyes fell to Addison before he murmured, "We're family. I came to back you up."

I nodded. That was how we were.

My eyes never left Addison the entire ride back home. And when we arrived, instead of going to her floor, I took her to mine and laid her in my bed. We called a doctor, and once he'd looked her over, treated her injuries, and given her pain medication, I let her sleep.

When I emerged, Carter waited in the kitchen, along with more of my men. Everyone knew this meant we were going to war again, but for tonight, I decided we would wait.

I returned to lean against the wall of my bedroom, watching Addison's breathing. After a while I slid to the floor and waited for her to wake up.

I never moved.

CHAPTER THIRTY-THREE

ADDISON

Gentle fingers woke me. Someone was brushing my hair from my forehead, and as my eyes opened, I heard a soft croon.

"Hey, hey." I could hear the smile, then a relieved laugh. "You're waking up. It's me."

The corner of my lip twitched. I knew who it was.

"It's Sia."

I opened my eyes, and there she was, looking like she'd just showered. Her hair was wet, and she was—I tried to lift my head so I could see better. Was she wearing sweatpants and a hoodie? I wrinkled my nose, or tried. She wouldn't wear a ratty-looking sweatshirt. But then I caught the Georgetown logo. It was Jake's. Sia would totally wear her boyfriend's clothes—relish them even.

"Is something wrong with me?" She looked down at herself.

I shook my head. There was nothing wrong. Absolutely nothing. "It's good to see you," I tried to say, and when I actually heard a scratchy whisper, I grabbed her hand and squeezed. I could talk again!

Sia laughed. "Whoa, ease up Miss I'm-Dating-a-Serious-Badass-Now." She slid her hand free, but laid it back on top of mine. She gently squeezed, and tears welled up in her eyes. "It's really good to hear you. I heard you couldn't talk when Cole found you. He's not here, by the way. He had to leave to do something, so that's why I'm here."

I lifted my head, wanting her to see the question in my eyes.

She waved her free hand in front of her face, trying to dry her unshed tears. "I'm an emotional mess. Gah. But I guess that's what happens when your best friend is kidnapped and tortured, and you get woken up when a mafia hit man rings your boyfriend's elevator, right?" She kept laughing, and a note of hysteria edged in. "My goodness. Wow. Okay. If I'm this shook up over what happened to me, I have no idea how you handled what happened to you. How did you handle it? Seriously?" She waited, scrutinizing me. "Do you take meds?" Then she snorted. "Well, I guess you do now, but okay. I'm stalling. I don't even know how to process everything, much less talk about it, but here goes." She patted her hair. It was in a messy ponytail, but that was what Sia did when she was trying to regroup. Her eyes closed. She took a quiet and calming breath, then looked at me again.

I tried to smile. I had no clue if it worked or not. I wasn't feeling the most myself at the moment.

"So…" Her voice wavered. "I should start from the beginning, right? When I went nuts at my own event at the Gala? Honestly, I don't think I'll ever be looked at the same way. I was behind you, talking to Mrs. Gallig and kissing her ass. She was so pissy because she'd had to wait for the bathroom, but then your boyfriend tapped me on the shoulder." She chuckled. "Mrs. Gallig looked ready to pass out. The entire room was buzzing. Everyone knows who Cole Mauricio is now. Word got out somehow, and when he came up to us, Mrs. Gallig squealed. I couldn't tell if she was scared or turned on. It was the funniest thing ever. But that didn't last long." Her voice dipped low. "He asked if you were still in the bathroom, and when he said those words—oh, man. I knew something was wrong. I just felt it. I don't believe in psychics, but if someone told me I was psychic at that moment, I would've believed them. I just *knew*, Addison. I knew."

She paused and laid her forehead against my arm for a moment. Then she was back up. "He had security guards on you. Did you know that?"

I shook my head. Carol told me, but I hadn't known before that.

"I couldn't do a thing. I froze up like a Popsicle. I could only stand there, gaping at your insanely hot boyfriend, and he took over. And boy, he really took over. He started barking out orders, and the doors were locked. Guards came out of everywhere. I think a third of the people there worked for him. Maybe not. I guess not. You wouldn't have been taken if that was the case, but okay. Yes. His guards began sifting through everyone. They searched, like, every person, and after Cole's guys deemed them 'civilians'—their words, not mine—they were allowed to leave. And when I say leave, I mean they were ushered outside. There were men outside the Gala, too. They watched all the people as they left. I don't know why, but they were thorough. I think everyone was on high alert—like, the guards messed up and your kidnappers got away, so they were going overboard to compensate so Cole wouldn't kill them." She gave a soft, slightly unhinged chuckle. "I mean, probably not that, but you know what I mean."

I wanted to ask when she went crazy, but it took too much effort to talk.

"They found you on the security feeds. I guess your bitch of a mother-in-law had good timing because the second you were whisked out, one of your boyfriend's security guards rounded the corner. It was eerie how close it was. In one of the frames, the back of your dress was just disappearing around the corner when he came in."

Sia shivered, shaking her head. "But yeah, that's when I went nuts. I got so mad. It welled up in me, and I let loose. I was breathing fire. I think it was because I was right there. I was in the frame the whole time. I could see myself as I watched Carol stick you with that needle, and then a guy swooped in behind her. Well, he'd been there the whole time, but as soon as she got you with the needle, he turned around and caught you. No one else noticed anything happening. You were there; then you were gone. And after seeing that, I raged out. I yelled. I threatened everyone—your boyfriend, too. I was ranting about Carol. Thank God, most of the room was emptied by then. My business rep won't be the same, but who knows. Maybe no one will mess with me again."

She didn't believe what she said. I could see it in her eyes, but I just squeezed her hand back.

"Anyway, Jake gave me a sedative. He wanted to call the cops, but Cole said absolutely not, and that was it. Cole and his team left, and we didn't hear anything about you until this morning when Carter Reed rang Jake's elevator. Jake was trying to keep it together, but I could tell he was geeking out like he did after the first event. *Carter Fucking Reed was in my living room* — that's what he kept saying once he left."

Sensing another ramble, I whispered, "What did he say?"

"Not much, to be honest. He said you were upstairs at Cole's place, and he wouldn't leave your side, but he needed to. Carter asked if I'd sit with you. He said that was the only way Cole would 'take care of business.' I don't know what that means, and I didn't ask, but here I am. Jake asked to come up, too, but Carter said no. And I don't have a phone. They wouldn't let me bring one up here. If I need to call out, there's a landline I can use." She glanced over her shoulder. "There are two big guys out there, and I'm sure a whole bunch more are stashed away somewhere. Your boyfriend might look like he goes around on his own, but he doesn't. I've seen, like, thirty guys come in and out of this building this morning."

"How long?"

It felt like a rock was stuck in the middle of my throat, and I had to talk around it. When I did, the edges scraped against me, drawing blood. It fucking hurt.

"It's a little after seven o'clock now. I've been with you since about nine this morning. I heard some of the guys talking. They brought you in early this morning sometime. Then Cole made everyone wait or something." She beamed at me, forcing a cheerful note into her words. "But I'm sure he'll be back soon, and you can snuggle up to your big bad boyfriend. By the way, I totally approve after seeing him in action Friday night. If he doesn't say it, I'm telling you: That man is in love with you."

I mustered up some strength. I had to know. "Where?"

Sia shook her head, her mouth curving down in sympathy. "I don't know where he is, but whatever he's doing, I'm sure it's for you. He'll be back. He didn't want to leave you. Even when I got here, he didn't want to go. It took almost everyone convincing him that you'd be fine. Carter Reed was telling him to go, all the guys, or most the guys—and side note, they're mafia guys, so I thought there'd be this whole 'I take orders, but don't say anything else' kind of thing." She shook her head. "Not the case. Your boyfriend's their leader—I got that—but the guys were talking like they were a team or something. It was kind of cool. They all love him. I could tell. But anyway, even Dorian came up and reassured Cole that the entire building was locked down. Guards are everywhere. All the doors are under surveillance..." She trailed off.

It had been him.

Dorian.

It was him—the memory exploded in my head.

The hallway door opened, and the light lit up the room. One brief second...and I saw him. I saw the man who had interrogated me. I saw his back, then his profile as he turned down the hallway.

I saw him.

My entire body turned cold. He was a traitor. And I hadn't told. I hadn't been able to tell, and then I forgot when I woke up. How could I forget? I cursed myself silently, feeling tears of frustration on my cheeks. I had to tell Cole. He had to know.

"Addison?" Sia straightened up in her chair. She winced, trying to pull her hand away. "You're killing my hand."

I had a death grip.

"Addison, seriously. You're going to break my fingers. I didn't know you were this strong—" She squeaked, prying her hand from mine. "Holy shit." She shook it out slowly, feeling her fingers and frowning. "What's wrong?" She started to get out of her chair. "I can get someone. Dorian's here. He can tell you you're safe. No one's getting in here to get you."

I shook my head, jerking it from side to side. She couldn't do that. "No!" My damn voice—it was barely a loud whisper.

"No?" She stood by the bed. "Addison, you're freaking me out. What's wrong?"

"I—" My throat started to spasm. I couldn't talk, or I couldn't rush it, at least. I had to go slowly to get the words out. Taking a big damned calming breath, I forced myself to speak slowly, "Phone. Call Cole."

"I can do that." Sia grabbed the phone next to the bed and held it out. "What's his number?"

Our gazes caught—I had no idea. She grimaced, then perked back up. She began searching through drawers. "I'm sure he's got his number around here…maybe? Maybe not. And you know, they didn't want me to have my phone so I can't even use that some way." She gestured to the hallway. "Let me ask Dorian. I'm sure he has Cole's number."

No, no, NO! I shook my head as fast as I could, but the words wouldn't come out. She left, and along with her, my only hope.

Fuck that.

Every part of my body was hurting, but I slipped from the bed—and crumpled to the floor. I landed hard, feeling stabbing pain shoot up my legs, but I gritted my teeth and scooted to the bathroom. I didn't want to leave Sia on her own, but if she didn't know, maybe he'd leave her alone? It was my only chance, so as I heard her coming back, I grabbed the phone and went into the bathroom.

"Addison?"

I looked back. She was coming around the corner, another shadow behind her. A larger one, and he turned with her, almost towering over her. I paused, the phone in one hand and my other reaching for the bathroom handle. Our eyes met, and his narrowed.

"Addison, what are you doing?" Sia asked.

Dorian's nostrils flared. His hand came down on Sia's shoulder, and he began to pull her behind him. He surged toward me, and I slammed the door shut. I hit the lock a fraction of a second before he was there, yanking on the handle.

"Ms. Bowman." He sounded so damned professional.

I kicked at the door, then regretted it. My ankle began to throb. I grabbed it, just holding on as he knocked on the door again. "Addison, if you tell me what's the matter, I can probably assist you."

Asshole. I couldn't say a word, and he knew it. He'd hurt Sia.

"Addison? Come on." Sia was becoming impatient. "This is ridiculous. You wanted me to call Cole. Dorian can do that for you. That's what you wanted, right?" Her voice grew quieter. "You can do that? You'll call Cole for her?"

"Mr. Mauricio is out handling business. I'm sure he'll call as soon as he's able."

"Yeah." Sia bought it. "You're right." She stepped closer to the door. "Did you hear that? Cole will call us. I'm sure the second he has his phone, he'll call. Dorian's right. Come on, Addison. Come back out. We can both snuggle in that bed of his—have you seen the bed? It should have its own Instagram page. It's like nothing I've seen. Huge. And the sheets?" She groaned. "I felt them before. I'm pretty sure that's Egyptian cotton."

A growl formed at the base of my throat. She wasn't helping, and I couldn't say a goddamn word. I hit the door with my fist, still holding my aching ankle in the other hand. The longer I kept quiet, the better chance Sia would remain alive.

Enough was enough.

I didn't want to involve the cops, but I had no other choice. Lifting the receiver, I dialed 9-1-1 and held my breath, hoping this would save the day without putting Cole behind bars.

"Addison?" Sia pressed against the door.

"Ms. Bowman." Dorian was right next to her. I could see their shoes.

"Emergency. What is your loca—"

The line went dead. I hung up and tried again. Nothing. I kept hitting the hang-up lever to try again, but nothing. I started crying. This couldn't be happening.

"Why'd you do that?" Sia asked, her voice suddenly different.

I froze, phone in hand.

"You yanked out the cord," she said. "Why…I mean, why would you do that?"

No, no, no! She couldn't ask more questions. I tossed the phone aside and began hitting the door with my palm. She needed to shut up.

I kept banging, as hard as I could. Maybe the other men would come in. There had to be more than Dorian. Sia said there were two. I hit the door with my entire arm, then both arms. I couldn't yell, so I kicked with my good foot, too.

I whaled on the door until I heard a loud thud on the other side.

Then I stopped, my heart pounding.

What had happened?

I looked under the door, and their shoes were gone. I heard the soft tread of footsteps, and I gulped as Dorian's feet reappeared.

His voice came through right at my level; he must've squatted down. "If you don't come out of there, I am going to kill your friend."

"Don't," I said, still so hoarse. "Please."

"She'll stay alive, but only if you come with me."

I still didn't know why Dorian was doing this. Who was he, really? I just knew he was a killer. He'd kill Sia. I had no doubt, and I had no options. It was my life for hers. My vision tunneled as panic and icy calm battled within me. I needed a weapon. Looking around, my head felt suddenly heavy, and I couldn't see anything. God, I needed something—the phone! I yanked out the cord that connected the receiver and the base, and tucked the receiver into my…what the hell was I wearing? I had on a shirt and pajama pants. There were no pockets, nothing. I tucked the receiver into the waistband at the back of my pants and pulled them tight to keep it there. I gripped them in the front, hoping Dorian would think I was just scared. Which I was.

With near hysteria slicing through me, and my legs feeling like lead, I scooted back and unlocked the door.

There he was. He had squatted down, and his eyes were so hard. He smirked, looking like the murderer he was. "Good girl."

CHAPTER THIRTY-FOUR

My stomach twisted with disgust.

Dorian clamped a hand on my bad arm and yanked me out of the bathroom. The pain was almost blinding, and I bit back a scream as he said, "We don't have a lot of time. I don't know what you did in there, but if a call got through, you might've just gotten a whole lot more people dead."

Sia was on the bed, her eyes closed and her head bleeding.

"What are you talking about?" I rasped. The pain was almost numbing now as he dragged me out of the room.

He paused, glancing down. "I see I didn't crush your throat enough. You can talk, huh?" His eyes held the same murderous glint as they had when he was interrogating me. "I'll have to fix that real soon."

I could see his grip crushing my hand, but I didn't feel it. Sia had said two men, but as Dorian pulled me all the way from Cole's bedroom down to the kitchen, I saw no one. They were gone.

"Ah. You're looking for help, huh?" He *tsk*ed me. "You're going to be a pain in my ass, aren't you? No one's here, Addison. They're gone, and you want to know why? Because I'm the building manager. I've been with Cole since the beginning, even before he came back. I was one of the first he put in place, so that means they trust me. They all trust me."

We moved through the kitchen to the elevator. Then he let me go. My hip hit the floor with a thump—a fresh burst of agony. Layers of pain on top of more pain. It was all starting to blend.

Dorian put the code in, calling the elevator, and as we waited, he glanced down at me.

He was smiling.

The asshole was smiling.

"Oh, don't give me that look," he said, shaking his head. "You have no idea what I've been through or what I've had to do. Do you know what it's like? I've been loyal to the Bertal family for years, and when they said they needed a rat in the Mauricio family, I volunteered. They told me I was going in deep, and they weren't kidding."

He squatted, looking at me with narrowed eyes. "I buddied up to Cole when he was in hiding. I waited six weeks, and then I made the call. I knew what party he was going to, what car he was riding in. I gave them directions. They were supposed to kill him, and my job was supposed to be done. But it didn't happen that way. The fucker killed them instead. Some of those guys were good guys. They were my friends, Addison."

The elevator arrived. When the doors opened, his hand clamped around my ankle, and he threw me inside. I hit the back wall and crumpled to the floor as he stepped in with me, whistling. He hit the override, and then the button for the basement.

He leaned back, folding his arms, and winked. "We can't have any surprises. Cole and his men are gone. I gave them the location of one of the Bertal warehouses. Told 'em it was another tip. The drive out there is a good four hours each way. The guards left behind are circling the running track. There was a breach by one of the exit doors there, and apparently I saw someone slip out. They'll be searching for a good hour." He grinned, so smug. "All the cameras are down, and the only one who could do anything to stop me is Ken. Too bad someone knocked him out. Oops."

Fucker. "Why? Why are you doing this?"

He laughed, rolling his eyes. "That's the funniest part. This is all because of me, but everyone thinks it was because of you." He shook his head, his laugh lingering. "This all started before your husband died. In a way, it's the reason he died."

I frowned. "What?"

The elevator stopped, but he hit the button to keep the doors closed and locked the elevator in place. "This might take a while, so bear with me. Once I get you in the car, that'll be it. I'll shoot you, throw you in the trunk, and ditch you as soon as I get to my spot. But you can die knowing why you're dying. I mean, I'd want to know."

I sneered. "How generous of you."

He frowned. "You don't have to be snooty. If you don't know want to know…" He reached for the button to open the doors.

"No!" I cried. "I want to know. Please. I want to know."

He held my gaze, studying me.

I held my breath. *Please, God—I need more time.*

He withdrew his hand, folding it over his chest once again. "Okay. I'll tell you, and then that's it." He sat on the floor of the elevator with me, softening his voice. "Your husband was a counselor at Haven Center, the place where my brother, Dusty, was a patient. He's an addict. He was in for treatment, and he trusted your husband because he came from Bea's line and because everything's confidential, patient/counselor privilege or whatever the hell it is. COPA? COBRA? No. HIPPA. That's it. Anyway, apparently Dusty ran his mouth about the family, and about me, too. I'd just been promoted because I volunteered for deep cover. Everything was fine until one day my brother was leaving his session, and as he walked out, a Mauricio walked in. Another fucking patient, can you imagine that? So my bro recognized this guy, and he backtracked. He watched as the dumbfuck went inside and went right to your husband. And you know what those two did?"

Clearly he didn't expect an answer. He barely paused to take a breath. "They shook hands. That was it. That was all Dusty saw, but it was enough. In one instant, your husband went from alive to dead. I heard he was a nice guy. Dusty told me later he probably kept the secrets like he'd promised. But he died anyway, so it didn't matter. Everything got shelved away."

My stomach flipped over. If I'd had anything in it, I would've spewed it out, right on Dorian's feet.

"I was in deep cover doing my thing, keeping watch over the fucking spoiled kid. I didn't find any of this out until I got back, but a war started between my family and the Mauricios. Sure, there's peace now—well, not now, but there was. And we'd had moments of peace before then until the Mauricios, they wiped us clean. A lot of good guys were killed by that fucker Carter and your boy. We kept getting hit, and we had no clue how they found us, but they did. There was a lot of stuff happening at that time. Some of Cole's uncles turned on him—one of them was the reason I was put in place, but then the war was over. They told me to stay put, just in case Mauricio backtracked, trying to find out who tipped off the Bertals about his car. That was the first of two breaks. Cole came back, and guess who he found still in place? Me. I was still there, pretending to be his buddy. But inside I was mourning my friends who died. I didn't know what to do. I had no mission anymore, and I wanted to make someone pay." He rolled his eyes. "I said all the right words, and it worked." A cold gleam resurfaced in his gaze. "Your boy asked me to work for him, and voila! I've been in his trusted circle ever since."

"He made you his building manager." I spat. "How trusted is that?"

"Shut up, bitch." He smacked me across the face.

I tasted blood in my mouth, but I clamped down. No way was I going to cry out, no way I'd give him that satisfaction. I spoke, swallowing some of the blood, "What does this have to do with me?"

"Oh." He chuckled. "Oh yeah. That was all me. I'm sorry. You see, I'm tired of being in deep cover. There has been peace between the two families, so until something happened where I'd be forced to blow my cover, I've been stuck here. I've been busy. I've been looking for a way out. I was the one who gave your friend the building's phone number. I did my research. She was your only friend, and I had to make sure you were the only one she'd actually give the number to. Once I was sure, I slipped her the piece of paper and sat back and waited. I wasn't sure what I'd do if you didn't take the bait, but you did. Eventually."

He shrugged. "I might've given you a push to be sure. I saw the bags under your eyes and figured maybe you weren't sleeping. So there might've been a recording of your husband's voice that I played sometimes. It was on an eight-hour loop. Did that work? Was that what pushed you to come here?"

He seemed eager to know, like a little boy who wanted approval, or even congratulations. I offered nothing, glaring at him.

"Whatever." He leered at me. "But yeah. That was all me. Once I got you here, I knew the conspiracy theories would start. I reported that you'd moved in right away, and the wheels were in motion. The Bertals started wondering if Liam told about me. They didn't think so, but they were still worried." He scowled. "They weren't worried enough, though. They were willing to wait it out, so I had to up everything. I told them you were sleeping with him, and that was it. I'd been holding on to that gem. You never know when you might need an ace up your sleeve, but I had to relinquish it, and it did the trick. They decided to grab you. And now, here we are." He was smiling again. "We're in a position where I have to blow my cover to take you out, and trust me, I am more than willing."

He was almost gleeful as he stood back up and hit the button.

Now. I had to do something. I stalled for time, saying quickly, "You said you got two breaks. The first was Cole coming back to get you. What was the second?"

I was half listening. I didn't care what he was going to say. I reached back to grab the phone receiver still in my waistband.

"Oh." He fell quiet.

Uncharacteristically quiet. I stilled, focusing on him again.

"Yeah. That." His mouth twisted. "It was your husband."

The doors opened.

He stuck his hand out, holding them in place.

"What?" An impending doom rolled in. I felt it coming, covering me like a dark shadow.

"There was a hit on him, but I told you it didn't matter in the end. He died anyway, but it wasn't us."

I shook my head. I knew this. "It was a drunk driver."

"No. The driver wasn't drunk, and no statements were taken by the police. You never knew that?"

"What?" I didn't… I couldn't… What was he saying?

"I have cops on my payroll. Your friend is going to find out, but I can delay it."

Cole said that.

"No." I had it wrong. "No way."

"We weren't the only ones who had a hit on your husband, and we weren't the ones who fulfilled it."

"You're saying—no. I don't believe you."

"Believe me, Addison. It was your boyfriend who had your husband killed. That 'drunk' driver was also *your* driver, until recently."

Carl…

I started dry heaving, but no—I couldn't. It wasn't over. There was no more stalling as Dorian bent to grab me, taking hold of my ankle again. He was going to drag me to his car, but as he started to turn back around, I swung. Everything in me wanted to cry, curl up, and give up, but I didn't.

I swung with everything I had. I was on the ground. I couldn't run away. I'd have to crawl, but I knew I had to fight. I had to make him hurt, even just a little bit. I swallowed blood, tears, and bile as I followed my swing with my entire body. I flipped all the way over, breaking his hold. I connected with his face, but even as I felt the contact, I knew it wasn't enough.

He fell back, but just barely.

I fell against the wall once again, and I could only sit there a moment, stunned. When I lifted my gaze, I knew he was going to kill me. He was going to shoot me right here and now.

His eyes burned with rage, and his hands balled into fists. He stood staring down at me, envisioning all the ways he could hurt me—I could feel his thoughts. A cold shiver went down my spine. A red mark had already started to form on his cheek where I hit him. I got a little satisfaction from that, but it was small.

So fucking small. I wanted to scream.

"You bi—" Dorian started for me, but someone appeared just behind him. She swung, hitting him in the back of his head, and unlike my hit—hers counted. His eyes rolled back in his head, and he whirled around, holding on long enough to see who'd struck him.

Dawn stood there, holding a pan in her hands. She was panting, but as he took a step toward her, she got him again, hitting him across the face and spinning all the way around from the force. She paused—her cheeks puffed out in concentration, her forehead wrinkled—then swung a third time. Right at his crotch.

Dorian fell, slamming into the cement of the parking lot.

Dawn looked back at me. "Cast iron skillet. Figured it was the best to knock him out." She let go, and the pan fell to the floor with a clang.

I frowned, trying to make sense of everything. Sia's words came back to me, *"He has security guards on you."*

"Are you a guard?"

"No." She grinned, looking almost ready to teeter to the ground herself. She raked a hand through her hair, making it more of a mess. "Just the building's shut-in. It paid to be nosy this time, huh?"

I wanted to laugh, but all I could do was cry.

Liam…

CHAPTER THIRTY-FIVE

I should've run. I didn't.

I should've hidden. I didn't.

I should've cried. I couldn't.

I should've raged, thrown something. My hands never left my side.

I should've done something, anything.

But I sat in my apartment, and I waited. That was what I did.

Jake and Sia showed up not long after Dawn knocked Dorian out. She called them, and they came down. Jake called an ambulance, and the cops right after that, and soon the parking lot for The Mauricio was filled with flashing red and white lights and uniforms walking around. The police took Dorian into custody, but I had no doubt Cole would get him eventually. Someone found Ken and loaded him into the ambulance. Dawn went with him, crying because apparently she always brought supper down to him every Tuesday night. They sat and ate spaghetti together, every week for the last seven months.

The paramedics tried to take me with them, too, but I refused. They checked me over and couldn't find any new injuries that alarmed them enough for a trip to the hospital, so I stayed back. There was a conversation I wanted to have. And I wasn't moving until it was done.

So here I was, a few hours later, and I finally heard the elevator start. My panel beeped, and then the door opened. Sia and Jake had been here earlier, but I made them leave. I knew it wouldn't be long before Cole arrived, and I didn't want them here.

I had them leave my bedroom door open, though. I wanted to hear him coming.

And in a way, I did, but I didn't.

I heard the elevator.

I heard when he overrode the code to open my door.

I heard the door open.

I didn't hear him.

There was no sound—as he walked down the hallway, passing the kitchen, turning by the living room—until he was standing in my bedroom doorway. Suddenly he was just there, and even though I was expecting him, my heart still jumped in my chest.

This man, who stared back at me with a fierce light heating up his eyes, his hands balled into fists against his legs, didn't look anything like the tender lover I'd heard whisper "I love you" earlier. No. I saw the killer I always knew was there, who I had witnessed myself, but it was more than that.

I searched for some guilt in Cole. I held my breath just a moment, and I saw it. I felt it.

I saw the rage barely blanketed under his control. I saw the ruthlessness in him. I saw the cold blood that someone with his life would need when they pulled the trigger, or when they had someone else pull the trigger.

My gut flared up, and I knew. He could've done it.

I asked, hoarsely, "Did your family kill my husband?" My throat barely worked, but I didn't think it was because of Dorian's hand. I blanched. I couldn't hold back the real truth. I asked one more time. "Did you kill Liam?"

And I waited.

His chest rose as he drew in a silent breath. He never broke eye contact, and maybe that was why it hurt so much—because I saw it as I heard it. It felt like he was delivering my sentence when he said one word: "Yes."

I only had one response in return. "Get out."

Five Ways To Mend After That Guy Got Past Your Walls

Okay, ladies. It happened. You tried to safeguard yourself against him, but he weaseled past your walls. Where do you go from here? Hopefully, he reciprocates your feelings. You're together now, and you get to enjoy romantic strolls in the park, holding hands, the joys of touching in a darkened theater. Those are the good days. Those are the days you're hoping for, but what if things aren't ending with happy ever after? In that case, you need to move on (again). This is what you do:

- **Booze.** Lots and lots of booze. Normally you're probably careful about your alcohol intake. This is the time you can throw that out. Write it down, then rip it apart. Burn the paper. In this circumstance, the more booze, the better off you are. Just be safe, of course. No driving, no drunk dialing, and know your limits!
- **If alcohol doesn't work for you, go the healthy route.** Focus on exercise. Get a gym membership. Become a runner. Power-walk your ass off. If you can't numb the heartbreak, use it to fuel something productive. Get high off those endorphins, ladies!
- **Music!** Sad music. Happy music. Blues. Folk. EDM. Whatever works. Fill up your phone, and blast it any time you need a dose. Combine number three with number two, and off you go into the healthiest, best-looking you ever. You can combine number three with number one, too. Number three can go with anything.
- **Food.** Now, while I've controversially recommended unlimited booze to numb your feelings, I have to offer this

option with stricter guidelines: Indulge in food for the first weekend only! Ice cream. Pasta. Pizza. Whatever is on your forbidden list, order it in for that first cry-fest. Feel the food. Feel the emotions. Anger. Sadness. Whatever you need fill that hole he left in you, use food, along with booze or music, to help you ease the pain. But when the tear ducts stop working, because eventually they will, put the food away. Start on number 2.

◆ **Friends/Family/Fun.** The three Fs. Use them. Have your friends to take you out, make you laugh—put them through the wringer. That's why they're your friends. Lean on your family. Go to them if you need support, or just to forget reality. If you need to revert back to your early childhood years when everything was safe, go there. Embrace this time when you can be selfish. You're the one hurting. You'll hold them up later, when you *can* hold them up. Until then, be selfish. Enjoy their support, and above everything else, seek to have some fun at the end of the day. That will chase the heartbreak away, little by little. And if all else fails, go on to number six.

◆ **One-night stands.** Getting under someone new can be the best way to jumpstart getting over someone old. But just be safe about it. Don't let a one-night decision, or a more-than-a-few-nights decision, alter your future. And if you go this route, empty a drawer and fill it up with condoms. Take charge, ladies. Don't rely on the guy. After all, that might be why you're in this mess in the first place.

With that said, drink up, eat up, let the tears flow, use the anger, and proceed with whatever helps you endure the pain. You'll have your walls back up in no time.

CHAPTER THIRTY-SIX

I left.

Sia drove me to my parents' house, a few hours away. When the door opened and my dad appeared, wearing his usual blue plaid flannel pajamas, I couldn't hold the tears back any longer.

This was when I raged, when I threw things, when I screamed, when I let everything out. But when it was over, the next week, I wasn't sure who I was grieving: Liam or Cole.

My parents were speechless when they first saw me, but I ignored their reactions. I didn't have the words to explain, so Sia did once my dad had carried me inside. I heard their soft conversation on the porch as I waited in the kitchen, tears pooling on the table. And that night, when they came back in and after Sia asked for the seventh time if she should stay and I told her no again and walked her out to her car, my dad pulled out a bottle of whiskey.

My parents didn't drink a lot. The alcohol was for special occasions, maybe one glass on holidays. But that night, my parents were lushes. My mom kept crying. She'd wipe her tears away, remark that they shouldn't have let me have my space even though I'd requested it, and get a forlorn look in her eye. Over and over. And every time that look appeared, she'd refill her glass.

My dad was much the same, except he wasn't crying. From time to time a murderous rage came into his eyes. His hands curled into fists, and the veins bulged out in his neck. Then he'd refill his glass with whiskey.

After a month, Sia and Jake offered to help pack up my apartment. Of course I would want to move, and of course they understood why I wouldn't want to come back, to face the place where I'd fallen in love with Cole. They understood. They were more than willing to help me move on with my life, but the only problem...every time I tried to think of that, I couldn't. My brain would shut down. The words to answer Sia never came out of my throat, and when we talked on the phone, it was always about my parents, about me being back home, or about her life. She told me about her job, how the Gala was doing great, and how her relationship with Jake was going as well.

I couldn't bring myself to ask her to help me move on. I tried. I did. I attempted to force the words out of my throat. But they never came, and every time after I hung up the phone with her, I was flooded with other memories instead. They weren't the ones I needed to remember, but they were torturous in their own right.

I'd remember the first time in Gianni's, when Cole walked in with his friends. I remembered how I woke up, like I'd been asleep for the last year.

I'd remember seeing him in the elevator, holding Carl up. My body burned as it had then. I felt it all over again, how much I'd wanted Cole, even then.

The sight of him on that running track, how my stomach had gotten butterflies and my palms were sweaty, like I had a schoolgirl crush on him.

Then I'd remember the table at our first dinner together, how we didn't order and went back to my place—the feel of his lips, the way he held me, the way he carried me. The way he made me groan, as I raked my fingers through his hair. The feel of him inside me.

The feel of him all the other times, too.

And I always asked myself the worst question, the one that plagued me:

Did he miss me like I missed him—utterly and completely?

CHAPTER THIRTY-SEVEN

THREE MONTHS LATER

"Addison, can you clean out Taffy's stall?"

"Who was that?" Sia asked over the phone.

I tucked my phone more securely between my shoulder and neck, gave Kirk the thumbs-up, and began heading to the opposite end of the barn. Horses looked up in every stall as I passed by.

"That was the guy I'm helping," I told her. "My mom got tired of me moping around the house. When the barn manager for our county fair mentioned he was looking for volunteers, guess who she suggested?"

"She didn't."

"She did."

I stopped halfway to Taffy's stall. My bags were stashed next to the food bins. I grabbed some of the apples I'd brought and kept going. When it came to the alpha mare, I'd learned bribes went a long way.

"It's been fine for the most part, and honestly, it really does get me out of the house."

Sia made a noncommittal *Mmmmm* sound as Taffy stuck her head over the stall door. She had large doe eyes and a long white blaze down the middle of her brown face. Her nostrils flared as she smelled the apples, and she nuzzled against my hand.

"Besides, some of these horses have better attitudes than humans," I told her. "Like this one." I ran my free hand up the front of Taffy's face, all the way to her forelock. "Oh, yes. You, Miss Taffy. You're a bossy mare, aren't you?"

"Are you flirting with that horse?" Sia asked.

I laughed and grabbed the phone, switching it to my other ear. Taffy picked up the apples and pulled her head back, content to let them drop in her stall so she could eat them.

I leaned against the stall door. "I am, and I don't care."

Sia laughed, then was quiet a moment. "You're not coming back, are you?"

"What?"

"You sound happy. Or, well, you've been sounding happier the last few times on the phone. You're not coming back, are you?"

I could hear her disappointment. "Uh…" What did I say? My stuff was still there. Waiting. Gathering dust. Sitting alone. "I don't know, Sia. I really don't."

"I still had hope since you keep turning us down, but now I can hear it in your voice. You can tell me. You're really not coming back."

I looked at the ground, holding my phone so tightly. My throat swelled. "Uh…"

"Never mind. I didn't say that to make you feel bad. I'm sorry. I just—I'm going nuts not having my best friend here."

"I know." I sucked in a breath. "I'm sorry."

Her voice dropped to a whisper. "I think Jake's going to propose." She rushed on before I could say anything. "I have no proof. It's not like I found a ring or anything, or even a receipt, but every time I go on his computer, ring ads pop up on the side. And when I'm searching for clothes, suddenly dress ads have started showing up, so that means he's looking, right?"

I already knew he was. Jake had called a week earlier to ask for my "permission." He'd laughed as we talked, but I heard how nervous he was. "I know you're not her mom and dad, but you're the reason I met her, and you're her family," he'd said. "I figured, well, this feels right to be asking you. I'm going to ask her parents, too, but to be honest, she's way closer to you. I know it'd mean more to her if I asked you, so here's me—" He laughed again, ending at a high pitch. "—asking you if I can marry your best friend?"

"Yes," I'd told him. My cheeks had hurt from smiling during that conversation. "A thousand times yes. She loves you so much."

"Yeah?"

"Yes!"

He'd sounded so happy, and it'd been a struggle to keep quiet since then.

"Well, if he does, he's a very smart man," I said now to Sia.

She snorted. "You're damned straight he's smart. He was a genius to seal the deal with a quickie that first night. Insta-love, Addison. I swear. It was during that first dinner at his place, after we found William's stash—when he finished and before quoting Derek's T-shirt."

"Do I want to know this?"

"You remember that shirt? Or wait. Was it his coffee mug? I think it was a mug. God…" She chuckled. "He brought his own mug to a dinner party, and he still does! The same one. *Don't Worry, I Won't Byte,* it says. When we were in the bathroom, Jake said, "Don't worry, I *will* byte." And then he spelled out byte as we climaxed. Okay. Yeah, that was too much information. But I was laughing so hard." She still was. After a moment she composed herself. "That's when it happened. That's when I fell hard for him. I just didn't know it till later."

"Well, that *is* a good story." I had to give her that.

"Not too much information?"

"Oh no, definitely too much info, but it's fine." I was smiling like a dumbass, and I knew she was, too. Taffy nudged the back of my shoulder, and when I turned back around, she sniffed my hand. "I should go. I've got a certain mare looking for food. She's eying my phone like it's her next meal."

"Okay. Listen, uh—before you go, I have to tell you something."

My stomach dropped. "What?"

"I saw him the other day."

I knew instantly who *he* was. My throat started to burn.

"He's lost weight." She faltered, coughing to clear her throat. "He's not around that much. I mean, I never used to see him at all, but that's according to Dawn."

My heart pounded. I always felt like I was holding my breath when it came to Cole.

"She said he's been gone, but now he's back. We saw him in the lobby the other night. Jake and I were leaving with Doris and William. That's who we've been reduced to hanging out with—our hippie retired neighbors, who are awesome and hilarious. I need to add that. Oh, and Derek is going to ask Dawn out. We had another resident dinner the other week, and she apologized to me for some phone thing. I had no idea what she was talking about, but she kept asking questions about Derek the whole night, so I think he'd already asked her out. I think she's thinking about it. I hope, anyway. She seems less obsessed with Jake, so that's a plus."

"Sia?"

"Yeah?"

"Cole."

"Sorry. I get nervous when I talk about him, you know? But okay. Yes. We saw him. Doris and William were freaking out afterward. I think William had toked up right before we left. He was more nervous that Cole was going to kick him out because there's a no-drug policy—which is how ironic? The landlord is a mafia boss, and there's a no-drug policy—"

"*Sia!*"

"Okay. Yes. I know. Uh…he asked about you."

I figured. "And you said…?"

"I didn't know what to say, so I just babbled. Gah. I never get like this except when it comes to you and him, but man. Addison, why did you leave?"

I was instantly hot and cold, all at once. "Because he killed Liam."

"Yeah, but…" Her voice got so quiet. "It just doesn't feel right. I don't think he'd be this wrecked, not if he really did do it, or ordered it. You know?"

What was going on? "Is this why you guys stopped talking about moving out? You don't believe he did it?" Taffy kept nudging my shoulders and arms. I ignored her. "Cole said he did." Man. I drew in a breath. I'd just said his name, out loud. It'd been so long…

…so long.

"I know." Sia sounded quiet now, like she'd shrunk in size. "I know, but…what if he lied, Addison? Have you thought—"

I didn't want to think about that. I could feel my throat close up. "I, uh, I have to go, Sia," I cut her off.

I was about to hang up.

"He asked if you were happy."

I stopped, my finger poised over the end call button. I couldn't breathe. My lungs were on fire, and I gripped my phone like a lifeline. "What'd you say?"

She rushed out, "I told him you were. He seemed happy to hear that. So, yeah. There you go. I'm sorry if I wasn't supposed to say that to him."

"No, no." I shook my head. I didn't know what to say.

He'd asked about me.

He knew I was "better."

He was happy to hear that.

I couldn't… I couldn't put together a thought, so I choked out, "I have to go."

I hung up before she could say anything more. My phone went in my pocket, and I stood as everything whirled—twisting, shaking, and churning inside of me. A hurricane was caught inside my body, and I could only stand there and stare at…I looked at what I actually was focused on. A piece of straw on the floor. A single, sad, lonely piece of straw. I felt at one with that straw right then.

I missed him. I felt the tears threatening to spill and blinked rapidly, brushing my hand over my eyes. They couldn't spill. Not anymore. Not still.

I needed to get over him. He'd told me he killed Liam. I shouldn't be feeling any of these emotions. I shouldn't even be thinking of him.

He should be dead to me, but my God—as I turned toward Taffy, I knew that wasn't ever going to happen. I would keep trying, but I knew Cole would always be a part of me, no matter how wrong it would be to go to him.

An hour later, I was sweaty and covered in dirt and straw when Kirk stopped at the stall. He rested a hand on the opened door and looked inside. "I didn't realize her stall was that messed up. John must not have mucked it out on Tuesday like he was scheduled to."

"Nah." I paused and wiped an arm over my forehead. "I took my time with Taffy before I came in. It's fine."

"Still." He frowned, eyeing the corners. "It should probably be rinsed out." He gestured outside. "Go ahead. I'll finish up. Taffy can stay in the other stall for the night."

"You sure?"

"Oh yeah. Besides, you got a visitor."

"I do?"

There was no warning, no car parked outside, no giant-sized security guards at the entryway—none of that, but a tickle started in the bottom of my stomach. I didn't need to ask who it was. As I stepped out from where Taffy was nudging my shoulder, I knew. The tickle grew. I walked through the barn, and it kept growing. Past the stalls, out to the cement stairs in front of the barn, and I felt him. He was right there, waiting for me, his hands in his pockets and his head turned away.

I drank in the sight of him. A buzzing started in my ears. I ignored it.

Sia was right. Cole looked thinner, and the bags under his eyes made me ache, but he looked so beautiful. A part of me hated that, a part of me loved it. I wanted to launch myself at him and feel his arms wrap around me, but I didn't. I couldn't. Instead, I stood there, and my mouth watered. His dark hair looked like it had been recently cut short again, a crew cut, and he wore a snug-fitting shirt over jeans. He looked lean, dangerous, mysterious, and altogether too gorgeous.

Then, as if he felt me the way I'd felt him, his head turned to me. His eyes. God. I stifled a sigh. I had missed his dark eyes and those long eyelashes.

A shadow crossed over his face before he asked, "Can I be here?" His voice was low, raw-sounding.

My heart dipped, hearing the pain there. "What do you mean?"

"Can I be here? Is that okay? If it's not..." He hesitated, his head lowering as he winced. "I can go, if you don't want me here."

I did want him. I *do*. I only said, "It's fine."

He gestured to an alley beside the barn. "Over there?"

The barn was tucked next to the wall surrounding the fairgrounds, so the alley was empty, except for two horses being primped farther down. They were tied to the wall, and their owners were combing them, but they were too far away to hear. They didn't pay us any attention.

Cole didn't say anything right away. Neither did I. My mind raced. *He was here. He had come.* I should've hated him on sight. I should be throwing up right now, or pulling out a knife to stab him. I did none of those things. I clasped my arms behind me because they wanted to touch him. Disgust filled me, but it was at myself, not him.

"Horses?" he asked.

"My mom volunteered me." Because I kept walking down the road to watch our neighbor's ranch. Because I took my dog for walks, and I never meant to end there, but I always did. Because when I looked at the horses, when I watched them, when I was around them, I felt like I was with Cole. It was all about him.

"I didn't kill him," Cole said.

Liam? My heart lurched, pressing against my chest.

"Dorian. I don't know if you wondered, but I didn't kill him. I handed him over to the Bertals, figured they'd deal with him on their own. They'll execute him, because he's the reason we broke into their whorehouse. I was going to kill him, for what he did to you, but then there'd be another war. One war took your husband already. So I handed him over." He was almost whispering, "I did that for you."

I couldn't... I could only blink at him. "What?"

"Dor—" He started to say again.

I interrupted, "I don't care about Dorian. Liam. I care about him." I cared about the reason I couldn't be with him, whether he really had killed him or not.

Sia's words echoed in my head, filling me with so much hope, too much hope. "But...what if he lied?" I'd only asked him once. He'd only answered once. He could've...maybe guilt made him say those words? He'd felt bad that I was attacked and kidnapped? He'd said that word to push me away? Because he was in the mafia, and he wanted to keep me safe? Sudden and ridiculous hope overwhelmed me. Maybe, just maybe. Did I dare voices those questions?

Suddenly, a savage curse left him. "I should go. I came because I wanted you to know that. I'm sorry. This was a mistake."

"Did you lie?"

He froze, his eyes clinging to mine. Or maybe I was the one clinging to him? I wasn't sure anymore. He didn't say anything, so I asked again. "Did you lie to me?"

"What are you talking about?"

"You didn't come to tell me about Dorian." I knew that much. "You could've told Sia. She could've told me. Why are you here?" My heart pounded, deafening in my ears, and I took a step toward him. I licked my lips. I couldn't keep my hands behind me anymore. I felt them reaching for him. I just wanted to touch him, just once.

One last time.

But then—

His mouth was on mine.

Finally. That was all I thought as I sagged into him.

He pushed me back against the barn. His hands cupped my face, and I kissed him back. Four months of anguish poured into that kiss. We were both starving. We tried to fill each other up, erase the hunger that had been there. I pressed against him, needing more, just needing so much more. As hungry as his lips were, mine were ravenous. As demanding, as tender—I matched him and wound my arms around his neck, lifting myself up on my toes. I couldn't get close enough.

I had him.

I was in his arms again. I didn't care about anything else. I just wanted him again.

I heard whispered laughter—it was the horse owners—and I ignored them. He didn't. He pulled away and stepped back. I went with him, but he touched my shoulders, holding me in place so my arms had to fall away. His hands went back to his sides. "I'm sorry. I didn't come here for that." He raked a hand through his hair.

"Then why did you? Did you kill Liam? Did you lie to me?" *Please say you lied. Please.* I wanted the feel of his lips on mine again. I wanted his arms around me. One last night.

He shook his head, pain tightening his features. "I didn't. No."

"What do you mean?"

Did that mean…? He didn't kill Liam?

"I didn't lie to you."

The ground fell from underneath me. Again. I looked down, as if I could actually see the black hole under my feet.

"But—"

I lifted my head.

"My family did."

"What are you talking about?"

"I told you some of my uncles betrayed me. Do you remember that?"

I nodded; my head felt so heavy. "Yeah." Why did that matter?

"One of my uncles ordered the hit on your husband. What Dorian said *was* true. But I had no idea until he told you himself. There's a hidden camera in the elevator. He must've forgotten about it. I heard everything he said to you, but it doesn't matter who it was. I mean, he lied about Carl. It wasn't him that killed your husband, but he was somewhat right. It wasn't me who ordered the hit. But it was my family, and it was one of our other drivers."

His eyes gleamed with unshed tears. "As for what you asked before, you're right. I could've had Sia tell you." His mouth opened. He was about to say something, then the look in his eyes fell flat. He seemed depleted now. His shoulders dropped. "I should go. This isn't fair to you."

"Then *why* are you here?"

He paused, torment evident on his face, and he let out another soft sigh. "Because I couldn't stay away."

CHAPTER THIRTY-EIGHT

"Hey, Addy."

I looked over from the kitchen. "What?"

He lounged on the couch in his boxers with a newspaper opened on his lap. Frankie ran to him, wagging his tail, and Liam's free hand petted him. "What's an eleven-letter word for requiem?"

"Are you joking? How am I supposed to know that?"

"Wait. Lamentation!" He gestured to his laptop. "The good ol' world wide web."

Then everything switched, and he gazed at me, somber all of the sudden. "You know," he said, "we don't talk about that stuff, but I don't want you to do that for me."

My stomach got a funny feeling. "I don't like where this is going. You want pizza tonight?" I picked up the phone. "I'll order it."

"I mean it. If something happens to me, don't waste your life. I mean, yeah, be sad. Be really sad. Look at me." He gestured to himself. "I'm a fine piece of ass. I'd mourn myself, too, but after a while, move on, okay? Promise me. Don't feel guilty about being happy, even after I'm gone."

My mouth went dry. "You're not going anywhere."

"Promise."

"Okay." I rolled my eyes. "I promise."

"He knew," I said, remembering.

"What?" Cole asked.

But I spoke to myself. "He knew something was going to happen. He was trying to tell me." I felt the same funny feeling in my stomach. "Two days before he died, he knew something was going to happen."

Cole stepped close.

I closed my eyes, feeling his warmth so near. I could turn and bury my head in his shoulder. He could hold me. He could make me forget everything, which is what he'd been doing. I'd forgotten about the reality of this life, of the mafia. I'd lost one love already. I couldn't lose another one. I couldn't lose Cole. I'd never survive.

I looked at him. I *really* looked at him.

He could be killed right in front of my eyes. It could all happen again. I should say no. I should walk away. I should leave, never see him again. I could do it. I could do all of that, though it would leave half of me bleeding on the ground right now.

I couldn't.

The truth resonated inside of me. It'd been four months. Four months of me believing he'd killed Liam. Four months of trying to let him to go, knowing I should hate him, that I should never want to see him again.

Four months of hell.

Four months of aching, because I couldn't do any of those things. I only missed him. I only loved him, and right now, as I stared at him, studying him, I knew what I was signing up for.

I opened my mouth, ready to share everything I'd just been thinking, when his words halted my own.

"I live in a building with other residents. Carter thinks I'm stupid. Yes, I'm in the mafia. Yes, you were pulled into this even before I came into your life. Yes, I can imagine that this is all a horrible story. But it's not a mafia story. It's a love story, and it's one that you should want a quick exit out of, but hear me out." He moved closer, lowering his voice. "*Please.*"

He didn't have to ask. I was already listening, and I knew I was looking at him with so much love. It must've been shining from me. How could he not see?

He started again, taking a step closer. His voice was so soft. "I live in a building with other residents because I used to live in a barn." He wasn't looking at me, like he couldn't bring himself to do it. Like he was ashamed. "That's ridiculous, isn't it? I'm the head of a mafia family, and I don't ever want to be alone."

"Cole—"

He raised his voice, but he still didn't look at me. "It's why I have people living there. It's why I liked to go to your place, not mine. It was never about not wanting you at my place or having it be a secret or anything. I lost everyone in my life. I lost Carter, too. It was just me for a long while. Me and—" He gestured to the barn behind us. "—horses. That's who I lived with. I didn't let myself love the family that helped me. I wouldn't because I knew one day someone would come to kill them. I knew every person in my life would eventually die. And they did. I lost three good friends. I have lost a *shit* ton of people, Addison."

He was right in front of me now. Living. Breathing. He was so warm. He looked at me then, and instantly I felt the difference, like he gave me oxygen. He touched my hands, interlocking my fingers with his. I felt the heat emanating from him. It was wrapping me in a safe shelter, pulling me in, tempting me. I leaned toward him.

"I'll always lose people. That's the life I live."

I bit down on my lip. It was all I could do to keep from wrapping my arms around him, pulling him to me, sinking my fingers into his shoulders, holding him close...

...never letting him go.

"So I won't."

My eyelids flew up. "What?"

"I won't ask you to come back. I shouldn't have come."

"What?" I had to ask again. This wasn't what I wanted.

"I'm letting you go."

He held my hand and pressed his lips to my forehead. It was a farewell kiss. He was pulling away.

"Goodbye, Addison."

"Cole," I started. If anything happened to him…

He turned to go, but I grabbed his arm.

Images flashed in my mind. When he walked into Gianni's.

The elevator.

The running track.

Our first night. Our second night, when he stepped off that elevator and held me.

The fundraiser night, when everyone was staring at Cole, who was staring at me.

When he came to me that night.

When he left to protect me at the horse ranch.

When I drove him home.

And the last time, as I was strapped in that bed. The gunfire, and then he'd opened the door. He'd saved me. I remembered his words, *"I love you."*

"You told me you loved me," I blurted.

"What?"

"When you saved me. I heard what you said to me." I let go of his arm and touched where his lips had been. My fingers lingered there. "You told me you loved me." I made sure to look right into him. I wanted him to know the truth, *my* truth. "I love you, too."

His mouth twisted, looking pained. "Addison."

I grabbed his shirt. "I love you."

"No, Addison. I'm letting you go. I'm trying to do the right thing. I'm in the mafia. That'll never change."

It didn't matter. I shook my head. "I'm standing here, and I'm staring at you, and I'm thinking all of those same thoughts. He's in the mafia. He's dangerous. He could die. I could see him die." I dipped my head, but I kept looking at him, holding his gaze. He needed to see that I meant every single word. "I could see *you* die. All over again. The same nightmare. But it doesn't matter. That's the truth that keeps hitting me. It. Doesn't. Matter. My heart might still be pounding. I might still be walking, talking, breathing when I'm away from you, but I'm not living. That's what I've realized these last four months. I could wait another three, another six. It doesn't matter, because it's you. I'm choosing you, just like I chose you the night we were attacked." The words wrung from me. "I *choose* you."

He paused, looking right back into me, and I saw the wall lift. It was staggering. The relief. The sadness. The hope. He was like me, struggling to do the right thing, to walk away, but we were wrong. To stay— that was the right thing.

He crushed me to him. His mouth on mine, once again, where it was supposed to have been this whole time. I felt his desperation, still as hungry as I was.

He murmured, his words a caress against my skin, "Thank God."

Then he kissed me, and I hoped he'd never stop.

EPILOGUE

SIX MONTHS LATER

"I love you."

I grinned before I even opened my eyes. This was how every girl should wake up every morning. Cole's lips touched mine again before he moved down to my throat. I raked my hands through his hair and asked, with my eyes still closed, "Why do you love me?" I loved when he told me.

He laughed, his breath tickling my skin. He kissed my neck. "I love you because of the way you laugh. You didn't laugh in the beginning, but now I just want to make you laugh all the time."

I opened one eye. "Yeah?"

He grinned, his eyes twinkling as he kissed the right side of my neck. He was stretched out beside me, leaning on one of his arms. He murmured again, "I love you because you go running with me every morning. Well, most mornings."

I barked out a laugh now. I hadn't gone the morning before. Sia's bachelorette party had proved too much of a hangover for me. But Cole had come back and awoken me in a whole other way. I was hoping for a repeat today.

I opened my other eye. "Come on. Keep going."

His eyes darkened, and he dropped a light kiss to the left side of my neck. "I love you because you go riding with me, and you don't mind mucking a stall or two."

I groaned. "It's so hard to come back to the city every time we're at the ranch. It's beautiful out there."

He shifted, moving farther down, and I felt his lips in the valley between my breasts. His free hand moved to cover one of them, his thumb rubbing over my nipple.

I murmured, "Keep going. I'm loving hearing all these reasons." I winked.

He shook his head, just slightly, before he pinched my nipple.

"Hey!"

He ignored me, running his tongue around the nipple.

"I love you because you crashed Dawn's Tuesday Spaghetti Night with Ken."

"It's not fair. If she gets to eat with Ken, I want to eat with him, too." I stuck out my bottom lip, remembering Dawn's protests. "She acts like she's the only one who can be sneaky, or eat with Ken. She's not the only one who adores him."

"And." He moved up, gazing down into my eyes. His hand raked through my hair. "I really love how you embrace everyone in your life."

"Oh." That one touched me more the others. He wasn't talking about Sia, Jake, and Dawn, or even Ken. He wasn't referring to the rest of the residents in the building. He was talking about Emma, who had become a close friend over the last six months. My throat closed with emotion. "I'm the one lucky to have Emma as a friend. She's a good person."

"She's family to me. I know you made more of an effort for me." He dropped his lips to mine, whispering there, "Thank you."

"Sia's still a little afraid of her." I laughed lightly, my lips brushing over his. "I love Sia, but I think that makes me like Emma even more." I sobered. "I wish they weren't leaving tomorrow."

Emma had flown in for Sia's bachelorette party. Cole spent the evening with Carter. I didn't ask what they did, but when I came home, there'd been paintball gear left on the kitchen table. I had a hard time imagining Cole and Carter Reed playing paintball, but I guess it was ironic in a way.

"We're flying to see them in a few months."

"That's right." I nudged him, bumping my hips up against his. "I don't understand why you lied to me before. You could've told me you were part owner of The Octavia."

He smirked, snaking an arm under me. He pulled me tight, tugging my body down until he fit right between my legs. He settled in, and I could feel him there, pressing against my opening. His eyes grew more serious.

He brushed some of my hair from my forehead, his touch tender. "I own a lot of places, and you could've researched the owners of The Octavia. I worried you would find out about me sooner than I intended."

"About you being in the mafia."

He nodded, his eyes watching mine. "I didn't mean for you to find out the way you did. I wanted to tell you. I just..." He hesitated, drawing in a deep breath. His chest moved against mine. "I wanted to make sure it would stick, what we had."

"You didn't think so after you flew me out there?"

"I hoped." His smirk morphed into a rueful half-grin. "I more than hoped."

An ache stirred in me, and I wound my legs around him, pulling him into me. The love talk was nice, but I was becoming impatient. When his eyes met mine, I murmured, "I'm glad everything happened the way it did."

"Yeah?"

"I was already falling in love with you then." I remembered the jittery feeling in my stomach, the confusion, the euphoria. It was there, but I hadn't wanted to identify it. I hadn't been ready.

He brushed his thumb along the side of my mouth. "I love you."

"I know." I laughed as I pulled him down. I met him halfway, my lips searching for his, and then I said, "Now show me. Again."

And he did just that.

THE END

Stay tuned for more Carter in *Carter Reed 3,* coming soon!

For more details, go to www.tijansbooks.com.

ACKNOWLEDGEMENTS

Oh boy. I started writing *Cole* so long ago. It wasn't intended to be a secret project, but my creative process was blocked to the book I was supposed to be writing. The characters in Cole just kept popping into my head and so a little over a month and a half, I had the first rough draft done. I didn't tell a lot of people, just a few because I wanted to surprise everyone and now I'm writing the acknowledgements. The feeling is very surreal. I can't believe it's almost ready to go for everyone to read! Thank you, thank you, thank you to my agent (Kimberly), my team that always is there when I need something either critiques or just reassurances: Debra, Cami, Eileen, Heather, Autumn, Paige, Chris, Kerri, Kara, and Pam! You guys are amazing! And Elaine, the best formatter ever! ;) You always work me into your schedule and you have no idea how thankful I am for that. And Jessica!! Gah. You're a miracle worker and so extremely patient, flexible, and just amazing to work with. Thank you guys!!

And the Tijanettes! You guys have no clue how that group helps me out. You guys make me want to keep writing. I mean, I'll always write. I have to because I'm addicted to writing, but there's been some days when I've felt crushed and I saw a post in there that took some of that feeling away.

Thank. You. So. Much!

NYT & USA Bestselling Author
TIJAN

CHAPTER 1

Douchebag's here.

That was the first thought that went through my head as I crept into our apartment. It was my apartment—*mine*—and I had to slink inside because my roommate's boyfriend was a pervert. I always snuck in when I saw his car in the parking lot, but this time was different. They were in the living room and my roommate cried out. I heard the slap next as he backhanded her and that stopped everything. I couldn't move, but I could see them. Then he growled at her to shut up before he went back to his business. She still whimpered, but quieted as he kept thrusting into her.

I couldn't look away.

He was raping her.

Sickness blasted me. I couldn't believe what was happening in front of me.

He kept thrusting as he held her down in front of him. His legs held her trapped and he was leaning over with one of his hands holding both of her wrists together. He kept going. My roommate lay there in surrender. He had defeated her, broken her, and I was witnessing it all.

Vomit and hatred spewed up in my throat, but I clamped them down. They wouldn't burst out of me, not when I had a chance to do something that I knew I would regret. But even with that thought, the decision had already been made in my mind.

Mallory cried out again. Her agony was heart-wrenching. My hand trembled before he ordered her to shut up again. Then he thrust harder, deeper. He kept going, clueless as to who else might've been in the apartment.

This was my home.

This was her home.

He was not welcome, but he didn't care. He kept going into her. Then he growled in pleasure. The sound of it went straight to the pit of my stomach. I wanted to spew my guts once more, but instead my eyes hardened and I went to the kitchen. There was a whole drawer of knives, but none of them would do. Not for him.

I went past the kitchen and knelt at the floorboards of our patio. I removed one of them and gripped the box that I knew my brother would've hated to know I had. Another scream ripped from behind me and my resolve grew.

My arm didn't shake.

I found the gun my brother had never wanted me to know about. I gripped it and lifted it free from the box before I put the floorboard back together. Then, with my heart going slower than it should've been and clearer eyes than I should've had, I turned for the living room again. The sounds of his thrusting continued. The couch slammed against the wall with each thrust. My roommate cried out with each movement. It never seemed to stop, but I held on tighter to the gun before I turned the last corner.

He had readjusted them. He sat her up against the wall as he kept pumping into her. Now her head bounced against the wall. She was pale as a ghost; fresh tears fell over the dried ones. Her eyeliner streamed down with them so that her face was streaked black, with bruises starting to fill in the rest of the space on her face. Her cheek was already swollen and red from where he had slapped her. There were cuts at the top of her forehead. Blood streamed from them. He had sliced her and pulled her hair out so much that it bled.

Her eyes met mine over his shoulder. A whimper left her again, but his hand slammed over her throat once again. He squeezed with more and more pressure, her mouth gaping open for oxygen. As he gripped tighter, his hips jerked even harder. He was getting off on it. Then she started to thrash around—she couldn't get any air.

He squeezed harder.

When her eyes started to glaze over, I saw a flash of something in them. It was meant for me. I knew it. And my hand held even tighter to the gun as I lifted it in the air.

I felt his gurgle of release before I heard it. I felt it in the air, through the floor, through my roommate. It didn't matter. I knew he was near to climaxing and nothing had ever disgusted me more, but my hand was steady as I held the glock. Then I removed the safety and I cleared my throat once.

He froze.

He didn't look around. He should've, but he didn't.

I waited—my heart starting to pound, but he just started thrusting once again.

"Jeremy."

My voice was so soft, almost too soft, but he froze anyway and twisted his head back to look at me. When he saw what I held, his eyes went wild—and then I shot him.

The bullet hit the center of his forehead. I wasn't surprised when Mallory started to scream, still in his hold. His body held her against the wall even as he slumped. He would have kept her in place if not for her frantic hands pushing him off. His body fell to the ground, as much as the bones and tendons allowed. His knees were still bent, but the blood seeped from him slowly. It formed a pool underneath, and as I stood there, it grew and grew.

Still screaming, Mallory scrambled from him and collapsed to the ground not far from his body. She scooted against the wall until she found the farthest corner and curled into a fetal position. She was sobbing, hysterical, as more screams ripped from her throat.

I went to her, but instead of soothing her like I should've, I put my finger to my lip and made a ssshing sound. When she quieted, I whispered, "You have to be quiet. People will hear."

She nodded but gulped for breath as her sobs grew silent.

Then I turned and slid to the space beside her. I couldn't look away from him. The pool of blood encircled him now. It seeped under the couch.

Absentmindedly, my hand found Mallory's exposed and bleeding knee. I patted it to soothe her, but I couldn't tear my eyes from him. I had killed him. I had killed someone. I couldn't think it or comprehend it, but everything was wrong. I should've been at the gym. I should've been trying to flirt with the new trainer, but I had been tired. I skipped the gym, just this once, and came home instead. When I saw his car, I almost turned around. I hated Jeremy Dunvan. He was connected to the local mob and he treated Mallory like crap. Still, I hadn't gone back to the gym. I figured I could sneak inside. They were always in her room anyway.

Jeremy's face had fallen towards us somehow. I remembered that she had shoved him away from her so his body bent at an awkward angle, but his eyes looked at me. He was dead so they were vacant, but he could still see me. I knew it. A shiver went down my spine as I looked the guy I had murdered in the eye. He was damning me to hell with those eyes.

"Em," Mallory sobbed.

This time her crying broke through my walls. The sound was now deafening to me. My heart picked up. I worried that they could hear in the next apartment, maybe below us or above us. They were going to call the police. We should call the police, but no—I had killed someone. No, I had killed Jeremy Dunvan. We couldn't call anyone.

I found her hand and gripped it hard. One of them was cold and clammy. Mine. My hand was pale while hers was warm with blood. I turned and saw she had her other hand to her mouth. She kept taking gulping breaths as she tried to contain her sobbing.

"We have to go."

My voice sounded harsh to my ears. I flinched from the fierceness in it.

She nodded, still sobbing, still gulping, still bleeding.

"We have to go." My hand squeezed hers. "Now."

Her head jerked in another nod, but neither of us moved. I didn't think my legs worked anymore.

Everything after that was blurry, only remembered in flashes.

We were sitting in a gas station parking lot as we looked at each other. Mallory needed to be cleaned up. Did we go to the hospital? Did I need a camera to prove that she'd been raped? Then she started crying some more, and I remembered who I had killed. Jeremy's father would come for us. No police would help us, not when half of them worked for Jeremy's father, who worked for the Bertal Family. His body would be found in our apartment, I hadn't the stomach to dispose of it.

The bathroom was connected to the outside so I had to get the key. She couldn't be seen like this. One of the two lightbulbs didn't work so the lighting wasn't the best, but I used my phone as I inspected every bruise on her body. She was covered from the top of her head to the two large welts on her calves. When I saw them and looked up, she whispered, "He kicked me."

I got Mallory sunglasses and a scarf to cover her head. She looked like she was from a different country, but it hid the damage. No one spared us a second glance as we went into a diner and ordered two coffees. My stomach growled, but I couldn't eat. Mallory's hands shook so much she couldn't pick up the cup so both of our coffees grew cold as we sat there. I'd grown numb long ago, but her lip still quivered. It'd been quivering for hours now.

It was past midnight. Neither of us ordered food. When the servers changed, I ordered a new coffee. This time I could finally sip it. Mallory gasped. My eyes shot to hers and then I felt the warmth in my mouth. I had burnt myself, but I barely felt it. After my second cup, I waited ten minutes before I picked it up. I knew it wouldn't burn me then. Mallory still couldn't pick hers up.

It was morning now. Both of our phones rang, but we only looked at them. I couldn't speak. I could barely order more coffee from the new server. Mallory's lip had stopped quivering, but I knew her hands still shook so she kept them in her lap. Then she choked out as she reminded me to go to the bathroom. We went together.

We were back in the car again. The staff had started to whisper about us so we left. We didn't want them to call the police, but now we didn't know where to go again. Then Mallory said, "Ben. We can go to Ben's." I looked over. "Are you sure?" My hand was so cold. I barely felt the steering wheel when I turned the car around. She nodded, some tears slipped down again. She had started crying when we left the diner. She said, "Yes. He'll help us. I know it." So we went to her co-worker's house.

The force of what happened hit me full blast after we had been at Ben's for a few hours. He opened the door, took one look at Mallory, and swept her up in his arms. She'd been sobbing ever since, and now all of us were huddled around his kitchen table. He draped a blanket over both of them at some point, but I couldn't remember when.

As she told him what happened through her sobs, I slumped in my chair. Jeremy Dunvan. He had been living twenty-four hours ago, breathing. Oh my god. I had killed him—I felt punched in the stomach. No. I felt like someone tied up my hands and legs, threw me in the highway and waited as a bus ran over me, and then ran over me again. And again.

I was going to die. It was a matter of time.

Franco Dunvan worked for the Bertal Family. They killed my brother. It was my turn now. Icy panic seared through me. I couldn't hear Mallory anymore. It had been in defense. He was going to kill her. He'd already been raping her. I killed him because he would've killed me too, but it didn't matter. As I started struggling to breathe, I tried to remain logical. The police wouldn't have helped. Why did we take pictures of her bruises then? What did it matter? None of it did. We ran. We should keep running.

"We have to go, Mals," I choked out.

She looked up from Ben's chest. He wrapped his arms tighter around her, and if possible, she paled even more. "We can't."

"We have to." They were going to hunt us down and kill us.

"Please, Tomino, please." My brother had begged for his life, but they shoved him to his knees and took a bat to him. AJ watched me the whole time. As he stared past the alley where they found him, we both knew they couldn't see me. He made me crawl behind a vent before they saw him in the alley. My hands gripped each other as I kept myself from crawling out and helping him. He shook his head. He knew what I wanted to do.

"Emma!"

I jerked back to the present and saw Ben frowning at me. "What?"

Everything seemed so surreal. It was a dream. All of it was a dream, it had to be.

He snapped at me, "Christ, the least you can do is be there for her." Then he pushed off from his chair and stormed past me.

What had happened?

"Carter's going to come for you."

I went back to that alley. I heard my brother warn them as he gasped for breath. He was choking on the blood, but they laughed at him. They fucking laughed!

"Whatever. You're a nobody, Martins. You're a waste of space. Your boy's going to get the same as you if he comes after us. In fact, we want him to come to us, don't we, boys?" Tomino had spread his arms out wide and the other three snickered with him. Then he lifted the bat once more.

AJ looked at me. He mouthed the words, *"I love you."*

Then the bat came down at full speed.

I fell off my chair and was slammed back to the present again. I was on the floor now.

"Jesus, Emma. What the fuck's your problem?" Ben grabbed my arm and hauled me up. He pointed to the bedroom. "I finally got her to sleep and now you're going to wake her up? Do you know the hell she's been through? I can't believe you. Have some consideration."

Have some consideration?

I yanked my arm away from him and glared back. "Are you fucking kidding me?" Was he? He had to have been. I shoved him back and then followed to get in his face. "I killed him, you asshole. I killed that rapist for her. I saved her life!"

Now I needed someone to save mine.

For more information on *Carter Reed* or any other books by Tijan, please go to www.tijansbooks.com.

CPSIA information can be obtained
at www.ICGtesting.com
Printed in the USA
LVOW10s1923220317

528099LV00015B/1534/P